ROCK STARS DO IT

JASINDA WILDER

This is a work of fiction. Names, characters, places, and incidents are either the product of the author's imagination or are used fictitiously. Any resemblance to actual events, places, organizations, or persons, whether living or dead, is entirely coincidental.

Previously published in serial format as ROCK STARS DO IT HARDER, ROCK STARS DO IT DIRTY, and ROCK STARS DO IT FOREVER.

ROCK STARS DO IT

ISBN: 978-0-9882642-8-1
Copyright © 2013 by Jasinda Wilder

*To all of my amazeballs readers,
bodacious bloggers, and rock star reviewers.
You give me a reason to sing.*

Thank you!!!!

ONE

THE PAIN IN ANNA'S EYES when she caught sight of him on the stage sent a bolt of agony through Chase Delany's heart. It was the ultimate rejection, even more than her words. She'd told him in no uncertain terms she didn't love him. Even that didn't hurt quite so much as seeing her soft, sweet, expressive gray eyes blaze with pain and surprise and anger at the mere sight of him.

Since she'd rejected him, Chase had thrown himself into the band, into tours and concerts. He wrote like a madman, pouring his pain and anger into songs that got progressively darker as the weeks passed. His bandmates noticed, but they didn't say anything. The darker music drew the fans, drew the crowds to swelling numbers, filled the stadiums and the bars and the casinos. Sure, they weren't headliners yet, but of all the opening acts, Six Foot Tall drew the most attention, garnered the loudest applause.

None of that mattered. Not to Chase.

The fans could scream their heads off, but it wouldn't fill the ache in Chase's heart, the hollow in his belly. Only she could fill him like that, and she'd chosen someone else. Even when fans sneaked backstage after shows and pressed their bodies against him, he couldn't find a single moment of contentment.

He'd let a girl take him all the way once— and only once—after Anna broke his heart. He'd rejected dozens of girls up until then, all skinny girls with small, hard breasts and waists he could span with his hands, ribs showing when they lifted their tops to tempt him with their pale, frail bodies. He'd rejected them all, politely but firmly.

Then a different kind of girl found him backstage, bribed security to give her a few minutes alone with Chase before a set. She was tall, with wide hips and heavy breasts, a luxurious fall of black hair, and bright green eyes. For the first time in weeks, Chase felt the stirrings of desire. He let her peel her shirt off, pendulous breasts swaying in front of his face, her areolas dark dimes against her pale skin. She'd pushed her skintight pants down to her feet and stepped out to stand before him naked and gloriously beautiful, a pale Diana. The cold air of the dressing room made her nipples stand on end, hard little beads.

Chase sat, waiting, heart thudding, his pose deceptively casual. She didn't say anything, just unbuckled his belt, tugged his pants down to his ankles, slipped her legs astride his, and impaled herself onto him, moved above him, her green eyes locked on his, full lips pressed thin, heavy breasts swaying. His body responded, but his mind stayed frozen and cold, his heart empty and black.

She isn't Anna. He pounded the thought through his mind, a harsh reminder, but to no avail. Black hair flashed into blonde locks, green eyes turned gray. Her name was poised on his lips, whispered in the cold air.

Her nostrils flared and her eyes narrowed, the black-haired beauty, but she smiled and said, "I can be your Anna, if that's what you want."

She moved faster above him, her eyes closed, and her breath came faster as she neared climax.

He came, and the release was brief and unfulfilling. She rose off him, plucked a few Kleenex from the box on the counter behind Chase. He watched with a kind of detached, apathetic disgust as she cleaned the white trickle from her thighs, swiped down the line of her lips, and then threw the tissue in the small metal trash can on the floor. She dressed, pulled her long black hair into a ponytail, and opened the door. Before she departed, she pulled a small white rectangle from her purse, a business card, and set it on the filing cabinet by the door.

"If you get over Anna and you want some real company, call me." Then she was gone.

Chase sat, his pants still around his thighs, cock limp and sticky against his leg. A fist knocked on the door, jerking Chase from his blank stare, and he tugged his pants on, buckled his belt, and called a hoarse, "Come in."

The security guard poked his head in. "You're on in five." He saw the card on the cabinet, and flicked a grin at Chase. "Nice, huh? That chick had some big ol' titties, right?"

"Yeah."

"Gonna bring her backstage again after?"

"No." Chase felt a flood of self-loathing wash through him. "In fact, don't let anyone else back here again."

The security guard lifted an eyebrow in surprise. "You sure? You don't want—"

"No, I don't."

"All right, man. If you say so."

After that Chase had taken to hiding in the green room, or in a crowd of other musicians. He'd started to heal, started to forget.

And then, a few weeks after the black-haired girl, he'd gone out onstage in Vegas, some music festival in a casino way off the Strip. The lights had gone up, the crowd had been wild, manic, infusing him with a crazed energy. The first number had killed. Then he'd paused, scanning the crowd, seeing only a sea of faces. Just as Chase was about to give the signal to kick in the next number, he'd seen a flash of blonde hair, an all-too-familiar face only a few feet away from the stage.

Anna.

One look, and his heart had crumbled all over again.

He'd written dozens of songs about her, but he'd only written one song *to* her, *for* her. It was, perhaps, his best song to date. The band had learned it, but they hadn't planned on performing it yet.

It was time, he decided.

Chase spun in place and waved for his band's attention. "We're doing 'I Found You.'"

"Now?" This was Gage, his bassist, and one of his oldest friends.

"Yeah, now. She's here. She needs to hear it."

Gage shrugged. "If you say so, man."

"Make it burn, boys," Chase said. He turned away and fixed his eyes on Anna.

Mic to his lips, he addressed her. "This next song is...special. It's brand new, so you guys are the first live audience to hear it played. I wrote it during a time of heartbreak and loss. Just listen—you'll see what I mean." Chase paused to tamp down the emotion rising within him. "I hadn't planned this, but the person...the woman I wrote this song about, she's in the audience today. Makes this performance especially personal. Anna, this is for you."

He watched her eyes darken with pain, and then the drumbeat kicked in and the music carried him away. He screamed himself raw, that song. But it didn't matter. She turned away, and he knew she'd made her final choice. Just as well. He was so hurt, so full of blind rage, he wouldn't have been able to speak to her.

He saw *him*, Jeff, standing behind her.

"Take care of her." Chase's raw, hoarse voice boomed into the silence of the stunned audience.

Jeff only nodded, and Chase was satisfied. Even through the boiling anger and searing pain, he wanted her to be happy, and it was clear Jeff made her happy.

The rest of the set flew by, and he collapsed in the green room, completely spent. He sipped water and settled in to wait for his bandmates to finish partying with the rest of the festival bands. He wasn't up for a crowd, not then.

The door opened, and he started to bitch out the security guard, but the face he saw poking through the gap stopped his heart. She hesitated, unsure.

"You?" Chase's voice cracked into a whisper.

"I know you probably don't want to see me, of all people, but—"

"No, it's fine. Come on in." He set his bottle down and tried to gather his scattered wits. "What—uh, what are you doing here?"

She shrugged. "I don't know." She held up a backstage pass. "I have this...Anna—sorry, *she* gave it to me. That looked like it was pretty rough, and I thought you might need someone to...I don't know. But here I am."

Her eyes held sorrow for him. That hurt, in an odd way. She cared about him? She saw his pain, clearly. "Here you are."

The silence stretched out, neither of them sure what to say, or do, or feel.

God, she's gorgeous. The thought struck him, unbidden.

For the first time in months, Anna was nowhere in his mind.

Jamie Dunleavy licked her lips and tried to slow her breathing. Chase was staring at her, his gaze inscrutable. He was sweaty, dark eyes narrowed, chest heaving, a bottle of water in one fist. His hand was so big it made the bottle of Ice Mountain look tiny.

She knew she shouldn't be there, with Chase, backstage. It was just asking for trouble. He wasn't with Anna anymore, but he was still off-limits.

A best friend's ex was a big no-no, in her book. She'd fucked more guys than she'd care to count or admit, but she'd never, ever slept with the ex of anyone she cared about. She had *some* standards, after all.

So why am I here? No reasonable answer popped into her head.

He'd just looked so...angry and broken when Anna finally, truly, and literally turned her back on him. The look in his eyes, before he'd shut himself down, was one of soul-deep hurt. And Jamie was a sucker for troubled, hurting guys. She seemed pulled to them. It wasn't so much bad boys that she was drawn to as guys with serious issues. Endless hours of self-psychoanalysis and girl talk with Anna had given her enough insight to understand why she was drawn to the fixer-upper, dark, and dangerous types: She saw herself in them, and hoped they'd have at least a chance of understanding her, of getting why she was the way she was.

So far, no luck.

Lots of sex, some of it pretty damn spectacular, but that was about it. Lots of walks of shame, lots of guys who disappeared after a tumble or two.

Chase seemed to be the ultimate in tall, dark, and fucked-up. He was lounging in a chair, sweat pouring down his face and beading on his clean-shaven head, a pair of supple, faded black leather pants hugging his thick legs and showing off a bulge that had her throat going a little dry and her pulse pounding. He had a ripped, sleeveless Led Zeppelin T-shirt on, tight around his torso and showing his burly, toned arms. His wrists were adorned with thick leather metal-spiked bracelets, and tribal tattoos peeked out from beneath his shirt onto his shoulders and arms. His ears were pierced and gauged. His brown eyes were so dark they were almost black, narrowed and struggling for expressionless apathy.

Jamie saw through his efforts, though. He was hurting. She had no idea what she, of all people, could for him, but she knew she couldn't just walk away and leave him to hurt alone.

"I don't know why I'm here, honestly," she said a second time. "Shit. I already said that. I just...I guess I wanted to see if you were okay."

Lame, lame, lame. Jamie kicked herself. Usually she was pretty good at saying exactly what she was thinking. To a fault, actually. She had tendency to take brutal honesty to a whole new level some- times. But now, faced with Chase, her best friend's ex-lover, Jamie found herself tongue-tied, stam- mering, fumbling for complete sentences.

Chase swigged his water before responding. "Okay? I mean, I'm here. I'm alive. I'm..." He trailed off, rolling the water bottle over his fore- head. "Fuck. No, I'm not. I'm not okay at all."

That was all the opening she needed. Jamie moved into the room and closed the door behind her. There was only the one chair, so she sat half on the counter, her back to the mirror and the too-bright light bulbs. She was within arm's reach of Chase, but not suffocatingly close. She tried to ignore how being this close to him had her feeling shaken up and out of sorts.

"Can I help?" she asked.

Chase laughed, humorless. "Help? What are you going to do? Get Anna back?"

Jamie flinched and stood up. "No, I can't do that. She's happy with Jeff. I just...I know how it feels. I—" She shook her head angrily. "You know what? Whatever."

She stomped toward the door, cursing herself mentally. She was stopped by strong, gentle fingers on her arm, spinning her around. Her lungs froze and her brain melted. Chase was suddenly inches away, his huge, hard body frighteningly close. She could feel the heat emanating from him, as well as the confusion and the hurt. And the attraction.

His eyes were on her, but she still couldn't make heads or tails of what he was thinking.

"I'm sorry, Jamie. That was a dick thing to say."

"Fucking right it was." *Damn it, there goes me and my mouth again.*

Why was he closer now? The glittery heart on her tank top, bulging with her breasts, brushed against his Led Zeppelin shirt. The contact, even that little bit, had lightning bolting through her. Her nipples weren't even hard, but she was still shivering when each of her breaths had her chest expanding and pushing her against him.

"Well, I said I'm sorry. It's just—I'm just—"

"No, now I'm the one being a dick," she said. "I shouldn't be here. I'm her best friend, and I'm probably just making things worse."

His hand was still on her arm, circling her bicep. He was so close now she had to tilt her head back to meet his eyes. His gaze was intense, and Jamie felt something in her stomach clenching at the way his stare washed over her, glancing from her face to her thick, curly hair and down to her cleavage. Her shirt wasn't low-cut, but it was tight enough that the outlines of her bra were visible.

And now, under his eyes, her nipples peaked and poked through her bra and thin cotton tank top to dimple the material.

She felt his body respond. *Oh, god. Oh, god. He's huge.* She felt her body quivering and straining to feel more, get closer. *Get your ass out, Jamie.*

She didn't listen to herself. He wasn't holding her arm so tightly that she couldn't have gotten away, so why was she stuck in place like she was about to kiss him?

No. No. *No.*

Yes...

She was falling forward…

His lips were salty with sweat, soft yet firm, scouring her mouth with something like desperation. His hand tightened on her arm, his other hand slipping to the small of her back and pulling her close. She moved into him instinctively, crushing herself against him before she knew what she was doing.

Then reality hit like a palm-strike from Jesus. *What the hell am I doing?*

Jamie threw herself backward out of his arms, away from his kiss. It hurt. It physically, mentally, and emotionally hurt to pull away so forcefully. He tasted, felt, and smelled like man-heaven. Hunk-nirvana. Sex-Valhalla. Were there other kinds of heaven she could compare that ten seconds to? Probably, but her brain was too fried to come up with them.

She'd kissed *him*. It hadn't been his fault. It was all her. She was a terrible, terrible best friend and an awful human being.

Jamie's fingertips touched her lips, as if to keep the memory of his kiss close. Her back was to the door, and her breath came in ragged gasps. "That… that shouldn't have happened. God. I'm so sorry." She ducked her head so her copper curls draped in front of her face. "I don't know what the fuck I was thinking. I'm sorry, Chase. I shouldn't have—" she cut herself off and groped for the doorknob.

Time to beat a hasty retreat before he could come up with a scathing response. Or worse, kiss her back. 'Cause that would be terrible. Wonderful, amazing, incredible…and totally wrong. If he kissed her, he'd be a cad. If she let him, it would push her past having just made an innocent mistake and into heinous-bitch territory.

He took a step, licking his lips, brows furrowed in confusion. "Jamie, wait. Just hang on a second. That was—"

"A mistake," she filled in for him. "Never going to happen again. It can't. I'm Anna's best friend, and you're her ex. Us…that kiss…it's not just 'hell, no' territory, it's like…full-on 'fuck no' country."

Chase's lips quirked. "You drop the F-bomb a lot, don't you?"

Jamie shrugged. "Yeah, I do. I know it turns a lot of guys off, but it's just how I am."

"I think it's hot."

Jamie backed up. "You're not allowed to think I'm hot."

"Why not?"

"Because. You just can't. It makes this that much harder."

"Makes what harder?" He took another step toward her.

She turned and spoke as she walked away. "This. The part where I do the right thing for once in my life. I'm gonna walk away, and we're both going to pretend nothing happened."

"But it did happen." He was chasing her, moving through the bustling hallways after her, shouldering aside techies and band members and stage crew. "Jamie, wait. Just hang on and let's talk about this."

She shook her head, curls bouncing. "No way. Not happening, Chase. Don't push me."

She tried to ignore him. She saw the exit just ahead, the red-lettered sign shining in the distance, a thin bright line of white spearing through the backstage gloom as someone stepped out. She scurried for the exit, not looking back, trying to ignore the part of her that was begging, *Just one more kiss, Jay. Just one more. It can't hurt anything.*

She made it. She hit the crash bar with her hip and stepped out into the oppressive, dry desert Las Vegas heat, squinting at the sudden brilliance of the day. She fumbled in her purse for her sunglasses and slipped them on, thankful for the emotion-blocking quality of the mirrored aviator shades.

But of course, he was right behind her. His hand was on her hip, spinning her around. How did he do that? She wasn't a small girl, and she worked out. She took kickboxing. Jamie knew she was buff. He shouldn't be able to manhandle her like she was some sprightly little thing.

"Jamie, just hang the fuck on for a second." His voice was a low growl. "Look, I'm not gonna pretend it didn't happen, but I know why you're bugging about this, and you're right. It's...complicated. But I don't think—"

Jamie smacked his hand away from her body, needing clarity, and god knew his hand on her wasn't helping. "Don't think what? Think it won't be a problem? Think we can just hook up and no one will be any wiser? She'll know, Chase. She's my best friend, and I can't lie to her. Trust me, I've tried. We're like...psychic with each other. She's lied to me, and I've known when she was lying. I know when she's hiding something, and vice versa. Not to mention, it's wrong. You don't fuck your friend's exes, Chase. You just don't."

"Who said anything about fucking, or hooking up? It was just a kiss."

Jamie snorted. "Sh-yeah. *Just* a kiss. Right. And I'm the Virgin Mary."

Chase smirked, the first real humor to enliven his face. "Then what would you consider it?"

"A gateway drug?"

Chase laughed, a belly laugh. "A gateway drug, huh?" He sobered and closed in on her; Jamie wanted to back away, but she was rooted to the spot, pinned by his intense gaze, his fierce presence. "Then I'd be interested in seeing what the hard stuff would be like."

Jamie forced herself away again. "No, Chase. That can't happen. How can you be thinking about that at a time like this?"

"You expect me to pine for Anna forever? I've had weeks to forget her, to move on. This was the clincher. Just…salt in the wound. I can't live my life in the shadow of her rejection."

"Bullshit." Jamie poked his broad chest with a finger. "You're not over her. I saw the look on your face."

Chase's face closed down. "I didn't say I was over her. I said I had to move on."

"Well, this isn't the way. Hooking up with me isn't the way."

Chase frowned. "You keep talking about hooking up. I never said or did anything to suggest that. You did."

Jamie clenched her teeth and turned away. "You're right. My bad. Have a nice life, Chase." She walked away again, and this time he didn't follow her.

Jamie found herself tensed and expecting to feel his hand on her; she was torn between hoping he would and fearing the consequences if he did.

TWO

CHASE WATCHED JAMIE LEAVE, wondering why his heart was palpitating. It might have had something to do with the way her fine, round ass swayed, cupped by denim so tight it left little to the imagination. It also might have had something to do with the searing memory of her kiss on his lips.

Ten seconds of time, but he knew he was ruined for other women, other lips. He'd gone from limp to raging erection in a single breath, a single brush of her balm-slick, strawberry-tasting lips.

It also might have had something to do with her unequivocal rejection. She'd kissed him, then bolted as if stung. Chase understood her reservations, and damn it all if she wasn't absolutely correct, but that didn't make it any easier.

Neither did how soft she was, how perfectly she fit in his arms, how her curves had molded to his body like puzzle pieces snugging into place. She'd enjoyed the kiss as much as he had; she could deny it all day long, but Chase knew she'd felt the same things he had.

He wanted Jamie, hard.

But the way she'd walked off with her jaw set and her emerald eyes blazing with determination left little doubt that he'd ever see again.

Which really, really, *really* sucked. Chase knew he'd walk through the Mojave Desert stark naked if it meant getting just one more kiss from her. But she wouldn't let that happen.

Chase turned away with a whispered curse. She was right. Goddamn it, she was right. He had to forget about Jamie. He was still broken up over Anna.

Being faced with her so suddenly, apropos of nothing...that fucking hurt. She'd seemed so surprised, so conflicted. As if merely seeing him had pained her. Which just went to show that she wasn't as over him as she'd tried to make it seem.

One look at Anna's sweet, innocent face, blue eyes and blonde hair and lush curves...and Chase had been lost all over again. Wishing he could hold her, kiss her, hear the low, passionate moans she used to make for him as she came. She'd been so eager, so hungry, like no one had ever paid attention to her, like she just had no clue how sexy she was. It was a turn-on all by itself, her strangely erotic innocence. She'd changed the way he saw sex. He'd thought he was teaching her, and all along she was showing him how much more than mere hormones and pheromones and orgasms it could be. Sex had always been fun for him. When he first met her and invited her back to his place, he'd thought it would be an enjoyable night in the sack with a hot girl who had some killer curves. But then it had changed. No warning, no clue. Just... it was more. From the first kiss in the car, stolen as she drove away, Chase had seen her hang-ups and had wanted to fix them. She didn't see her own sexiness, and he'd made it his mission to show her what she was, what she had that men wanted.

In the end, she'd shown him that sex could have meaning. And goddamn if he didn't want that again.

But Anna was gone forever. She'd chosen Jeff over him. Chase had seen enough to know she really, truly loved Jeff. She was happy with him, and Chase wasn't going to begrudge her that. She deserved happiness.

He wished it could have been with him, but that wasn't meant to be, and he had to move on.

He just didn't know how. That random groupie who had seduced him...he could have pursued her.

She might have distracted him for a while. But he hadn't.

Now Jamie had to go and show up, kiss him, rock his world, and ruin the little bit of progress he'd been making.

What now?

"Hey, Chase, there you are." Gage popped his head out of the door. "We need you inside, dude. Cleo from Murder Doll Asylum is looking for you. She wants you to do a couple songs with her."

Chase followed his bassist inside and through the backstage area. "Murder Doll Asylum?"

Gage shrugged. "Yeah, I know, right? Bizarre-as-hell name, but I listened to a couple of their songs on the way down, and they're fucking bru-tal, man. She's got a killer voice." He quirked an eyebrow at Chase, grinning. "And having met her, she's got a killer body to go with it. Could be fun, if you know what I mean."

Chase waved his hand. "I'll do the set, but that's it, man."

Gage made a disgusted face. "Dude, listen. You're all hung up on that chick. I know you liked her, but you've gotta get over her. You've been a mopey fucktard for weeks, man. Distract yourself. That one chick a few weeks ago, Shannon? The one with the black hair and the huge tits? You tapped that, right? She was asking us at the after-party why you weren't there. She wanted you, bro. Like, hard."

Chase could only shrug. "Yeah, I hit it. She was hot and all, and it was good, but...I just don't know. She didn't hold my interest. I don't know what else to say. I'm just not interested."

Gage shook his head again. "Well...I guess it's whatever you want, man. But we've been friends since ninth grade, man, and this ain't you. You're all...*depressed* and shit. We're on the way up, man! We're playing Madison Square Garden next week—how huge is that?"

"We're opening for the openers, Gage," Chase said. "But I know. Okay? I know. Just give me some time. I'll come around."

Gage slapped him on the back, playfully hard. "Just do me one favor?"

"If I can."

Gage grinned lecherously. "Don't count Cleo out before you've met her, bro. She's hot. Like... *hot*. And I'm pretty sure she's into you. I mean, fuckin' *every* girl on the *planet* is into you, but Cleo is fine as hell, and she can scream like a banshee, man. Their tracks are sick."

Chase forced a grin and a laugh so Gage would get off his case. "I'll try to keep my mind open."

"That's all I'm asking."

Murder Doll Asylum was an all-girl screamo band led by Cleo Calloway. They'd made a name for themselves as a band that could rock as hard on stage and play as hard off-stage as any of the all-male metal outfits. Six Foot Tall wasn't strictly metal, but they had enough hard numbers that they could fit in with billings that featured harder acts. This gig in Vegas was with a ton of metal bands of several subgenres, headlined by acts like Hatebreed, Devil Driver, and Otep; it was the hardest grouping of bands they'd ever played with, and all the guys in Six Foot Tall were finding the process of adjusting from the tamer rock acts they usually played with to the darker, harder thrash, screamo, and death metal bands on this gig to be a strange but fun adventure.

Chase idly twisted the spiked bracelets on his wrists as they neared the stage. He could feel the music in his bones and his belly before he could really hear anything specific. Until you were close enough to hear the feed from the monitors, the music heard backstage was a wall of sound, thick and impenetrable, rumbling and grumbling in your body.

Now that he was in the side-stage curtains watching, he could hear the band's signature sound, a steady, growling bass line overlaid by high, squealing, technically stunning lead guitar work. Through it all, the drums pounded mania-cally, topped by Cleo's unintelligible but emotive screaming, chanting vocals. Chase wasn't usually a huge fan of screamo bands, preferring a more melodic and artistic approach himself. He could appreciate the talent he was seeing, though. Cleo's face twisted and contorted with angst and rage, her thin, porcelain-pale features curtained by a thousand thin dark purple dreads as she bent over at the waist, mic held sideways to her lips, cupped by her other hand. He couldn't make out a damn word she was saying, but she sure did seem to feel it from the depths of her soul.

The number ended, and Cleo stepped off-stage as the lights darkened between numbers.

She grabbed a water bottle proffered by stagehand and stood next to Chase. "Hey. Wanna do a couple numbers together?"

Chase grinned at her. "Sure. I don't know any of your stuff, though."

She waved a hand dismissively. "We can do some covers. We're more than just screamo, you know."

"Cool. What do you want to cover?"

"You know 'Cowboys From Hell'?"

"Hell, yeah." Chase bobbed his head; the boys were all huge Pantera fans.

The bassist, a tall, willowy girl with blonde pigtails, tapped in a thrumming line, followed by the kick drum, and then the lights came on, bathing Cleo and Chase in twin spots. Cleo leaned in close to the lead guitarist, a short but svelte girl with black spiky hair and earrings rimming her ears from lobe to tip, muttering the song they were going to do. The guitarist nodded and strummed a few chords as the rest of the band cued in.

Then they were off, blazing through the beloved metal anthem, Cleo and Chase alternating verses and harmonizing on the chorus as perfectly as if they'd rehearsed it. They did "Sanitarium" by Metallica next, and then closed the set with "Killing in the Name of" by Rage Against the Machine. Chase was skeptical when Cleo suggested it, but Cleo assured him the band knew it backward and forward, and had covered it before. He found himself pleasantly shocked when the guitarist did indeed do justice to Tom Morello's guitar work.

Chase had paid close attention to Cleo while they performed, and she was as sexy as Gage had suggested. She was thin and pale, with small breasts and boyish hips, which was as far from Chase's taste as you could get, but she was beautiful, with wide hazel eyes and an expressive, kissable mouth.

Maybe she would provide enough distraction to help him forget; he had a lot of forgetting to do after all. Anna, Jamie…between the two, he wasn't sure he'd ever truly be able to forget, but he had to try.

It was midnight, and Chase was hammered, more than half-naked, and about to lose his third straight hand of strip poker. Of course, he wasn't necessarily playing to win, and neither were the girls from Murder Doll Asylum. Chase smirked as he thought, *Losing has never been so much fun.* And neither had winning. He was down to his leather pants, earplugs, and his socks, but then, the girls were faring about as well. He'd won twice as many hands as he'd lost, so Cleo was down to her bra and panties; Leah, the bassist, was topless in her Catholic schoolgirl–style miniskirt; and Kylie, the guitarist, was in a T-shirt and panties.

They'd been partying for hours, ever since their set ended earlier in the evening, with the drummer and rhythm guitar from MDA having gone with the other guys from Six Foot Tall to some after-party somewhere in Vegas.

Which left Chase to entertain three hot chicks on his own. He figured he could handle it.

He fanned his cards and examined them again, as if they might have changed. Ace of hearts, ace of diamonds, and three of hearts. A pair, but not enough. He was pretty sure Leah had a straight, and Cleo was holding something to beat that—a full house, maybe. He wasn't sure what Kylie was holding, but he was pretty damn sure it beat his hand.

Chase sucked in a breath and let it out slowly. Leah had just raised on his bet, which meant he was beaten three ways. "All right, ladies. I'm not gonna see that. I've got a pair of aces."

He laid his cards down and tried to keep his face neutral.

Leah whooped. "Hells, yeah! Straight, baby. Take 'em off, Delany."

Chase grinned and stood up, ran his hands over his abs teasingly. He watched as all three girls froze in anticipation. He decided to toy with them; he drew off one sock, and then the other.

"That wasn't the bet!" Cleo yelled. "Your pants, Chase. The bet was, if you lose, you take off those sexy leather pants."

Chase looked down at himself, as if surprised to see his customary leather pants. "The pants?" He glanced with overdone incredulity at the three girls. "You want me to take my pants off?"

"YES!" all three girls said in chorus, and then burst into a fit of giggles.

Which was funny in and of itself, since none of them were the giggling type. They were the type of girls who could hold their own in the most brutal of mosh pits, who could breed a sonic massacre onstage and then drink half their male counterparts under the table afterward. And they were giggling.

Chase laughed, swaying in place. Those last two shots of Patrón were starting to catch up to him. "Well, let it never be said that Chase motherfucking Delany ever welched on a bet," he announced, a little too loudly.

He eyed each girl in turn, his gaze lingering on Leah's perky C-cup breasts, and then unbuttoned the top of his pants. He grinned when Cleo licked her lips, shifting in her chair. The zipper went down, and now they were loose around his hips, his semi-rigid cock bulging in his skin-tight CK boxer-briefs.

And then he paused. "I have an idea. How about the three of you play one last high-stakes hand." He poured a shot for each of them, handed out limes and the salt, and then, when everyone was ready, he lifted his shot glass in a toast. "Winner of the last hand helps me take off my pants."

Leah, Cleo, and Kylie exchanged looks, then grinned. Cleo scooped up the cards, shuffled, and dealt. Chase planted himself unsteadily into his chair, blinking at the double images he was starting to see. Time to slow down a bit; they were just starting to get down to the fun part of the night.

He watched the girls play, each one keeping her face straight and hard, giving nothing away. Watching them play, he started trying to figure out each girl's tell. Leah was worrying at her bottom lip with her teeth absently, fingering one of her cards with her thumb. Kylie was blinking a lot and uncrossing and recrossing her legs—either nervous, or she had to pee. Cleo was the hardest. She was perfectly still, no obvious sign of nerves or excitement. Then she glanced at Chase and licked her

lips, pink tongue swiping with exaggerated slowness between her black lipstick–painted lips.

She's going to win, he realized. She wasn't nervous or excited, only confident, which meant she
had a killer hand and she knew it. Chase found
himself hardening at the thought of Cleo's hands
stripping him of his pants. She was pretty sexy, in
her own way. She had knowing eyes, busy hands,
porcelain-doll features. Like a china doll turned
goth-anime.

Chase shifted in his chair. This would definitely
be a welcome distraction. He'd hoped the night
would provide a few hours of forgetting, but he
hadn't dared hope it would go this well.

He pushed away the doubts concerning what
was about to go down. He owed no one anything.
He could do what he wanted. If he wanted to
spend the night in a *ménage à quatre* or whatever
this would be called, then he had every right to.
He was a goddamn rock star, for fuck's sake. Rock
stars fucked three girls at once.

Cleo's whoop of triumph jerked him back to the
present. Leah and Kylie were pouting while Cleo stood
on the table, gyrating her hips and pointing at Chase.
"Get over here, Delany. You're mine, now, bitch."

Chase stood up slowly, eyes on Cleo across the
table from him, Leah and Kylie between them. He
circled behind Leah. He paused with his lips at her
ear and put his index finger on her bare knee near

the hem of her skirt, then dragged it up her thigh, hiking her skirt higher as he went. He felt her breathing cease entirely as his finger moved up her hip to her naked side. She gasped when his finger traced the underside of her breast, and then whimpered when he flicked her rigid nipple.

"Don't worry, sweetheart," he whispered in Leah's ear, his eyes fixed on Cleo's. "I haven't forgotten about you."

He pinched her nipple, nipping her earlobe, letting his hot breath huff into her ear. She tipped her head sideways to offer him better access, and he took it, planting a hot kiss on her neck.

She deflated when he moved away, letting her breath out, her head lolling back on her shoulders. Kylie was next, and she was watching him out of the corner of her eye, palms flat on the table, drawing slow, deep breaths. He paused behind her as he had Leah, but instead of immediately touching her, he simply stood behind her, mouth against her ear, his hands planted to either side of hers. She was frozen, head turned slightly so she could see him. He waited. Chase could feel the anticipation rolling off her in palpable waves.

"I haven't forgotten about you, either," he whispered.

Kylie turned in place so her lips brushed his. Chase felt a bolt of lust hit him when her soft, moist lips touched his.

"What are you gonna do?" Kylie asked, breathless.

"I don't know. What do want me to do?"

She shrugged. "I'm awful hot in this shirt."

Chase grinned and touched her lip with his tongue, tasting the salt and the tequila and faint traces of lipstick. "Hmmm. I might be able to help you out with that."

Kylie sucked in her belly when Chase's fingers brushed the skin of her abs, lifting her tight red baby-doll T-shirt up over her head and off. Her spiky black hair was mussed by the shirt's removal, so Chase took the opportunity to run his hands over the spikes. She shivered when his palm grazed down her neck and across her shoulder, hesitating on the shoulder blade before plunging down her chest to her breasts, cupped by a plain black bra.

Chase dug his fingers into the cup and lifted one breast free, tweaking the rosy bud of her nipple. He lifted the strap and let it snap back. "Is this in the way, too?"

She nodded, unable to speak. Chase winked at Cleo, who watched the exchange with an amused lift of her eyebrow, arms crossed over her chest.

"You're next, Cleo," Chase said. "And you have a bet to keep."

Cleo just smirked. "Bring it, sexy pants."

Chase froze. "What did you call me?"

Cleo frowned. "Sexy pants. Why?"

Mr. Sexypants. Anna's voice echoed through his head, her nickname for him tugging on his heart.

He shook his head to clear it of the memory, and her voice. That was past. This was now, and he had three beautiful, willing women waiting for his attention.

"Something wrong, Delany?" Cleo asked.

"No, sorry. It's nothing." He turned back to Kylie, slipping the bra strap off her shoulder, then the other. "Now, where was I?"

Kylie reached behind her head to slide her hands over Chase's back, clawing with her nails. "I think you were helping me off with my bra."

"Oh, yeah," Chase said, "now I remember."

He deftly unhooked her bra with one hand, nibbling on her ear and cupping a breast as the bra fell away. He felt Leah's eyes on him, hungry. Cleo was watching, too, and he tried to decide if he was seeing hints of jealousy in her eyes or not. Cleo shook her head slightly, poured a shot of tequila and downed it sans salt or lime, then turned her attention back to Chase, who was prowling around the circumference of the table once more.

He stopped beside Cleo, who turned in her chair to face him. "My turn?" she asked.

"Your turn." Chase ran his thumbs around the inside of the waistband of his underwear, but didn't lower them. "You're the only one who's wearing a top," he pointed out.

Cleo laughed. "It's not exactly at a top," she said. "But I take your point. Want to fix that?"

Chase smiled, licking his lips, then lowered his mouth to her ear. "It would be my *extreme* pleasure."

He suited action to words, unclasping her bra and tossing it away from her body in a single motion. Cleo stared up at him, lifting her chin defiantly, as if refusing to feel embarrassed by her nudity. Chase let his gaze rove down her body, taking in her small breasts with their nickel-sized areolas and beaded nipples. He reached down and carved a narrowing circle around her nipple with his finger, feeling the skin tighten under the pad of his fingertip.

Cleo bit her lower lip, sliding her eyes closed slowly and then opening them again. "I don't think this was part of the bet."

"Nope."

"So what are you doing?"

Chase shrugged. "Three sets of beautiful bare breasts? How can I not touch them?"

Cleo didn't answer. She continued to stare up at Chase, then hooked her fingers through the belt loops of his pants and tugged them down. They were tight enough that his boxers shimmied down with them, revealing the broad tip of his cock, now fully erect.

Cleo grinned. "Well, that works." She tugged again, and Chase stepped out of his pants, naked now. "The bet was just the pants, but I'll take this, too."

Kylie and Leah glanced at each other, then burst into giggles again. They whispered to each other, then stood up and wove their way, a little unsteadily, around the table to Chase. Cleo poured four shots, and they each downed theirs. Chase looked at each woman in turn, all of them now clad in only panties—or, in Leah's case, a miniskirt.

Leah stood to one side of Chase, Kylie on the other, with Cleo still sitting facing him. No one moved for several long moments, and then Leah lifted her hand and slid it down Chase's chest to his belly. Kylie did the same on the other side, and now both girls' hands were on his belly, inches from his straining cock.

Chase, his eyes still locked on Cleo, who seemed to be battling some kind of discomfort or embarrassment, ran his hands up Kylie's and Leah's thighs. Both girls pressed closer to him, and then Kylie turned into him, pressed her lips to his arm and wrapped her nimble guitarist's fingers around his thick shaft. Chase slipped his palm under her panties to caress her ass, pushing the cotton boy-short panties down. Kylie wriggled her hips and shimmied out of them. Chase searched the hem of Leah's skirt until he found the zipper, and then, with one hand still kneading Kylie's firm, tight ass, he unzipped Leah's skirt and shoved it down, working his palm down one hip and then arcing across her flat belly to the other hip. Cleo sat motionless the entire time, her hazel eyes piercing into Chase's.

If he was going to be honest with himself, Chase knew he would rather have been alone with Cleo, and if he was any judge of her expression, Cleo was wishing for the same thing.

Instead, Kylie's delicate fingers were slowly stroking his cock near the tip, and then Leah took him in her hand as well, near the base, their pumping hands meeting in the middle.

Chase held himself absolutely still, except for his exploring hands, which were drifting up to curl around Kylie's and Leah's waists to cup their breasts and roll their nipples.

"I dare you to lick it, Cleo," Kylie said, her free hand grazing over Chase's ass.

Cleo hesitated, glancing from Chase's face to his cock.

"Yeah, Cleo. Come on," Leah urged. "Suck on his pretty cock."

"You first," Cleo said.

Leah shrugged. "I'd love to," she said, sinking to her knees.

Cleo's brows knitted as Leah put her lips around the broad crown just above Kylie's still-stroking fingers. Chase's breathing grew ragged, but he didn't move a muscle, even his hands frozen as Leah began to get into it now, sucking on the tip, licking around the groove, her fist pumping him near the base, her other hand gripping his ass.

Chase once again pushed away doubts, which were buried deep, and not enough to put a halt to this.. This felt good. Two hot women were all over him. This was awesome. Epic. He'd never been with more than one woman before, and this was shaping up to be even better than he'd dared imagine.

Except...Cleo.

She seemed as unsure as he felt, deep down. She wasn't touching him, her eyes locked on his.

Pour a shot, he mouthed to her. She nodded and poured shots. He need more liquid courage to really go through with this. He snaked his arm out from behind Kylie and took the shot, feeling his inhibitions burn away under the smooth burn of the Patrón.

Kylie knelt down on his other side now, and Leah moved away to make room for her. Kylie's lips wrapped around him, and she took him deep into her mouth. Leah had only worked his tip, never taking him deep. Kylie did the opposite, sliding him into her mouth as deep as she could before backing away slowly, only to deep-throat him again.

Chase closed his eyes and swallowed, his throat dry and his muscles burning from the effort to keep still, to hold back. "Girls, you have to stop now. I'm close."

Kylie laughed, her voice buzzing on his cock, and he flinched. She took him deep, and then moved away. Leah took her place again, working his tip with her tongue.

Chase frowned, realizing they had no intention of stopping. Cleo watched all this, her face struggling for impassivity. She abruptly stood up, and Chase shot his hand out to grab hers, stopping her from walking away. He slid his palm up her arm, stopped at her breast, then moved up again, slipping around the back of her neck beneath her purple dreads. He pulled her close, closer, and then his lips met hers. She gasped, stiffened, and tried to pull away, but Chase held her in place, darting his tongue between her lips. She melted slightly, and then eased into the kiss.

Chase pulled away after a moment, his forehead touching hers as he struggled to hold back. His hips were circling against his control, and now Leah backed away, too.

"You want it?" Leah asked Kylie.

Kylie didn't answer, wrapping her lips around him again and taking him deep. Her hand, along with Leah's, began to stroke him faster now, and Kylie's bobbing head matched the speed of her hand.

"I'm...I'm right there," Chase gasped. "I'm about to come..."

Cleo moaned into his mouth as he began to growl, and then she kissed him. Chase ran his hand over Cleo's ribs, then palmed her breast. She moaned again, then slipped her hand down between Kylie and Leah to cup his balls, pressing her middle finger against his taint. Chase let his head flop back, and his spine arched as he came with a loud roar. Kylie took him deep into her throat as he spurted a second time, and then her lips were replaced by Leah's, and she sucked his tip furiously, drawing a third spasm from him, hollowing her cheeks to glean every drop from him.

She drew him out of her mouth with a *pop*, and then Leah gave his tip one last lick.

Chase sagged, stumbling. Kylie and Leah stood up, pushing Chase toward the queen bed, and he crawled onto it. Cleo remained where she stood, hesitating. Chase held his hand out to her, meeting her gaze with his own.

A long moment passed before Cleo lifted her chin in a defiant gesture, then wriggled out of her panties and climbed onto the bed.

Chase planted sloppy kisses on her skin as she moved onto the bed with him. *She's going to be the first to come*, Chase decided.

Leah was already pressing herself in on his right side, Kylie on his left, their hands smoothing over his body, roaming his chest and stomach and thighs and cock. Cleo was perched awkwardly over his knees, her hands on Chase's shoulders to support her weight. Chase grasped her wrists in his hands and tugged her toward him, kissing her lips as she reached him, then pulled her higher yet, ignoring her confused expression. He planted his hands on her ass and lifted to settle her knees next to his head, her legs under his shoulders so her soft, damp, shaven core was hovering over his mouth.

Planting her palms on the wall, Cleo arched her back with a low, hesitant moan as Chase swiped his tongue along her crease. He adjusted her position slightly, then licked at her again, and still a third time before flicking at her clit with the tip of his tongue. Cleo gasped, a breathless sound that turned into a drawn-out moan as he circled her clit.

Chase was reminded of the girls to either side when their lips pressed moist kisses on his chest and stomach, their hands still exploring his body. Chase slid his palms on their bellies, and both Kylie and Leah sent up their moans of pleasure as he dipped his fingers between their thighs. Chase found his ability to multitask put to the test as he swirled his tongue around Cleo's clit while establishing a delving rhythm with his hands inside the other two girls' desire-wet clefts.

A chorus of moans filled the hotel room, Cleo's the loudest. Chase slowed his rhythm, finding his tongue and fingers working together. Each girl gasped in protest when he slowed his ministrations to nearly nothing, teasing their pussies with finger-tips and tongue moving just enough to stimulate, but not enough to let them reach orgasm.

"Chase, god, please!" Cleo groaned.

Chase chuckled low in his throat. "Please what, Cleo?"

"Fuck you, Delany. Don't make me say it."

Kylie giggled on his left, her diminutive but nimble fingers stroking his limp but slowly solidi-fying cock. Leah was working his balls, massaging them gently in her hands, pressing a finger to his taint and rolling it in tiny circles as Kylie began to pump his now semi-rigid shaft. He felt Kylie leave the bed then come back, guiding his fingers back to her cleft. He didn't spare a glance, but he heard the crinkling of a condom wrapper, then felt the rub-ber stretch over him, rolled hand over hand down his length.

Chase sped up his rhythm, licking at Cleo's clit quickly, circling, flicking and sucking the small, hard, sensitive nub until she was writhing above him, gasping loud moans, arching and bowing her spine. She was at the edge, Chase realized.

He slowed his tongue, keeping his fingers mov-ing inside Kylie and Leah, flicking his two long middle fingers over their G-spots.

"Say it, Cleo," Chase demanded, then speared his tongue at her clit.

Cleo tried to resist, groaning and lifting up, away from Chase, but then lowered herself back down to his mouth. "Goddamn it, Delany." She moaned again when he licked her pussy in slow, torturous circles. "I won't beg you."

"I'm not asking you to beg. Just say what you want."

Cleo growled. "You're a bastard." She whimpered when his tongue ran in narrowing circles around her nub, then shrieked when he flicked it again with his tongue. She was close now, only a few swipes of his tongue away from coming. "Goddammit, Delany. Fine. Please, *please* make me come."

Chase rewarded her with an increased tempo, licking her clit until she was undulating above him, caught up in the sensation and helpless to quiet her shrieks as she came apart.

Leah was right behind Cleo, moaning softly as she gyrated her hips on the bed, lifting her clenching pussy into his fingers as she came, her hands going still on his balls. Kylie was last, letting her voice rise up in a long scream when she came, slowing her fist on Chase's cock and curling into his side as she writhed in ecstasy.

Cleo was gasping, panting, sliding her core down Chase's chest to rest her breasts on his face.

He took a nipple in his mouth, gently suckling until she wriggled on top of him, hypersensitive. She lifted up to meet his gaze, and for a split second, he saw something in her eyes, a moment of vulnerability swiftly erased.

Leah clambered over Chase's legs to slip between him and Kylie, turning away from him to face the other girl. Both girls giggled and then tangled their legs together, Leah half-straddling Kylie as they locked lips. Chase watched in fascination for a long moment as the two women scissored their legs together, palms scrubbing over breasts, groping and grabbing with a frenzy that shocked him.

Cleo laughed in Chase's ear. "Don't mind them. That's just what they do."

Chase ran his hands down Cleo's back to caress her ass, then grabbed her hips, pushing her downward until her cleft was brushing the tip of his cock. Cleo moaned, rolled her hips slightly, then lowered herself to impale him into her.

"Oh...my...god..." Cleo gasped, thumping her head onto his chest and swiveling her hips to help him find her sweet spot. "Right there, oh, god, yes, right there."

Chase thrust into her, trying to ignore the sounds of the other girls next to him, wet kissing, fingers moving inside pussies, giggles and moans. He was slightly embarrassed to be witnessing

Kylie and Leah together, but in end gave himself over to being turned on by it. Their soft, sinuous bodies writhed together, pale skin flashing in the lights of Vegas shining through the open curtains. Their laughter faded as they neared release, moans becoming frantic, feminine gasps of ecstasy rising in an erotic chorus.

Chase let himself grunt as he moved inside Cleo, raising his hips to meet hers, his large hands nearly spanning her tiny waist, lifting her negligible weight to crash her back down on top of him.

"I'm so close again, Chase," Cleo whispered in his ear, "but I need you on top."

Chase grinned up at her, then flipped her effortlessly, propping his weight on his elbows, his hips fitting between her parted thighs. "Like this?"

"Fuck yes," she moaned, wrapping her legs around his ass to pull him against her. "Harder, please."

Chase complied, driving into her slow and hard, drawing out and thrusting in. Cleo's hands clawed down his shoulders as she rolled her pussy against him, their bodies meeting in a slap of flesh, their mutual moans of pleasure counterpointed by Leah and Kylie next to them coming with tangled screams and shrieks.

Chase's low male growls braided with the three female gasps, and then all became a symphony of orgasm as they released together, Cleo curling around Chase and growling a high-pitched scream, Chase rasping low in his throat, Kylie's and Leah's moans echoing in harmony.

Then all was still and silent but for desperate panting for breath.

Chase moved his weight off Cleo, resting half on, half off the bed, one leg planted on the floor, the other across Cleo's legs. Kylie and Leah took up most of the bed, tangled together in a splay of limbs, their breathing soft and rhythmic, gentle snores.

Chase tried to relax and get comfortable, but there were simply too many bodies in the bed, so he slipped off the bed, tugged his boxers on, and made his way onto the balcony. The Vegas air was warm and dry, the sound of cars rushing in perpetual traffic, voices filtering up from the sidewalk a dozen stories beneath him.

He was still a little drunk, he realized. The lights around him were blurring and twisting. He heard the sliding glass door open and then close. Cleo joined him, his T-shirt not quite covering her ass, showing she hadn't put on panties. Her bare skin flashed in the darkness, and he felt a stirring of desire for her, something strange and out of place that he didn't understand. He'd just had sex with her, but he felt awkard staring at her bare pussy peeking out from beneath the shirt. He looked away, and Cleo tugged the shirt lower.

"Couldn't find my panties," she said, sounding as awkward as he felt. "And I need a smoke." She smacked a new pack of Parliament Lights on her palm three times, then ripped the cellophane off, withdrew a cigarette, and lit it. She'd brought the nearly empty bottle of Patrón out with her, and she took a swig from it before handing it to Chase.

Cleo's pack of cigarettes sat on the railing with her clear orange Bic lighter, and Chase, feeling an odd compulsion, took a cigarette and lit it.

"I didn't think you smoked," Cleo said, blowing a plume of smoke out of the side of her mouth.

"I don't. Or at least, not anymore. Used to, back in high school."

"Why start now? It's a nasty-ass habit, but I love it too much to quit. At least not till I stop touring."

Chase shrugged, coughing as the acrid smoke hit his lungs for the first time in more than ten years. "Not sure. Had a craving, I guess."

Chase took the bottle from Cleo and drank from it, wincing at the burn. Cleo hit it after him, then set it down next to her foot, the shirt riding up to bare her small, tight ass. Once again, Chase looked away, unable to shake the strange embarrassment he felt at seeing her naked body, now that he was out of the passion of the moment.

They were standing next to each other, close, thighs brushing, arms touching. Cleo drew on her cigarette, snorted the smoke out of her nostrils, then turned her head to meet Chase's gaze.

On impulse, Chase closed the distance between them, his lips touching hers. Cleo froze in surprise, then eased a little, kissing him back. Their lips moved together, and it wasn't unpleasant, but it just felt...off.

Chase pulled away first, his brows furrowed in confusion. "Cleo, I—"

"That was weird," she said, cutting him off. "Not bad...just...not right."

Chase shook his head, then inhaled smoke, coughing once more. He glanced at the cigarette and tossed it away half-finished. "Not doing it for me," he muttered, then looked back at Cleo, who was examining the glowing orange tip of her cigarette.

"Cleo, listen—what happened, with us, in there..." Chase waved his hand at the glass door. "I'm not sure...I mean..."

Cleo laughed, puffing smoke from mouth and nose. "You don't have to explain, Delany. I get it. It happened. It was good, in the moment. You're...I won't deny, in one way that was the best sex I've ever had. But in another way, it was really, *really* fucking awkward. I've never gotten it on in a bed with other people." She drank from the bottle again, hissing as it went down. "That's more Kylie and Leah's scene. I've never shared a guy before."

"I've never done anything like that either," Chase admitted. "And like you said, in a way, it was great. Having all three of you go down on me...that was intense. But with you and me—"

"If we'd been alone, I think it might have been different," Cleo said, cutting in over him.

"Yeah."

"But as it is..." Cleo shrugged. "I don't think I could do anything with you again and not have the image of tonight in my head. Even now, all I can see is Kylie and Leah taking turns on you while you kiss me."

Chase ducked his head, a feeling of mutual understand washing between them. "Yeah, exactly."

Silence stretched out, and Cleo finished her smoke, tossed it away, and swigged from the bottle. Chase finished it, and they stood side by side, watching the three a.m. Vegas crowds hustle and bustle below them.

Finally, Chase broke the silence with the question burning unspoken between them. "So...you and I...is there something there?"

Cleo didn't answer right away. "I don't know, Delany. I don't know." She crossed her arms beneath her small, hard breasts, turning to face him. Her hazel eyes met his, and they searched each other silently. Eventually, Cleo shook her head. "No, I don't think there is. I think there could have been, but..."

Chase nodded. "Yeah, I know what you mean. I almost want to say, 'I'm sorry,' or that I'm kinda disappointed. You're a cool chick, and you're hot, and talented. I think there really could've been something."

Cleo shrugged, a little lift of one shoulder. "But that back there...it was fun, but it's not something I'll do again."

"Me, either."

Cleo tilted her head, considering her next words. "Also, Chase? I'll say this totally honest. I don't think you're over that other girl. The one you sang the song to."

Chase looked away. "That's complicated."

"Meaning you don't want to talk about it."

Chase stared at the yellow headlights coming at them, the red taillights moving away; as a kid, he'd always thought of the stream of headlights as "bees" and the river of taillights as "wasps."

"I *am* over her. I mean, I know she's gone, that she doesn't want me. I'll admit that still hurts, but I'm past hoping it'll change. She's with Jeff, and she's happy. That's good enough for me. I'll move on. I'll be fine."

"I know it's none of my business," Cleo said, "but I don't think this is the way to go about getting over her." She waved at the hotel room again, meaning what had gone on earlier.

"No, you're probably right. But...I don't know. It's not something that makes sense out loud. I'm not trying to forget her, just...god, how do I say it? I need to get rid of the hold she has on my heart." Chase ran his finger back and forth on the railing, staring at the path of his finger rather than meeting Cleo's too-knowing gaze. "For a long time after she made it clear she didn't love me, I couldn't do anything. I couldn't make myself care about anyone. All I could do was play and write music. Which is all well and good, but...I can't let the pain rule me. I have to get over her."

"I thought you *were* over her."

"I said it's complicated."

"Meaning you have no fucking idea what you're feeling, because there's just too much going on."

Chase laughed. "Yeah, pretty much."

"My advice, for what it's worth? Give it time." Cleo rested her head against his shoulder, and they stayed like that for a long time. Eventually, Cleo pushed away. "Now get out of here."

"What about Kylie and Leah?"

"They'll be fine. This is what they do. They're... complicated. I'll tell 'em you said 'thanks for a good time.'"

After he got dressed and left the hotel, drunk and dizzy and confused, Chase wandered Vegas on foot, trying to sort out what he was feeling.

He'd told Cleo the truth about Anna; he was as over her as he would get, this soon. Seeing her had hurt, had dredged up a lot of emotions he'd worked to bury. But it had also reinforced the fact that she was gone.

But what he hadn't told Cleo was how Jamie had affected him. She was still there, in his head. Under his skin.

When he'd kissed Cleo on the balcony, the reason he'd pulled away was because all he could think of was Jamie. The pained, tortured look on her face when she'd torn herself away after their kiss. It was brief, but that one kiss had held more tantalizing pressure than Chase had ever felt. He'd been ripped apart by that kiss.

Cleo, Kylie, Leah...he'd had fun, but now, alone after the fact, all he could think of was Jamie. Where was she? What was she doing? Was she with someone else?

He imagined her at a bar, a bottle of beer in her hand, leaning into some half-drunk asshole with groping hands. The thought of some other guy's paws on Jamie's full, hypnotizing hips sent a pang of hurt through Chase. The idea of her going home with that guy, stripping for him, kissing him, caressing him, letting him touch her ivory skin...it made Chase crazy with irrational jealousy.

He tried to banish the images, but he couldn't. All he could see was Jamie's fiery curls and green gaze, and then he would see some faceless male clawing at her skin, the sweet flesh that should belong to Chase, but didn't.

He could feel her palm scraping over his scalp as she kissed him, her balm-slick lips sliding on his, teasing him, her full breasts pushing against him, nipples pebbling against her bra hard enough to feel through the cotton.

"Fuck," Chase growled aloud.

He swerved off the sidewalk and into a doorway, the bumping bass line from within the club promising a few hours of distraction, at least. He sat at the sticky, scratched bar, watching fake-breasted strippers undulate against silver poles. He stuck to beer, lost count, lost track, lost time. The strippers became the same person after a while, delirious images of Jamie, naked, dancing just for him.

Eventually, he felt Gage slump onto the stool next to him, pry the bottle from his fingers, and drag him out of the club. Gage never said a word, just propped up Chase's dead weight and dragged him into a cab, into their hotel, into bed.

Day came, and with it the oblivion of hangover pain, the haze of travel, setup, performance, and the familiar ritual of going from one show to the next, now drowned in a constant ocean of alcohol.

Women came and went, but none of them stirred his interest.

Jamie stayed in his thoughts, until eventually numbness set in.

THREE

JAMIE WAS DRUNK. Like, really, *really* drunk. The kind of hammered where she couldn't remember where she was, how she'd gotten there, or what was going on. She was conscious, but unable to form coherent thoughts. She'd been this way for a while, she thought. She was starting to gain some control over herself, over her awareness.

Focus, Jamie, she told herself. *Wake up.*

She wasn't really asleep, but it felt that way. She needed to get her bearings. Something was happening, something was going on. Something not right. Deep breath, think hard, blink…blink.

Jamie breathed in, cleared her vision, squinting straight ahead. A blur of colors, a wash of inchoate images: the faint scent of booze on someone's breath close by, aftershave, male deodorant, male musk; soft breath on her face, the sound of male grunting above her, flesh against flesh, the wet sucking sounds of sex. She focused again, forcing coherency to the world: blank white above her, a ceiling with a trapezoidal area of brighter white from a window. Jamie squinted to her right, saw a window in triplicate, shadows beyond, an orange dot of a streetlamp, a gibbous moon.

The sounds of sex continued, and then Jamie became slowly aware of physical sensation. The sex was happening to her. Another sound filtered through the haze of alcohol: feminine moans of sex enjoyed. *Her* voice, moaning softly. *She* was having sex.

Jamie gathered herself together and focused once more, this time on the blurry pale skin and dark hair and pale blue eyes above her. No one she knew. Thick, shaggy brown hair the color of walnut shell, unkempt, uncut. A goatee, thick as an overgrown shrub, with a few days' worth of growth on his cheeks between the goatee and his long sideburns. Pale blue eyes watching her, slightly unfocused, dilated, reddened. A weak chin,; thin features; thin, dry, cracked lips. Jamie continued her perusal of the man she was having sex with, almost apathetically. She wasn't sure who he was or why she was having sex with him; he certainly wasn't attractive, not in the way she usually liked her men. He looked young, younger than she, more of a manling, a man-boy, which was also not her type. He was skinny, all hard angles and thin, wiry arms, hairy legs. Again, so not her type.

Jamie focused on the rest of her awareness. He *did* seem to know what he was doing, sexually. Decent rhythm, stroking evenly. He filled her well enough. Not huge, but not tiny. She could feel him inside her, so that was okay. He didn't weigh much, so she wasn't being crushed. That always sucked. He wasn't grunting like some kind of hog, which was nice, just softly groaning low in his throat, a constant sound.

Time to finish this and figure out what the fuck was going on. Jamie pushed at his shoulder. "Roll over."

"'Kay," he said, and complied.

She settled onto him, making sure to keep her weight evenly distributed. He was just a skinny little guy—no sense in breaking him. She would have to hold back a bit; besides, she was feeling queasy and dizzy, and not really in the mood for a wild frenzy.

Jamie adjusted the angle of her hips and set a slow rolling rhythm, supporting her weight with her hands next to his face. A little close for comfort, since she didn't know him and wasn't attracted to him, but she could feel a little orgasm coming along nicely, so there was no sense in stopping now. Maybe if she closed her eyes, it would help.

She arched her back and rolled her hips, and let herself gasp a little louder as the tip of his cock hit close to her G-spot. Not right on, but close. Close enough.

Then she felt a palm on her side, running up her ribs to cup her full, swaying breast. *Wait a second.* There were already two hands on her waist, holding her in place. The extra hand gripped her boob, too hard, groping and fumbling awkwardly.

What the fuck?

The hand roamed over her back and down her spine to explore her ass. Jamie turned her head, craning to see who else was in bed with her. She was too drunk to panic, and this seemed like consensual sex anyway. But...two guys? Hell, no. The hand slipped up her back and over her shoulder, then back under to grope her tit again. It was a pudgy, hairy hand, short fingers, greedy fingers. Strong, clumsy fingers.

She peered dizzily behind her and saw, yes, another man. This one was the polar opposite of the guy beneath her. Short, stocky, a bit of a belly around the middle, a mat of hair on his chest, small, beady eyes and wet, thick lips. Watery, bloodshot brown eyes, moon-face features. Way, *way* not her type. And he was on his knees behind her. Was he...? He wasn't. No. No....

Yes, he was.

The moon-faced second guy was on his knees behind her, gripping his short, thick, uncircumcised penis in his hand and stroking it along the crease of her ass.

Um, no.

She croaked, but couldn't get words to come out. She was close to coming, which wasn't helping matters, but having moon-face behind her ostensibly preparing to anally penetrate her was one hell of a turnoff.

She croaked again, trying to get the "fuck no, you aren't doing that" out past her lips, but it wasn't working.

Then Moon-face spoke. "Are you ready for Big Ben?" As he said this, he gestured with his penis, probing her ass-crack with the tip of his cock.

That got her powers of speech working. "'Big Ben'? Did you just refer to your penis as...'Big Ben'?"

The guy beneath her choked back a laugh. Jamie felt an orgasm quavering within her, absurdly, impossibly timed. She couldn't stop her body's rolling rhythm now. Couldn't.

Moon-face—whose name was probably Ben... she seemed to hazily remember meeting a Ben... and a Brad—hesitated, licked his lips, assessing whether she thought this was funny and/or hot.

"Yes?" he said, his tone of voice lost between a statement and a question.

Jamie, coming now, couldn't quite express her disbelief. "Are you—oh, god, oh, god—are you fucking serious? Big Ben? Does that make the rest of you—oh, god, yes—Little Ben?"

The guy beneath her laughed out loud now, and then groaned as he came. Jamie didn't feel the hot rush of seed when he spasmed, so he was wearing a condom, thank god.

Jamie felt something hot and hard probing her ass again.

"No, asshole." She threw herself clumsily off the guy beneath her, away from the probing nastiness of Big Ben/Little Ben. "And I also mean that literally. No asshole. Not for you. Not for anyone. Not ever."

Jamie may have been…experienced, sexually, but she drew the line at anal. Not gonna happen. Especially not like this. Not with him.

Ben shrugged, his face pouting comically. "Um…okay, then."

Jamie was overcome by a rush of dizziness, and lay back in the bed, palm over her eyes.

"So…can you at least help me out, here?" Ben asked. "You can't leave me hanging like this."

Jamie squinted at him, feeling floppy and disconnected from herself, severed from reality. She was beginning to come down a little, and she found herself not caring about anything, especially now that her virgin little asshole was safe from probing.

Ben was lying down next to her, not too close, thankfully. The bed they were all three in was big, king-sized, probably. Good thing, too. Jamie watched her hand reach out, wondering what it was doing.

Oh, that.

Her hand fisted around Ben's penis and began to pump. He grunted, porcine, thrusting his hips into her hand. Jamie felt her lip curling in something that would have been disgust if she'd been able to feel anything, but, thankfully, she was numb emotionally and mentally.

And that, she abruptly remembered, was the reason she'd gotten so hammered in the first place: to achieve numbness, to forget him.

Ben grunted one last time, hips thrust up, and then came onto her hand and his belly. Jamie's eyes were closed, sparing her having to watch. She cracked her eyes open and stared at her hand, barely suppressing a shudder of revulsion.

What...the fuck...am I doing?

Jamie slid down the bed and off the foot end, glancing around the room. The only article of her clothing she could find among the piles of towels and jeans and boxers and T-shirts was her panties. She scooped them up and donned them, grateful to not be totally nude anymore.

The guy whose name she hadn't remembered yet—but who she strongly felt might be Brad—got up and found her bra and T-shirt, handing them to her wordlessly before getting a pair of gym shorts from his dresser next to the window. Ben didn't move, just watched the proceedings disinterestedly. He stared openly, not even bothering to disguise his blatant ogling. Jamie tried to ignore his leering gaze as she hooked her bra beneath her breasts and then spanned it around her body to stuff her boobs in.

Eventually, she snapped. "Would you look somewhere else, please? Big Ben ain't gettin' nothin' else from me, I can promise you that."

The other guy, tugging his shirt over his head, glanced at Ben. "Dude. Enough already. Get the fuck out."

"I'm tired, now, man."

"I don't give a shit. Get the fuck out."

Ben frowned, shrugging. "Fine, man. Whatever." He stuffed his feet into a pair of shorts that hung past his knees, then tugged a Bob Marley shirt on. As he exited the room, he said, "Call me later, Brad. We'll blaze. I'm getting an 'O' from my hookup tomorrow."

Brad nodded. "Sure thing, dude."

Jamie watched all this in dawning comprehension. She pulled her shirt on, saw her Steve Madden sandals by the door, and slipped her feet into them, stumbling from one foot to the other. "You're a stoner?"

Brad shrugged. "I smoke down, yeah. Why?"

Jamie just shook her head. "I'm really hammered. I don't remember...well, shit. I don't remember a damn thing. I wasn't even sure what your name was until 'Big Ben' said it."

Brad's face pinched in confusion. "You don't remember anything?" He stuffed his feet into a pair of ADIDAS sports sandals. "We met at Duggan's. You sat down with us and started flirting. We did some shots of tequila, and then you suggested going back to my place for a threesome. I thought you were joking, but...you weren't. I couldn't believe my luck."

Jamie rubbed her forehead. "I suggested it? Shit. With you two?" She left the bedroom and found the kitchen, saw her purse sitting on the counter by the microwave.

"'With us two'? What's that supposed to mean?"

Jamie washed her hands in the kitchen sink, almost frantically. "Nothing. Don't worry about it. Did I drive here? Please tell me I didn't."

Brad shook his head. "I only had a beer and a shot, so I drove."

"Were you high?"

He shrugged, a tiny roll of his shoulders. "A little." He took a box of Cheez-Its from a cabinet and opened them, offered them to Jamie, who took some. "Does it matter? I wasn't drunk, and I wasn't, like, crazy-blazed. I was fine."

Jamie suppressed her desire to tell him driving high was just as stupid as driving drunk. He was her ride back to her car, so she held her tongue.

They munched on crackers, and then Brad pulled a pair of Dr. Peppers from the fridge.

After a while, Brad said, "Sorry about Ben. He's kind of a douche. He has this hookup for some seriously amazing bud, so I hang out with him. But...he's a douche."

Jamie studiously examined a cracker. "If he's a douche, why the hell did you agree to a three-way with him?"

Brad shook his head and shrugged. "I don't fucking know. You're the hottest girl who's ever paid attention to me, so I guess I just went with it for the chance to get with you. I may have been a bit more blazed than I thought, though. Now it seems like kind of a bad idea."

"You think? 'Are you ready for Big Ben'? Who the fuck names their cock that?"

Brad laughed. "Right? I can't believe he actually said that. Like, he was totally serious."

"No, he really was." Jamie laughed, but only to cover the shudder of disgust.

Brad was silent for a while. "I kind of feel like I should apologize. If you don't remember anything, you must have been pretty hammered when you sat down with us."

Jamie sighed. "Yeah. It's probably my own fault, though. I'm the kind of person who you can't tell how drunk they are. I could be obliterated, and you wouldn't know it. If you can see me looking impaired, like I'm stumbling or slurring or whatever, then I'm probably beyond schwasted and about to pass out."

Brad toyed with the tab of his soda can, not looking at Jamie. "So...you really don't remember anything?"

"No, honestly. I sort of came to in the middle of having sex with you. Everything before that is a blank."

Brad kept his eyes averted. "Oh. I guess I thought we sort of hit it off at Duggan's. I thought you and I...maybe we could—"

Jamie winced. "Brad, listen, I'm sorry. This whole thing is weird and uncomfortable for me. I don't know you. I don't remember meeting you, and that's just the hard, honest truth." She set her empty can by the sink. "I'd really like to just go home. Is there a bus stop nearby? Or..."

Brad shook his head. "A bus stop? Have you ever actually ridden a SMART bus? It's terrifying, and that's not even mentioning the crazy people." He set his can down next to Jamie's, staring at the two cans together as if they represented something that could have been but would never be. "I'll take you to your car. Come on."

The ride from Brad's apartment, which was in Hazel Park, back to Duggan's in Royal Oak was one long, awkward silence. Woodward Avenue was empty at three-thirty in the morning, a single SMART bus rumbling along the right-hand lane, spewing clouds of diesel exhaust. Duggan's was dark, Jamie's battered blue Buick LeSabre one of a few cars left in the lot.

As Jamie was sliding out of Brad's old red F-150, he touched her elbow to stop her. "Could I call you sometime?"

Jamie sighed, not turning around to look at him. "Brad, I'm sorry. I'm gonna be brutally honest here. I just want to go home and try to forget this ever happened. It's not really you, per se. You're a nice guy. Sex with you was nice. But I'm just...I'm fucked up, okay? This was a mistake, an awful drunken mistake. There's so much I'm trying to forget, and this is just one more thing." She shook her head, almost angrily. "I'm sorry, I don't know why I said all that."

Brad didn't answer for a long moment. "It was 'nice,' huh? That's the kiss of death for a guy. I get it, though."

"I'm sorry, Brad. Really. I wish I knew what else to say—"

"No, it's fine. It really is. I had a good time, except for—"

"Except for Big Ben," Jamie filled in. She turned and grinned at Brad as she stood up, leaning down to look into the open door. "A word of advice, from a woman to a man? Next time you try to score with a chick, leave the creepy douchebag out of it. Things might have gone differently if he hadn't have been there harshing my mellow, or whatever it is you stoners say."

Brad just laughed. "Yeah, I'm starting to see that." He put the truck in Drive. "Anyway, you're here. So...thanks. And Jamie? Good luck forgetting. But remember, sometimes you can't forget, and shouldn't. Sometimes you need to remember the bad shit, so when the good times come along, they'll mean that much more to you."

Jamie closed the door, and Brad drove away, back south down Woodward. She stood watching his taillights recede, hearing his last words echoing in her head.

Maybe forgetting Chase was impossible. Maybe she should just go on with her life and try to let go, rather than wishing for the impossible and hating life when it didn't happen.

Jamie drove home to her apartment in Clawson, barely seeing the road. With every mile, something hot and acidic rose in her gut, as much emotional as physical. By the time she was unlocking her front door, she was holding it back by force of will.

She slammed her door behind her and ran into the bathroom, dropping her purse on the floor as she fell to her knees and vomited into the toilet. She brought up everything she'd had to drink, everything she'd eaten, and then vomited more. When she felt done, she sank back sit on her thighs, her feet tucked beneath her, wiping her mouth with the back of her hand. Then her vindictive subconscious brought up an image of Ben, kneeling behind her, waving his chode-like penis at her, and then she had a sensory memory of Ben spooging onto her hand, and she vomited again, bringing up bile this time.

She slumped with her cheek against the toilet rim, holding back what felt suspiciously like tears.

She couldn't cry. She didn't cry. Not about guys. Not about doing the walk of shame. Not about waking up in strange apartments, or having sex with guys she didn't know. She did *not* cry.

She needed to talk to someone. Jamie dug her phone out of her purse and dialed Anna, knowing she'd answer even though it was four in the morning.

Anna answered on the third ring. "Jay? What's up? It's four a.m., hooker."

"I know, I'm sorry to call you at this hour, but...I fucked up, Anna. Really fucked up. Can you come over?"

"Shit. Are you hurt? Pregnant?"

"What? No. Not like that. Just...I need my best friend."

Anna paused before answering. "You broke your vow of celibacy, didn't you?" Jamie didn't answer, just sniffled as she struggled to hold back the tears, and that was enough for Anna. "Oh, shit. You're crying? I'll be there in a few minutes."

As she disconnected, Jamie heard Anna talking to Jeff in the background, telling him she didn't know when she'd be back. Jamie tossed the phone in her purse, stood up unsteadily, and brushed her teeth. She stripped, turned on the shower, and let it run hot, staring at herself in the steam-fogged mirror.

She stepped under the stream of scalding-hot water and scrubbed herself until her skin was red and raw, and then let the water soak her until the hot water ran out. Jamie was sniffling nonstop now, but refused to let the tears fall. She put on her favorite sleep T-shirt, an ancient thing with Eeyore on the front that used to be black but was now faded closer to gray.

Jamie climbed into bed, curled into a ball, and focused on not crying.

She'd been holding it back for so long. Not just tonight. The thing with Ben and Brad was the last straw, the tipping point. She'd been denying herself the emotions, pushing them down, bottling them up and ignoring them.

Now, whether she liked it or not, they were all coming up, coming out.

She heard the apartment door open and close, and then Anna appeared in her bedroom door, a box of donuts in one hand, the other holding a cup-tray with two Tim Horton's cups. Anna was sleep-mussed, long blonde hair tied up in a messy bun, wearing yoga pants, Uggs, and a several-sizes-too-big Dopey T-shirt every bit as old as Jamie's Eeyore one. She had makeup smeared under her eyes, and as she sat down on the bed, Jamie caught a whiff of sex from her.

"I brought you a hazelnut mocha, extra whipped cream. Plus, a dozen assorted donuts, with a few extra honey crullers." Anna set the donuts and coffee on the dresser, kicked off her boots, and sat cross-legged next to Jamie. "Talk, Jay. What happened?"

Jamie tried to sit up, but couldn't. She rolled to her back and met Anna's worried blue eyes. "I got drunk."

Anna frowned. "Well, that's not too unusual, though, right?"

"No, Anna. I mean, really, *really* drunk. Blacked-out drunk."

"Oh."

"And I woke up in a strange apartment."

Anna winced. "Shit."

"Yeah. Except it wasn't really waking up, exactly. It was more...coming to...in the middle of having sex. With a guy I don't remember meeting, whose name I didn't know until afterward."

Anna's eyes slid closed. "*Jamie.*"

"I know. Shut up, though. It gets worse."

"Worse? How the hell can it get worse?"

Jamie squeezed her eyes closed, near panic as the tears welled up. "There was another guy in the bed." Anna made a strangled noise, but Jamie spoke over it. "He...I was on top, and the guy I was having sex with had his hands on my hips, you know how they do, holding on right where your legs meet your hips? Well, then I felt this other hand start touching my boobs. And then I saw this guy behind me. God, Anna. You don't understand how drunk I was. It was hard to see anything. Like, past seeing double. I saw this guy, right? And you know what he was about to do? Yeah, you can guess, can't you?"

"You didn't, Jamie. Tell me you didn't let him."

"Hell, no. He had his short little chode-dick in his hand and he was...god, I'm gonna puke again... he was tickling my ass crack with it."

Anna put two fingers to her mouth and puffed out her cheeks, making a heaving noise.

Jamie laughed, a choked, humorless sound. "This is the best part, though. Or worst, depending on how you look at it. You know what this guy said to me? As he was about to anally penetrate me, he said, and I quote, 'Are you ready for Big Ben?'"

Anna blinked several times, processing. "Are you serious? He actually said that?"

"Yes, he did. And no, he wasn't joking. His name was Ben, and he named his dick Big Ben."

"That's...I don't even know what that is. Terrible. Funny, but terrible."

Jamie nodded. "Yeah. So I put a stop to the anal real fast. But I guess I lied when I said that was the worst part."

Anna covered her face with her hand. "There's *more*?"

Jamie closed her eyes and drew a deep, shuddering breath. "Let me just preface this with a reminder that I was still drunk, and I had no idea what was happening. I think I thought it was all a bad dream, or something. I still want to think it was. But...anyway. This Ben guy. He was sitting there, all pouty, with this pathetic hard-on. And he begged me to help him out."

"You didn't. Please, Baby Jesus, tell me you didn't go down on him."

"Well, no, I didn't do that. I gave him a hand job. I have this image in my head now. I mean, I didn't want to touch his dick. But part of me seemed to be...I don't know...acting by itself or something. I watched my hand reach out of its own volition and grab him. I closed my eyes at that point, but I can't get this memory out of my head of him coming on my hand. With the right guy, I don't mind that, you know? I mean, I'm not a money-shot kind of girl—that's nasty—but if I'm into the guy, I don't mind having his come on me. But this guy...I can't describe him 'cause I swear to god I'll puke again if I do. He was such a creeper. It wasn't how he looked, exactly, it was just...him. I was getting dressed, and this guy was just *staring* at me. Watching me get dressed. With what he'd said and was about to do to me...no lube, no prep, nothing? It was creepy." Jamie shivered dramatically, choking back bile and tears.

Anna slumped back against the headboard. "Jamie. Ohmigod, Jamie. How—and *why*—do you get yourself into these situations?"

"I don't know, Anna. I don't know. I wish I knew," Jamie heard herself say.

She knew it was a lie, though. She knew precisely why she'd gotten herself into that situation. She'd gone out drinking to drown out thoughts of *him*, of Chase. Then, at some point, she'd decided to try and erase her need for Chase with other guys.

She couldn't tell Anna any of this, though.

What she said was, "Anna, I'm tired of being a slut."

"You're not—"

"I *am*. We've been over this. I...am...a... slut. I know it, and I own it. I like sex. I *love* sex. I'm a twelve-step program away from being a nymphomaniac."

"So choose not to be."

"It's not that easy, Anna. I wish it was. I tried. I kept my vow from Vegas until now, no sex, not even my own fingers. Not even Mr. Pinky McVibrator. And you know how much I love my Mr. Pinky."

"Yes, Jay. I know you love him. I loved my Mr. Pinky, too."

"Then you found Jeff, and now you don't need Mr. Pinky, 'cause you have Mr. Long Hard and Attached to a Real Man Who Loves You."

"So what happened?"

"I don't know." Jamie hated the lie, hated that she could see the knowledge of Jamie's lie in Anna's eyes.

"Jay. I'm your best friend. Tell me."

"No."

"*Ja*mie."

"*An*na."

"Okay, fine." Anna stood up and paced away, grabbed her coffee, and sipped it. "There's something you're not telling me. If you need your secrets, then fine, whatever."

"It's not that I don't want to tell you. I just... can't. Not yet." Jamie managed to sit up as she said this.

The hurt in Anna's eyes was more than Jamie could take. One tear slid down her cheek, and then another, and then a third, and then she was bawling helplessly, curled up around a pillow, wracked with bone-shuddering sobs.

Anna knew there was nothing to say, so she sat grabbed the box of Kleenex from the back of the toilet and sat down next to Jamie with it, stroking the curly red hair out of her face as she wept.

When the storm of tears quieted, Anna drew Jamie's head into her lap and looked down at her best friend. "You know I love you, Jamie. You know I'll never judge you. You know there's nothing you could do to make me not be your best friend. I won't ask you again. Just know…I'm here, okay? If and when you're ready to spill, I'll be ready to listen."

"I know. And thanks."

Anna drew a deep breath, and Jamie knew the ass-kicking was about to ensue. "You know, too, that I can't let you get away with this bullshit without kicking your ass."

"I know."

"It's not about the vow of celibacy, Jay. That was just my attempt to help you see that you can enjoy life and enjoy being yourself without sex. Especially without *cheap* sex." Anna twirled the end of one of Jamie's curls between her index finger and thumb. "But in the end, you have to want to be different inside yourself."

"I know, Anna."

"No, I don't think you do." Anna met Jamie's eyes, her blue gaze hard now. "Have some goddamn self-respect, Jamie. Quit putting out for chumps and douchebags. Wait for a real man, a good man. If that guy—*the* guy—comes along, and you have no standards, no self-respect, then he won't respect you. And a guy who doesn't respect you will walk all over you. You'll be little more than his sex slave. You have to want better for yourself."

Jamie couldn't help the renewal of tears Anna's brutally honest words engendered. "Easy for you to say."

Anna drew back, stung. "Really? You think so? You were there when I was with Bruce. You think I just magically figured all this out? Everything that happened with Chase...running off to New York to fuck him, and then running back to Jeff? God, Jamie. I hate myself for leaving Jeff like I did. I was too chicken to see what I had with a damn good man who loved me, so I ran off to be with someone else. Someone like Chase."

Jamie couldn't help defending him. "What's wrong with Chase?"

"Nothing. It's not about Chase. He's a good guy. He'll make someone very happy someday, if he ever learns to settle down. But he's a rock star, and you can't expect a rock star to be faithful. I can't live like that. He wouldn't have been able to give me the attention and love I needed. He's too focused on his career."

"You don't know that. Maybe he could have."

Anna looked at Jamie with suspicion in her eyes. "No, maybe you're right. But I've made my choice, and I don't regret it for a moment. Chase wasn't right for me. I didn't love him. I never did. Maybe I could have, but I'll never know that, will I? Why are you pushing this?"

Jamie wiped her eyes. "Sorry. I don't know. I just...I don't know. You have Jeff, and you're deliriously happy. I'm happy for you." She couldn't keep the jealousy out of her voice."

Anna sighed. "It'll happen for you, Jay. It will. Just...learn to be okay within yourself. For yourself. It'll happen. Probably when you least expect it."

Jamie felt exhaustion creeping over her. "I know. I will." She peered up at Anna through sleep-heavy eyes. "Just make me one promise."

"What?"

"Love me forever and be my BFF, no matter what?"

"You know it, hooker. No matter what."

Jamie pretended to fall asleep, listening to Anna let herself out. Real sleep soon washed over her, but not before the inevitable thoughts of Chase made their way through her mind and heart.

She couldn't tell Anna what she was feeling for Chase. Not yet. Maybe not ever. Anna had promised to be her BFF no matter what, but if Jamie and Chase were to be together, Anna would be reminded of everything that had happened between her and Chase every time she saw him. And considering how close Anna and Jamie were, that would be often.

Jamie sank into sleep, knowing Chase was an impossibility.

That didn't stop her heart from crying out for him, or her body from needing him.

FOUR

JAMIE SIGHED AS SHE PLACED the last stack of folded Cacique panties on the display table. She'd been folding and putting away the stock order for hours, after an insanely busy Saturday afternoon rush. She was exhausted, emotionally, mentally, and physically.

It had been a little more than two months since her drunken debauchery with Ben and Brad, and in the intervening weeks she'd kept almost strictly to herself. She worked a huge amount of hours at Lane Bryant as it was, and then she'd been promoted to assistant manager, and her hours had only increased.

The busyness had been good for her. She worked, went to the gym, and went home. She'd been studiously avoiding her drinking buddies, knowing if she went out with them, she'd fall right back into her old ways. Meaning, she'd end up doing the walk of shame again.

She'd gotten back on the celibacy wagon, which was good but sucked. She was busy, she was in shape, and she was learning to be content by herself.

But then, that was the problem: Jamie was lonely.

Anna was busier than ever with Jeff and their ever-expanding DJ business, so Jamie didn't even have her BFF to hang out with as much as she used to. That was fine, she told herself. Anna was happier than she'd ever been. Good for her.

Jamie was keeping her legs closed and staying off her back. That was a good thing.

Maybe when she met Mr. Right, sex with him would be, like, the best ever. The problem was, if she was keeping to herself all the time, how was she supposed to meet him?

The other problem, the real problem, was that Chase wouldn't leave her thoughts. She hadn't seen him in nearly three months, and all those weeks, all those days hadn't dulled her desire for him. He was still on her mind when she fell asleep, still in her heart when she sat in the bathtub with a bottle of wine and Mumford and Sons on Repeat.

Yeah, she still drank too much; she just did it alone. Which was even more pathetic, in her opinion.

Jamie glanced around the store one last time, making sure everything was in place for the opener tomorrow morning. She'd let the other two girls go home early once the rush died down, so she was locking up alone.

Just as well. No one to goad her into going out with them.

She shut off the lights, locked the doors, and made her way across the parking lot, nose buried in her phone as she checked Facebook. The status updates weren't helping, of course. It was Saturday night, just past midnight, and all her friends' statuses were the same. Everyone was out, and drunk, and having a great time.

"Lynn tagged you in a photograph...." But of course, the pic was a self-taken shot of Lynn and her boyfriend Aaron making out at The Post Bar, and the caption was, *Jamie u whore where the fuck are you,* chica! *You should b partying with us rt now!*

The Post Bar. Ugh. Posers and douchetards getting hammered and pretending to be cool.

That used to be me, Jamie realized. Suddenly, it didn't interest her as much. Yeah, she was turning into a lonely old hag, and she was probably only a few dozen cats away from being the cat lady, but for some reason going to the bar to get blitzed and flirt with guys who'd bathed in cologne and popped their collars and shuffled around in their Puma shoes just didn't seem as appetizing as it used to be.

Jamie unlocked her Buick and opened the door, scrolling through her Facebook feed until she reached posts she'd already seen. She heard a vehicle approaching from behind her but didn't turn to look as she slid into her car, the leather cold on her thighs.

"Jamie!" a male voice called. "Get in!"

Jamie clapped her hand to her chest, having jumped clear off the seat in surprise. She glanced up to see Vince hanging out the window of his silver Excursion. Vince's girlfriend Nina waved from the passenger seat, and then the window behind Vince's rolled down to reveal the one face she couldn't say no to: Lane, her openly gay *other* best friend.

"Jamie, darling, we're going to Harpo's," Lane announced, throwing open the door, hopping out to drag Jamie toward the mammoth SUV. "We've got an extra ticket since my loser boyfriend got called in to work tonight. You're coming."

Jamie had to make a token effort to say no. "Lane, I can't. I'm exhausted. I worked a double today, *and* we had the inventory order come in. I just want to go home and collapse."

Lane stuck his tongue out at her, shoving her into the car, pushing on her ass to get her through the door. Lane was a twink, thin, absurdly beautiful with startling blue eyes and angelic features, manicured fingernails, and impeccable fashion sense. Jamie could have flattened him with ease if she wanted to, but she also knew Lane wouldn't take no for an answer. He would just pester and whine and harp on her until she agreed.

Besides, she'd been good for months. She could afford to unwind a little.

"Jamie, *chica*, you've been avoiding us for months. It's time to get out and have some fun." Lane reached across her body and buckled her in, then wrapped his arm around her shoulders and gave her a squeeze, kissing her cheek. "I can only let you be lame for so long, then it becomes my honor-bound duty to drag you out for a fun night of drinking with your gay husband."

Jamie laughed, Lane's irrepressible humor and infectious sense of fun getting to her and lightening her mood. "Fine, but you have to have my back."

Lane pretended to swoon as if mortally wounded. "Of *course* I have your back. How could you even doubt me?"

"I mean you have to keep me out of trouble. Drinking a bit, fine. Letting me do the walk of shame, not fine."

Lane lifted his index finger. "Ah. Now *that* I can do. When did you join the nunnery, if I may ask?"

"Don't be a dick, Lane. I'm not a nun. I'm just taking a break from my role as a hopeless slutbag."

"You're not hopeless," Lane said, smirking.

Jamie smacked his shoulder. "So you agree I'm a slutbag, then?"

Lane narrowed his eyes. "This sounds like a verbal trap, but I'll go ahead and spring it. Baby girl, you're probably the only person who's fucked more guys than me. And *that's* saying something."

Jamie sighed. "That's what I was afraid of. I mean, I knew it. But...maybe I don't want that to be me anymore."

Lane, ever on his toes, nodded, his expression serious and genuinely concerned. "Well, sweetie, all I can say is, if that's what you want, then you have to make it happen. Matty turned me around, that's for sure. I haven't so much as kissed another boy in the year and half I've been dating Matty. Which for me is a record. Usually I'm bored and sucking cock in the bathroom by week three."

Jamie laughed because it was funny, but also because it was true. Her expression sobered quickly, though. "Are you in love with Matt? Are you happy?"

Lane glanced past Jamie out the window, thinking before he answered. "Yes, I think I am. When my need to keep him happy and faithful to me out-weighs my desire for all the shiny new boytoys, you know he has to mean something important. I don't want to let Matty down by being a ho, so I choose not to be a ho." He shrugged as if it was simple math.

Jamie nodded, but inwardly questioned how easy it really was. "Well, if works for you, it can work for me. I just need to find the guy to inspire me down the straight and narrow."

Lane laughed. "No, honey. The straight and narrow is a myth. I'm still kinky as hell. I just get everything I need from *him*. That's why it works."

They chatted for the rest of the ride down to Harpo's, and Jamie never even thought to question who they were going to see play. It didn't matter, after all. She wasn't going for the music.

When they entered the club, a band was fin-ishing up their set with an instrumental hard rock number. Jamie and Lane got their drinks from the bar and then made their way to the railing over-looking the pit. Vince, Nina, and John and Kelly, who were friends of Nina's that Jamie didn't know, went down to the pit to get good spots for the next band, who it seemed they were there to see.

Jamie and Lane made small talk as the techies cleared the stage and reset it for the main act, and then the lights went down and the distinct sounds of the band warming up clattered over the crowd.

"Do you know who's about to play?" Jamie asked Lane.

Lane shrugged. "No, not really. I've heard Vince and Nina talking about this show for weeks, but they bought the tickets. I'm just along for the fun. I'm more of a Britney fan anyway, you know that. Hard rock is *so* not my thing."

The lights came up slowly, purple and red and blue washing in strobing pools over the stage. Then a spotlight lanced through the gloom to illuminate the lead singer.

Jamie's heart stopped.

"Hey, guys. It's great to be back in D-town. How's everybody doing?" The crowd went nuts, and when they settled down, he continued, "Awesome. Well, we're Six Foot Tall, as you might have guessed, and I'm Chase Delany. So tell me, are ya'll ready to rock?"

Jamie was frozen to the spot, one hand clutching her third vodka cranberry, the other gripping the railing in a fist so tight her knuckles were white. *No. No. Not now. I was just starting to be okay.*

That was a lie. She wasn't okay. She would never be okay as long as Chase Delany was alive and not hers.

She watched him rile the crowd all through the first number, getting them pumped and wild, moshing with violent abandon, psyching them into a frenzy. She couldn't take her eyes off him. She was close enough to see his features, but too far away to make out anything detailed. She needed to see him up close. She needed him to see her; she was afraid of what would happen if he did see her.

Jamie turned to Lane and sank her clawed hand into the muscle of his arm. "It's *him*."

Lane looked at her as if she'd sprouted horns. "Retract the claws, kitten, you're hurting my arm." Jamie forced her hand to her side, and Lane shook his arm, wincing. "Damn girl, you got some grip. Now what the hell are you talking about? You know him? I admit, he's one fine-ass piece of man-meat."

"It's Chase. *Chase*. Anna's Chase."

Lane's eyes widened. "Oh, shit." Lane looked from Jamie to Chase, who was standing at stage-edge, his eyes locked on Jamie, never missing a beat of his Kid Rock–style rap number. "Wait. You said 'him' like he meant something to you."

Jamie turned away, realizing she was danger-ously close to admitting something no one could ever know. "No. Never mind."

Lane leaned back, examining Jamie as if seeing her for the first time. "Girl, you're lying through your teeth. It's me we're talking about here. If you can't tell your gay husband about it, who can you tell?"

"No one. Never. It's nothing. There's nothing to tell." She drained her rocks glass and shook it.

"Whaddya know, I'm empty. How about another round?" She turned away to escape to the bar.

Lane grabbed her by the shoulders and span her around to face him. "I don't think so, sweetheart. You're not getting out of it that easy. Now, let me see if I have this straight. He's your BFF's ex. If I remember correctly, that was a messy situation, in which he ended up with a broken heart. Yes?" Jamie nodded. "And you're in love with him. I can see that much for myself. You don't even have to say it. The question is, does he know? Does he love you back?"

Jamie licked her lips and squeezed her eyes shut, refusing to let her emotions fly away from her. "It's impossible, Lane. *Impossible.* Completely and totally. There's no point in even discussing it."

"Nothing is impossible when it comes to love, kitten. Trust me on this. Matty is as far away from my type as a man can get, but it works. It may seem impossible, but you never know what can happen, right?"

Jamie shook her head, staring at the ceiling, refusing to even blink. When she had control over herself, she said, "No, Lane. He and Anna...they can't see each other. It would cause both of them too much pain. I just...I have to get over him."

Lane's voice was achingly tender. "Jamie, baby. You know I love you, so you know I'm saying this out of an attempt to help you. You're seriously about three seconds away from ugly crying over this guy right here in the middle of Harpo's. That's not something you can just get over."

"I have to," she whispered.

Lane shook his head. "No. Live your life for you. Anna's your BFF, she'll understand. She may not like it. It may be awkward, it may break every rule in the girlfriend handbook, but when love comes knocking, you answer."

"Lane—"

He cut her off with a palm over her mouth. "You listen to me, Jamie Grace Dunleavy. Go down there and *do* something. Just talk to him. Ancient Chinese proverb say, 'A journey of a thousand miles begins with a single step.' So take a step." He pushed her gently backwards, turned her toward the stairs leading to the pit and slapped her ass. "Go. And if things go FUBAR, you can blame me."

Jamie hesitated, then glanced at the stage. Chase was prowling across the stage like a caged lion, growling a metal number, but his eyes never left her. She made her way through the jostling, moshing crowd to the very front of the stage and stared up at him, her hands at her sides, perfectly still amidst the chaos of the pit. The song ended, and their signature ballad "Far From You" started, a haunting guitar refrain underlaid by a grumbling, chugging bass and almost jazz-like snare-drum taps. Chase sang the entire song crouched at the edge of the stage, his eyes locked on Jamie's.

She looked at him, unflinching, watching a bead of sweat run down his scalp to drip off his nose, then another runnel down his temple and drifting into a smear on his stubble-dark cheek. He was shirtless, a plain white T-shirt gripped in his fist, which he wiped across his brow every once in a while, and he wore a pair of leather pants and knee-high shit-kicker boots crisscrossed by straps and buckles and studded by short metal spikes. His thick, toned arms glistened with sweat, and his rippling abs moved as he breathed and sang, the sheen of sweat glinting, teasing, tantalizing.

Jamie wanted nothing so much as to jump up on stage, shove him to the floor, and rip his pants off, lick the sweat from his body and rub her hands across his slick skin. She wanted to feel his cock in her hands—she wanted to taste his come in her mouth and feel him fill her pussy as he thrust into her.

She wanted to let him tie her up and tease her for hours. She wanted to blindfold him and torture him with a thousand kisses over his flesh and on his stone-solid arousal until he begged and pleaded with her to let him come.

Jamie bit her lip, picturing these things. She felt her nipples harden, felt her core grow hot and damp. She found her fingers drifting down to the waistband of her skirt and slipping beneath it.

She wanted to touch herself, thinking of Chase
naked for her, tied up and blindfolded, laid out to
her mercy. She wanted to make herself come thinking about Chase's cock dripping with pre-come,
smeared with her juices and her saliva, the thick
purple veins standing out on the silky flesh.

Jamie gasped, realizing she was actually touching herself right there in the middle of the moshing
crowd, with Chase watching her. She jerked her
hand out of her skirt and wiped it on her blouse,
then smelled her fingers out of some odd reflex. She
stank of female arousal.

She glanced up at Chase, who seemed trans-
fixed, his eyes wide, the cords in his neck standing
out, his fist gripping the mic so tight she could
see the straining tendons of his hand. He was still
performing, still singing the final chorus of the ballad in his deep, rich voice. But as he stood up and
turned away from the crowd, she could see a huge
telltale bulge in his pants. His bassist nudged him
and said something, laughing, and Chase shook his
head irritably.

Chase didn't turn around for a few moments,
waiting as the next number began, this one
another driving metal song. Jamie stood watching
him, keeping her thoughts away from dangerous
territory.

Then, after an amount of time Jamie couldn't
have measured, their set ended, and Chase left

the stage with a backward glance at Jamie. A few seconds later, she felt a huge hand wrap around her arm. "Miss? Please come with me. Mr. Delany asked me to bring you backstage."

She complied, ignoring the jealous murmuring of the other girls around her who'd overheard. She followed the security guard, who was roughly the size and shape of a silverback gorilla, through the crowd to the backstage area. He led her to a door, knocked once, then opened it, ushering Jamie through. She stepped in, and the door closed softly behind her, latching with a *snick* of declarative finality.

Chase sat on a threadbare couch, one long arm slung casually across the back, one leg stretched out across the cushions, the other gripping his T-shirt in a tight fist.

Jamie stood with her back to the door, her breath coming in ragged, panting gasps. It took every ounce of willpower to keep from crossing the room and covering his magnificent body with hers, tangling her tongue against his, tasting the sweat and cold water on his mouth.

He rose up from the couch in a lithe, graceful movement, his expression roiling with emotion. Then he licked his lips, opened his mouth as if to speak, and Jamie was undone. The sight of his mouth, lips parted, teeth white...she *had* to taste him.

She lunged, crossing the three feet between them, crushing her breasts against his bare chest, wrapping her palms over the back of his head and neck. Her lips met his with desperate need.

He tasted as she'd imagined, as she remembered, of sweat from his lips, of ice-cold water from the bottle on the floor by the couch, and faintly of alcohol.

Jamie moaned as she kissed him, and that sound spurred him into life. His huge hand curled around her waist to rest on the small of her back, his other burying itself in her curls near her ear.

They kissed until their breath merged, until they were gasping, chests heaving. Jamie felt his erection at her belly, and her core surged hot and wet at the feel of him.

"I want you so fucking bad," she whispered into his lips.

"I'm right here," Chase growled. "And goddamn it, I've dreamt of you every night. Wet dreams of you naked, touching yourself like you did out in the crowd."

Jamie felt herself flush. "This is still impossible."

"I know. But...I don't care. I need you." He rumbled in his chest, a sound of frustration. "I don't care if that makes me weak for admitting. I *need* you, Jamie."

She sagged into him. "I need you, too. So what do we do?"

Chase shrugged. "Fuck if I know. I can't think for needing you, wanting you. All I can think of is kissing you again." His hand clawed into the muscle of her ass, sinking into the silk of her skirt, pulling her against him. "I want to take you on the couch, right now."

Jamie whimpered. "Don't you fucking dare say shit like that."

"Why not?"

"Because I want that so bad...so bad. I'm about to let you. I'm *this* close to ripping those stupid, sexy leather pants off and raping you on the goddamn floor." Jamie was trembling from head to toe, shaking with fear and need and lust and excitement.

Chase's hands were shaking, too, his breathing shuddering, his cock a hard rod between them. "Fuck, Jamie. We can't. We can't. If we do, there's no going back."

Jamie laughed mirthlessly. "There's already no going back."

"I know."

Jamie lifted her chin to gaze up at him, her palms caressing the stubble on his scalp at the back of his head. She knew she shouldn't be here. She knew this couldn't be, couldn't happen, but it already was happening.

She lifted up on her toes to kiss him, and something deep in her heart caught, tripped, and shattered. His lips were tender on hers, tasting her mouth, not demanding more but exploring, treasuring.

His palm slid down her ass to pull up the skirt, and she desperately, frantically wanted him to lift it, to touch her bare skin.

No. She couldn't do this to Anna.

Jamie snatched at the last vestige of self-control she had, a spider-silk tendril of hesitation. She stumbled away from him, backward, back against the door, clutching the doorknob in her fist.

She ignored the single tear slipping down her cheek. "*Goddammit.*"

Her heart was cracking, but she made herself turn the knob, thinking of Anna's face when she'd seen Chase in Vegas. It would be like that every single time they saw each other. That thought was impetus enough to twist the knob and slip out, her lips tingling, her body trembling, her skin on fire and her core throbbing with unsated need. She wiped the tear away with her knuckles and let herself feel the hurt.

Pain was better than need.

Chase watched Jamie slip away once more. She kept running from him, sneaking out of his grasp. She was right—he knew she was. He'd seen the thoughts pass across her face, seen the determination settle onto her features.

Anna's face crossed his mind, her eyes when she saw him onstage in Vegas. That moment...the surprised pain, it was reason enough to stay away. Anna and Jamie were closer than sisters, and Chase knew Anna still had feelings for him. They might have been buried deep and overshadowed by her love for Jeff, but if she saw Chase again, especially on a regular basis, those feelings would find their way to the surface. Which was a surefire way to break up a friendship.

He couldn't do that to Anna, or Jamie.

She was gone now. Really gone. He was back out on the road tomorrow; they had a show in Kalamazoo and then Grand Rapids, followed by Marquette and then Green Bay. He would stay far away from Detroit. Far away from Jamie.

He'd stay away if it killed him.

Chase slumped onto the couch, aching in his heart, aching in his body. He rubbed his hand across his scalp, trying to hold on to the feel of Jamie's hands on his head, on his face.

He nearly jumped up and followed her, then sat back down.

A second time he got up and paced to the door, then turned away. *No fucking way, dickhead. Don't do it.* But it was no use.

He needed her too badly.

He threw the door open and ran after her, needing to catch her, if only for one last kiss.

FIVE

Jamie heard Chase's feet behind her, heavy boots smacking the concrete. She ducked her head, doing her damnedest to pretend she didn't hear him. To pretend she didn't know what would happen if she turned around.

Jamie didn't turn around. She made it to Dale's car, gripping the leather strap of her purse in a white-knuckled grip. A part of her wanted to haul around and deck him. Another part wanted to haul around and kiss him, then take him somewhere, *anywhere*, and finish what they'd started.

She was tugging futilely at the locked car door when he caught up to her. His hand wrapped far too gently around her upper arm, near her armpit, his knuckles brushing her breast. She dragged a deep shuddering breath in, placed her palm on the window, refusing to turn around.

"What do you want, Chase?" Jamie hated how quivery and breathy and damned *needy* her voice sounded.

"You." His voice was raw, growling, as if the admission had been dragged out of his chest.

"Well, you can't have me."

"I know, but…" His grip tightened on Jamie's arm, and then he let go with a long, expelled breath. "That doesn't mean I'll ever stop wanting you."

She clenched her teeth and squeezed her eyes shut; the visceral pain in his voice tore at her heart.

"Chase…" Jamie could feel the intensity radiating off him, and she just *had* to turn in place to see his eyes. "God, you think I want—you think I don't—"

"Then why can't we make this work? Anna will be okay. She has Jeff. I'll be okay around her, if I have you."

Temptation raged through Jamie. "That's like… it's so wrong. I can't. I can't. It'd be ripping open wounds every time you two are in the same room."

She was standing against his chest, her hand curled up between them. She wasn't sure how that had happened, but it felt so right. And so wrong.

"It would get easier. Time heals all wounds, right? You heal the hurt inside me. You make it all go away."

Jamie blinked hard and bit her lip until it hurt. "*Stop*, Chase. *Please* stop. It would be a betrayal of Anna. My best friend. The one person I have in this world who's like family. I can't." The admission of her own feelings bubbled on Jamie's lips, and she choked them back. "I'm sorry. I'm *so* sorry."

She stepped away from him, and the hurt in his eyes deepened until Jamie thought she might be seeing the raw material of his very soul gleaming in the cracks of his heart, visible through his eyes. She felt a tear dragging down her cheek. Jamie knew this was the correct decision, but it still felt so wrong, so terrible. Chase was already hurt; she was only driving the dagger deeper.

She watched his eyes harden, watched as the shutters slammed down between them, between him and the world.

"Fine. I get it. You're right. She's your best friend. Your family. I'm just...some guy, right? I wish you all the best, Jamie." His voice was dead and cold, his words like stones. He turned and walked away.

"Chase, no, it's not like that. You're not just some guy, you're—"

He spun around so fast it startled her. "*Don't*, Jamie. Don't mitigate it. Okay? You can either heal me, or hurt me. Not both. That's not an ultimatum, it's just facts. I'm not going to try to make you choose between me or her."

"But that's exactly what you *are* doing."

"You're doing it, not me. I think it would work. I think it would be tough, but eventually, it would be okay."

"No, it wouldn't!" She slumped back against the door of the car, struggling for breath, for control. "Why do you have to make this so much harder on me?" Jamie slid along the side of the car, away from him; his nearness was intoxicating, suffocating. "What do you want to hear from me? Yes! I want you! Is that what you want to hear? But this *cannot happen*! I can't betray my best friend like that. Not even for you."

Chase backed away, his eyes dark, fathomless chasms. "Message received, Jay. Loud and clear. I won't bother you anymore." And then he turned away again.

He walked back into the building, shoulders tense, palm scrubbing frantically over his scalp. Jamie let him go, the hurt she could feel from him as powerful as the hurt inside herself.

He'd called her "Jay." No one but Anna ever called her that.

After Chase was gone, Jamie texted Lane, begging him to get her home. Lane appeared a few minutes later with Dale's keys and drove Jamie to her car. He didn't ask her any questions, didn't say a word the entire drive from Harpo's to Lane Bryant. He just drove, one hand on her knee.

When he pulled up next to her car, he unbuckled his seatbelt and leaned over to hug her. She clung to his neck and choked back her tears, focusing on breathing until she had control over herself again.

"Thanks, Lane."

He nodded and kissed her cheek. "You know I love you, sweetie, and you know I'm here for you."

"I know." She pulled away and opened the car door, swung a leg out. "I'll call you later and we'll talk, okay?"

Lane smiled. "No worries, kitten. Just take care of yourself, okay?"

She made it home without breaking down, somehow. She made it into her bed before unleashing a torrent of tears that didn't stop until she was simply too exhausted to weep anymore.

Anna showed up. "Jay?" she called from the kitchen. "Something told me you needed company."

Jamie didn't answer. She felt Anna's weight on the bed next to her, then fingers brushing curls away from her eyes.

"What happened, Jay?"

Jamie could only shake her head. "Just...life sucks."

Anna sighed, an irritated huff. "Jamie. Why aren't you talking to me? There's something big going on with you, and you're holding out on me. I'm starting to get mad."

"I can't tell you, Anna. It's complicated."

"Meaning you're afraid."

"Shitless."

Anna didn't answer right away. When she did, her voice sounded distant. "Okay, well, I can't make you talk to me. You know I love you. You know I'd never judge you."

Jamie sat up and faced Anna, working her feet beneath her into a cross-legged position. "Anna, please. Listen. It's not that...I don't know...it's not that I don't trust you or that I want to keep things back from you. You know I tell you everything—"

"Except the one thing that I've ever seen make you cry on a regular basis." She gestured at the bed they both sat on. "I've found you here, in your bed, bawling, more times over the last few months than in all the years I've known you. And we've been friends forever."

Jamie didn't know what to say. She fidgeted with a loose thread on her comforter. "Anna—god. I want to tell you. You're my best friend. You're the only one I've ever been able to tell everything to. But this is...it's fucked up, Anna."

"Are you in some kind of trouble?"

"No, it's nothing like that. It's just..."

"What? Just what?" Anna jerked the pony-tail holder out of her hair, untangling her blonde locks with her fingers before smoothing it back and retying it. "I'm not gonna ask again, okay? If you won't tell me, fine. I get it."

Jamie flinched at the hardness in Anna's voice. "Why does this feel like a turning point between us? Like if I don't tell you, things won't be the same between us?"

Anna shrugged, a tiny lift of one shoulder. "I'm not trying to make demands or ultimatums or whatever. I just...I guess I sense this somehow has something to do with me, and I'm worried."

Jamie sighed, a frustrated expulsion of breath. "God. I need vodka."

"Me, too."

"No, I mean for real. If I'm going to do this, I'm going to need vodka." Jamie wiggled off the bed, wiping her face.

"Do what?"

"Tell you all of this."

Anna twisted to watch Jamie scrub the smeared makeup off her face at the *en suite* bathroom sink. "You're going to tell me?"

"I guess I have to. It does concern you. And... if I'm going to lose him over you, I might as well tell you, right?"

A pregnant pause, and then the question, in a low, tense voice: "Him?"

Jamie shook her head. "Vodka first." The two women went into the kitchen, and Jamie pulled a bottle of Grey Goose from her freezer. "I've been saving this for an emergency. I think this qualifies."

She poured two generous measures into a pair of juice glasses, then a hint of orange juice over them. She knocked hers back immediately and poured a second while Anna sipped hers more slowly.

"Jeez, Jay. Don't get drunk without me." Anna tried to laugh, but the worry in her eyes had Jamie swallowing the last of her second shot and pouring a third.

Jamie poured juice over the third measure and leaned back against the kitchen counter across from Anna. "Not drunk. Just tipsy enough to be able to get this out." She sipped, and then set the glass next to her. "Just remember when I'm telling you this, that nothing actually happened, okay?"

Anna frowned. "Okay…?"

"In Vegas, when you left the casino…the Six Foot Tall show. You gave me the backstage pass. I'm not sure what I intended to do, but…I ended up in Chase's dressing room. You should have seen him, Anna—well, I guess I'm glad you didn't. He was so broken up. I just…I hated seeing him hurt. I mean, you could see how upset he was from the audience. I just wanted to make sure he was okay, you know?"

"What *happened*, Jay?"

"It was like…being hit by a bus. Something about him just struck me, deep inside. You know? It was more than his looks or charisma. I remember how you talked about him. Like he's got this magical presence. You just can't help yourself when he's around—he just takes over a room."

Anna's voice was quiet. Too quiet. "I remember."

"Well, this was more than that. It was…something totally different."

"Are you in love with Chase, Jamie?"

Jamie sucked down vodka, coughing before answering. "Maybe. I don't know. I haven't let myself think that far." She wiped her mouth with the back of her hand. "We kissed. In Vegas, back-stage. I've never felt anything like it in all my life, Anna. I'm sorry. I can't even pretend to know how this is making you feel, but you wanted the truth."

"I'm not sure this is what I was expecting."

"Yeah, how could you, right?"

"How could I expect it? Or how could you do this to me?'"

Jamie shrugged, looking at Anna over the top of her glass. "Both?"

"I honestly don't know. Maybe I *am* thinking both. Keep going."

"Well, it was like that one kiss was more…I don't know…more intimate, or meaningful than *any*thing I've ever shared with another guy in my entire life. Like that one kiss was…a promise of everything he and I could have, and god…it was like an earthquake, it was so intense."

"Damn, Jay."

"Yeah. Damn. But then I remembered who it was I was kissing. I ran. I mean…of all the people in the world for me to finally feel a real connection with, it had to be *him*? Of course it did."

"So that was it?"

Jamie snorted. "Not hardly. I told him I couldn't do it, couldn't let anything happen between us. You're my best friend, and he's your ex. No way. Taboo, right?"

"Right." Anna's voice was oddly strained.

"So I managed to get away from him, which was like ripping out a chunk of my heart. We had your wedding and went home, and I worked my ass off, got the promotion. I tried to forget."

"And then you got drunk and had an accidental threesome with a pair of neanderthal potheads."

"Yeah. Fucking awful. Especially since it didn't help. It just made it worse. And not just because they weren't Chase, which was bad enough, but because even though we weren't together, I still felt like being with those two gumps was like cheating on Chase. Stupid, but it's how I felt, and it was rotten."

Anna rubbed her face. "God, Jay. No wonder you were so upset that night."

"Yeah." Jamie finished her vodka and poured a fourth, seeking oblivion, even though she knew it would never come. "I managed to bury myself in work enough to almost feel like I was moving on, and then Lane and the gang showed up after work tonight and dragged me out with them."

"Uh-oh."

"Yeah. They had an extra ticket to a show. They didn't tell me who was playing and I didn't ask, 'cause why should it matter, right?"

"Right. But let me guess. It was Chase."

"Bingo. So he brought me backstage this time, and we had another moment. It was all tortured and angsty and shit. We kissed again, and it was just as epic as the first time, only more so. I can't even put it into words. I never wanted to stop. I..." Jamie set the glass down and rubbed her face with her hands. "Anna, I swear, I never meant for this to happen. I don't know how it *did* happen. But I can't get him out of my head, no matter how hard I try."

Anna seemed to be at a loss for words. "Jay, I'm not even sure what to say, or what to think, or how I'm supposed to feel about this."

"Sshh-yeah. Tell me about it."

"I mean, in one sense, I want to be happy for you, but on the other side, you're my best friend and Chase is my ex. If I had to see him every time you and I got together, or something...it'd be impossible. It would hurt. I broke his heart, Jay. I did. He has every right to be pissed off at me. To never want to see me again. And I *hate* that I hurt

him." Anna's eyes were downcast, as if the depths
of her mixed drink contained some kind of answer
to the situation.

There was a long silence then, during which
both women sipped their drinks and tried to figure
out what to say next.

Eventually, Anna broke the silence. "If he's
what you want, Jamie, I'll deal with it. I love you
enough to make it work."

Jamie groaned. "I already—shit. I already told
him it could never work. I couldn't do that to you,
Anna. I broke his heart again."

"For me?" Anna said, her words barely a murmur. "Because of me?"

"Not just—I mean, yeah, sort of. You're my best
friend. You have such an intense history with him,
and..." Jamie turned away and rummaged in the
fridge, emerging with a bottle of cranberry juice.
"I've had enough drama in my life. I don't need a
relationship predicated on the kind of intense bullshit anything between Chase and me would come
with."

"But, Jay...this is breaking your heart, too. I
can see it."

Jamie shook her head. "It's done. Maybe in
another life we could've...I don't know. It's moot
now. He's gone."

Anna crossed the kitchen and wrapped her
arms around Jamie. "Oh, god, honey. I'm so sorry.

I wish I could—I don't know. I just wish it was different for you."

"Me, too." Jamie whispered the words so quietly they were barely audible.

Jamie sat alone in a bar an hour's drive from anywhere she knew. She'd been working sixty-hour weeks for nearly three months straight, working close-open shifts, doubles, extra inventory shifts, then working out at a twenty-four-hour gym, only going home when she was so exhausted she could barely make it through a shower before collapsing into bed.

Even still, she dreamed of him. She saw him on a stage, dark eyes boring into her, sweat running down his temple, down his chiseled cheek. She felt his scalp under her palms, woke up with her hands tingling from the vivid memory/dream of their stolen kisses. She woke up damp between her thighs, frustrated and alone and angry.

So, one day, she called in sick and drove away, pointing her car north on I-75 and just going. She blasted HIM and Hinder, Mumford and Sons and The Fray and everything on her favorite playlist until she was almost out of gas, and then she pulled off the interstate and found a bar.

And then she drank.

And drank some more.

She was in that pleasant place between buzzed and drunk, far enough gone to not care about what happened next, but sober enough to enjoy it. It was six in the evening on a Tuesday, so the bar—a just-off-the-freeway dive bar—was sparsely populated by a few isolated truckers and a table of drunk locals wearing John Deere hats and stained blue jeans. The only person of interest was a man who seemed to be none of the above, someone out of place, like Jamie. He was sitting at the end of the bar, a fitted baseball cap with a curved bill pulled low, sandy hair curling up from under the back edge. She couldn't see much else, but his jeans were dark and tight and clean, and his arms seemed thick and muscular, stretching the sleeves of his T-shirt.

Jamie pretended to watch the Lions-Falcons game, checking him out in brief sidelong glances. He never really looked her way, but she thought he might be doing the same as she was, watching her out of the corner of his eye.

Maybe I just need another distraction, she thought.

Then she mentally snorted, knowing it would be futile. She also knew she was going to go through with it anyway. She could tell from the way his finger traced patterns in the sweat on his beer bottle that he was preparing to make a move.

Yep, here it comes.

He stood up, strolled over to her, and sat down next to her. He lifted his beer bottle and tipped it toward her. "To passin' through, yeah?" He had a British accent, which did something fluttery to her stomach and made her toes curl in a way she hadn't felt in a long time.

Jamie clinked her glass of shiraz against his. "To passing through."

They both sipped, and then Jamie let herself give him a long once-over. He was hot, that was for damn sure. Gorgeous, piercing blue eyes in a classically beautiful face. His hands were strong-looking but manicured, large enough to make his Coors bottle seem small.

"So, where're you from, Blue?" he asked, his voice deep enough to pleasantly rumble in her ear.

She quirked an eyebrow at him. "Blue?"

He laughed. "It's an Aussie thing. People with red hair get called 'blue.' Haven't the foggiest why, though."

"You sound British."

"Well, I am. But my mum's from Perth, and I spend summers with her, so I've picked up a few mannerisms."

"You still spend summers with your mom?" Jamie said, amused but slightly worried.

He just laughed again, an infectious, unselfconscious sound that made her grin. "Not like you're thinking. I take a month every summer and go on holiday to visit her."

Jamie lifted an eyebrow at him. "You take a month-long vacation every year?"

He shrugged. "It's not uncommon, actually. For Europeans, at least. You Yanks are so obsessed with work you never take more than two weeks. A month is standard for most of Europe."

Jamie sighed wistfully. "A whole month off? God, I'd kill for that."

"Make it happen, then."

She shook her head. "I wish, but no. It's pretty much impossible." Jamie stuck her hand out to him. "I'm Jamie."

"Ian." His handshake was firm but gentle, his hand swallowing hers.

Jamie felt another flutter in her belly. Maybe this distraction would be more effective than she'd anticipated.

"So, Ian, where are you headed?"

He shrugged. "Actually, this is the time of year I'm usually in Australia, but Mum is traveling this year, so I came to America for my holiday."

Jamie laughed. "You came to Buttfuck, Michigan, on a vacation?"

"Is that the name of this place?" Ian asked, laughing. "I knew you Yanks were weird, but that really takes the cake. Kind of a strange name for a town, innit?"

Jamie found herself giggling. "I know you must get this a lot, but your accent is hot."

Ian swigged from his beer. Jamie got the sense he might be embarrassed.

"I might have gotten that before, yeah." He grinned at her, wiggling his eyebrows suggestively. "So...feel your panties dropping, then? 'Cause that's what one bloke told me, just this week past. He said, 'Your accent is a panty-dropper, man.'" He said the last part in a passable American accent, which Jamie found supremely odd-sounding.

Jamie shrugged nonchalantly. "Keep talking, and we'll see what happens."

"So your knickers *are* feeling a bit loose, then?"

"I'm not sure I'm wearing knickers."

Ian choked on his beer. "I didn't take you for that sort of girl, Jamie. Knickers is just another word for panties."

Jamie laughed. "Oh. Well, I am wearing pant-ies, yes. But they *might* be feeling the slightest bit wiggly. Especially if you buy me another round."

Ian lifted his bottle at the bartender, then ges-tured at Jamie's glass, holding up one finger. "In that case, we should toast to sexy accents and dropping panties." He chuckled, making it seem like a joke.

Jamie clinked her glass against his bottle again, laughing with him. As she sipped, she wondered if he had any idea how close to the truth their toast was.

I'm back to my old tricks, I guess, she thought. *'Cause I'm about to take this boy back to his hotel and fuck him silly.*

She let him buy her a few more drinks, discovering over the course of two more hours that he was an IT consultant, and he was actually in Michigan on a mix of business and pleasure. He'd finished his contract in Detroit and had decided to venture northward with no real destination in mind. She also discovered that he was an only child, unmarried, and that he lived in London.

A couple more rounds revealed that he was staying in a motel just down the street from the bar.

"So, Jamie. What are your plans for the rest of the evening?" Ian asked.

"Don't really have any," she admitted.

She'd managed to avoid answering too many questions. Mainly, she didn't want to admit she was trashed in a bar hours from anywhere.

"Well, why don't you come back to my room with me?" Ian said. "Just...you know, till you sober up a bit?"

Jamie nodded, trying to calm her hammering heart; she wasn't sure why she was nervous, but she was. Being nervous was a good thing. "Sure. Sounds good."

"I hope you don't mind a bit of a walk, though," Ian said as he stood up, "seeing as I didn't drive from the hotel."

"No, that's fine. Probably do me some good."

"That it will, love. You seem a mite wobbly, if you don't mind me saying."

Jamie laughed as she stood up, swaying unsteadily. "Yeah, just a mite." She exaggerated her unsteadiness, using it as an excuse to wrap her hand around Ian's arm. "Mind if I hold on to you?"

Ian glanced down at her; standing up, he towered more than six inches over her. "Not a bit. Wouldn't want to go and have a spill, now, would we?"

Jamie just shook her head in response, concentrating on the feel of his thick arm, corded with muscle. It was a nice sensation. He smelled good, too, she realized, leaning into him. Faint cologne, not overpowering, a spicy, male scent, along with deodorant, and that other more indefinable scent of clean man.

Ian laugh rumbled through her. "Did you just sniff me?"

Jamie giggled in embarrassment. "Um. Maybe? Shut up. You smell good." She leaned in again and sniffed at his shirt. "A man who smells good is as much of a panty-dropper as a sexy accent."

"So...if I've got both..."

Jamie glanced up at him through her lowered eyelashes. "I plead the Fifth?"

Ian just snorted. "The Fifth Amendment is an American thing, love. I'm British, so it doesn't work on me."

"Oh, damn."

Ian didn't push it, and she let it go. She had to be a *little* hard to get, after all. *Right*, she thought. *'Cause this is hard to get.*

They were following the main road, walking across parking lots and stretches of yellowing grass, cars whizzing by to and from the freeway. A hotel sign about a quarter mile down announced their destination. They reached it after a few more minutes of walking in a surprisingly companionable silence.

Ian led her to a ground-floor room, unlocking the door and throwing it open with a flourish. "It's not much, but...well...that's it, really. It's a hotel room. Sorry I can't offer you better."

"We *are* in Buttfuck, Michigan. I can't really expect the Ritz, can I?" Jamie said.

She didn't spare the room much of glance; it was the same as any Best Western anywhere in the country. There was a pile of clothes on the bed, and Ian rushed over and scooped them into a Samsonite suitcase, which he closed and tossed into a corner.

"Sorry about that," he mumbled. "Wasn't expecting company."

"No problem," Jamie said.

An awkward silence ensued, in which Jamie wondered how long she should wait before attacking him with her face. Ian seemed, if Jamie was any judge, to be wondering the same thing.

"I'm not as drunk as you think," Jamie blurted. "I mean…I was kind of hamming it up. So I could hold on to you."

She heard the words coming out but couldn't seem to stop them. Embarrassment was shooting through her, centered in her belly as a knot of nerves. She hadn't been nervous around a guy in…a very long time. Since high school, probably. Even with Chase she hadn't been actually nervous; she'd been anxious, flooded with uncontrollable need and burning desire. She'd been mixed up around Chase, an emotional wreck, a physical mess. He turned her inside out and upside down and set everything about on fire.

Ian was different. He was…comforting. Familiar, somehow. And yet, she was nervous. She wanted him, but she didn't want it to be like all the guys she'd picked up at the bar. He was only in the U.S. for a month, she assumed, so it was a limited-time offer only. Maybe that was the source of her nerves. She wasn't really sure. She only she knew she didn't mind being nervous. It was a new feeling, something besides the ache in her heart and the coiled knot of need low in her belly.

Ian regarded her with something like amusement. "Yes, I'm aware. I wasn't going to say anything, since it seemed to be working in my favor."

Jamie shifted her weight from one foot to the other. "This is where I say 'I'm not usually this kind of girl,' except...I kind of am."

Ian lifted an eyebrow, the corner of his mouth quirking up in a smile. "Well, I guess we're evenly matched, then, because I'm in the same boat, more or less."

Jamie laughed. "Un-mix your metaphors, Shakespeare."

"I just mean I'm supposed to say something like, 'I don't normally bring girls home from the pub,' but I do, rather often, actually. I'll admit I'm relieved you said it first, though."

Jamie relaxed then. She sat on the edge of the bed, her purse still hanging from her shoulder, and glanced at Ian. "I'm in the middle of a big internal conflict, actually. Not about you, exactly, just... life. Myself. This tendency of mine to go home with guys from the bar. I promised myself I wouldn't do this anymore. But then there was this guy...and it was all Shakespearean forbidden love and whatever. So now that's over and I'm trying to go on with my life, but it's not that easy and you're here and I'm here, and—"

Ian crossed the space between them in a single stride, kneeling between her thighs and kissing her suddenly, silencing her. His hands were on her legs, and he tasted like beer and faintly of spearmint gum. "I get it, Jamie. I do. You don't have to explain."

Jamie wasn't sure what to say, for once. She *wanted* to explain. She wanted him to understand what he was getting into, but she wasn't sure what it was herself. It didn't feel like a one-time-only hookup, and nothing had even happened yet. They both clearly knew the score. They both knew how it was supposed to go: They'd fuck, and then Jamie would sneak out at some point in the early hours of the morning and walk back to her car. Only... she didn't want to.

She kissed Ian back, hesitantly, exploring the sensation of lips on lips, his hands daring up her thighs to curl around her hips inches above her ass. She felt butterflies in her stomach at his touch. She was looking forward to feeling him peel her shirt off, strip her of her jeans. It wasn't fire in her belly, but it was enough.

Ian might even be more than a distraction, she thought. She could run with that.

When he pulled away to slide up onto the bed next to her, Jamie kicked her shoes off and set her purse on the floor. She watched as Ian untied his shoes and tossed them near the table by the window.

"Ian?"

"Yeah?" He sat cross-legged and barefoot in the middle of the bed, combing his fingers through his shaggy blond hair.

"What if I said I didn't want to do the walk of shame tomorrow morning?"

He shrugged. "Then don't."

She picked at a loose thread on the comforter. "I mean...wake up here, tomorrow. I mean, we both know how this usually goes. This is your hotel room, so normally I'm the one who's supposed to sneak out at four a.m. But...I don't want to. I'm not sure what that would make this between us, but... yeah. What if I just want to do things differently?"

Ian nodded. "Ah. I...you know, normally that would make me rather uncomfortable. We've been honest with each other thus far, so I'll go ahead and continue the trend. I actually asked a girl to leave once. She was just...lingering. All bloody morning, she was there. Tea and breakfast, and checking her email and whatever, and I just wanted to tell her that wasn't how it worked. So I asked her if she would mind being on her way. I said I had business to take care of, only it was Sunday and I didn't. I felt like rubbish all the rest of the day. I kept seeing her disappointed face, like she thought we were going to *be* something and it was awkward. I hated that. I've never gone looking for a relationship, you know? I had one once. A serious one, too. Introduced her to Mum and Dad and went on holidays with her, all that rot. It was nice for bit, having someone to come home to, someone to watch the telly with." Ian's accent, fairly unpronounced until then, had grown stronger. "She was a beautiful girl, Nina was. Great in the sack. But... she was a slob around the flat. Couldn't make a decent cup of tea to save her life, either. And it was shite like that that did us in. The little things. No one cheated on anyone, we never really fought, and I really did enjoy having her around, but it was just...it wasn't *right*, you know?"

Jamie nodded, unsure where he was going with it. "Relationships are hard," she said, just to fill the silence. "I'm never sure how they're supposed to work. I always feel like it should be just sex, and he obviously thinks it's something more, but I never know what it's supposed to be, you know? Like, it's fun, and they're nice, and it's great not being alone at home all the time, but..."

"What's the point?" Ian finished for her.

"Exactly. If it's not just sex, and we're not getting married, what's the point?" Jamie pulled the thread free, popping seams until she had a few inches of clear thread like thin fishing line. "So... yeah. I guess I'll go, then. I really don't want to do the whole hook-up thing. I'm tired of it. I don't know what I do want, but I know I *don't* want that." She stood up, slipping a toe into her sneaker.

Ian looked up sharply, confusion on his face. "Go? No, that's not what I meant. I'm not sure why I said that. I shouldn't have told you all that. I'm sorry." He scooted across the bed and pulled her down by the hand so she was sitting on his lap. "Stay. Please? Stay here tonight. Let's both of us try something new. No expectations either way. You don't do the walk of shame, and I won't wake up alone, stuck somewhere between relieved and disappointed."

"So no expectations either way?"

"Right."

"I can do that." She let herself settle onto his lap, wrapping her arms around his neck. "I have to warn you, though, I'm pretty sure I'd make a shitty cup of tea."

"I drink coffee, too." Ian grinned, sliding his hands under the hem of her shirt to touch the skin on her back.

Jamie explored the muscles of his shoulders and back through his shirt. "Well, you're in luck then, 'cause I make a killer pot of coffee."

His lips touched her neck on the side an inch above her shoulder, then moved down to her throat, kissing the hollow at the base of her throat. Jamie let her head fall back, feeling an exhilarating rush of pleasure at the touch of his mouth on her flesh. She found the bottom edge of his shirt and lifted it up over his head, tossed it aside, then resumed her roaming of his torso with her palms. His skin was fair and smooth, his body toned and muscular, but not overly developed. He continued kissing her throat, then slid to the right, moving the neck of her shirt aside to touch his lips to her shoulder blade. With his other hand he touched her belly, dragging his fingers upward, lifting her shirt as he went. Jamie pulled back and raised her arms over her head, and Ian drew the fabric off, tossing it aside.

His gaze roved over her body, her full breasts held in by the red lace of her bra. "You're very beautiful, Jamie." He reached up and brushed one of the bra straps off her shoulder. "Very beautiful indeed."

Jamie glanced away. "Thanks."

His fingers slid the other strap off, and then he was unhooking the back with one hand, his eyes never leaving hers. Jamie held his gaze as her breasts fell free, and then her eyes slid shut involuntarily when his fingers grazed the underside of one breast. She clutched his forearm, and he cupped the heavy weight of one breast in his hand, then pinched the nipple between two fingers, rolling it. Jamie let herself gasp. She wriggled her bottom on his lap, feeling his erection thickening. Slipping sideways off him, Jamie lay back and pulled Ian down over her, tangling her fingers in his hair as he dipped in to kiss her lips. She felt her pulse quicken as their lips met. Butterflies again, more of them now, fluttering in her belly.

She slid her palms down his spine, curved around his waist and found the button of his jeans, popped it open and unzipped his fly. He was on his hands and knees over her, his palms by her face and his knees on either side of her hips. She pushed his pants down and he lifted up to let her get them off. She grasped his shaft in her hand, her pulse go from a rabbiting patter to a hammering thunder. He was well-endowed, thick, straight, pointing away from his belly. She slid her fist down his length, then paused at the base as he lowered his mouth to her breast, and she gasped when he sucked her nipple between his teeth. He reached between them and stripped her of her jeans quickly, then let his fingers roam along the outside of her hip, running in along the swell of her hipbone, across the dip where leg met groin, then down between her thighs.

Jamie let her legs fall apart, stroking his length as he slid a single finger along her crease. She reveled in the sensation of a man who knew what he was doing. He didn't just plunge in, but let the tip of his finger tease her, dragging up and down her pussy before probing in, ever so gently at first, then more and more, until his finger was inside her to the first knuckle, and then the second. She rubbed her thumb over the tip of his cock, drawing the pre-come out and smearing it over him with her fingers. Jamie let her hand move down to cup his balls, testing their weight, exploring them gently before resuming her slow and steady stroking of his cock.

He circled her clit with his middle finger, slowly, teasingly, then brushed the nub quickly, once, twice, and then she was arching her back and whispering a moan. He had her moments away from coming already, and they were just starting. This boded well. He slipped his fingers deeper into her, curling in to unerringly find her G-spot, then flicked his fingertips across it, pushing her closer to the edge, rubbing it, and now she was there, *right there*...Ian added his thumb, pressing it lightly against her clit, and that was all it took. Jamie gasped, shuddering, as the orgasm ripped through her. She pulsed her fist on his cock as she came, and then when the waves lessened, she pulled him toward her.

Ian pulled away. "Wait...wait. My trousers. I have a rubber in my wallet." He hung off the bed and dug his wallet out of his jeans while Jamie watched.

She was on the pill, obviously, but she didn't stop him. An aftershock rippled through her, and she pulled him to her as he sat up with the wrapper in his hand, moving toward her.

She took the condom from him, ripped it open, and slowly rolled the latex over his cock. He rolled his hips into her grip, then settled himself over top

of her again. He paused, his ocean-blue eyes pinning hers, and his mouth opened as if he was going
to speak. She met his gaze evenly, waiting for him
to say whatever was on the tip of his tongue. But
he didn't. He just smiled at her, a half-curve of his
lips, and then swiveled his hips to caress her nether
lips with the tip of his cock. Once again, he didn't
simply drive in but took his time, weight on one
elbow, the other brushing her red curls away from
her eyes and drifting down to cup her breast.

She ran her fingers through his coarse blond
hair, then down his back, and cupped his firm ass,
pulling at him, wanting him inside her.

He just shook his head. "Not just yet."

She didn't answer, held onto the hard globes of
his ass and waited. His strong hand explored her
body as he probed into her pussy with slow, soft
rolls of his hips, teasing, teasing, and now he was
inside her but only a few inches, and oh, god, he
was right at her G-spot, gliding into her and away,
sliding across that perfect place in a deliciously
slow rhythm, driving her already orgasm-sensitive
flesh wild. She clawed her fingers into the muscle
of his ass, wanting to pull him in, pull him harder,
but instead she merely held on and let him go at his
own pace.

She felt his cock thickening inside her, felt his
pulse beating hard against her chest, felt his muscles quivering and sweat sheen his pale skin as he

moved inside her, slow, then a few quick strokes, then slow again until she was almost mad with frustration, wanting him to settle above her and drive in hard. But he didn't. She wrapped her legs around his hips and pulled at him, but he only laughed into her mouth, kissed her, and moved slower and more unpredictably than ever.

"Goddammit, Ian. Just—oh, god, that feels good. Just fuck me. Hard." Jamie whispered the words raggedly, her hips now fluttering against his with a life of their own, pushing in when he pulled away, pulling away when he began to drive in.

"You want me to fuck you hard?" Ian adjusted his position so he was directly over her now, his palms next to her ears and his hips between her thighs, his mouth next to her ear. "Is that what you want, Jamie?"

She clung to him, shuddering as the waves of her second orgasm began to tremble low in her belly. "Yes, Ian. Yes. Fuck me hard. I'm so close."

He planted a kiss on her neck and drove into her, deep, hard. Jamie whimpered, meeting his thrust with her own. "Like that?"

"Yes...yes...just like that. Again." Jamie arched her back, planting her heels to get herself closer, to get him deeper.

But he didn't drive in hard again. He fluttered at her entrance, shallow bursts near her G-spot, pushing against the ribbed flesh there until sensation overwhelmed her and she flopped back to the bed, whimpering helplessly, mad with need, close to orgasm but not there, while a new kind of detonation crashed through her, not quite orgasm, but like it. It was an emotional sensation, something entirely wrapped up in Ian, in this experience with him.

Ian shifted again, moved upward and began thrusting slow and deep, his body close to hers, and now she felt true release build up, pressure rising as his pubic bone slid along her clit, his shaft moving deep inside her.

It was then that Jamie recognized the emotion tangled up with the physical release: relief.

She had been worried she would never be able to truly enjoy being with a man if it wasn't—she stopped herself from even thinking the name—if it wasn't *him*. Even though she'd never actually been *with* him, she was worried no one else would be able to meet her needs, to spark her desire the way he did.

This, with Ian, was as close as she'd ever come to the intense welter of desires *he* ignited with Jamie. It wasn't the same, but it was close. And it was good.

She shook the thoughts free, feeling Ian begin to move with increasing desperation now, driving harder, if not faster. She was close, again. The pressure was a balloon inside her, pent-up need, layers of frustration building layer upon layer like a pearl in an oyster. The first orgasm had only added to the buildup, and now she was nearing a second, and felt a dizzying fear that this too would only add to the snowball effect.

It was just there, suddenly, that pulsating inferno of frustration, stress, pent-up need. It had been building up within her ever since she first saw Chase in the back room in Las Vegas, and now that she saw it for what it was, she couldn't see or feel anything else. It was like panic. She needed release, but she didn't think mere orgasm would do it; this was emotional in nature, internal, mental, psychological, not physical. The first orgasm Ian had given her had only put more on top of the pile. This second one was going to be intense, and Jamie found herself hoping desperately that it would give her the relief she needed. She felt doubt sneaking up on her, though.

The pressure mounted, and Ian's thrusts grew frenzied, his back arching and beaded with sweat. She clung to his shoulders and met him thrust for thrust, her legs around his hips, pleasantly filled by him, his tip striking her at just the right angle to give her the most pleasure. She heard herself moaning, felt the intensity building, felt the waves rolling through her. Jamie bit Ian's shoulder as she came, raked her nails down his back and cried out. The explosion of physical release made her writhe and cling even tighter to Ian, and then she was sent further into abandon when she felt him come moments after her, groaning and burying his face in her neck, grinding madly into her, and then they were still together.

Ian rolled off and lay next to her, breathing heavily. "Bloody hell, Jamie." He rolled his shoulders. "You took a layer of skin off, I think."

Jamie pushed him over so she could look at his back, wincing at the eight parallel gouges running down his back. "Damn. Yeah, I did. Sorry. Guess I got carried away."

Ian just chuckled and pulled her over to rest her head on his chest. "No worries, love. I wasn't complaining. I haven't had it off that well in an age."

"Me, either," Jamie said. "Assuming that last part means it was good for you."

Ian rumbled in sleepy laughter. "Precisely. It was more than good for me, darling."

Darling. Love. Jamie listened to his breathing as it slowed and evened out. Those were just casual words for him, she reminded herself. Not actual terms of endearment.

She was dizzy, drunk, fairly well-sated... and disappointed. Still burning with frustration. Need. The mountainous weight inside her was still there. She wasn't as sexually frustrated as she had been, but the root cause of her ache hadn't changed. She listened to Ian's sleeping breaths, felt his heart beating under her ear, watched his chest rise and fall, admired the contours of his body. He was damn sexy, and a good lover. A girl could do worse. He had a good job, a hot-as-hell accent, and he could make her come twice in a row, while they were both drunk. She should hold on to this one while she had him.

Maybe it would turn into love. Or at least... something like it. Something as close as she could come without—*no*. She wouldn't, *couldn't* go there. That wasn't a possibility. She'd made her choice.

Her instinct to flee kicked in. It was that time. Ian was asleep, her car was waiting, and by the time she made it to her car, she'd be sober enough to drive. Or she could just sleep in her car. Or even get a room in this same hotel.

As if sensing her inner dilemma, Ian's arm curled around her waist and held her tight against him. Jamie kicked the flight reflex down, choked it down, shoved it down. This was good. Ian was good. She reached down and tugged the flat sheet and the comforter up to her breasts, covering herself and Ian. This was nice. He was holding her. She'd be here with him when they woke up. They'd have breakfast together. She might even learn his last name.

This is good, Jamie told herself.

The problem was, she didn't quite believe herself. Not deep down. A voice in the shadowy corners of her soul, that place where one's darkest truths reside, was telling her this was still just another futile attempt to bury her heartache.

She felt the pressure in her belly, the burning need for release. She *wasn't* sated. Not by a long shot. Maybe she could wake Ian up in a few hours and go again, take the edge off. He'd be game, most likely. She knew, though, that for as long as she was with Ian, the edge would still be there. He simply wasn't capable of satisfying the blood- and soul-deep desires within her. He could—and would—try his best, and she'd let him. But it wouldn't be enough, and she knew it.

She fell asleep wondering how long she could keep this up.

SIX

THE MUSIC WAS FIRE IN HIS VEINS. It was raw, primal fury pounding through his blood and his muscles and his brain. The shrieking guitars and chugging bass and pounding drums, the poetry flowing from his mouth in the growled and sung lyrics—these were the only things capable of drowning the hurt, capable of disguising the cracks in his heart.

Chase crouched on top of the speaker stacks, shirtless, sweating, screaming into the mic as thousands of fans watched, rapt. They could see the agony in his performance. He didn't try to hide it. Rather, he used it. He left his soul on the stage every single night, and the fans ate it up. Music journalists and bloggers were watching him carefully, offering write-ups praising his "raw, soulful, and deeply tortured performances," as one writer put it. Chase didn't care for any of that. Let them blog and tweet and and whatever else. Let them talk. The music was what drove him. He wrote on the tour bus, ignoring the wild parties, the joints and fifths his bandmates indulged in around him. Ignored the gaggles of topless girls. He wrote, worked out the melody, and gave it Gage and Linc to perfect.

The guys were increasingly distant. Or rather, they recognized his need for space and distanced themselves, left him alone. Didn't invite him to after-parties, didn't offer him the joints or the bottles. He hadn't had a drink in over a month by the time the tour schedule allowed them a few weeks off, and hadn't touched a woman since the experiment in Las Vegas with the girls from Murder Doll Asylum.

Back in Detroit, Chase didn't know what to do with himself. Without the rush of the performance, without the fans and the music, he was left loose and numb.

He'd long since used the money fronted him by the record label to pay off his house. He had a cousin drop by once a week to keep the place from looking abandoned, so when he finally walked into his house in the suburb of Sterling Heights, it was clean, the lawn mowed, the fridge empty of molding food and spoiled milk. He'd called his cousin,

Amy, from Chicago and let her know he was coming home, and she'd stocked his kitchen with some food staples. In return, he'd mailed her money and a ream of tickets to the next Detroit show.

He stood in his living room, trying not to remember the last time he had been here. He had stood in this very spot, just to the left of the faded suede couch, while a certain blonde-haired, hazel-eyed DJ had stolen his heart, one stripped-off article of clothing at a time. Her bra and panties had been blue, lacy, and too fucking sexy for his own good. God, what a night that had been.

Chase shook himself. No sense in thoughts like that. It wasn't Anna on his mind or in his heart anymore, anyway. He hadn't really been truly in love with her, he had long since realized. He had been falling in love with her, but hadn't been there yet. She'd run off before that could happen.

Not that he was at all bitter about it.

Then Jamie had come along while he was at his most vulnerable and had wormed her way into the aching space in his heart. She was all curls and curves, red hair like fire-lit copper and fierce green eyes, soft lips that tasted of vodka and cranberry and lip balm. She'd given him the slightest taste of what it would have been like to be her lover, and then snatched it away from him.

Not that he was at all bitter about it.

He rummaged in the fridge, found a case of Harp lager, popped one open, and sipped from it while he made himself a sandwich. He was back in Detroit. Jamie didn't live too far away. Finding her would be a piece of cake.

No.

Chase scrubbed his face with his palm. That was over. She'd made her choice clear. She didn't want him. Although that wasn't true, exactly. She *did* want him, equally as much as he wanted her. She just refused to let herself have him. Sure, he understood her reasons; they were perfectly reasonable and correct reasons, after all. It's not like he *wanted* to see Anna all the time. It would have been difficult and awkward as hell.

But Jamie...she would have been worth it.

Would have been.

Chase finished his beer and swirled the suds on the bottom around, wondering what the hell he was supposed to do with himself now.

He picked up his phone and scrolled through his contacts until he found the one he was looking for: Eric Meridian. Eric owned a gym and kickboxing studio not far from Chase's house, and he had often gone there before the band really took off, sparring with Eric, pumping iron, or just pummeling the heavy bag until the stress was reduced to a manageable level.

Chase needed to vent. Badly. He sent a text to Eric asking if he had time to spar and waited for a reply.

Within minutes, Eric texted back: *I've always got time to spar bro. Drop by whenever you want.*

Chase grinned, changed into workout shorts and a tank top, packed a clean change of clothes, and drove to the gym. When he got there, Eric was taping his fists. Tall, wiry, nondescript of feature with short brown hair and brown eyes, Eric didn't seem to be the kind of person you should be afraid of, but he was. Eric was deadly proficient in several styles of martial arts, mainly Muai Thai, kickboxing, and Jiujitsu. He wasn't hugely muscled, didn't have any tattoos or piercings, and would pass on the street for an accountant or CPA, but Eric Meridian was, in reality, one of the hardest and toughest people Chase had ever met.

Chase taped his fists, stretched out, and then he and Eric stepped into the small roped-off ring. They began circling each other, fists raised, bodies twisted sideways to present the smallest possible target. Chase, full of angst and suppressed pain and anger, struck first. He didn't hold back, knowing Eric was perfectly capable of handling with ease anything Chase could throw at him. Chase lashed out with a right cross, which Eric blocked easily, then lifted his knee, leaping into Eric to provide impetus to the blow. Eric quick-stepped backward, grabbed Chase by the bicep, threw himself to the floor, and planted his heel in Chase's chest, kicking up and back to flip Chase over his head.

Landing with an *ooomph*, Chase was winded but scrambled to his feet, throwing up crossed arms to block the flurry of quick jabs Eric threw at him, designed more to distract and disorient than actually do damage. The real blow came suddenly as Eric danced backward then darted forward, left heel flashing out to catch Chase in the chest, winding him further and propelling him backward. It was enough to spur Chase into a fury. He launched himself forward, using Eric's own tactic of a flurry of jabs to distract, then plunging in with a knee, then a snap-kick to Eric's ribcage.

From there, the fight turned savage, in a friendly type of way. Eric seemed to sense Chase's underlying tension and began pushing Chase harder and harder, putting real force behind his blows and letting fewer and fewer of Chase's strikes through his defenses. After almost ten full minutes of all-out sparring, both men had bloody noses and bruised ribs. The core reason for Chase's distress hadn't changed, but at least he no longer felt like he was so on edge, so about to implode or explode, or just simply combust into a million pieces of sexual frustration and broken-hearted despair.

They sat on a bench side by side and swigged from water bottles.

"What's eating you, bro?" Eric asked.

Chase shrugged. Eric was a good friend and great source of stress relief, but he used the word "bro" in every sentence. It grated on Chase's nerves after a while, which was why he usually kept their conversations to a minimum. "Just life," he ended up saying.

"Life? I'd think life would be great. You're a fuckin' legit rock star, bro. Things should be off the chain."

Chase suppressed a sigh; Eric also spoke in an endless series of slang phrases and terms. "Yeah, well. Even rock stars have problems, man. I just need to blow off some steam. Thanks for letting me stop by."

"Hey, I getcha. No worries, bro. I've got a date in a couple hours so I'm gonna bust outta here, but you go ahead and do what you need. You know your way around." Eric bumped fists with Chase and then swaggered off to take a shower.

Chase finished his water, then refilled it and moved to the heavy bags suspended from the ceiling a few feet away from the ring. Chase rolled his shoulders, then slipped a soft right jab at the bag, an exploratory touch. A second, then a third, and then a pair of snap-kicks, followed by a roundhouse heel kick. With that, Chase was off in a frenetic rhythm of punching and kicking, letting out all of his anger and hurt, pummeling it all into the bag. He heard noises around him, people talking, the grunts and shuffles of a pair sparring in the ring, clinking and clanking of weight machines, but none of it penetrated through his awareness.

When he finally stopped to rest, his hands on his knees, dragging in quick, deep panting breaths, he realized someone was watching him from the heavy bag nearest him. She was tiny but full-figured, barely five feet tall but blessed with curvy hips and breasts even a sports bra couldn't hide. Her thick black hair was twisted into a braid dangling over one shoulder, and her eyes were a vivid green. Too green. Too reminiscent of—Chase cut that line of thinking off with brutal finality.

She had a quirky grin on her lips. "That poor bag must've really pissed you off, huh?" She had her fists taped, and sweat was beading on her face, neck and chest. She was breathing almost as hard as he was.

Chase found himself turned on for the first time in weeks. "Yeah. I caught it talking about my mom, so I had to beat the shit out of it."

"Remind me not to get on your bad side, then." She crossed over to him and stuck out her hand, which was dwarfed by his when they shook. "Tess."

"Chase." Chase smiled at her, a genuine smile. "It's a pleasure to meet you, Tess. Come here often?"

She lifted an eyebrow at him. "Really? You're using *that* line on me?"

Chase laughed, and felt the pall of numbness receding. "It's not a line, I swear. I don't come here often, so I'm honestly wondering if you do."

"Uh-huh. Sure. It's a pick-up line if I've ever heard one, but I'll take the bait." She rubbed her wrist across her forehead and shook her head to toss her braid away so it dangled down her back.

Chase found himself wanting to wrap that braid around his fist and use it to hold her in place while he drove himself into her from behind; faint shock rippled through him at the ferocity of the sudden desire. He felt a smile curl his lips, a feral, seductive smile. He felt satisfaction at the way Tess reacted, nostrils flaring, breasts swelling as she dragged in a deep, steadying breath. Her fingers tightened into the leather of the heavy bag, and her eyes narrowed. Chase took a few steps toward Tess until he loomed over her, staring down into her eyes. She didn't back up, but he could tell she wanted to. Instead, she seemed to swell in presence, meeting his gaze head-on, the corners of her mouth lifting in a smile as hungry and feral as Chase's.

Without warning, she shoved the bag at him, hard, knocking him back. While he reeled, stumbling for balance, she snapped a kick at his stomach, which he didn't quite block. He was knocked farther back, heaving in a breath. She didn't relent, however, and closed in with him, curling in a pair of swift uppercuts to his ribs. She wasn't trying to hurt him, he could tell, but she wasn't holding back, either. Her eyes gleamed with adrenalized excitement, and even as she crushed her knee into his chest, her eyes betrayed her desire.

Chase slapped away a straight right punch with his wrist, then darted his own blow at her ribs, hard enough to let her know he wasn't fooling around, but not enough to really hurt. He'd never sparred with a girl before, and it unnerved him. She was clearly skilled, more so than he was, Chase realized, but he still couldn't bring himself to open up the way he would with Eric. Chase might not have had much good to say about his upbringing, but at least his old man had drilled into him a bone-deep respect for women, a refusal to ever strike a woman under any circumstances.

Tess was inviting him to come at her, though. She was dancing around him, having lured him into the ring, bouncing from one foot to the other, fists up, braid-end swaying in a serpentine rhythm. She was a tiny ball of energy, quick and fierce and wild. Chase snapped a kick at her, worried it was too hard. If he connected wrong, he could easily send her flying, injured. He need not have worried, though. She dodged it with ease, knocking his heel upward with a forearm and lunging in underneath it to crash into him with her body. She might have been small, but that body-blow had a huge amount of force behind it, her fae frame slamming into him hard enough to topple him backward. He landed on his back, winded once more, gasping for breath like a fish out of water.

He felt a weight settle on him, blinked hard to clear his vision. Tess was above him, on top of him, green eyes glinting merrily, barely breathing hard. Her knee was in his groin, a subtle warning that nonetheless managed to be an erotic promise.

"Yeah, I come here a lot," she said, her face mere inches from his.

"I can tell," Chase gasped.

He wrapped his fingers around her wrists next to his head, holding but not restraining. Tess tensed, eyes narrowed, chin lifting in defiance, her knee shoving ever-so-slightly harder into his crotch. Chase moved his hands up Tess's arms slowly, non-threateningly, until he reached her shoulders. Tess was frozen now, eyes locked onto Chase's, waiting for his next move. Chase held her gaze as he slid his palms down her spine, hesitating at the small of her back for a millisecond before continuing down to cup her ass. Tess's eyes widened and her breath caught. Chase gripped the firm globes of her ass, kneading the flesh through the thin, skintight fabric of her knee-length yoga pants. Tess moved her hips—involuntarily, it seemed to Chase—so her ass worked deeper into his grip. Chase let his fingers spread apart, exploring the expanse of each cheek, then tracing the crease between them. Tess shivered above him, widening her knees and pushing her hips backward to open herself to him.

Chase felt his erection stiffening between their bodies, and Tess licked her lips and let her gaze flicker down to take in the bulge in his gym shorts. Without warning, Chase gripped Tess's hips and flipped them over so he was on top, one hand pressing her hips to the floor, the other capturing her wrists and pinning them above her head. Tess writhed beneath him, bucked and kicked, but Chase had his knees between her thighs, preventing her from gaining leverage against him.

Lowering his lips to her ear, Chase whispered, "How about this: I'll take you out to dinner, wherever you want, and then I'll bring you back to my house."

Tess bucked again, this time less to get free than to remind him she wasn't going to go down without a fight. Then she said, "Sure. But what are we going to do at your house?" Her voice was low and sultry, breathy against his cheek.

Chase nipped her earlobe with his teeth. "Hmm. We could play euchre?"

Tess laughed, a seductive, rippling sound. "You need four for that." She returned the bite, worrying at his ear with her teeth. "I don't share."

"Oh. Well. Hmmm." Chase shifted his position so his rigid shaft brushed against her cotton-covered mound. He could smell her arousal, a dizzying musk. "I have an idea. How about I bend you over my bed and fuck you from behind until you're screaming my name? I'll wrap my fist around that sexy braid of yours and make you come a dozen times before I let you leave."

Tess's mouth opened in a breathless gasp of surprise. When she found her voice, it was shuddering and broken with desire. "Only a dozen?"

"Greedy? I can make it more, if you want. Maybe I'll tie you up and see how many times I can make you come before you pass out?"

Tess writhed her hips into his, and he nearly forgot they were in a public gym—empty, by the sounds of it, but still a public place. He had to tense every muscle in his body to keep from ripping her pants off and taking her there on the mat of the sparring ring.

"How about I give you three hours to make me come as many times as you can? If you can give me more than four orgasms in three hours, I'll do whatever you want, or let you do whatever you want to me, within the limits of safety and consensual agreement."

Chase laughed. "Is this a bet?"

"Yep. I don't think you can do it."

Chase narrowed his eyes. "Doubting me already? We just met, honey. You have no idea what I'm capable of."

"Oh, I'm not doubting *you*, I'm doubting *me*. I've never in my life orgasmed more than once in a row."

Chase laughed, but this time it was a rumble of pleasure containing a promise. "Then you've been with all the wrong men, sweetheart."

"Maybe I have," she said. "But I guess we'll see, won't we?"

"I guess we will."

They used the gym showers and dressed, then took Chase's rental car to dinner at P.F. Chang's in the Somerset Collection. They learned a bit about each other during their leisurely dinner. Tess was a flight attendant for Northwest Airlines, was currently single following what Chase gathered was a pretty bad breakup, although she glossed over it with a few curt phrases of dismissal. She was the youngest of three children, and the only girl, and her much-older brothers were both in law enforcement, so she'd learned young how to defend herself. For himself, Chase told her about his band's recent success and left out any mention of Jamie or Anna, saying only that he'd been single for quite a while. Tess's eyes narrowed when he said this.

"You know my brothers are both cops, right? I did mention that? You should realize they've taught me how to detect a liar, and how to cause intense physical pain to men who lie to me."

Chase didn't answer right away, dragging his last pea pod through the sauce on his place without looking at her. Finally, he met her eyes. "It's a lie of omission. Let's just say it was a complicated situation that I don't want to talk about. If it's something that needs to be told, eventually, then I'll tell you."

Tess nodded. "Eventually, hmm? I can live with that. As long as you're not secretly married or something." She finished her glass of red wine, then twisted the stem between her fingers. "Are you planning on there being an *eventually* between us?"

Chase shrugged. "I honestly hadn't thought that far. It's not impossible."

"Fair enough," Tess said.

"About our bet," Chase said.

"Yeah?"

"What do you get if I lose?"

Tess gave him an amused grin. "Hmmm. I'm glad you asked." She ran her tongue along her upper lip suggestively. "If you lose, you agree to be my bitch for three days. Sexually and otherwise. Everything. Do my dishes, vacuum my floor, wash my car...shirtless. Go down on me whenever I want without having the favor returned. Rub my feet."

Chase tilted his head to the side. "Damn. You drive a hard bargain. How about that's the bet both ways? I lose, I'm your bitch. If you lose, you're mine. Including the topless car washing."

Tess lifted her chin defiantly. "Deal." She extended her hand and they shook to seal the deal. "But you'd better bring your A-game, buddy, because I'm telling you, you've got your work cut out for you. It's really difficult for me to reach climax, and I'm a mess afterward. Just sayin'. Be ready to be my bitch."

Chase leaned forward and kissed the corner of her mouth, a tease, a promise. He sat back without delivering on the kiss, leaving Tess with her lips parted in anticipation, her eyes half-closed, nearly panting.

"Pay the bill so we can go," Tess whispered. "I've got a bet to win."

"There's just one stipulation," Chase said, sliding cash into the black bill-folder. "You can't cheat. No pretending I didn't make you come."

An older couple sitting at the table nearest them glanced up as Chase and Tess left their table; the older couple gave them a look of profound disgust and offense.

Chase drove them to his house, and when he closed the door behind him, Tess stood in the middle of the living room, hands crossed over her stomach, grasping the hem of her shirt in preparation to strip it off.

"Not wasting any time, are you?" Chase said, crossing the space between them and capturing her wrists in his hands. "We're doing this my way, sweetheart. And my way involves stripping you myself. Slowly."

Tess released her shirt and stood, waiting. "Your way, huh? What if I don't want to do it your way?"

"Well, if you're having trouble coming, then maybe your way isn't working." Chase ran his hand between the bottom of her shirt and the top of her calf-length skirt, brushing her skin with the calloused pads of his fingers.

"Maybe you're just a cocky bastard," she said, gasping, the breathy catch in her voice stealing the vitriol from her words.

"Or maybe I just know I can make you come as many times as I want. Maybe I just I know I can play your sweet little body like a guitar."

Tess let her head loll back on her shoulders as he lifted the hem of her skirt up, dragging his fingers along the insides of her pressed-together thighs. "If I'm a musical instrument, I'm more of a mandolin: round at the base and strung tight."

"You're not self-conscious about your figure, are you?"

She shook her head. "Hell, no. I may be tiny, but I'll kick your ass. I've got wide hips and big tits, and I'm so short I'm nearly a little person. If you don't like it, that's your loss."

"I like it. I like it a lot." Chase brushed her silk-covered slit with his fingers, feeling her grow damp as he touched her. "In fact, I plan to spend the rest of the night showing you how much I like it."

"That works. I'd hate to have to break your arms."

"You wouldn't break my arms."

"Yes, I would. Especially if you don't quit teasing me and touch me already."

Chase was slowly working his middle finger under the elastic leg-band of her panties, tracing the outer edge of her labia. "All in good time. I'm not sure you're ready for me to touch you yet. You don't want it bad enough."

Tess clawed her fingers into his bicep, trying to tug his finger closer, deeper. "Yes, I do. I do. I want it."

"How bad?"

"Really bad."

Chase swiped his finger along her slit, feeling her slick, hot juices as they coated his fingers. "I don't believe you."

"I'm not gonna beg, Chase. You're the one who has to prove yourself to me, remember. If you lose, you'll spend three days licking my pussy and rubbing my feet."

His middle finger dipped deeper, curling into her tight channel and rubbing against the ridge of her G-spot. She shuddered; her knees buckled, and she stiffened her legs to catch herself. "Maybe I shouldn't tell you this, but that doesn't sound like a loss for me."

"You say that now..." she started, then trailed off as Chase hooked his fingers inside her panties and tugged them off with a single sharp motion, guiding her legs to step out of them one at a time.

Tess started unzipping her skirt, but Chase stopped her. "Not yet. You're going to have your first orgasm fully clothed."

"Except for my panties, you mean." Tess ran her hands over his shoulders as Chase knelt in front of her.

He slid his palms up the backs of her legs from ankle to buttocks, tickling and tracing the strong curves. Her skirt was still draped down around her calves, disguising the way his hands were slipping between her thighs from behind, spreading her stance until her feet were shoulder-width apart, granting Chase access to her desire-wet nether lips. He cupped her buttocks, then traced a finger down the crease of her ass.

"Is this off-limits?" he asked, letting his finger move in near her anus.

"For now? Yes." She pushed his hand away, moved it to her hip. "Ask me again later if you've managed to win our bet. I may change my answer."

"Fair enough."

Chase ran his hands down the front of her thighs and then back up, twisting his palm so it was facing up, cupping her mound. Tess's legs buckled again, and her weight bore down on his palm; she wiggled her hips so her clit rubbed against the heel of his palm, and she let out a soft moan.

"You're wet and tight, Tess. I think you might be ready," Chase said, dragging two fingers through her folds.

"About...oh, god...about damn time," she said.

Chase lifted her skirt up to her hips, steadying her with an arm around her ass. He curled his two middle fingers into her hot, wet pussy, flicking his fingertips across her G-spot. When she gasped, he sucked her clit into his mouth, turning her gasp into a moan. Her hands scraped over his stubble-dark scalp, her fingers turning into claws as he licked and flicked at her folds. Her breathing turned to panting, her knees began to dip and buckle with every swipe of his tongue, every feather-light brush of his fingers over her G-spot.

"I can't believe it...oh, god, oh, god, I'm close already." Tess's hands cupped the back of Chase's head in a familiar way that did something deep in his heart, something between pain and desire, its source nebulous and difficult to pinpoint.

He pushed the thoughts away and renewed the vigor of his tongue's assault on the sensitive, cream-wet nub of her clit. She clutched him tight, and his arm kept her upright when the first wave rolled over her. Chase felt it start low in her belly, heard her breathing grow frantic as her orgasm neared. As she closed in on climax, Chase slowed and then paused, drawing a curse from Tess.

"What? Why the hell are you stopping? I'm so close, you bastard!" She writhed into him, seeking release.

Chase let the fabric of her skirt droop around his face, obscuring him. He slipped his free hand up her belly and tugged the cup of her bra down to reveal her breast. Pinching it between two fingers, Chase began again with his tongue and fingers, rolling the tip of his tongue in circles around her taut clit, pressing his fingers against her G-spot and working in circles to match the motion of his tongue.

She was almost instantly on the cusp of climax, but Chase drew it out, increasing his pace until she was frantic once more, then slowing down, repeating this cycle until Tess was nearly mad with need for release.

"Goddamn it, Chase! You're making me crazy!" She clutched his face against her, shamelessly pushing him into her folds. "Fuck me, I'm so close."

"I know you're close, sweetness." Chase paused to answer, gently tweaking her nipple. "And believe me, I plan to thoroughly fuck you. And then some."

She tried to speak, but her words were subsumed beneath a strangled shriek of ecstasy as Chase pushed her closer and closer to climax with now-relentless fingers in her cream-drenched sex, his tongue whipping at her throbbing clit. He felt the pulse in her clit, felt the throb, felt the quavering in her belly and the clenching in her inner muscles.

Two fingers deep in her sex, Chase extended his pinky and pushed it against the tight bud of her anus, and as she came, he pressed just the tip of his littlest finger against the knot of muscles, not quite entering her. She screamed then, a full-voiced howl of release. Her body undulated as she came, her knees giving way even as she fought to stay upright. Chase continued to flick and suck and wiggle and pinch her every nerve ending until she was wrung limp. He caught her and carried her to his room, kicking open the door with his foot, settling her on the bed gently. Her body shook and shuddered with aftershocks, and her breathing was ragged.

Chase unzipped her skirt, slid a palm under her backside and lifted her, tugging the skirt off with a jerk. Then he peeled her shirt over her head, Tess cooperating with floppy limbs. He unhooked her bra and tossed it aside. She was naked for him then, and he was hard with desire. He felt the all-too-fa-miliar pang of misplaced guilt rush through him as he pressed kisses to her breasts, the awful, unshake-able sensation that he was doing something wrong by being with someone *else* than Jamie.

Tess was oblivious to the thoughts racing through him, of course, and he was thankful for that. He nibbled on her nipple, worrying the taut bud with his teeth, eliciting a sexy little mewl from her. She was regaining her senses finally, and was clawing at his shirt, pushing it up over his head and exploring his torso with eager hands, then ripping at the button of his jeans and pushing them down.

Chase had left all his leather pants with the tour bus, so he was stuck with jeans, which he disliked and rarely wore. He let her strip him, let her look at him, let her take his turgid shaft in her small hands. She slid her palms along his length, rubbed her thumb over the broad mushroom head, caressed his cock with quick, soft, skilled hands. He knelt above her, letting her touch him until his felt himself begin to respond, begin to rise.

"No more touching. I'm yours to do with as you wish if I lose," Chase said, pushing her hands away and over her head, then tracing a line from neck down between her breasts to test her swollen folds with his index finger. "For now, however, you have three more orgasms to go."

Tess arched her back as he ever so gently began to move his finger inside her. "Shit...shit...that was so intense, I'm not sure I'd survive another one."

"Well, then, I hope you have life insurance, sugar, because that was just the beginning."

Tess moaned as he lapped his tongue around one nipple, working the other with the fingers of one hand and circling her clit with the fingers of his other hand. He was using the opposite hand in her sex as he had used before, and he could smell her musk on his fingers, along with another, darker scent from his pinky. She'd said her second entrance was off-limits, but she hadn't protested when he'd touched her there before, so he decided to push his luck a bit. The first orgasm had wrenched through her like a tidal wave, so if he drew this one out even longer, the second would be even more intense.

He worked her clit slowly with his fingers, getting her hips moving in gentle circles before slacking off, letting her subside a bit, then bringing her back up again, biting at her nipple, sucking on it, flicking and pinching the other. And then, abruptly, he moved down her body and lifted her legs over his shoulder, lifting her hips to bring her sweet wet folds to his mouth. She writhed in place, moaning nonstop now as he suckled her clit, slathering her own juices downward over the tight muscles of her anus. She groaned when his pinky touched her there, and then sucked in a ragged, whimpering breath when he penetrated up to the first knuckle. He didn't move his pinky, just left it there to let her adjust, slowing his pace and working her throbbing bud with soft, slow licks of his tongue. He was able to reach her nipples still, so Chase rolled one between finger and thumb in torturously slow pinches.

Tess was wiggling and arching and undulating as he drew out the process, working his pinky inward with careful, delicate pushes, timing them with thrusts of his tongue against the straining nerves of her clit. When he was inside her to the second knuckle, he began to work his finger in and out, once again synced with the rhythm of his tongue against her folds and his fingers on her breasts.

Tess began to buck into his finger, driving him deeper, her voice raised in a keening shriek. He felt her pussy muscles clench and quiver; her back arched and her heels dug into the bed. He pushed his finger and pulled it, licking furiously until his jaw ached and his tongue was on fire, pinching her nipple until he was sure the twinge of pain was adding to the pleasure.

She came with a cry, bowed upward in an arched bridge, only her heels, head, and neck touching the bed. Wave after wave crushed through her, shaking her, ripping shuddering sobs from her as she lowered her body to the bed. Chase relented then, and kissed his way up her flat, taut belly, kissed each breast, then her neck, then her mouth, tasting the salt of sweat and tears on her mouth and cheeks. Tess clung to his neck, shaking uncontrollably.

He kissed her neck and shoulder as he fished a condom from the bedside table drawer, ripped it open with his teeth and rolled it over his straining cock. Tess was oblivious to this, gasping for breath.

"Ready for number three, sweetness?" Chase said.

"What? Oh, god. Oh, god...I can't—I'm not ready. I'm not ready." Tess was barely able to whisper, the words mumbled drunkenly. "It's too much."

"You asked for it, babe." Chase probed her entrance with the tip of his cock, working himself slowly inside. "Too much? Want me to stop?"

Tess's fingers scrabbled at his back as he filled her, stretched. She was tight, so tight, almost too tight. He went as slow as was humanly possible, working himself in an inch, then pausing to let her adjust before pushing gradually farther in. He watched her face work through a myriad of emotions, surprise, delight, even fear.

He paused again before he was fully inside her. "Seriously, Tess. I don't want to hurt you. You're so fucking tight. Should I stop?"

She shook her head, the snake-tip tail of her braid jiggling near one of her breasts. "No...god, no. Please don't stop. Just...like you are. Slow."

"Slow," Chase agreed, thrusting incrementally.

He'd been straining with need to release for what felt like forever, turned on by the noises Tess made as she came, the sight of her tan skin and rounded curves, but still he held back, squeezing his eyes shut in concentration as he felt himself drive in to the hilt, almost too big to fit inside her tiny channel. He had to be careful with her, he knew, even after she'd adjusted to him, even after climax had her loose and pliant.

He moved into her in sinuous thrusts, barely moving still, but enough for her to feel it, enough for him to feel it. Tess began to whimper again, mewling noises in the back of her throat, moving her hips with his now, meeting him careful thrust for thrust. Her fingers tightened on his shoulders and her legs circled his waist, holding him deep inside her.

Chase decided to give her the illusion of control for a while; he flipped her so he was on the bottom, and she readily adjusted to ride him, knees wide to straddle his hips, palms flat on his broad chest. Her braid dangled over her shoulder to tickle his throat. He grabbed the braid and tugged gently until she was sitting upright, and then he held her in place with his hands on her hips. His middle fingers were mere inches apart on her belly, and he began to lift her, guiding her motions. She arched her spine inward, tipping her head back and moving on her own, now, finding her rhythm on top of him.

Chase was barely thrusting, letting her do the work while he held himself back. He had to give her a break, let her recover before he brought her to climax again. She wasn't ready yet. He let her move on top of him, surging up and down now, impaling herself on him, driving herself deeper than he'd imagined she'd be able to take him. She collapsed forward after a few minutes, writhing with increasingly desperate movements.

Now.

He lifted her off him, bodily removing her, ignoring her frantic moans of protest. He put his lips to her ear and whispered, "You didn't think I'd forgotten my promise back in the gym, did you?"

She shook her head. "No...what? What promise?"

He slid off the bed and drew her after him, flipping her onto her stomach and pulling her toward him by her ankles. "I'm going to bend you over this bed and fuck you from behind."

"Oh, my god, Chase. I can't take that. I could barely handle your finger." Real fear was evident in her voice.

He settled her on the bed's edge so her feet didn't quite touch the floor, so she was at his mercy. He carved his palms over her arched spine and to her ass, tiny and taut. He gently caressed each cheek, then teased her anus with a finger. Tess whimpered, pushing into his questing finger even as he could feel her shivering with a mixture of fear and anticipation. Chase spat saliva onto his hand and smeared it onto the knot of muscles and worked his ring finger around the circle of muscles, while with his other hand he gripped his shaft at the base and probed her pussy with the tip. He hadn't inserted his finger into her yet, and he gently, carefully pushed in as he thrust into her wet, ready folds with his cock.

"Oh, god," Tess whispered, relief in her voice.

Chase leaned over her. "I would never do that. I would never hurt you," he murmured. "The tip of my pinky finger is one thing. That is something else entirely."

He was telling her the truth, in that he would never push a woman past what she wanted and what she was capable of doing with enjoyment, but he didn't mention how much he *wanted* to take her like that. He was riding a knife-edge of control, his ring finger now in her to the first knuckle, his shaft moving into her sex in small, shivering thrusts. He wanted to plunge hard and fast, but he held back, riding gently into her pussy, her fine, firm ass quivering gently with each thrust.

He was learning her noises. She began to mewl again, a kitten-like noise high the back of her throat, a sound that he now knew signaled her impending orgasm.

Chase allowed himself one concession to the fury pounding through him: He wrapped her braid twice around his fist and gently but firmly tugged until her back was arched and her head lifted off the bed. She planted her fists on the bed and undulated her body into him. She was still unable to reach the floor, and Chase began to plunge up into her, lifting her up with each driving plunge, still holding back, still restraining himself from crushing into her with the kind of intensity he desired.

Tess took all of him, though, and gave back with everything she had, losing herself in the delirium of sexual abandon. She lifted herself up with her torso muscles and back, then let herself crash down onto him, spreading her thighs farther apart and wiggling to get his finger deeper into her asshole. Chase gave her what she wanted, more of his finger, pushing in until his other fingers were splayed against the muscular flesh of her ass, until his finger was impaled inside her as far as it would go, and he began to thrust his cock into her harder and harder, never fully penetrating, knowing he might hurt her if he did so. He held on to her braid and let himself drive into her, and now, finally, she began to lose the rhythm in the frenetic frenzy of orgasm.

Chase felt her muscles clamp down, squeezing his finger as she came. He finally let himself loose then, coming with her, driving as deep as he dared in slow but powerful thrusts. Tess was wild, thrashing beneath him, shrieking and writhing and sobbing. Chase came hard, desperate from having held back for so long, from having gone so long without sex.

After nearly a minute of body-wracking climax, Tess went still, but for her ragged breathing. Chase withdrew from her, lifted her to the middle of the bed and drew the blankets over her. He went into his *en suite* bathroom and discarded the condom before washing his hands twice. When he approached the bed again, Tess was snoring.

He smiled to himself, then slipped on a pair of gym shorts and got himself a beer from the fridge. He hiked himself up onto the kitchen counter and drank his beer, head slumped back against the counter, lost in thought. After a trackless amount of time, he finished his beer, and then a second, and then a third, his mind and heart a muddle of half-formed desires and fears and worries.

Foremost in his mind was the knowledge that he was far, far from sated. He'd ravaged Tess and left her passed out in his bed. She really was a fiery, spirited little thing, but he'd simply wrung every last drop from her. He didn't think she'd be complaining come morning, but he knew for as much fun as he'd have with her, eventually it would end.

He, however, was still burning with need, adrenaline, desire, and pent-up frustration.

Tess simply couldn't give him what he needed. It was through no fault of hers, though, and that was the part that left him sad. Throughout their dinner conversation, he'd come to like and respect her, and the fact that she could kick his ass in the ring turned him on something fierce. He wished they were more compatible in bed.

He drained his fourth beer and then slipped into bed next to Tess. She moved against him, instinctively spooning with him.

She half-turned to face him, opening one eye. "You lose the bet, Chase."

"What? No way. I'm not done yet."

Tess laughed. "I hate to say this, but I am. I can't take any more. I really can't. I'll be sore as hell in the morning as it is. I cannot physically handle another orgasm. The bet was four in three hours, and that's not happening. Therefore, you lose."

Chase laughed. "Fine. I concede."

"You would. Bitch."

He laughed again, and Tess smiled sleepily at him, then turned back over and was soon asleep once more.

Chase fell asleep thinking of green eyes. Only, these green eyes were framed by red curls as fiery as the woman beneath them.

SEVEN

A FALL WIND BLEW HARD down the corridor of Michigan Avenue in Chicago. The sidewalks were full of pedestrians burdened with shopping bags and the streets jammed with taxis and buses and private cars. The sky overhead between the towers was gray and heavy. Flecks of something cold and wet—possibly snow, or rain, or a mix of the two—spattered against Jamie's face as she bustled from the door of the high-rise condo building. She had her phone in her hand, an iMessage in the gray bubble: *Meet me at the corner, babe. Dinner reservations in twenty.* Her response, in blue: *K. B right there.*

She flipped the collar of black pea coat up and hunched her shoulders, hustling through the post-Thanksgiving shopping crowd to meet Ian. His mother had relocated to Chicago, and Ian had ended up moving to Chicago with her. He didn't live *with* his mother, but nearby. Laura Collins, his mother, was a short, sweet woman with iron-gray hair and steely blue eyes. She adored Jamie, but had hinted in more than one conversation that she didn't think Jamie was entirely happy.

Which was true, of course. She'd put everything she had into making things with Ian work. She commuted to Chicago every Thursday after her last shift and spent Friday and Saturday with Ian and his mother, then made the four-hour drive back for work Sunday afternoon. Ian met her in Detroit a few times a month as well, and overall, things worked. They worked.

But...Jamie was restless. She spent most of the four-hour trip twice a week trying not to think about how much longer she could pretend she was okay.

Ian knew. She saw the knowledge in his eyes at times, in the way she'd catch him gazing sadly at her, expectantly. Waiting.

Ian had something planned for today. He'd made reservations, which was unlike him. Usually they did burgers and beers at a local pub, or ate in. This was *an event*. He had something to say to her, and she knew it. It was probably a preemptive strike. His way of sparing her feelings, in an odd manner.

She found Ian waiting at the street corner, watching her approach. The sad look was in eyes again, distant and semi-hollow.

"Hello, love," he said, with false cheer.

She kissed him, a brief touch of the lips. They pulled away at the same time. "Hey, yourself."

"Hungry?" Ian took her hand, and they walked through the crowd together.

"Famished. Traffic into the city was hellish."

"Sorry to hear it, darling. I worry about you making the drive so often in that dodgy old auto of yours. I'm always afraid it's going to go tits up on you halfway here."

Jamie chuckled at his turn of phrase. "Yeah, it's definitely a possibility, I guess. But it's fine for now. Besides, if it does go tits up, I'll just call you, and you'll rescue me." Out of habit, she nudged closer and smirked at him. "And then as a reward, *I'll* go tits up for you."

Ian laughed. "Oh, god, I *really* don't think that phrase means what you think it means."

Jamie shoved him with her hip. "Oh, shut up. I know exactly what it means, I was just using it in another context."

"And *I* know *that*. I was just teasing you."

They had a long, leisurely dinner, filled with the idle conversation of a couple familiar and comfortable with each other. It was laced with tension, though. Jamie felt it, and she saw it in Ian's eyes.

Finally, she leaned back in her chair with a sigh. "Out with it, Ian."

He shifted uncomfortably. "I—I'm not sure where to start."

"Just start with the truth." She flagged the waiter and held up her wine glass.

Ian sipped from his own wine and then set it aside. "You aren't happy. With me, I mean."

Jamie pinched the bridge of her nose. "No, it's not that. Not really. It's...complicated."

"Un-complicate it."

"God. That's a lot easier to say than to do. As cliché as this is, and as much as I hate how it's going to sound...it's not you, it's me."

"That's fucking bollocks, Jamie."

"I know, I know. But it's *true*." The server arrived to pour Jamie another measure of cabernet, and she sipped it greedily. "There's just—"

"Someone else?"

"Yes. No. Sort of. There isn't anyone else in the sense you're thinking. I haven't been seeing anyone else. I promise. But my heart is...I just can't—" Jamie cut herself off with a huff. "Shit. I'm making a mess of this."

"Sorry, darling, but you kind of are making a bit of a muddle of it. Just spit it out. You're in love with someone else. I get it."

"It's not that simple, though. It's just one of those things that won't go away, you know? No matter how hard I try, I just can't seem to let go."

Ian scratched his jaw and then fiddled with the cloth napkin on the table. "I do remember that conversation we had. In my hotel room in Buttfuck, Michigan. You said some rot about forbidden love. You said you were over him."

"It wasn't rot, Ian."

"It's just a word, Jamie. I know it wasn't. I just meant I remember you mentioning this other guy. And you're still not over him enough to be happy with me."

"It's not like I don't want to be over him, Ian. I do. I really, *really* do want to be over him. But I just...can't seem to do it."

"And I can't do this with you if you're not." Ian tossed back the rest of his wine and watched Jamie's reaction.

She only nodded. "I know. And I'm sorry. I'm sorry to have wasted so much of your time." She stood up, leaving her half-full wine glass, and turned to walk away.

"Jamie, wait. You didn't waste—shit." He cut himself off when he realized Jamie wasn't listening.

She was already out the door and into the flurries of hard, stinging snow. She wasn't crying. Not again. Her eyes were stinging from the wind, was all. There was no reason to be upset. She knew it was coming. She would have done it herself soon. She wasn't being fair to Ian, or to herself.

It still didn't explain why the hole in her heart ached so badly.

Chase flopped over onto his back, and Tess let out a long, contented sigh.

"Chase, baby. I don't know how you do that to me every time," Tess said.

Forcing a smile onto his face, Chase turned over and kissed her. "I'm just that good," he said.

Tess pinched his thigh. "And you're just that arrogant."

"It's not arrogance, it's confidence."

"Same thing, babe." Tess scooted out of bed and gathered her clothes, tossed them in her suit-case, then dug out a clean pair of panties and a bra. Her uniform was already pressed and hanging on the rack near the hotel door.

Chase watched her diminutive form as she moved around the room, gathering the rest of her things and packing them away, then hopped in the shower. He was every bit as attracted to her as the day he'd met her three months ago, but his ability to pretend she satisfied him was waning. He hated the pretense. Hated feeling like shit when he had to paste on a smile and act exhausted after a vigorous session in bed with her, when the truth was he was always holding back and was usually just getting started when she was finished, left partially sated and entirely frustrated.

He had an inkling she knew, but he hadn't had the courage to broach the subject. She had a flight to Boston in a few hours, so he doubted the discussion would happen right then. He had a gig himself in a while, headlining at the Mayne Stage here in Chicago.

He liked Tess, a lot. He had a good time with her.

But…it just wasn't enough.

Tess emerged from the shower to find Chase standing naked at the eleventh-floor window, staring out at the swirling snow. She stood next to him in silence for a while, then looked up at him.

"This isn't working, Chase."

He glanced down at her. Serious green eyes gazed back up at him, calm and collected. "No, I guess not." He turned back to the view of downtown Chicago. "I'm sorry."

"Why are you sorry?"

"I don't know. It's…I'm just sorry this didn't work. You're an amazing girl, and I wish—"

"I can't keep up with you. I know I can't. But I think that's only a part of the problem. There's something else. That thing you said you'd tell me 'eventually.'" Tess leaned her head against his arm. "This is eventually, but you still don't have to tell me. It's someone else. I see the way you look at me sometimes. Maybe I look like her, or something. I don't know. But that's what it is."

"Yeah, sort of. But it's—"

"Complicated," Tess said in sync with him.

"Yeah," Chase said. "It's really complicated."

Tess turned away from him, dropped the towel, and stepped into her panties, then hooked her bra around her middle and slipped it on. "I don't need to know the details. But I'll tell you this: A lot of the time, when someone says something is complicated, what they really mean is they're afraid of the truth. They're afraid of what will happen, afraid of the consequences." She turned back to Chase. "Good things often come with tough consequences. It just makes us appreciate the good that much more."

"You're right," Chase said. "But it's not me you have to convince. It's her."

Tess shrugged. "*I* don't have to convince anyone. *You* do. And if it's meant to be, it'll happen." She put on her flight attendant uniform, zipped her bags, and then set her rolling suitcase on end, handle extended. "I care about you, Chase. You're a good man and an incredible lover. I really am sorry this didn't work out, too."

Chase thunked his head against the cold glass, then moved toward Tess. "I haven't been fair to you, Tess. And that's what I'm sorry for."

She smiled at him, a little sadly. "I knew this was coming a long time ago. I knew it was coming when you said you didn't want to talk about it back in Eric's gym. I was just being selfish. I wanted a piece of you for myself."

"Well, you got a piece. A big piece." He grinned lecherously, but his heart wasn't in it, and neither was hers. "Seriously, though. This goodbye sucks."

Tess nodded. "Yes, it does. All goodbyes do."

He leaned toward her and kissed her, careful not to smudge her makeup or wrinkle her uniform. When he let her go, Tess took a deep breath and let it out.

"Goodbye, Chase."

"'Bye, Tess." He watched her leave, wondering what he was supposed to do with himself now.

He took a long shower and dressed, packed his one duffel bag, and left the hotel. The snow was bitterly cold against his shower-hot skin, and the wind was even worse, snatching his breath away. He walked aimlessly, trying to empty his heart, snuff out the turmoil inside himself. He shrugged deeper into his thick coat, eyes downcast, attention wandering. His bag was slung over one shoulder, and his hands were dug into his pockets. He thought he might be capable of just walking, walking, walking until the snow buried him or the cold froze him, or the hole in his chest ate him from the inside out.

Then he rounded a corner, and something soft yet firm slammed into him, knocking him backward. He slipped on a patch of ice, tangled up with whoever he'd run into, and tumbled to the sidewalk, slamming his head into the concrete. He saw stars, squeezing his eyes shut against the pain. Then something familiar spiked through the fog and the thunder in his skull to his awareness. It was subtle at first, a combination of scents, lotion and perfume and shampoo, woman-scent...and then a series of sensations, the way her body fit against his, a tickle of hair on his face, and the heat of an intense gaze.

Chase cracked his eyelids open to see the burning jade orbs that had haunted his dreams for months staring down at him.

"Y-you?" Her voice broke.

Chase tried to catch his breath and speak, but the wind scoured past his nose and mouth, taking it, and the pain in his head and the ache in his heart all conspired to keep him gasping. Most of all, it was her beauty that left him breathless.

Her hands were on his chest, resting lightly. Her lips were inches from his, red and full. Her breasts were crushed against him, and...he was instantly erect, hard as a rock and near to bursting in the space of a single heartbeat. And all Jamie was doing was looking at him.

Then he truly looked at her. Her eyes were red, and unshed tears were pooling, threatening to spill out. "Jamie? Are you okay?"

She could only shake her head. She tried to get off him, to stand up, but she couldn't. Chase let his head touch back down to the cold concrete, snow drifting around his eyes, and gazed up at her.

"Yeah, me, either," he said.

Jamie laughed, a choked sound. "Help me up. I can't…"

Chase stood up gingerly, helping Jamie to her feet. He didn't let go when they were upright. He drew her instinctively into his arms, and she went willingly, seemingly unconsciously. "What's wrong, Jay?"

"Everything. You. Me. Just…everything."

Chase laughed again, knowing what she meant, somehow. "I wish I didn't understand that, but I do. All too well."

"Why are you here? Why do you always show up at the worst times?"

"I wish I knew." He felt truth boiling on his lips. "But then…I do know. I keep showing up because we're meant to be."

"It can't be."

"But it is."

Jamie sobbed into his chest, as if a dam had burst open, then cut herself off just as quickly. "Why? Why, Chase?"

"Why what?"

Jamie pulled back to meet his green piercing brown. "Why did you have to make me fall in love with you? I wasn't supposed to fall in love with you."

Chase felt something hot and wet burn down his cheek. "I don't know, Jay. But I've been wondering the same thing. Why, oh, why did I have to fall in love with the one girl I can't have?"

Jamie's eyes slid closed, fluttered, then opened. When her eyes met his again, he saw a new kind of determination in them. As if she'd made a decision. The hot wetness stung his eyes, almost as if he was crying, but that wasn't possible. He hadn't cried since he was in elementary school, if not before. Certainly not over a girl.

Then he felt moist, soft, wet lips touch his cheek where the saltiness stung his skin, heat on his cold flesh. Again and again her lips touched his face, cheek, chin, forehead, throat, neck, then…a pause…bated breath…and her lips touched his. Chase's eyes were closed tight, blocking away the world, and he almost flinched away, so intense and visceral was the sensation of her lips on his. Like hot wine, like a drug.

He had no chance of resisting.

He kissed her back, softly at first. So softly. Then her lips pulled away, and he heard her drag in a shuddering breath. He opened his eyes and saw her, tear-tracks on her cheeks, trembling fingers wiping them away. Chase mimicked her gesture, kissing away the salt of her tears, trailing kisses across her face, over her lips, tasting hesitantly, then taking hungrily. She met him with equally sudden ferocity, and they were lost together then.

Chase pulled away first. "If you walk away again, if you tell me no again, I'll be broken in a way that can never be fixed," he said.

Jamie shuddered, and then collapsed into his chest. "Me, too." Her words were muffled by his coat, but he heard them.

"Is this happening? Us?" he asked.

She nodded. "It has to. It can't not." Jamie looked up at Chase and let him see into her heart through her eyes. "I'm terrified."

Chase licked his kiss-swollen lips. "Me, too."

"Where do we go? What do we do?" Jamie asked.

"Well, first I have a show to play. Then I'm going to find a hotel, and I'm going to kiss you and make love to you until you beg me to stop."

Jamie shuddered into him, but this was a different, more feral and salacious, kind of shudder. "I'll never want you to stop." She arched into him, wind-blown red curls tangling around them both, and he felt fire blaze through his body, instant heat, instant need. "Never."

"Then I never will," he answered.

Chase kissed Jamie again, and this time it was slow and languorous and full of promise. Their eyes met again as they pulled apart, and the heat flying between them was hot enough to melt the snow as it drifted between their bodies.

The promise in her eyes had him ready to explode, and he knew when they finally came together, it would stop his world.

EIGHT

SNOW SWIRLED, SMALL STINGING FLECKS drifting and windblown and never accumulating, touching Jamie's nose and cheeks like frozen fingers as she rested her face against the scratchy wool of Chase's coat. Her heart thudded crazily in her breast, adrenalized with the knowledge that she was indulging in something forbidden, something that surely would come with a high cost. She was giving in to something that felt inevitable, as unavoidable as the movement of the stars across the sky, as unstoppable as gravity or time or each breath drawn into shuddering lungs.

Chase's arms were wrapped around her, strong and thick and comforting, holding her close to his warmth and spicy male scent, blocking out the world. The cold around them only added to the sense of isolation, the feeling that they two were the only ones in the world. Jamie had spent so long denying her feelings for Chase, reminding herself why she couldn't be with him, why it was wrong, why it couldn't happen. Now here she was in his arms, and nothing had ever felt so right. Standing chest to chest, breathing in his scent and his strength...nothing had ever felt so much like home.

For Jamie, whose life had been one ratty, bare-ly-able-to-afford-it apartment after another from the age of sixteen, home was a nebulous concept, a thing to be desired but never had. Home was the latest one-year lease, non-refundable deposit, one-room apartment with a galley kitchen and blank white walls. Home was wherever she had a bed and a bottle of vodka.

Now, home suddenly had become this man, wherever he was. She'd spent weeks and months traipsing from suburban Detroit to Chicago, back and forth every weekend, until she was more familiar with the inside of her battered blue Buick LeSabre than the inside of her battered Clawson apartment.

Home. Jamie breathed in again, deeply. Wool of Chase's thick navy peacoat, his cologne—some spicy, citrusy smell that seemed at once exotic and deeply masculine—tangled up with body wash and the smell of fall morphing into winter, the smell of fresh snow and cold, crisp air. She tightened her grip on Chase's shoulders, her arms curling up from underneath his armpits, clinging to his shoulder blades for dear life, as if he might be ripped away.

"You don't need to crush me, Jay," his voice rumbled, amused. "I'm not going anywhere."

"Yes, you are." She fought the overwhelming rush of emotions threatening to choke off her words. "You're always going away."

Chase laughed, another rolling rumble. "Hate to break it to you, babe, but you're the one who kept running from me."

Jamie sniffed—from the cold, of course. "I had to."

"So...what changed?"

Jamie shrugged, a small movement almost lost against Chase's bulk. "Nothing. I just can't fight it anymore."

"Fight what?" Something in his voice had Jamie thinking Chase knew the answer but wanted to hear her say it out loud.

She pushed back a little and tucked her hands in between them, gazing up into his dark eyes. "You know."

"Yeah, but I just want to hear you say it again."

Jamie let her forehead rest against his chest. "Fine," she said, wrapping her arms around his neck, "if you must hear it again. I love you, Chase Delany."

His eyes burned, lit from within, fiery brown locked on her wavering green. "You love me."

"Yep."

His hands rested on her waist, skated up her sides to her shoulders, then cupped her face, powerful callused paws cradling her cheeks with tender gentility. "I might like you a little bit, too."

Jamie frowned. "*Like* me? A *little* bit? I'm not so sure this'll work if that's all you've got for me." She pushed up on her toes and bit Chase's lower lip between her teeth.

Chase turned the bite into a kiss, and, unlike the others, this kiss was not the product of desperation. He took her mouth and her lips with hungry determination, devouring her breath with his, driving his tongue into her mouth and exploring it with possessive need. His thumbs brushed over her cheekbones and his lips crushed hers, his tongue tasted hers, and his body was hard and solid against hers. Jamie melted into the kiss, feeling the edges of her soul bleeding into his, the joining of their mouths only the beginning, only the visible tip of the mountain.

"Does that help?" Chase asked.

"Nope. I need to hear it. I need the words." She pressed a kiss to the hard line of his jaw. "I need you to *show* me."

"I can do that," Chase murmured. "I've loved you since the second you walked into my dressing room in Las Vegas."

"Now we're getting somewhere," Jamie said. "About showing me…?"

Chase laughed. "Well, I have a show. Have to be on stage warming up in an hour. Come with me."

"Like you could pry me away from you at this point," Jamie said.

"Hungry?"

Jamie shook her head. "No, I just ate."

Chase cocked his head. "Something tells me I won't like the answer if I ask who you ate with."

Jamie's eyes narrowed. "No, you wouldn't."

"Is that why you were crying when you ran into me?" Chase said.

"I wasn't crying when I ran into you. I was trying *not* to cry. Then I smacked into you, and that's what started me crying."

Chase pulled her into a walk and tangled his fingers in hers. "Who was he?"

"Why do you want to know?" Jamie glanced up at him. "Does it matter?"

"Yes. If he made you cry, then I need to kick his ass."

Jamie snorted a laugh. "If you're gonna kick the ass of the person who's made me cry the most in my life, then you'll have to kick your own ass."

"There's something confusing about that statement, but I'm not sure what it is." Chase shook his head. "But for real? You've cried about me?"

Jamie ducked her head, watching the snow drifting in circling swirls between her feet. "Chase, I've never cried so much in my whole life as I have since I met you. It's not...it's not really your fault, directly. It's just the situation. I'm not a crying type, honestly. I don't go bawling into a pint of Ben and Jerry's every time something shitty happens. But something about this whole situation between us just fucks me up in the head."

Chase nodded. "I know what you mean." He squeezed her hand. "Tell me about him, though. This situation is fucked up enough without any secrets."

"It's not a secret. But fine, if you must know. His name was Ian. He was from London. I met him..." She trailed off, laughing. "Actually, I met him when I was trying to run away from how I felt about you. I ended up somewhere north of Flint in a shitty dive bar off the freeway. He was the only one there who wasn't a trucker or a gap-toothed yokel."

"Good reason to like a guy, I suppose."

"I liked him because he made me feel something. I'd been trying to just *not* feel for a long time. He wasn't you, but he was nice. Kinda sexy. Had a hot accent." Jamie sucked in a long breath. "Ian was...wonderful. Treated me great. Eventually moved here to Chicago to be with me. He claimed it was because his mother moved here, but I think she moved here to be closer to him. I don't know. I've been coming to Chicago to be with him every weekend for months now."

"He made you come to *him* every weekend?" Chase sounded incensed.

"I did it voluntarily. He came to Detroit, too, but I liked driving down to Chicago, because driving was...a relief. I could shut down and just drive."

"Am I missing something? You said he was wonderful, but it sounds almost like you were trying to get away from what he made you feel."

"Damn your insightfulness." Jamie dug her other hand into her coat pocket. "I didn't love him. I couldn't, and I didn't try to convince myself I did. I just wanted to not be alone. I couldn't have you, but I thought maybe if I tried hard enough, I could be happy with *some*one. If it could have been anyone, it would have been Ian."

"But?"

"He knew I wasn't happy. I met him for dinner a few blocks away, maybe two hours ago. He just wanted to know what was going on, why I wasn't happy. I tried to explain...well, no, I didn't. I knew he wouldn't get it. How do you explain this thing between us?"

Chase expelled a breath heavy with sympathetic understanding. "You don't. Fuck, I didn't even *try* to explain it to Tess. She broke up with me just before you ran into me."

"Tess?"

"My version of Ian. My attempt to be okay without you."

Jamie glanced up at him. "Didn't work any better than mine, did it?"

Chase huffed a sarcastic laugh. "Not hardly. Clearly. Staying away from you...it's like...trying to defy gravity."

"Gonna sing me some *Wicked*?" Jamie teased.

Chase quirked an eyebrow at her, then did a surprising rendition of the iconic song in question. Jamie found herself stunned. Chase's voice, what little she'd heard of it, was lower, growly, more of a rock voice, and she hadn't thought him capable of hitting some of the notes in that song. He did, though, and amazingly well.

"You just can't help it, can you?" Jamie asked, laughing.

"What?"

"Being incredible."

He shrugged, grinning. "Not really, no. I was just joking with you, though, singing the song. It was shitty, too. That song is written as a duet, and it's *way* out of my range."

"I didn't notice anything off."

Chase waved a hand dismissively. "Most wouldn't. I did it fair justice, but a real Broadway singer would have cringed."

"I don't know. I thought you sounded amazing. You shouldn't doubt yourself."

He just shrugged. "I'm not doubting myself. I'm in a rock band. I have no designs or aspirations on Broadway. I have enough of a musical ear to be able to sing pretty much anything I hear, but my voice just isn't that kind of voice." He glanced at her. "You know I majored in musical theater in college?"

Jamie stopped walking, staring at him. "Are you shitting me?"

Chase rubbed the back of his neck. "No. Why is that so surprising? I've always loved music, and yes, I've always loved being the center of attention."

"I guess I shouldn't be shocked," Jamie said, walking with Chase again. "I guess you just seem so much like a natural born rock star that I can't picture you prancing around singing 'Maria.'"

Chase laughed. "Actually, I did that show my sophomore year of college. I was a kick-ass Tony, I'll have you know."

"I'm not about to debate that," Jamie said, trying to picture Chase with slicked-back hair and tight black jeans. It wasn't a difficult image to summon, oddly.

Chase stopped into a pizzeria and got a couple to-go slices, ate them as they made their way to the venue where Six Foot Tall was playing. Jamie sat at the bar and nursed a glass of wine while she watched the band set up and warm up. She watched Chase test his microphone. Doubts crept in.

What the hell am I doing? She shouldn't be here. Shouldn't be considering what she was considering. A couple of kisses, a declaration of love… those were all good and well, but nothing had changed. Being with Chase would still be fraught with problems.

She should just get up and leave. Not tempt either of them anymore.

Jamie stared down into the rippling red depths of her wine, arguing with herself. If she walked away again, she wasn't sure she would ever recover. She'd turn into a cat lady. Or a dog lady, since she hated cats. Or maybe a fish lady. One of those really, *really* crazy people with fish tanks on every wall. Chase would be okay, right? He'd get over it. Just like she would.

Right.

Part of her kept wondering why she was fighting this so hard. Hadn't Anna said she'd find a way to deal with it if Jamie and Chase got together?

Chase's deep voice rumbled in her ear. "Not thinking of bolting on me, are you?"

Jamie started, not having heard him approach. "What? No! Yes. Maybe. No." She took a swallow of her wine to cover her nerves.

Chase dragged a fingernail across her hand clutching the wine glass, then to her wrist, then up

her forearm. Jamie shivered and swiveled her gaze
from the ruby liquid to his intense mocha gaze. The
heat in his eyes had the doubts melting like an ice
cube under a summer sun, had desire pulsing from
a flicker into an inferno. The only point of contact
between them was his finger trailing a line of fire
from her elbow up her shirt sleeve to her shoulder,
but that was enough to push a balloon of pressure
into her womb, to send heat cresting between her
thighs.

If he touched her any more intimately, Jamie
would combust on the spot. He brushed his finger
back down her arm, slicing down the skin mere
millimeters from her breast. She ached for his
touch suddenly. If he would just nudge the outside
of her breast, even through her shirt and her bra,
she might find some satisfaction. Some release.
The pressure, the mountain of frustration piled up
within her, was heavier than ever, pushing at the
walls of her sanity. She *needed* Chase. It wasn't a
matter of desire. Not anymore.

She *had* to feel him. Hold him. Touch him.
Taste him. His face was an inch away from hers,
his spicy male scent filling her nostrils, his breath
on her neck, his finger now teasing her, tracing
the curve of her breast. His freshly shaven scalp
gleamed dully in the dim lights, and Jamie couldn't
resist scraping her palm over the smooth skin,
drawing his lips closer to hers, drawing his mouth

against hers, from sucking his tongue into her mouth and running her tongue over his teeth and tasting the faint tang of toothpaste layered under the pizza and the more recent beer he'd been sipping as he set up.

His body closed the space between them, his hips between her legs, his mouth returning her kiss with equal fervor, his hand kneading the denim clinging to her thigh, his fingers tickling the underside of her breast. He was her world, the distant thump of the drums being tested fading, the hum of a guitar and the rumble of a bass drowned beneath the rush of blood in her ears, the pound of need in her mind, the crush of desire like sun fire in her veins.

"I want you..." she gasped, the words torn from her lips as the kiss broke.

"I need you..." he answered, murmuring the words in a ragged rhythm, his lips moving against hers.

Her legs wrapped around his waist, her arms around his neck, and they kissed once more, or perhaps it was the same kiss continued, broken and resumed. *That was it*, Jamie decided: they'd only kissed once over the blocks of months they'd been denying their love for each other. It was only one kiss, interrupted.

Howls and wolf whistles finally had them splitting apart.

"If we don't stop now, we'll never stop," Chase said, his voice a husky whisper.

"But I don't want to stop," Jamie said.

"I don't, either," Chase said, "but the things I want to do to you are best done in private."

"What are you doing to my privates?"

"A lot of things," Chase promised, "but none of them here."

"At least give me a hint?"

Chase kissed her again, slowly, driving his tongue into her mouth, dipping in and retreating, laving her lips and tongue. "I'll do that to you…" he whispered, "over…and over…and over."

"Oh, god…please?" Jamie's voice was a pleading whimper. She sounded desperate, and she didn't care, because she was desperate. "What else are you gonna do to me?"

"Hmmm," Chase rumbled. He scratched her jeans on her thigh, high up, dangerously close to the "V" where she wanted his touch, his fingers moving in a mocking rhythm. "I might do this to you…and if you're good, I might even kiss you and touch you like that at the *same time*. I might even let you come."

Jamie laughed against his mouth, her smile mirroring his. She reached between them to cup his bulge through the leather of his pants, felt a thrill of satisfaction as she realized he was huge and hard inside his pants, aching for her as she ached for him. She traced the hard lines of his cock with her thumb and forefinger, stroking him through the leather. "And I might just do this to you," she whispered back to him. "I might just let you come, too. *If* you're good. I might just put my mouth on you and let you come down my throat. You want that? Hmmm?"

"Oh, god." Chase's voice was thick with barely restrained desire. "God...do I want that. *So* bad. So bad."

"Well, then...you'd better be good. And you'd better finish this show so you can take me home." Jamie felt a pang of emptiness shoot through her as Chase backed away, watching her for several backward steps before turning away and swaggering to the stage. The ache between her thighs was an all-devouring pressure now, a pounding, pulsing, fiery burn.

It was going to be a long show.

NINE

CHASE KNEW HE'D NEVER BEEN MORE ON FIRE as that night on stage. The knowledge that Jamie was waiting for him at the bar infused him with a manic energy, a contagious drive that had the band playing better than they ever had. The crowd felt it, too, and turned the concert into a wild party, several mosh pits starting in various areas. Chase worked them up into a fury, adjusting the intended playlist to include numbers the crowd could participate in, goading them into singing back to him. He bounded across the stage, feeling the music in his veins like liquid fire. Every once in a while he would glance to where Jamie watched from her seat at the bar, and he would feel a new rush of energy burst through him at the sight of her.

By the time the show was over, the crowd was insane, and began chanting for an encore until the band had to go back out and play another mini-set. Chase was impatient by this time. As much as he loved the rush of performing, he was ready to be done, ready to scoop Jamie up and find the nearest hotel room. He crossed back and forth at the edge of the stage, eyes now locked on Jamie in the distance, finishing their last encore number.

Off-stage, Chase had a quick celebratory shot with the guys, who knew his moods well enough to know he wasn't in the mood for a party. They'd grown used to him taking off on his own while they partied.

Gage followed him away from the group, cornering him against a doorway. "Something happened." Gage knew him better than anyone, and knew there was a reason for his renewed energy.

Chase shrugged into his coat and moved to push past him. "Yeah, something happened. I'll catch up to you guys."

Gage narrowed his eyes, blocking Chase's exit. "You've doing better recently. Since you've been with Tess. The guys need you on point, man. I don't know what's going on with you, but something's changed."

"Tess broke up with me."

Gage rocked his head back on his shoulders, eyes closing, scrubbing his palms down his face. "Shit."

"It's okay, though. It had to happen. I knew it, she knew it. It's better this way."

"You don't seem real broken up about it." Suspicion crossed Gage's face, his pale blue eyes searching Chase's.

"It's complicated. We're in Milwaukee next, right?"

"Yeah, why?"

Chase shrugged, going for nonchalance. "Go without me. I'll meet you there. I've got some shit to take care of."

Gage's lips quirked. "Does the shit you're taking care of happen to have curly red hair?"

"Might."

Gage shook his head slowly and blew out a long breath. "Just be on stage in Milwaukee on Wednesday, man," he said. "That's all I ask."

"I will. You know I will."

Gage clapped Chase on the shoulder and turned away, then stopped and gave Chase a long, level look. "Also, because you're my best friend... be careful, okay? When everything happened with Anna, man, you were a hot fucking mess. Having you on an even keel makes everything better for all of us."

Chase nodded and gave Gage a man-hug, their right hands clasping as if arm-wrestling, then bumping chests and right shoulders. "I know. That was kind of a shitty time for me. Thanks for putting up with my bullshit. This thing I've got going on now…it could be good. Really good."

"And if it doesn't go the way you're hoping?"

Chase didn't answer immediately. "It will. It has to."

Gage gave Chase a hard shove toward the exit. "Go. And good luck."

I don't need luck, Chase thought. *I just need her.*

He found her on the same stool where he'd left her, finishing a side of cheese fries, dipping the last one in ranch. She had a nearly empty glass of red wine in front of her, and she tossed the last bit back as Chase approached.

"That was a seriously great show," she said, standing up and putting on her coat, then slipping her palms around to the backs of his shoulders. "You kicked ass."

The familiar affection in the way she touched him sent a thrill of excitement through Chase, the kind of upwelling of emotion that had his throat closing and his heart pumping harder. He fitted his hands to the swell of her hips, holding her tight against him.

"Thanks," he said. "I was pumped. I felt good. Knowing you were watching…it just gave me this jolt of energy."

Jamie pressed even closer to him, crushing her breasts against his chest and gazing up into his eyes. "So now what do we do?" She curled her fingers into the muscle of his shoulders, nails raking through the thin cotton of his T-shirt, sending chills of arousal shivering down his spine and into his balls.

"Now...we have three days to ourselves. My next show isn't until Wednesday."

Her lips touched his jaw between ear and chin, then his throat; Chase had to focus on catching his breath each time a kiss planted fire on his skin. "And what could we possibly do for those three days?" Her voice was low and sultry and thick with overt suggestion.

Chase let his fingers crawl down to caress the upper curve of her ass, scratching the denim. "Hmmm. I might be able to think of a few things."

"Less thinking, more doing." Jamie bit him, a sharp nip of the skin on his neck near his shoulder. "I can't take the waiting anymore. I need you. Right now."

Chase rumbled a husky laugh in reply, turning away and taking her hand in his. He pulled her into a swift walk, leading her out of the club and into the cold Chicago night. The air was still and thin, cold as the upper atmosphere, dark as space. A yellow cab drifted by, its light off, tires buzzing against the road. A few isolated flecks of snow skirled through the street, blown from some secret place. The sky above was clear and cloudless,

blackest black between sky-scraping towers. A
sliver of gibbous moon glinted low in the sky, and
Jamie's hand was warm in Chase's.

He took a deep breath of the frozen air, glanced
at Jamie. "There's a hotel just around the corner.
We can go there."

"The closer the better."

Chase pulled her into a walk in the direction of
the hotel. "Eager, much?"

Jamie shoved him playfully. "Yeah. You're not?
Maybe I misjudged the situation, then."

Chase pulled her into him and grabbed a handful of her ass and kneaded it roughly. "I'm about
two seconds away from bending you over that car
and taking you right here," Chase growled, "so
don't tempt me."

Jamie gazed up at him with serious eyes. "You
don't hear me protesting, do you?"

Chase just shook his head and pulled her back
into a walk. They reached the hotel soon, and
Chase stood at the concierge desk arranging for
a room. The lobby was deserted except for the
concierge. As he worked with the young woman
behind the desk, Chase felt Jamie's fingers slide
down over his stomach and down to his groin.
She found the shape of his cock behind his zipper
and traced its length with her fingers. Chase gave
her a look in warning, but she only smiled inno-
cently at him. The concierge named the total for

the room, and Chase dug his wallet out of his coat pocket, working to keep his expression neutral and his hips still. Jamie's stroking of his shaft through the leather increased in tempo as he waited for his card to be run, and then as he signed the slip. He was growing harder with every stroke, burgeoning, thickening. He felt pre-come gather at the tip, soaking the cotton of his boxer-briefs. He sucked in a deep breath and let it out slowly, turning away and pushing Jamie in front of him to hide his arousal. They stood back to front at a bank of elevators, waiting for a car to arrive. As they stood, Jamie pressed herself back against him, subtly writhing her hips to rub her ass against his cock.

Chase hissed between his teeth, finding it ever harder to contain his arousal. He was nearing the point of having to physically hold himself back. He'd been so turned on for so long that he was near to bursting. He'd been turned on and ready to go since the moment Jamie slammed into him on the street, since she kissed him, since her body pressed against his. His arousal had only kind of gone away during the show, and every time he'd glanced at Jamie from the stage, he'd felt a bolt of desire.

He was so hard, so ready...and she was making it impossible to hold back, reaching behind herself to cup the back of his head, turning her face sideways to plant desperate kisses on his cheek and lips, writhing against his cock shamelessly. There was no one in the lobby at all, the concierge having vanished, but Chase still felt exposed.

"Goddamn, Jamie. You have me right on the edge," he said, whispering in her ear. "I'm close already. You'd better back up and give me a chance to get myself under control, or I'm gonna come in my pants right here."

The elevator doors opened right then, and they stepped into the car, pushing the button for the seventh floor. The doors swooshed closed, and as soon as the car began moving, Jamie turned to face Chase.

"Maybe I don't want you to have control..." she said, fumbling with the button of his pants. "Maybe I want you to come, right here, right now."

"That could be messy."

His pants were open now, and she was pushing his zipper down, freeing his rigid shaft and taking it into both hands. Chase couldn't breathe suddenly, could only hold himself absolutely still, every muscle tensed and locked, focused on holding back. Her hands were hot on his skin, soft and tender and greedy, working him steadily, her body pressed against his, backing him into a corner.

He felt himself rising then, against his control. Her eyes were on him, searching him. He had to close his eyes then, squeezing them shut and gritting his teeth, sucking in a breath and holding it, ducking his head and straining with every fiber of his being.

She didn't relent, kept up her slow, intimate ministrations, both fists on his length, gliding up and back down, rubbing his crown in her palm now as she pumped his base, then moving her fists on him hand over hand.

He gasped raggedly, then ground out the warning: "I can't...I can't hold it back. Goddammit... *fuck*." He clawed his fingers with crushing force into the denim and muscle of her ass, squeezing so hard she gasped. "I'm gonna come, Jamie. Right now."

She sank quickly to her knees and took him in her mouth, one hand stroking his cock at the base, the other cupping his balls, middle finger pressing against his taint and massing the muscle there. She sucked hard, taking him deep. Chase came with a soft grunt, fisting his hands in her soft curls, holding her but not pushing at her. She drew him out of her mouth to lick his tip, then sucked him deep again as his muscles clenched once more, releasing a second stream into her mouth. She was grinding her fist on his base in a furious rhythm, drawing his orgasm to a wild frenzy, her finger pressing against his taint and spurring him to a third spasm, her mouth bobbing on him, taking him deep and then backing away.

As he shot the last of his seed into her mouth, the elevator came to an unexpected stop on the fifth floor, the bell dinging and the doors sliding open. Jamie jumped to her feet at the *ding* of the bell, tugging his pants up. She pressed Chase into the corner, wrapping her arms around him and burying her face against his cheek, shielding his still-throbbing cock from the view of the elderly couple who got onto the elevator with them.

Chase heard her giggling, then heard her swallow and giggle again, her shoulders shaking. Her hands were cupping the back of his head, stroking his stubble, her breath huffing on his ear.

"You came a *lot*," she whispered, her voice so quiet as to be barely audible.

"I can't believe you did that," he said, his voice equally low.

The couple in front of them were whispering to each other as well, muttering and casting disapproving, disgusted glances at Chase and Jamie.

"I told you I needed you," Jamie whispered. "And I still do. That was…just a taste."

Chase chuckled helplessly at her turn of phrase. "Well, you did get quite a taste."

"You taste so good," Jamie said. "And your cock…it's perfect."

"Think we could get away with me tasting *you* on the elevator?"

Jamie laughed. "Maybe if I was wearing a skirt."

"You mean I have to wait?"

"Only a few more seconds."

The elevator dinged again, letting them off on their floor. As they exited, Chase still pressed against Jamie's front, they heard the man on the elevator mumble, "Damn kids. Smells like sex in here."

They broke into laughter as the doors closed. Their room was only a few feet away from the elevators, and as Chase reached past Jamie to slide the keycard into the slot, Jamie tilted her head back to whisper in Chase's ear.

"I need you inside me." She reached back and stroked a finger against his soft shaft, causing him to twitch and harden. "Hurry up and get the door open."

Chase was fumbling, inserting the key and pulling it out either too fast or too slow so the light wouldn't switch from red to green. Finally, after a few muttered curses, he got it open, and they stumbled into the darkened room. The door snicked closed, and Chase flipped on a light.

He stopped, pants unzipped and unbuttoned, his cock thickening in anticipation as he watched Jamie turn in place to face him, a hungry look in her eyes. She licked her lips, breasts heaving as she sucked in several deep, steadying breaths. She bit her lower lip, then crossed her arms and peeled her shirt off, revealing her full, ivory breasts pushed up in a violently purple front-clasp bra.

Chase felt his cock twitch and grow harder, and Jamie's eyes flicked down to it, a grin spreading across her face.

"I didn't really get to see it before," she said. "It's so pretty."

Chase glanced down at himself, then back to her. "If you say so." He took a step toward her, then another, stretching out a hand to caress her waist. "You're so fucking gorgeous, Jamie. You take my breath away. I get hard just looking at you. You're incredible. You're perfect."

Jamie shook her head, ducking her face to glance at the carpeting. "No. But I'm glad you think so."

"You are. You're perfect. Not just perfect to me, but actually perfect." He stepped closer yet, and his naked cock pressed hot against her warm, silk-soft belly.

"Perfect? I'm not, I'm—"

Chase shut her up with a kiss, a deep, endless, claiming of her mouth. She melted into him, digging her fingers against his back and pushing his T-shirt up, breaking apart to rip the cotton away and toss it aside before reclaiming his mouth with hers. Her hunger for him made Chase dizzy, wild with disbelief, breathless with anticipation.

She explored his body with her hands, roaming from his bare shoulders to his chest, his back to his stomach, scrubbing her palms over his bald scalp in a now-familiar gesture of affection that had Chase's heart seizing.

Jamie pushed his pants down, sinking to her knees and brushing his torso with hot kisses as he did so, then caressing his leg with her hand and lifting his foot from the leather, peeling it off one leg at a time, kissing each thigh as it was bared. Chase tried to lift her to her feet, uncomfortable with the kind of attention she was paying to him, overwhelmed by the sheer potency of the emotions she was displaying. She cupped his balls in both hands, pressing kisses to his belly, his thigh, the crease of his leg beside his sack, then touched her lips to his shaft. He gasped, and she turned her face sideways to take his length in her mouth, sliding her wet lips across his skin, tongue tasting his flesh. She wasn't giving him oral sex, he realized. She was kissing him, arousing him, showing desire for him. As if he needed further arousal.

He pulled away from her forcefully, feeling himself rising yet again. *Not this time*, he thought. *This time is about her.*

He pulled her to her feet, captured both of her wrists in one of his hands. "My turn," he said.

She let her hands go limp, stood straight, lifting her chin and gazing at him, cool and collected. "Touch me, please," she said.

Jamie's heart was pounding in her chest. She had the taste of Chase in her mouth, the musk of his seed from the elevator, the salt of his skin.

She couldn't put words to what she was feeling in that moment. Desire, need...these weren't strong enough. She hadn't meant to go down on him in the elevator. She'd just been unable to resist touching him in the street, or in front of the concierge, and then when they were alone in the elevator, she'd simply had to feel his skin in her hands, feel his huge cock fill her fists. And then she'd realized how close he was. She then simply *had* to feel him come, had to taste him. His cock felt so perfect in her hands, filling both hands and spilling over the top of her uppermost fist. She knew there might be cameras watching, knew someone could get on the elevator with them at any moment, but she didn't care. If he'd stripped her naked and banged her up against the elevator wall, she wouldn't have cared. Nothing mattered in the moment but Chase, nothing but his skin and his heat and his body and his heart, his emotions so potent and completely bared on his face, in his eyes.

She'd tasted him, taken him in her mouth, swallowed him, caressed him and brought him to completion, felt his seed fill her mouth, hot and salty and thick, felt his tip touch the back of her throat, felt his balls seize and clench, and she'd taken more, wanting all of him.

And now she stood in front of him, vulnerable, letting her love show in her eyes, nearly naked and shivering with need. Except...what she felt was so far past a paltry word like "need." Every atom in her body was vibrating with desire for him, with the blood-hot need to feel his hands on her bare skin, his lips on her body, his thickness filling her.

She stood stone-still, shirtless, breath coming in slow, deep gasps, waiting. His eyes were dark and hooded, his chest rising and falling with his desperate breathing. He was naked, gloriously nude, bared for her perusal. She openly stared at him, taking in his thick arms scribed with tattoos, his hands curling into fists and releasing at his sides, his narrow waist and hard, round ass, his proudly jutting cock, huge and thick and dark, purple-veined and heavy. His thighs were thick and hard, too, quadriceps cut and defined. His bald scalp was beaded with dots of sweat, and one drop trailed down his cheek. Why was he sweating? It was cold in the hotel room, and he was naked.

She forced herself into stillness, wanting to rush over to him, press her body against his and beg him to put his hands on her, his cock inside her, his mouth on her. She'd already asked him to touch her, and now she would wait for him to do so in his way, in his time.

Her hands trembled. She'd tasted him, touched him, given away her feelings. She'd given herself over to him, knowing there was never any going back now. That kiss on the street had done her in. She was his now, for better or worse.

Jamie swallowed hard past the lump in her throat. He wasn't moving, wasn't doing anything but staring at her, his gaze suddenly inscrutable. His hands tightened into fists at his sides, and his jaw clenched, his eyes narrowing.

Suddenly, fear shot through her. Maybe...*god, no.* Maybe since she'd gotten him off, he was done with her. Maybe all he'd wanted was a cheap thrill, and the rest of it had been a game. Maybe he was about to walk away. He was tensed, hard, almost shut down.

"Chase?" She couldn't help his name from escaping her lips. "I..." One of her hands reached for him, then dropped to her side again. "Was this not what you—"

He crossed the space between them with one bound, lips crushing against hers, his hands curling around her waist and pulling her body flush with his. His cock was a hard rod between them, thick and hot against her bare belly.

"I love you so much it hurts," he whispered.

Jamie's soul clenched. "What?"

"You heard me. I...you're so beautiful. So perfect. You're really here? With me? You're not going to leave again?" His face twisted, and his voice was low and hard. "I need you. Now. Always."

Jamie caressed his spine, then clutched the cool muscle of his ass. "I'm not going anywhere," she said. "I'm here. I'm waiting for you to make love to me. Please, Chase. Is that what you're waiting for? Me to beg you? Please, Chase. *Please* make love to me."

Chase's eyes blazed. "I should be the one begging you. I *am* begging you. Let me love you."

In answer, she reached up and unclasped the bra, pulled it off her shoulders, and dropped it to the floor next to her with a flourish. She reached for the button of her pants, but Chase stopped her.

"Let me," he said, and sank to his knees in front of her.

She caressed his scalp as he pressed a line of fiery kisses down her stomach, then gasped as he *thankgodfinally* freed the button of her jeans, unzipped them, worked them down her hips. She wriggled her ass as he shimmied them down to her feet, then stepped out of them. When she wiggled her hips, Chase's nostrils flared, and his mouth seemed to latch almost involuntarily onto her hipbone, his teeth nipping her skin, as if the sway of her hips drove him wild. She did it again, but this time to a rhythm, swaying side to side in his grip in a belly-dancing bounce. Chase growled, eyes sliding closed as if he couldn't contain his desire. His fingers scraped down her spine, stiffened into talons, raking off her panties—a purple thong matching her bra. She was naked then.

Kneeling in front of her, Chase merely gazed at her once again for several long moments, eyes raking over her full breasts to her wide, curvy hips, to her thick thighs. He reached up, traced his hand down her side, caressing the edge of her breast, then down farther to her hip. Her breath caught as his hands swept around her hips to clutch her ass, exploring the firm flesh, kneading, digging, caressing. His finger swept down the crease, and she instinctively widened her stance to allow him better access. She didn't care where he touched her, she just wanted, *needed*, his touch. Anywhere. Everywhere. She trusted him to touch her any-where, everywhere. He didn't push in, but simply explored her body with his hand, caressed the weight of each cheek of her buttocks.

She began to breathe a little then as he kissed her belly, sucking in long, shuddering breaths. He reached up to cup her breast, merely holding its weight at first, then exploring it more thoroughly as he had her ass. She let her head tip back as he rubbed his thumb over her nipple, felt it harden under his touch. Having been settled back on his haunches, Chase now rose up to his knees and kissed the underside of one breast, then the other. Jamie felt her lungs seize again when he took a nip-ple in his mouth, sucking it between his lips, past his teeth. She moaned gently, and then louder when he worried the nipple in his teeth, gasped when he pinched the other nipple in his fingers. His free hand carved down her ass, down the back of her leg, then back up her thigh, along the inside now.

Jamie let her legs widen a bit more, and his fingers found the damp heat of her entrance. He didn't enter her channel yet, but, as he had her breasts and ass, he merely explored at first, tracing the line of her labia, one side and then other, tickling, probing, touching. He was moving his mouth from one breast to the other now, his one hand clutching her ass, fingers of the other hand darting into the wet heat of her desire.

She smelled the musk of her arousal, potent and pungent, and then, to her mortification, she heard him sniff her, smelling her.

"God, Chase, don't do that!" she said, feeling her cheeks flush. "I smell—"

"You smell incredible," he said, cutting her off. "You smell so good. So good, I just want to…taste you, eat you."

"God…Chase…" This time it wasn't a protestation, but an affirmation.

He had accompanied his words with a swipe of two fingers into her pussy, and her legs buckled, her capacity for speech stolen along with her breath. Jamie rested her hands on the top of his head, rubbing her thumbs in tiny circles, letting her eyes shutter closed. He curled his fingers to explore her inner walls, stroking her insides, exploring her there as thoroughly as he had everywhere else, not seeking yet to bring her to orgasm, but merely learning her body.

Jamie loved his exploration. She would be content to let him explore forever, even if she never came. This touching, this tender, hungry searching of her body, sated her in way she'd never felt, filled the ache in her soul. Already the mountain of frustration was gone, replaced now by a wellspring of contentment, and they'd only begun.

He suckled her nipple into his mouth and drew his face away from her body, stretching her nipple to its fullest, almost painful extension, and then he released it with a wet smack. She felt his gaze on her, opened her eyes to see his wide and full of vulnerability. His hand was resting on her ass, holding her, and the other was delving in her womanhood, dipping and curling and swiping; now, his eyes locked on hers, he traced his middle finger up the wet crease of her pussy and began to circle her clit. He didn't make direct contact yet but merely let his finger drift almost lazily around it. Jamie held her breath, legs buckling to get her core closer to his touch, then, after an endless moment, he brushed the sensitive nub, seemingly by accident. Jamie expelled the breath on a short, sharp moan.

His touch was like fire, like magic. Nothing had ever felt so good. He seemed to know exactly how to touch her, how to give her the most pleasure. She kept her eyes on his, forced her heart open, letting her every thought, every emotion show in her eyes. She'd been holding herself in for so long, containing her feelings, pushing everything down, and now here he was, the man she'd dreamed about, wanted, needed for so long, here in front of her, kneeling before her and worshipping her body with his hands and his mouth.

The hand on her butt trailed down her leg, curled around her ankle, and gently guided her stance wider. She complied willingly, spreading her feet apart until she felt air cold on her bare, bald pussy. Then she held her breath once more as Chase slowly lowered down on his haunches, his gaze never leaving hers. She stroked his head, fingers playing across the ripples and ridges of his scalp, down behind his ears, tracing the hard, masculine line of his strong jaw, thumbs skittering lovingly over his cheekbones before resting once more on the back of his head. His gaze pulled away then, and turned to her core.

"God, Jamie. So sexy. So hot. So perfect." He kissed her belly, cutting a line of kisses across it, making it clear that he liked it, loved it, found it as sexy as the rest of her, and for once she believed him, knew he believed it and felt sexy for him, because of him; his mouth touched lower now, just above her pubis. "Your pussy is so beautiful, Jamie. Just like the rest of you. Hold on to me now.

I'm going to kiss you here. I'm gonna make you come *so* hard."

She clutched the back of his head and shamelessly, wantonly pulled his mouth onto her pussy. "Yes!" she cried out, the word a gasp of intense pleasure.

His tongue teased her clit, lapped up the crease from bottom to top and then again, licking her. His fingers had never left her, had been slowly working toward her G-spot and were massaging it gently. When he thrust his tongue against her clit, he began to work her G-spot harder. She arched her back and let her knees buckle once more, lowering herself to his mouth. He began a rhythm now, tongue circling her clit, moving his fingers against the sensitive ribbed flesh high inside her walls, free hand caressing and clutching her breast, cupping it, thumbing the nipple, pinching it.

She held on to him, held him against her, bobbing her body up and down into his tongue, into his fingers. She was close already, despite his promise to make it slow.

Then he pulled away, and she heard a whimper of frustration rip from her lips. "Chase! Don't stop, I was close—"

"I said it was going to be slow." He stood up, leaving his fingers inside her, moving them from her G-spot to her clit, circling and stimulating, but not enough to let her come. "You need to lie down, love. I wouldn't want you to fall."

"You seem pretty confident you're gonna make me come that hard, huh?" She tried to make her voice steady and flippant, but it still came out breathy and small.

"It's not confidence, babes. It's knowledge. I *know* how hard I'm gonna make you come."

"Oh, yeah? How do you know?"

He pushed her back toward the bed until her knees hit, then pushed her again so she was bending awkwardly backward, her feet still planted on the floor. He crushed his body against hers, his cock against her belly, hot and hard. She wanted it. She hooked her feet around his waist and jerked him toward her, reaching between them to grab his shaft.

He laughed and let her touch him, their wrists crossed and bumping as he mercilessly and skillfully caressed her stiffened clit with his fingers, her hand pumping cock greedily. He kissed her lips, and she tasted her own juices on his lips, his tongue, as she knew he tasted himself in her mouth. He crawled up onto the bed, forcing her to let go of him or risk hurting him, so she scooted backward until she felt a pillow beneath her head. He stopped, and then began to slip back down her body, taking his cock out of her reach. She wanted to touch him more, hold him, caress him, kiss him. She wanted him in her mouth again, in her pussy, against her belly and between her breasts, all over her. She wanted him everywhere—

Then his teeth brushed her clit, his lips forming a seal against her labia, sucking her nub into his mouth. She let her legs fall apart and went limp into his touch, gasping a whimper when he slipped his fingers deeper once more, pressing circles onto her G-spot, and she knew she was rising again, nearing orgasm again.

So, of course, he slowed down. She wanted to cry out in frustration, and opened her mouth to do so, but her growl turned into a moan as his free hand drifted between her legs, beneath his other hand and sought out her most secret place. She clenched up, legs squeezing, buttocks tensing.

"Chase...no...not yet."

He grunted, still swiping his fingers inside her. "No? Not ready for that yet?"

She shook her head, unable to get a word out past her trembling, shaking lips. She was on the verge of orgasm still, held there by his fingers inside her, by his tongue inside her. She wasn't able to fall over the edge, though, clenched up and tensed up and and quivering at the feel of his long middle finger waiting at the crease of her ass, mere centimeters from the tight knot of her anus.

He left his finger there, and she tried to forget its presence but couldn't, and that kept her just this side of orgasm.

"I want to come, Chase, please!"

"Then come."

"I can't—I can't. You...your finger. It's too close to my asshole. I'm...I can't. Not that. Not yet."

He moved his hand away, drifting upward with deliberate slowness to cup her left breast, the larger one, the one he seemed to favor. She arched into his touch, gasping, scratching lightly down his scalp with her fingernails. He shuddered and moaned when she did that, and the vibrations of his voice on her clit sent her spiraling over the edge, writhing uncontrollably beneath him, pushing her core into his mouth, shameless, needing more, more, and he gave her more, tonguing her relentlessly, milking her orgasm, sliding his fingers within her, pinching her nipple almost-but-not-quite too hard, just this side of painful.

She rode the waves of climax, clinging to Chase's head, pushing him between her thighs until she couldn't take any further stimulation, and then she pulled him upward. He let himself be dragged up to lie next to her, stroking her skin with his palms, roaming over her belly and arms and thighs, but giving her sensitive, swollen tissues a brief respite from his attentions.

Jamie held him to her chest, then pulled him to her mouth for a kiss, tasting herself on him even more strongly. The kiss sparked her need all over again, and she twisted on the bed so she was facing him, partly on top of him, tracing the contours of his chest with her fingers. She slowly drifted her touch downward, following the hard lines of his ribs, then the ridges of his abdomen, then the sexy V-cut leading to his achingly hard cock.

He gasped into the kiss when she took him in her hand, moaned low in his throat when she caressed his length.

"I want you inside me," she whispered, her lips moving against his.

He took her hips in his hands and lifted her all the way on top of him, then paused to grunt a single word, "Protection—"

"I have some in my purse." Jamie looked away, then back to Chase, their eyes meeting in an acknowledgement of the awkwardness brought on by the tacit understanding of what that meant. "I know that's—I'm sorry if—"

Chase slid out from beneath her and grabbed her purse from the floor, handing it to her. "I know. You don't need to be sorry. You're here with me now. That's all that matters, right?"

"Right," Jamie agreed.

She dug in the purse and produced an unopened box of condoms, set them on the table beside the bed. They both stared at the box. Jamie pushed away the niggling worm of doubt deep inside her, the part of her that wanted to bring up the reasons why there might be other things that mattered besides being there in the hotel room with Chase. She wanted so badly for that to be all that mattered, but there *were* other things.

"Chase, I—"

He flopped backward, rubbing his face with his palm. "There are other things that matter. That's what you're going to say, isn't it? I know, Jay. I know."

"No one has ever called me Jay except... except—"

"Except Anna. You can say her name, you know. I'm not gonna flip out or get weird. She's my ex-girlfriend, not my ex-wife. And honestly, I'm not sure 'girlfriend' is even the right word for what we had. We never discussed the nature of it, never put our relationship in a box. But whatever. That's completely beside the point." Chase sat up again and took Jamie's hands in his. "The point is, you don't have to tiptoe around the subject of Anna with me. I'm here. You're here. There are issues, yes, and I'm not saying I don't care about them, because I do. But...I don't want to care about them right now. I just want to be with you right now."

Jamie shifted on the bed, torn between awkwardness and worry and desire. "I want to be with you, too. I just...I'm worried we're...I don't know. Never mind. It's nothing."

Chase hissed in exasperation. "Oh, come on Jamie! Don't give me that 'it's nothing' bullshit. Say what you think. Say what you feel."

Jamie tugged the blankets down and tucked the flat sheet over her chest. "I'm worried we rushed into this."

"Rushed—Jamie...how can you think that? How long have we been denying what we feel for each other?"

"Not that. This," Jamie said, gesturing to their naked bodies, to the bed. "Both of us were with other people, like *today*."

Chase growled in frustration, rubbing his palm over his head, a gesture Jamie was learning meant extreme distress and helplessness. "Fuck. Fuck, you're right." He settled the sheet over his lap, hiding his softening erection. "I wish I could deny it, but I can't. I can't say it didn't mean anything to me, because it did."

"What did?"

Chase hesitated. "Being with Tess."

"Oh." Her voice was small. "I'm sorry, Chase. I wish...I wish this conversation could have waited until after we'd been able to—"

"No, it's probably better this way. I don't know what we're supposed to do, though. You know? I mean, yeah, I was with someone else earlier today. So were you. I don't like the thought of you with another man any more than you like the thought of me with another woman. But it's the facts, and you can't change facts." He took one of her hands in his, rubbing the pad of his thumb across one of her fingernails. "So are we supposed to wait a specific period of time? A day? A week? A month? How long is appropriate? We've already talked about why we were with other people and what it meant to us and all that. I don't see any reason to go back over all that."

"I don't want to wait, either, Chase, but—"

"How long is long enough? What's the right reset period, or whatever? I'm not being flippant. I'm not just trying to gloss over the problem so we can get it on. I'm asking honestly."

The sincerity and confusion and anguish in his eyes had Jamie scooting closer to him. Chase moved so he was leaning back against the bed, partially sitting and partially reclining, then pulled Jamie over to him so she was resting her head on his chest, the sheet covering both of them. Jamie took a few deep breaths, taking in his scent, the feel of his muscles under her cheek, his broad male bulk a comforting presence as much as it was a sensual turn-on. Her hand settled on his diaphragm, between his chest and belly, and he tangled his fingers with hers.

Silence stretched out as Jamie tried to come up with an answer, but all she could think of in the moment was how perfect and comforting and warm it was being held by Chase. His arm around her shoulders, tucking her close against him, his fingers tangled with hers, the rise and fall of his breathing, the faint thump of his heartbeat....

He felt like home.

"I don't know what the answer is, Chase. But I've just spent so long ignoring the truth about so many things, I can't—I can't do it anymore."

"What truths have you ignored?"

She snorted. "God. Everything. For most of my adult life I've ignored how lonely I was. How miserable and fucking pathetic my life was. I ignored how shitty I felt about myself, how trashy I knew I was."

"You aren't—"

"*Don't*, Chase." She cut him off sharply, almost snapping. "I *was*. I fucked anything with a cock from the time I was sixteen, okay? Sure, I had fairly legitimate reasons. But that doesn't change it. And I got good at pretending it didn't bother me, to the point that I almost believed it. But I can't pretend anymore. This doesn't even really have anything to do with you. When I met you in Vegas, Anna had dared me to go celibate for two months. The dare was no physical male contact. No kissing, nothing. I couldn't even go a day. I kissed you. Then I went home and did okay for a while, but then I got drunk and…well, bad things happened that I don't want to go into with you just yet."

"Jamie—"

"Shut up and let me answer the question."

"'Kay."

"I pretended a lot of things. I pretended I wasn't in love with you. I pretended I was okay without you, that this between us wasn't the most powerful thing I'd ever felt. And now...I can't pretend. I just want the truth out there, good or bad."

"So what is the truth for you?"

"I want you. Even still, in the middle of this whole heavy conversation, I can't stop wanting you. I'm partially wishing I could let myself just stop talking and get you hard and take you. Ride you. Suck you off again. Let you do whatever you want to me. But...I can't push away the truth that this thing between us is still impossible."

"It's not impossible. It's just complicated."

Jamie laughed. "It's impossible, baby. It is. We were both broken up with less than twelve hours ago. I have no clothes but the ones on the floor over there. Everything else is back in Ian's condo, including my car. I may be with you, now and in the future, but I still have to deal with Ian. I kind of ran out on him. What if he changes his mind and tries to tell me he wants to get back together, give it another shot? I wouldn't do it whether I was with you or not, because my thing with Ian was nothing but a distraction from how I really felt. I knew that from the beginning, but that was another one of those truths I pretended not to care about."

"I like it when you call me 'baby.'" Chase rubbed her knuckle with a thumb. "I know what you mean, though. My thing with Tess isn't as complicated to untangle, but it's still there. She has a few things at my place back in Detroit, but that's easy enough to take care of. My cousin can send them to Tess. The emotional thing is harder. I know…I know it's hard. I know it's tangled up and fucked up and complicated. But it's not impossible. We just…we have to be honest and take things one step at a time."

Jamie sighed. "Yeah. But none of this answers the original question. What do we do now? Is it wrong for us to be together like this so soon?"

"Wrong?" Chase shook his head. "Being with you can never be wrong, if you ask me. *Not* being with you would be wrong. Maybe we just stay like this tonight, just…sleep. Hold each other. Cuddle and shit."

Jamie giggled. "You're funny."

"What?" Chase sounded confused. "How am I funny?"

She shook her head, giggling into his chest again, helplessly lost in laughter. "Just the way you said that." She made her voice gruff and growly, at the bottom of her register, chin tucked against her breastbone. "'Cuddle and shit.' Like it would make you less manly to suggest we cuddle. It was just funny to me for some reason."

"Guys aren't supposed to want to cuddle. It's not a manly word."

Jamie laughed even harder at that. "Call it something else if you want, but you *like* this.

Holding me. Not having sex or foreplay or any-thing. Just…being together."

Chase turned his face to her hair, breathed deeply, clutching her against him. "Yes, Jay. I like it. I love it. Call it cuddling if you want. I'm secure in my manhood. Just don't tell the guys I wanted to cuddle. Especially *before* sex."

Jamie huffed, not laughing anymore. She turned her face up to meet his gaze. "I won't tell anyone. Your secret is safe with me."

His eyes bored into hers, and she felt warmth running from her cheeks down to her chest, filling her stomach with tingling anticipation. Their fin-gers were still twined together on Chase's torso, his arm around her shoulders, but suddenly Jamie was much more aware of his body, of his desire, of her own need. She felt mercurial, being a raging tem-pest of desire one moment, then an emotional mess the next, and then back to wanting his body again, all within a matter of twenty minutes.

"I'm sorry I'm so back and forth on you," she said.

Chase smiled at her, the kind of smirk that said he thought she was being ridiculous. "We're both back and forth. That conversation wasn't just you. I was thinking the same thing. You were just more willing to say it out loud than I was."

"I still don't know exactly what we should do."

"*Should* do, or want to do?" Chase asked. "They're very different things in this case, I think."

"And that's where my confusion comes from." Jamie untangled her fingers from his and let her hand roam over his chest, her eyes fixed on his chiseled, beautiful face.

Chase put his finger to her chin and tipped her mouth to his for a soft, chaste kiss. "My desire for you isn't going anywhere. I'm not going anywhere. We don't have to do anything right now. We can just *cuddle*." He grinned as he said it, tangling his fingers in her hair, cupping the side of her face.

Jamie twisted in his arms slightly so she was pressed against him. "Maybe we could just kiss a little bit. Make out like we're teenagers."

Chase smiled at her again, an indulgent, knowing smile. "Yeah. That sounds good. Just kiss."

He pulled her face closer to his, their lips brushing but not meeting. Jamie moved to close in for the kiss, but he darted back out of reach, then brushed her lips with his again, his hand in her hair, eyes open and searching her face. She tried to kiss him a second time, and he evaded it again, this time touching her upper lip with his mouth, then her cheek. Jamie caught on to the game, grazing his lips with hers, waiting, waiting, and then when he moved to kiss her chin, she intercepted him, crushing her mouth to his and claiming it, curling her hand around his head and holding him in place, stealing the kiss.

Chase sighed through his nose, softening into the kiss. Jamie smirked and pulled away, turning his game back on him. She touched her lips to the corner of his mouth, dipped her tongue against his lips, then darted away to hover near his mouth once more. He laughed and slid the arm that had been wrapped around her shoulders lower down, curling around her waist. Jamie unconsciously arched into his hold, turning more fully onto her stomach atop him, her weight more than half on his chest, the sheet tangled between them, a thin barrier between their skin.

Jamie shifted, pushing the sheet away so they were skin to skin, her left arm underneath her to support her weight. The fingers of her right hand skated over his bald scalp, down to cup his cheek as she moved in for a kiss, no games now in this one, only full passion, unrestrained. She slid her leg over his, toes digging into the mattress between his feet, shoving herself forward so she was directly above him, hips to hips, face to face.

The kiss opened up, heat breathing between them, igniting each of their desires. Jamie felt Chase's need in his kiss, felt it in the way his mouth moved hungrily on hers, in the way his tongue speared into her mouth to taste her tongue, trace her lips and her teeth. Jamie's heart began to thunder in her chest once more, the same lightning excitement at his touch thrilling through her body. His hand on her waist thrilled her, excited her. The prospect of his palm drifting down to clutch her ass excited her. His cock hardening between their bodies excited her. She needed this. She wanted it. She couldn't go another minute without it.

The issues remained, but when he kissed her like this, so raw, so full of vulnerable hunger...nothing else mattered. She could give in to this now, or later. The hunger wouldn't change. It would only increase. She'd been starved for this her whole life.

Jamie felt the truth in that thought and accepted it. She had been waiting for Chase all her life. She might not have known it, but the way he kissed her, held her, spoke to her...he was the thing that had always been missing, the element she had been searching for in all those other men, those other boys. Those guys. Chase was a man. He wasn't just a guy. Jamie wasn't sure what defined the difference, but she knew it was there, saw it and felt it. Chase was so much more than those other guys in her past had ever been.

He saw her, saw into her heart and her soul and her mind and knew her, completely. He might not have known the details of her life, but he knew *her*.

All this, in the space of a kiss.

Jamie pulled away and saw the fire in Chase's eyes, felt it in the way his hands curled on her stomach. He was waiting for her to tell him what she wanted. She couldn't speak, finding her words buried under a wave of need, a wildfire of hunger. She could only kiss him again, dipping down to touch her lips to his with aching, deliberate gentility, putting all of her heart into the contact of mouths. She felt her hair fall down around their faces, red curls framing their faces, curtaining them off from everything else.

She felt Chase's hands rest on her waist, both of them now, holding her sides, fingers splayed to touch her ribs. He hesitantly, almost gingerly, smoothed his palms down to hold her ass, cupping and caressing. She arched her back, gasping into the kiss, loving that single intimate gesture with all of her soul and body in that moment. Chase captured her gasped breath with his mouth, touching her tongue with his, inviting her passion to higher peaks.

Jamie responded by shifting her weight to fully straddle him, her thighs on either side of his waist, forearms on the pillow next to his face. She felt the broad soft tip of his cock touch her inner thigh, and was filled in that single instant of touch with an inferno of want, flooding her belly with clenches of desire, her slit with slicking juices. She was wet immediately, and she let her thighs split farther apart, spreading her nether lips wider. Without breaking the kiss, Jamie slid down his body until the crown of his cock was nudging her entrance. Chase groaned and swiveled his hips into hers, mouth stretching open, breaking the kiss. He let out a long, deep, rumbling moan when she rolled her hips up to work his tip inside her.

He didn't move to thrust in, though. She felt him stretch out his arm, grab the box from beside them, shred it open, and fumble a string of condoms out, rip one free. Jamie moaned into his mouth, then kissed his jaw, his chin, his shoulder, his throat. She couldn't help herself. She writhed her hips, wanting so desperately to drive him deeper into her, but knowing she had to wait.

He moved his hips down and rolled the latex over himself. Jamie rose up on her elbows, moving so he was poised at her slit once more.

She met his dark, hooded gaze. "Please? Now?" Her plea was breathy and desperate, and she didn't care.

"Yes, god, yes, now." He took her by the hips, hands holding her tight and pushing her down.

Jamie buried her face in the hollow of his neck, exhaled, and impaled him inside her. "Oh...my... god." Jamie heard the words escape from her as a sob of raw ecstasy.

She couldn't take him in all the way. Not yet. She wanted to savor every second, every inch. She only slid him in to the groove beneath his crown, then stopped, panting. He stretched her, filled her.

She bit his neck, arms wrapped beneath his head in an embrace, knees drawn up to spread herself wide.

"God...god*damn*, Jay. You feel so—so perfect. So incredible." Chase's voice was just as ragged as she felt, shredded by the potency of fulfillment after so long a denial.

At the sound of the nickname, Jamie clung to him even more tightly, then drew in a deep breath. She paused, breath held at the apex, torso stretched taut, hips drawn up...then exhaled once more and sank down onto him, slowly sliding his huge, incredible, soft yet iron-hard cock into her all the way, stretching her body down his until he was buried in her softness to the root, until they were joined fully.

"*Jamie...*" Her name emerged from his lips in a shuddering gasp, his head lifting from the pillow in a gesture of helpless intensity.

Then he thrust, once, slowly, and Jamie came. Without warning, without a breath to prepare, just a sudden tidal wave of clenching, ripping, juddering orgasm. Jamie sobbed into his shoulder and rode it out, rolling her hips on him.

"Yes, Jay, yes. Come for me." Chase whispered the words into her ear, breathed them so softly she might have imagined them.

But Jamie heard his words, and now she couldn't help but come even harder, lifting and lowering herself onto him in rhythmless abandon, sucking in deep, sobbing breaths and letting them out as high cries of climactic delight.

Chase fluttered his hips, rolling in and out in small thrusts, grunting as her inner muscles clamped down on his cock. Jamie felt herself clenching, every muscle contracting, especially her inner walls squeezing him mercilessly.

When Jamie went limp as the waves subsided, Chase rolled them over so he was on top. Jamie splayed her hands on his back, rubbed them up his neck to cup the back of his head, pulling his mouth down to her breast. He suckled her nipple and thrust into her, slowly and sinuously, one hand supporting his weight, the other fondling her breast.

"God, Chase. More." She arched her spine, shoving her breasts into his touch, lifting her hips to meet his in a steady rhythm. Jamie clawed her fingernails down his back lightly, then clutched his ass and pulled him against her. "I need more, Chase. More. Harder."

Chase lifted his mouth from her nipple and smiled at her, then deliberately slowed his thrust until he was sliding oh so slowly. He pulled nearly all the way out, so only the very tip of his cock remained inside her. He paused then, meeting her eyes, making her wait. She wanted him to crash into her, hard and fast; she also wanted him to go as slow as he could, to draw out this union as long as he could. She decided she didn't care how he made love to her, as long as she had him there with her.

"You want it harder?" Chase asked.

"Mmm-hmmm." Jamie caressed his ass gently, stroking his flanks and the hard muscle of cheeks. "I like it hard. But...slow and soft is good, too. Just make love to me. Please...please."

Chase dipped down to kiss her, still holding himself barely inside her. He pulled away from the kiss to meet her eyes. Jamie searched his face, memorizing his features, absorbing greedily the look of wonder and tenderness and love. Then she felt him move into her. He glided in with deliberate slowness, barely moving at all, and Jamie felt his entire body shivering with the effort to move so slowly. Jamie's mouth stretched wide in a silent scream as he filled her, and her fingers dug into the flesh of his ass in urgent claws, pulling at him with fierce power.

"*Chase...*" His name was a plea, a whispered epithet.

He repeated the action, pulling out almost all the way, pausing at her entrance, then sliding in as slowly as he could. Jamie scrabbled at his back with her hands, digging at the bed with her heels. Chase drew a hand back and curled his elbow around the crook of her knee, planting his hand near her hip so her leg was drawn up. Then he did the same with the other hand, and now Jamie was stretched open and her hips lifted up and her body bare for his pleasure.

"God!" she shrieked. "Yes!"

Jamie reached up behind her head to grasp the headboard, lifting up to meet his first stroke. He delivered the initial thrust slowly, as he had all the rest, worshipful and prolonged. Jamie waited, quivering, as he drew himself out, and then when he began to glide back in slowly, she lifted herself off the bed to meet him, hard.

Chase slumped over her, forehead touching her belly, breath huffing on her navel, his entire body trembling with restrained need.

"I need it, Chase," Jamie whimpered. "I need you. I *need* you. Please. Don't hold back anymore. Give me all of you. Hard."

Chase growled at her words, a primal sound of capitulation. He drew out, shudderingly slow, and then, with an infinitesimal pause, he slammed himself home with nearly savage force. Jamie loosed a scream of rapturous bliss, dragging her nails down his back so hard she knew she'd drawn blood. Chase growled, thrusting again, hard and slow, pulling out and crashing in against her in a rhythm now, and she could only return her hands to cling to the headboard and cry out in euphoric delight as he slammed into her, harder and harder now, faster and faster, feeling her body shaking and trembling with the coiled tension of impending orgasm.

Jamie met him thrust for thrust, using the headboard for leverage to get herself off the bed, crushing her folds against him desperately, wanting more even as he gave her more. She was unable to control the sounds emerging from her throat, tiny mewls, shrieks, screams, ragged sobs. Chase grunted and growled with each thrust, moaning with every furious pump of his hips.

Chase released Jamie's legs, and she wrapped them around his waist, clung to his neck with her arms, and pressed her lips to his ear.

"I love this, Chase," she whispered. "I love you. Yes...oh, god, yes."

They were moving together frantically, desperately.

"Jamie. Oh, Jay. I need you... Don't stop," Chase said, his voice guttural and thick.

"Come with me, Chase," Jamie said, feeling the waves begin to roll over her body. "Oh, god, I'm gonna come right now, so hard, so hard."

Chase lost the rhythm, grinding into her with stuttering, shattering force, groaning every time his body slammed into hers. "Say it again, baby."

Jamie knew exactly what he wanted her to say. "Come with me." She clung to him, her hands on the nape of his neck and the back of his head, holding his face against her throat. "Come with me, Chase. Now. Oh. Oh...oh, god, oh, fuck!"

Jamie felt lightning strike inside her, a detonation so intense she couldn't stand it, couldn't take it. She felt herself coming apart at the seams, shattering, splitting apart, full past bursting with all of Chase, with the infinite potency of his love, of his body inside her, of his arms around her, and all she could do was sob and cling and come, and come again and again while Chase undulated into her, making an incoherent sound in his throat that was part sob, part feral growl, and all man. He pushed and pushed and pushed, his mouth quivering between her breasts as he thrust frantically, arrhythmically. Jamie felt wave after wave of climax wash over her, each one more earth-shattering than the last, until she knew she was experiencing something far beyond mere physical orgasm.

Then she felt Chase unleash, felt his body tense and clench, then felt him judder and thrust hard, twice, and go still, lying on top of her, his lips pressing delirious kisses to her throat, chest, shoulders, cheek, and then her lips.

Jamie kissed him back, devouring his mouth, his breath, taking his love into her through the contact. Tears slipped out, trickled down her cheek and onto the pillow. She wasn't sure why she was crying, except perhaps for the sheer overwhelming amount of emotion running through her, from the intensity of her climax.

"Jay? Are you crying?" Chase carefully pulled out and rolled over with her, effortlessly shifting her to cradle her in his arms.

She nodded. "It's not sad tears, though. Promise." She breathed deeply, shuddering involuntarily as an aftershock rippled through her. "I'm just...overwhelmed. In a good way."

"That was crazy intense, wasn't it?" Chase said.

Jamie moaned in satisfaction, wriggling against him. "'Intense' is an understatement. Like saying the ocean is a little wet." She felt him softening against her leg. "You'd better take care of that and come back to me. I need cuddles. And shit."

Chase laughed. "Mock if you will. Real men cuddle."

Jamie agreed, but was too entirely sated to say anything and too fully enjoying the sight Chase's tight naked ass as he went to the bathroom to clean up. She also enjoyed the view as he returned, and enjoyed even more the feel of his arms curling around her as he drew her into a tangled embrace. She nestled into him, hearing his heart beat beneath her ear, his fingers toying idly with a curl, his breathing slow and steady, his body hard and strong but soft in all the right ways. Jamie closed her eyes and sighed deeply.

She was drowning in a sea of contentment, and nothing had ever been sweeter.

"Okay, baby?" Chase murmured.

"Never, ever been better."

"Good. Me, neither."

Jamie felt herself drowsing. She wanted to stay awake, to savor the moment, the feeling of being held and loved, but sleep was stealing over her, an unstoppable force. She shook herself awake and turned her face up to look at Chase.

He rumbled in laughter. "Relax, Jay. Just... relax. We're together now. Let me hold you."

Jamie felt like a child fighting sleep. She sighed again and let sleep sweep her away.

TEN

CHASE WAS DREAMING. It was a good dream, a pleasant dream. It was more than that—it was a fantasy, a wet dream. It wasn't real, he didn't think, because that would be simply too much to bear, too much wonder to contain. *She* was the dream, the one woman of whom he'd dreamed so often lately. The dream had been a long one, hours of ecstasy, it felt like. He'd dreamed of running into her after a show, and discovering she loved him after all, wanted to be with him despite the impossibility of such a thing. They'd gone to his show, and then to a hotel, and they'd made love. In that dream, she had taken Chase to a place he'd never thought possible, beyond sex, beyond climax, beyond anything that had ever been. He hadn't just come harder than ever before in his life; he'd felt her soul merge with his.

They'd fallen asleep together, in the dream.

And now, dreaming, he felt her lips on his body. Pressing fiery kisses down his chest, across his nipple, light lip-touches on his ribs, his side, his hip. Oh, god, what a dream. She was kissing his thigh, and her hands were carving hot lines of sensual contact over his arms and inner thighs and now... oh, shit, now she was *touching* him. Holding his aroused flesh in her fists. Stroking him slowly. Running her tongue up the side of his cock, licking his length as if he was a popsicle, taking him in her mouth and sucking hard.

"Oh, god," he heard himself say. In the dream.

It was all a dream. He would wake up alone in the hotel room, hard and aching and ready to burst with no way to release except his own hand.

She fisted him, then feathered her fingers over his shaft in achingly soft caresses, sucked his tip hard, and then moved her lips gently on his crown, so soft, so wet, so delicate and loving and...

"Jamie. Oh, god, Jamie, that feels so good." He heard the words, and the sound of his voice, in the dream, was ragged, thick and stuttering.

It felt so real, though. So real. Too real. But it wasn't, was it?

He didn't want to wake up.

"I love the way you taste," she said, then took him in her mouth again, deep now.

"It feels so good," Chase heard himself say. "Don't stop. Please don't stop until the dream's over."

He felt her pause. "Do you think you're dreaming, baby?"

Baby. The endearment tore at his heart, made it swell and fill.

"I'm dreaming. It's a dream. You're a dream. I don't want to wake up and still be alone." He shouldn't tell her that, even in a dream.

It sounded almost like she sobbed, then choked it off. "God, Chase. I'm so sorry you woke up alone so often." She caressed his cock with both hands, fist over fist, fingers trailing up his length, cupping the sensitive swollen flesh of his balls in tender hands, kissing him, deep-throating him, licking him, swirling her tongue around his tip. "What if this isn't a dream? What if you opened your eyes and it was real?"

Chase squeezed his eyes closed tighter, in the dream. "It's a dream. If it was real, I would die from happiness. I love you so much, and I don't want to wake up and not be with you." He knew he shouldn't tell her this. Not even in a dream.

She sobbed again, a sound of joy, he thought. Her voice sounded so real. Her hands on him, her mouth on him, her breath on his skin, it all felt so real. He felt a leg slide across his hip, then her weight settle on him. He felt her moist, hot entrance touching the tip of his cock, and he gasped in need. He wanted to touch her, take her hips in his hands and hold her, slide into her, feel her heavy breasts in his hands. He didn't dare.

He worried if he touched her the dream would pop like a soap bubble.

He felt her lips caress his chest, her hands rest on his pectoral muscles, and then she kissed his throat, and Chase couldn't help arching his back and tipping his head back to let her kiss him there again. He heard himself groan, a long sound of pleasure when her lips touched his adam's apple, and then his jaw, and then the corner of his mouth, and her breath was so hot on his lips, her mouth so wet and her tongue so demanding on his.

"Wake up, Chase." Her voice was a breathy whisper in his ear, and then she kissed him again, slow tongue in his mouth driving him wild with desire and heat and wetness and softness. "It's not a dream. I'm here. I'm real. I need you. Wake up and make love to me. Touch me."

Chase heard his voice raise in a moan of need, a raw, low, vulnerable sound of desperation. He wanted to believe the words of the dream-vision. He felt his hands unfisting from the sheet, which he'd been clutching with desperate strength, and drift up to touch the dream-her. She felt real, too.

Soft as silk, skin like velvet, like heat and love and softness and sex made flesh. Her thighs under his hands were thick and strong, yet still as soft as down. He was touching her, and the dream continued. He dared to touch more. Her hips, wide and round and intoxicating, curves like deepest fantasy in his hands, under his needy fingers. Her sides, her belly, her padded ribs, her spine and her long, sensual back. He breathed deep, almost panting with the fullness of his love for her, the drunken ecstasy of merely touching her. She was sitting on him, palms resting low on his belly, near his diaphragm, her thighs split wide across his hips, poised above his rigid, throbbing cock. Poised and waiting.

He wasn't ready to be inside her yet, even in this dream so like wonderful reality, like fantasy made truth, this dream he'd dreamed so many times and always woken to the emptiness of a dark hotel room. He slid his dream-palms up her ribs to cup her breasts, and yes, they were every bit as large and heavy and silky-soft as he'd always imagined.

Her voice came, like music. "Open your eyes, love."

"No, no. Not yet. I don't want to wake up yet." He ran his thumb across her nipple and felt it bead into a hard, stiff nub. "I want to make love to you before I wake. I need you, even if you're a dream."

She writhed on top of him, rubbing her wet slit over his tip, and he could've come just from that.

"I'm not a dream. This is real, Chase. It's real. I'm real." She leaned down and kissed him, full and furious and passionate and hungry. "Remember? We're in Chicago. I watched your show. We made love. And now I want you again. Wake up."

Chase moaned, running his palms between her breasts, up her collarbone and up farther, cupping her face, her neck. He buried his fingers in her curls.

So real. Too real.

He felt her palms on his chest, her hips writhing in undulating, sinuous circles, working the tip of his cock inside her soft folds, just the first inch slipping in and out. He smelled her: faint shampoo, perfume, sex.

The scent of sex was what woke him. He'd never smelled anything in a dream.

He cracked one eye open, hesitantly, then the other. Her weight above him didn't vanish with the return of sight. Her sweet beauty greeted him like dawn after a long night. Red sleep-tangled curls tickled his face and his shoulders as she leaned over him, smiling down at him.

"There you are, baby." She crushed her lips to his, then lifted up to gaze down at him. "You wouldn't wake up."

He had his hands fisted gently in her curls, so he tugged her down for another kiss, devoured her mouth greedily. "I didn't want to. I thought it had all been a dream."

"But it wasn't," Jamie said. "It was real. I had the same thought when I first woke up, so I had to touch you, make sure you were real. Once I started, I couldn't stop. I want you so bad it hurts."

"Thank god it wasn't a dream. I would've died, I think."

She lifted her hips, wide green eyes locked on his. "Me, too."

"But it's real. Right?"

"Right." She hovered there, just the tip of him inside her pussy. "But I think you'd better tell me you love me again. Just in case."

He released her hair, trailing his fingertips down her breastbone, over each nipple, down to the soft field of her belly, then slipped a single finger into her, brushing her clit. She gasped, arching her back as she writhed on top of him, driving him deeper.

"I love you, Jamie. I love you." He whispered the words, his voice low and fierce.

Jamie shivered, trembled, and then gasped his name as she sank down onto him, impaling him to the hilt, their hips colliding. Chase groaned in ecstatic relief as he felt himself filling her, and Jamie's voice rose to match his, and then they both began to move in perfect sync, moaning together, lips touching but not kissing, simply stretched wide in silent screams, breath shuddering in and groaning out.

Their motion together was slow, glacial, coursing in like a tide, drifting out like an exhalation.

Jamie's palms pressed onto his chest, her breasts swaying in the rhythm of her body's thrusting, her hips rolling, drawing him deeper. She took control of their pace, and Chase let her. She leaned forward, lifting up, hesitating at the apex, then sinking down, repeating this motion, drawing out every impalement, crying out as he dove deeper with every thrust.

Chase cupped one of her swaying breasts in his hand, scratching his fingers along her spine and clutching her ass as she undulated on top of him. He whispered her name as he moved, over and over: "Jamie...Jamie...Jamie..."

He felt himself rising, felt his climax nearing. He held it back, clenching every muscle, gritting his teeth as Jamie moved, gliding him in and out, her wet heat slicking his throbbing cock. She was so wet, so tight, and Chase struggled with every breath now to hold back.

"God, Jay. I'm so close. I can't hold it back much longer." Chase grabbed her hips to slow her motion, but Jamie resisted his hold and moved harder, faster. "Jamie...come with me."

"Don't hold back," Jamie whispered, and collapsed forward to lie chest to chest with Chase, burying her lips against his, moving only her hips now.

Chase felt his throat burn as he growled, hips juddering up against hers. He couldn't hold back.

She was milking him, working her hips on his in a relentless rhythm, and all he could do was let go.

"Jamie…" He gasped her name as he felt himself about to release. "Now, Jamie. I can't stop… Please don't stop."

He grabbed her hip with one hand and drove her down onto him, arching upward as he climaxed, scratching the fingers of his other hand down her spine. He felt her inner walls clamp down around him, and she screamed, coming with him. He felt liquid heat burst out of him, filling her, and then she crushed herself down hard onto him, riding a wave of climax, and he shot again, thrusting hard enough to lift his entire lower half off the bed.

Jamie collapsed, limp, onto him, shuddering and quaking with wave after wave of orgasm, and Chase couldn't stop, couldn't slow his manic plunging into her. She gasped breathlessly into his ear, making desperate sounds as Chase finally slowed.

They lay silent together, panting, shuddering. At long last, Jamie rolled off him, carefully drawing his softening member out of her.

"I have to pee *so* bad," she said, slipping off the bed.

Chase watched her naked body as she walked, feeling desire roll through him, even as he was still trembling with the aftershocks of climax. She was *so* beautiful. He felt his breath catch as she came back to him, breasts swaying slightly in a pendulum rhythm, hips gyrating from side to side as she walked. Chase rolled to a sitting position and shifted his legs off the bed. Jamie stopped just out of reach, copper curls wild around her shoulders, pale skin like flawless ivory, eyes like luminous chips of jade.

"God, Jay. You're so lovely, you take my breath away. Literally. I had to remind myself to breathe just now, watching you, naked and sexy and just-fucked."

Jamie's face twisted with emotion, clearly over-whelmed by his words. "You're too sweet, Chase."

"It's nothing but the truth, sweetness."

Jamie moved closer, one step at a time, until she was standing between Chase's knees. He reached up to hold her hips, and she rested her hands on his shoulders. "You like when I look just-fucked, do you?"

Chase laughed. "Yes, I do. I fully intend to keep you looking just-fucked as long as I can. I might feed you once or twice. I might even take you out to dinner, if you please me."

Jamie's eyes narrowed dangerously. "Oh, if I please you, hmm? And how do I go about pleasing you, *master*?"

Chase grumbled low in his throat, a ruminating sound. "Hmmm. You've done well so far. But I'm still feeling a bit...peckish."

Jamie huffed a confused laugh. "Peckish? What the fuck does that mean?"

"I means I'm hungry. I need to eat."

"Oh, I see." Jamie's expression told him she wasn't following yet.

He pressed his palms together, flattening his hands, and slipped them between her thighs, pushing them apart. "Yes. And at the moment there's only one thing I want."

Jamie let him part her thighs, thrusting her chest out as he pressed his lips to her belly, then trailed kisses lower and lower. "And...oh, god... and what would that be?"

Chase lay back on the bed, leaving his feet planted on the floor, and pulled her toward his face, causing her to climb up onto the bed on her hands and knees. He cupped his hands between her thighs to cup her ass from beneath, pulling her forward, then guided her torso upright so she was kneeling above his mouth, core directly over his lips.

"What would that be?" Chase murmured. "Can't you guess?"

"No." Jamie shifted, seeking balance. "This is dangerous, Chase. I've got no way to balance myself like this."

"I'll hold you." He extended a hand up and Jamie took it in both of her hands, clutching tight and sucking in a sharp breath as he flicked his tongue over her slit. "*This* is what I want. Your pussy."

"Chase...we just..." Jamie trailed off, mewling in her throat as he laved his tongue inside her.

"Don't care," Chase said. "Besides, I'm only going to kiss you *here*."

He suited action to words, pressing his stiffened tongue to her clit. Jamie whimpered and rocked forward, and Chase straightened his arm, holding her upright. Her legs buckled, and she forced herself back upright, then had to lean into Chase's arm as he began to circle her clit with his tongue, setting a fast, relentless pace. Chase's arm trembled as she leaned all her weight against him, lifting up and rocking her core back and forth into his tongue.

His index and middle fingers dipped into her folds and sought out her G-spot, and Jamie threw her head back and shrieked as he found it, massaging gently in rhythm with his mouth. Then, without warning, Chase's middle finger extended outward, tracing the line away from her pussy, backward.

"Oh, god, Chase...no..."

"Please? Trust me?" Chase broke away from her juice-wet slit long enough to murmur the words.

He tasted himself in her faintly, but she'd cleaned herself before coming back to bed, so it wasn't too strong. He didn't care, anyway. He had a mission now. He wanted to feel her come apart above him. He was going to make her next orgasm shatter her.

He pressed the tip of his ring finger to the hard knot of muscle but didn't push in. He continued to circle her clit with his tongue, occasionally flicking the taut bead, drawing a sharp intake of breath from her. She didn't demur when he moved his ring finger in small circles, ever so gently depressing into her tight channel. She growled as he worked his finger into her, carefully and slowly. He continued his assault on her clit, working his other two fingers against her ridged inner flesh, holding her upright with a burning arm.

She slid her legs apart and rolled her hips, still growling low in her throat at the invasion of his ring finger. He was nearly in to the first knuckle, and that was far enough. He began to move the finger in and out in tiny gyrations, working to keep the rhythm of all three fingers in tandem.

Jamie straightened her body, lifting up and giving Chase's trembling arm a respite. He felt the first quivers of climax begin, tremors in her belly against his forehead. She was chanting now, "oh, oh, oh, oh," and he felt her muscles clench. She went limp again, falling forward against his supporting arm, letting go with her hands and placing his palm against her breastbone, supporting her weight there.

She was rolling her hips against him helplessly, working his finger deeper into her tight, forbidden entrance. Jamie curled over his hand, and he had to use every ounce of strength to hold her upright. She was close now, so close.

He sucked her clit into his mouth past his teeth and pressed his fingers against her G-spot, digging his third finger deeper; Jamie came with a keening cry, and Chase milked her climax until she began shuddering.

"No more, no more, let me down, please..." she sobbed, gyrating her hips helplessly, her entire body shaking as she continued to climax.

Chase gently withdrew his finger and slid out from beneath her. She collapsed onto her hands and knees, gasping, heaving. Chase knelt behind her, stroking her back with both hands, rubbing in gentle circles, then down to her buttocks, cupping and kneading. Jamie moaned.

"Oh, my god, Chase. Fucking hell." She twisted to look at him over her shoulder. "Give me a minute. I'm not sure I can take another one just yet."

Chase laughed. "Oh, yes, you can." He moved closer into her so his erection was nestled upright between the globes of her ass. "And you will. Right...now."

He bowed his spine outward, grabbed his shaft, and guided it to her entrance. Jamie sucked in a breath and shifted her hips, lowering her spine and lifting her ass to meet him. He nudged her labia with the tip of his cock, rocking his hips to nudge in, one hand on her hipbone. Jamie moaned, buried her face against the backs of her hands on the rumpled comforter, arching for him to split herself wider, granting him access.

He slid in deeper, slowly, slowly, gliding silkily into her folds, groaning in his chest as he penetrated her. When he was impaled to the hilt, he paused. "God, oh, god, Jamie. You feel so fucking good."

Jamie could only moan in response, rolling her hips in an invitation for him to thrust.

"Oh, god." Then a realization washed over him. "Shit, Jamie!"

She heard the change in the tone of his voice, twisted her head to look at him over her shoulder. "What? What's wrong?"

"We haven't been using protection this morning."

Jamie huffed, something like a sigh or a laugh, Chase wasn't sure which. "It's fine, baby. I'm on birth control, and I was just tested last month."

Chase hesitated still. "You're sure?"

Jamie lifted up on her hands and pushed back into him, ducking her head between her arms, doing a half-push-up, then pulled forward and crushed backed into him. "God, yes. I'm sure. I'm sure..."

Chase let her reassurance push away all the worries and lingering doubts, the feel of her firm, soft ass meeting his thighs and her tight pussy clenching around him driving him wild. He shifted his knees farther apart, leaned over her back to plant kisses on her spine, then her lower back, then her ass.

"God, Chase…I need you deep." Jamie was panting, rolling her hips into him, waiting for him, encouraging him.

Chase took her hips in his hands and pulled her back as he thrust forward, a first slow, gentle surge. Jamie cried out softly, bowing her spine down to raise her hips, sinking back on her haunches to meet him. Chase pulled back slowly until he was nearly falling out, then, unable to hold back any longer, drove himself home, slow but hard. Jamie cried out again, and then Chase's control was lost.

"Jamie…I can't hold back. I can't go slow." He drew back and then slammed himself in, the slap of flesh against flesh cutting through their mutual panting.

"Don't—don't be gentle," Jamie gasped, rocking back and forth to meet his ever more urgent thrusts. "Fuck me hard…yes! Fuck me hard, just like that!"

Her words made Chase even crazier, fingers digging into her hips so hard she sucked in a breath. He forced himself to let go before he bruised her pale flesh. Harder and harder now, no semblance of control or sweetness or gentility. His back was straight, his hands scrabbling at her thighs and hips, resting on her back as he slammed into her again and again, her cries of pleasure, her breathless gasps of "yes yes yes, fuck yes…" sending him even further over the edge. She was meeting him stroke for stroke, her hands planted forward, her knees wide, her hips high, moving back into his nearly savage thrusts and encouraging him to give her more, more, more.

He was close then, and she felt it in his loss of rhythm. She snatched a pillow and shoved it under her stomach, bending down so her breasts and face were on the bed and her ass lifted as high as she could get it, welcoming the loud slap of his thighs into her ass. His balls were striking her folds with every stroke, his cock slamming deep, his body convulsing as he prepared to come.

"*Fuck*, Jamie, I'm gonna come so hard.."

Jamie's voice rent the air with a feral snarl. "Come for me, Chase. Fuck me hard!"

Chase felt her clenching around his shaft and knew she was close, too. He fumbled at the crease of her ass with his hand, finding the rosebud knot of muscle with the same ring finger as earlier, discovering it to be more pliant than the first time. He spat on his fingers and smeared it on her entrance, sliding his finger in.

"Oh, my fucking god, Chase!" Jamie could barely speak through the moans emitting from her throat, and she nearly collapsed as he worked his finger in to the second knuckle, then pulled it back.

He felt her quivering, choking on her breath and her screams. He was holding back, slowing himself down to long hard thrusts as he carefully inserted his middle finger. Jamie screamed out loud then, writhing against him and biting the bedspread.

"What are you doing to me? *Ohmyfuckinggod* that's good!" Jamie spread her thighs as wide as they would go, leaning back into his hand so her ass was stretched wide for him.

Chase let himself begin thrusting harder again, moving his fingers back and forth, not really in and out but merely insinuating the idea of motion. Jamie instinctively and unconsciously began to feather her hips into the movement of his fingers, timed with his thrusts.

"It...doesn't hurt...does it?" Chase asked between panted breaths.

"NO! No...it's fucking incredible." Jamie was lost in primal lust then, growling and groaning, shoving back against him, driving his fingers deeper.

Chase let his two fingers begin to actually move, and then, when he felt the muscles of her pussy begin to clench and clamp around his cock, her groans turning to full-voice screams. He had no idea how he'd lasted this long, since he was already dripping pre-come when he first thrust into her. They were moving in perfect sync then, his fingers deep inside her now, moving in with every slap of flesh meeting flesh.

"I'm coming, Jamie...come with me, love, *now*."

"Holy fuck, Chase! Fuck me harder...I'm so close..."

Chase gave it to her, pulling back and driving in so hard his pubic bone was bouncing off the flesh of her ass, harder than he'd ever fucked in his life. He gripped her hipbone with his free hand and jerked her back into him, even though she was already willingly ramming herself into him with every stroke.

And then they came, their voices shouting in unison, her voice shrieking, piercing, his a lion-like roar of ecstatic fury.

He unleashed his seed into her in a thick, hard rush, feeling it shoot deep, and then he was totally lost in her, frantically and arrhythmically driving into her, milking his orgasm along with hers. Jamie's inner muscles clamped down around his cock and his fingers so hard when she came that his thrusts were slowed by the coiled tension of her flesh, and he let himself go slack, moving languidly as his last throbbing spurts of come leaked into her.

He collapsed forward onto her ass, sweat sticking between them, slick and salty and stinging his eyes and mouth, his sweat mingling with hers. Chase extricated himself from her tight openings and rolled to the side with her, spooning her.

Jamie twisted her neck to kiss his lips, her mouth quivering with the intensity of her still-shuddering aftershocks. "Chase...Chase, baby. That was fucking intense..."

Chase laughed. "No, that was intense fucking." He kissed her throat behind her ear, lifted her hair with his clean hand and kissed her nape beneath her hairline, then her shoulders. "You think that was intense? Just wait till I fuck you in the ass, baby. You'll come so hard you'll think you're being ripped in half."

Jamie shivered against him. She twisted in his arms and put her lips against his ear. "You want to fuck me in the ass?" She clutched his ass and jerked him against her body. "You want me to let you do that? I just might let you, if it's anything like that last orgasm. I think I want it. I want your big hard cock in my tight little asshole. I want to feel you come deep in my ass."

Chase's eyes closed at the sound of her whispery breath in his ear, at her dirty words. "Good. 'Cause I'm going to." He reached up between them and tweaked her nipple, drawing a sharp gasp from her.

"But…" She traced her finger up his spine, then back down, lower, lower, until she was teasing the crease of his ass. "But you'll have to let me do something back to you."

Chase felt his ass clench tight in response. "Oh? What's that?" He went for nonchalant, but didn't quite make it.

Jamie laughed, a throat, sultry, amused sound that had his cock twitching with renewed desire. "Mmmm…not telling. It'll be a surprise. You'll like it, though. I promise."

Chase felt nerves shoot through him at her words. "Um. You're not putting anything back there."

"Nothing you haven't put in me. How 'bout that?"

Chase wriggled uncomfortably. "I don't know."

Jamie laughed again. "That's my terms, sweetness. You want to fuck me in the ass? You have to trust me back, then." She tilted away from him to take his flaccid cock in her hands. "You have to know I'd never do anything I didn't think you'd like. That's how this works, right? I trust you, you trust me?"

"I trust you, but—"

"There's no 'but' when it comes to trusting someone. I let you put your fingers in my ass. I've never let anyone do that. I was an ass-virgin. I trusted you." Jamie traced his length with her fingers.

"I didn't know that was your first time."

"It doesn't matter. It was awesome." Jamie kissed the round part of his shoulder. "Beyond awesome. Every time I come with you, it's better than the last. If that pattern keeps up, I might actually die from orgasm overload."

Chase rumbled a laugh. "I don't think that's possible."

"Well, if it is, you're determined to find out." Jamie closed her fist around him, feeling him begin to respond, pushing him onto his back and sitting up cross-legged next to him, facing his prone body.

"God, Jamie. You have me ready to go again. You make me feel like a teenager. Horny, insatiable, unstoppable."

"You *are* insatiable." Jamie began to stroke her fist up and down, achingly slow.

"So are you."

"Then we're a good match."

Chase met her eyes. "The best match. I've...I never knew I could feel this way about someone."

"What way?" Jamie's eyes told him she knew but wanted to hear him say it; he wanted to say it out loud.

"Like I can just let go."

Jamie's face scrunched up in confusion. "What's that mean?"

He rolled one shoulder in a shrug. "Just that I've always held back a little. With everyone I've ever been with, *everyone*—" The emphasis made it clear who he meant, without having to say more, "—I've held back. Emotionally, physically. I move fast, Jamie. I fall hard, and I fall fast. I mean, we've been dancing around this thing between us and avoiding it for months, but despite that, this is the most time we've actually spent together. But already I know, I *know* I'm in love with you. And I love that that doesn't scare you off."

Jamie laughed, a disbelieving scoff. "Scare me off? Chase, I don't think you understand how bad I have it for you. If you didn't return how *I* felt, *that's* what would scare me off." She continued to move her fist on his shaft as they talked, almost as an afterthought.

Chase just nodded, then said, "But it's also physical. I've always felt like if I just really let go, did everything I wanted...how I wanted, as hard and as intense as I wanted, it would hurt the person I was with, or scare them." His breath was coming in long gasps now as Jamie's fist on his cock began to pick up pace.

"Baby, listen. I know we've only spent this last, what, twelve hours together, but I feel like we've been together forever. Like, I know you. I know your soul. I know your heart. I know your body. I want all you have to give. All of it. Don't ever hold back." Jamie glanced down at his turgid cock, smiling hungrily as a pearly drop of pre-come glistened on his tip.

Chase couldn't get any words past his closing throat, past his gasping breath. She was stroking him with both hands, fist over fist. He began to move his hips into her hands, throwing his head back. Jamie slowed then, until one hand was nearly at his base, sliding molasses-slow, before she slicked the other over his tip, and she continued this erotically slow manipulation until Chase was thrusting up with his entire spine and nearly begging for her go faster. He didn't, though, because as teasing as her pace was, it felt like pure heaven, drawing his desire into a furious boil.

Jamie adjusted tactics then. She began to pump him with one hand, just as slowly as before, working her fist up his length, rubbing her thumb around the smeared pre-come and then gliding back down. With her other hand Jamie cupped his sack, merely holding at first, then massaging gently. The hand stroking his shaft clamped down around his crown and squeezed, and Chase gasped at the feeling. Still cupping his tightened sack, Jamie extended her middle finger to his taint, still squeezing his tip in a quick pattern of clenches. Chase shifted on the bed, not thrusting up but wriggling and writhing under her touch. She pressed her finger in circles around his taint until he began to moan, then slid her finger back farther, into the tight-clamped juncture of his ass.

"Relax for me, baby," she whispered, and plunged her hand down his length, squeezing his shaft in the tight sphincter of her fist.

Chase forced himself to relax, spreading his thighs apart, trusting her. Jamie loosened her hold on his cock, sliding her hand up and down loosely now, so loose she was barely touching him. Her finger worked its way in, toward his anus. He felt a bolt of fear, quickly squashed. She was touching him there finally, just a fingertip on the knot of muscle, the way he'd initially touched her. Jamie applied a hint of pressure as her fist began to pick up pace on his length, and Chase knew it wouldn't be long before he came. The boiling need to release was reaching an unbearable intensity, and her gently probing finger was only adding to the desperate inferno of pressure within him, hot and hard and ready to explode, despite how many times he'd already come with her that morning.

He felt her finger push harder, and he couldn't help his reaction. He pushed his torso downward, an involuntary motion, his legs falling apart as his heels pulled up higher. A welter of emotions tumbled through him, a slight twinge of embarrassment at his position, knees drawn up and back arched, with Jamie's finger beginning to probe deeper as his climax rose. The embarrassment grew as he began to roll his hips, feeling the tip of her finger now inside him, an alien, foreign pressure sending spasms through his entire body.

"Don't fight it, Chase," Jamie murmured. "Give in to it."

Chase forced himself to relax again, and his knees fell apart and his body began to move as her finger dipped in and pulled back, the same kind of *faux*-motion he'd used on her. And god...it *did* feel good. Strange and intensely powerful, pressure building inside him like a steam boiler gone wrong, about to detonate.

Jamie was stroking him at a middling pace, a steady rhythm. She leaned over as her hand reached his crown, forming a cup with the top of her fist, and spat into it, slicking her saliva over his shaft with a slow downward stroke. Chase gasped raggedly, then groaned in rapturous need when she began to work him more quickly, harder and faster, her finger not going any deeper but moving in and out more fully. Chase was wild, desperate, undone.

"Jamie, I'm...gonna—gonna come..." He could barely form the words.

She leaned over again and continued pumping him at the base, wrapping her lips around the very tip of him and stroking her fist up to her mouth and back down. He felt her tongue on his tip, and then she began to suck, hollowing her cheeks. Her hand moved in a blur on his cock, her finger working inside him, her mouth sucking with vacuum force.

And then he came, a feeling of his entire body emptying up and out, as if his very insides were being torn up and shooting out into Jamie's suctioning mouth. He couldn't make a sound, even the breath in his lungs emptying through his spasming shaft, all sounds, all breath, all sensation throbbing in his cock as he came, and came, and came, and Jamie drew it all out of him, stroking him relentlessly, his body bowing upward and her finger moving in and out and his brain scrambling.

He didn't think he could come any harder, but she didn't let up, milking him with her mouth and her hands until he was gasping for air and scrabbling at the sheets with his heels, and still he came, orgasming so hard his body ached.

Finally, she let his cock go with a wet *pop*, withdrawing her finger from him, slowing her fist on his shaft until she was merely holding him as he panted.

"Fuck, Jamie. Just...*fuck*."

She just smiled at him and lay down to nestle against his chest. After a long, comfortable silence, Jamie spoke up. "We should get cleaned up. We're all...dirty."

"I'm not sure I can move yet," Chase murmured.

"Don't, then. I'll go first." Jamie slid off the bed and went into the bathroom.

Chase watched her as she went, beyond sated, wrenched thoroughly dry, yet still finding a throbbing core of desire inside himself for all of Jamie. He watched her wash her hands, turn on the shower, and brush her teeth with the complimentary toothbrush and toothpaste. He watched her rinse her mouth and spit, and felt an ache in his chest at the beautiful normality of watching her doing such mundane things.

He watched with a welter of emotions, all of them centered around and springing out from love, as Jamie stuck her hand into the stream of steaming water, adjusted the temperature slightly, and then stepped in, sliding the curtain closed.

Her phone rang, a sudden, jarring, shrill interruption cutting through the silence of his thoughts and the sounds of Jamie showering. He contemplated answering it but decided against it. He thought about finding it and seeing who showed up on the caller ID, but decided against it. The phone went silent and then rang again a few seconds later. Silence, and then a third ring. The bleeping tone of a voicemail received.

Jamie emerged from the bathroom, wreathed in steam, wrapped in a thick white towel, her red hair wet and tangled and dangling down her back. "Did I hear my phone going off?"

"Yeah," Chase said. "It rang, like, three times. You have a voicemail, I think."

She crouched and dug it out of her purse, swiped her finger across the screen to unlock it, and tapped the screen, bringing up the "missed calls" screen. She tapped it a few more times, and then a voice came out of the speakers, male, British, and smooth.

"Jamie, love. I know we had a tiff, and I said some things I mightn't've meant. You know how it goes. I just...I'm sorry. I hope you'll come home, come to my flat, I mean." Jamie paled, falling backward onto her butt on the floor, scrambling to silence it.

"Shit," she said.

Chase sat up and pinched the bridge of his. "That complicates things."

Jamie looked up sharply. "No! No it doesn't. There's no complications. I walked out. I left him because I didn't love him, didn't want to be with him. I left him *before* I met you."

"But he clearly wants you back."

Jamie stood up and crossed the room to sit next to Chase on the bed, phone clutched forgotten in her hand. "But I don't want him. I never really did. That was the entire problem. I was trying to convince myself another man could take your place. I couldn't keep up the pretense, Chase. I just couldn't. And now that I've been with you—made love to you—I could never ever spend a single second with anyone else." She pivoted to sit cross-legged on the bed, and Chase's eyes were drawn to the shadowy vision of her folds between the gap of the towel. She took his face in her hands and forced his eyes to hers. "Eyes up here, Tiger. You need to understand what I'm saying to you. You've ruined me for all other men. You did that the first time you kissed me."

He felt a hesitancy it her words. "But?"

"No buts. I just have to get my things from his condo. Make sure he knows I'm really done."

"Want me to go with you?"

Jamie considered. "I don't know. That could get awkward. But I really don't want to go alone, either."

"How about I go with you, but wait in the lobby?"

"That would work," Jamie said. She pushed Chase toward the bathroom. "Now go clean up. You're crusty."

Chase showered and dressed, and they left the hotel. Chase felt as if something in the world had shifted, as if everyone should know how completely his life had changed since the last time he was outside. When he and Jamie had entered the hotel, he had been bursting with need, every fiber of his being aflame with frustration and love and lust. Now, leaving the hotel not even a day later, he felt like he was almost a different person. One night with Jamie, and she'd stolen his soul, hidden it within herself. She had shown him what he'd been missing his entire life, and now he couldn't fathom being without it...couldn't fathom being without her.

They caught a cab, and Jamie gave the driver the address. A few minutes later they pulled up in front of an upscale high-rise condo building right on Lake Michigan. Chase went into the lobby with her, holding her hand. He stopped with her at the bank of elevators.

"I'll come up with you," Chase said.

Jamie shook her head. "It's fine. It's not like I'm scared of him or anything. He's a good person, and...I don't know. I just feel like if I leave your side, even for ten seconds, this whole thing will pop like a bubble. Like you and I finally being together is a dream that I could wake up from any second."

Chase laughed in relief and put his forehead to hers, one arm around her waist, the other tangled with hers at their sides. "God, I'm glad I'm not the only one feeling that way."

The elevators dinged, and the doors whooshed open. A disbelieving huff of male laughter sounded from within the elevator directly in front of them.

"Fucking bollocks, Jamie. Didn't imagine you'd move on quite *that* fast." The British voice from Jamie's cell phone.

Jamie jumped in Chase's arms, gasping in surprise. "Ian...I—um..."

Chase felt her pulse leap into a frenzy. He stepped away from Jamie, still holding her hand.

"I don't guess there's much to say, then, is there?" The man, tall and good-looking with sandy hair and blue eyes, flicked his gaze from Jamie to Chase, his eyes alternating between angry and hurt and confused. "I'll just go."

"Ian, wait. I'm sorry for this, but—well...I don't know. I told you it was complicated."

"Complicated?" Ian laughed, a sarcastic sound. "Complicated is having feelings for another bloke when you're with me. Complicated I can deal with. Having a tumble with him in the lobby of my flat building is a bit different, I'd say."

"I wasn't—" Jamie started. "Listen, I just need my stuff, okay?"

"You've been fucking him all along, haven't you?" Ian said, fists clenched at his sides.

"What? No! Ian, don't make this into something it's not—"

"You stormed off yesterday, and I thought you'd just need some time to cool off. I thought...I thought you'd come back, and we'd discuss it a bit, figure things out. I—you—" Ian turned away, paced a few steps, and then turned back. "You ran straight to him, didn't you? Straight from his bed to mine."

Chase couldn't keep himself from intervening. "Now, hold on just a minute, pal. You don't have to like the situation, but you've got no call to insult her."

"Sod off. I'm not talking to you, Yank." Ian dismissed Chase with a flick of his fingers. "I'm talking to Jamie, so you can just shut your fucking mouth."

"Fuck you. You're being a dick."

"Chase, don't." Jamie pushed at Chase's chest. "Just let me talk to him."

"Like I said," Ian punctuated his next words with a finger poking hard into Chase's shoulder, "sod...off."

Chase knocked Ian's hand away and stepped in front of Jamie, putting his back to her so he was inches away from Ian. "Don't touch me."

Chase heard Jamie moan in frustration when Ian's fist flashed up and into Chase's stomach, knocking the wind from him. He saw red, lunging.

ELEVEN

JAMIE GROANED IN IRRITATION. *Fucking stupid posturing males.*

She saw Ian's fist move in slow motion, slam into Chase's stomach, then watched a transformation overtake Chase. He grunted, sucking in a breath, then straightened. His face was a rictus of rage.

She had to stop this before it got really ugly. She stepped in front of Chase and shoved him back as hard as she could, taking his face in her hands. His eyes dragged from Ian to her.

"Don't, Chase." She spoke so low only he could hear it. "Do *not* do this."

"Motherfucker sucker-punched me," Chase snarled.

"I know," Jamie said. "I know. But please just let it go. It's not worth fighting over. I hurt him, okay? He has a right to be angry—he's just being a child about it. Taking it out on you instead of me. Just walk away, okay? There's a pub a couple doors down. Go have a drink while I get my stuff. Please?"

Chase's chest heaved, and she saw the rage warring with his desire to please her. "Fine. Only for you." He spun on his heel and stormed off, fists clenched.

"Pansy," Ian's voice said from behind her, goading.

Jamie whirled, seeing Chase's shoulders tense and his strides slow. "Shut the fuck up, Ian! You're being a shithead. I just diffused the situation *you* created." She shoved him onto an elevator as it opened to let off a businessman. "Get on, Ian. Don't piss me off."

She stepped onto the elevator behind Ian and stood against the far wall, away from him. The ride up to Ian's condo was long and awkward and tense. Jamie followed him down the hallway and to his door, waiting while he opened it up, then stood in the foyer. Ian set his keys on a thin table by the wall, sighing deeply. His shoulders slumped, and he turned in place, scrubbing his face with one hand.

"I'm sorry, Jamie. I shouldn't have done that. I was just...I'm right pissed, and I've got every reason to be, I'd think."

Jamie flopped back against the closed door. "I know. And I'm sorry. I know you're hurt, and you do have a right to be. I haven't been fair to you."

Ian ran his hands through his hair, tilting his head and peering at Jamie as if exhausted. "Did I mean *anything* to you?"

"Of course you did, Ian. It was just...I don't know. It's hard to explain."

"You've said that before. I don't care to hear it again. Try to explain."

Jamie let her head thunk against the door. "You *did* mean something to me. I had a good time with you. You...you're wonderful. In any other situation, I think we really could have had a good chance at something long-term together."

"But?"

"But you never really had a chance with me, through no fault of your own. I've just...I've been in love with Chase for a long, long time. Since before I met you. I was running from my feelings for him when I met you. I told you all this yesterday."

"Feels like a thousand years ago."

Jamie blew a long breath out. "You have no idea." She looked up at Ian, who was leaning against the wall with one shoulder. "Look, I don't really know what to say to you that I haven't already said. I'm sorry I hurt you. I'm sorry you saw me with him like that. It's not like you think. I never even talked to him on the phone until yesterday. I literally ran into him in the street, and I just...I couldn't deny how I feel for him any longer."

"And how you feel about me no longer applies, is that it?"

Jamie couldn't answer, since it was true.

"I see," Ian said. "Well, then, there's only one thing left for me to do."

Something odd in his voice had Jamie glancing up to see Ian inches away and closing, hand scooping around the back of her head, his lips crashing against hers. Jamie froze in shock, felt herself melting just slightly—Ian was a damn good kisser, after all—and then she felt the rush of outrage and anger blast through her.

She pulled back, shoved him as hard as she could, and then slapped him. "*Seriously*, Ian? You kiss me? All that, and you kiss me?" She scrubbed her mouth with her palm, as if to wipe away the fact that she'd nearly let herself enjoy the kiss.

Ian shrugged. "I had to see. There is nothing left, is there? Was there ever anything?" Jamie opened her mouth to answer, but Ian cut her off. "That was rhetorical. Wait here. I'll get your things."

Jamie dug the heels of her palms into her eye sockets hard enough that sparks flashed in the blackness of her closed eyes. She heard his tread, lowered her hands to see Ian holding out two small duffel bags, the kind given out as freebies at the tech conferences Ian frequented.

"Pretty sure this is everything. If there's anything else I discover, I'll ship it to you."

"Thanks." A long silence expanded between them until Jamie broke it. "You're a good man, Ian, and I'm sorry for…using you, I guess. Wasting your time."

Ian sighed, and rubbed his jaw with his wrist. "You didn't waste my time, Jamie. You just broke my heart." He ran his hands through his hair, and Jamie had to look away from the raw splinters of emotion in his blue eyes. "I was falling in love with you. I'd thought about proposing."

Jamie let out a sound that was half-sob and half-laugh. "You were going to—? Ugh. I wish there was something else I could say besides 'I'm sorry.'"

Ian shook his head. "There really isn't anything, is there? Goodbye, Jamie."

She turned and opened the door, pausing to pick up her bags and glance at Ian. "I really am sorry. You deserved better treatment."

Ian didn't answer, besides a shrug. Jamie left, and the elevators closed on her vision of Ian standing in his doorway, one hand in his pocket, the other rubbing the back of his neck, his eyes betraying pain even from a distance.

She found her car in the garage, tossed her things in the back seat, pulled it out into traffic, found a parking spot on the street near the pub where she'd told Chase to go. She sat in her car, trying to collect herself. It had been harder than she'd thought it would be to say goodbye to Ian. To see him hurting. To know she'd been the one who hurt him.

The passenger door opening startled Jamie into alertness, but she knew it was him even before she opened her eyes. She smelled him first, body wash, cologne, faintly of beer, that male scent and the unique essence of Chase, comfort and desire turned olfactory.

"I'm sorry I made it a scene, babe," Chase said as he settled into the seat next to her.

She glanced at him in amused disbelief. "It was going to be a scene regardless. An ex and a current is always messy, no matter what. You were defending me, and that's...so sweet. And really, the fact you were able to walk away from the fight? I love you so much for that. Any guy can beat someone's ass for his girl. It takes a real man, a strong man, to walk away from a confrontation for his girl."

Chase reached out and took her hand. "Neither of us needed that." He examined her face. "It was pretty rough, huh?"

"That obvious?"

Chase laughed. "You look emotionally wrecked. Gorgeous and glorious as always, but you look like that took it out of you."

"He kissed me after I told him I'd been in love with you since before I met him. And then he told me he had been falling in love with me and that he was thinking about proposing."

"Shit."

"Yeah. It hurt."

"I'm sorry you had to go through that," Chase said.

"It's over now." Jamie noticed Chase had his bag on his lap. "You checked out?"

Chase shrugged. "Yeah. I figured we've spent enough time in Chicago."

"Sounds good to me. I have to be back in Detroit for work on Monday, but that's it. I'm free till then."

They headed away from Chicago, going vaguely west and north toward Wisconsin. They stopped at a Holiday Inn off the freeway about halfway to Milwaukee, checked in, and had dinner. Jamie felt antsy for most of the time, wanting nothing more than to erase the bad taste in her mouth left by the scene with Ian. She wanted to feel more of Chase, experience more of his many mercurial sides. She'd only scratched the surface of him, she thought. He seemed just as tense, just as full of coiled intensity. His head was freshly shaven, his jaw and chin clean and the hard lines of his handsome face accentuated by the low lights of the diner. His arms stretched the sleeve of a charcoal henley shirt, the sleeves pushed up to his elbows.

She wanted those arms around her, those hands holding her.

They went back to the hotel, and the door had barely closed behind him when Chase's voice washed over her. "Strip."

She turned in place to face him, her heart thudding. "Excuse me?" He was leaning back against the door, one leg crossed over the other, arms akimbo.

A faint smile traced his lips. His eyes twinkled. "I said, strip. Take your clothes off."

Her chin lifted. "Oh, yeah? Just like that?" She *wanted* to strip, but she also wanted to see where he'd take it if she refused.

He took a step forward, his gait loose and powerful, his eyes predatory. "Yeah. Just like that."

"And if I don't?"

"You will." He smirked again. "Well...you'll be naked in about thirty seconds either way."

Jamie sucked in a deep breath and let it out, then crossed her arms beneath her chest. "No."

Chase lifted an eyebrow and stepped toward her again, arms uncoiling. Jamie took an involuntary step backward at the intensity in his gaze. An excited smile played over her lips, and her heart crashed in her chest.

He lunged, catching her in his arms, squeezing them to her sides. She gazed up at him evenly.

"Now what are you gonna do to me? Spank me?" Jamie asked.

"Tempting," Chase said. "But no."

He returned her even gaze, and then, before she could blink, he had spun her in his arms so her back was to his front, both of her hands pinned in one of his, firmly but gently. Jamie struggled to free her hands, but she couldn't. She went still, waiting for his next move. His breathing was hot and loud in her ear, his chest hard at her back. With his free hand, he traced her cheek, following the line of his grazing fingers with his lips. Jamie tilted her head to the side as he lined kisses down her neck. Chase moved them forward so her torso was pressed to the wall, pinning her there with his hips, his erection against her jeans-clad ass. Jamie was wearing an old Counting Crows concert T-shirt, thin and tight; Chase released her hands, gripped the collar of her shirt, and ripped it open down the back and brushed it off her.

"I liked that shirt!" Jamie protested.

Chase just chuckled. He grabbed her hands again before Jamie could think about finding a way to get free, and besides, she didn't really want to. She was interested in where he was going with this. But, for form's sake, she had to put up a fight. So—in the name of the game—she writhed her ass against his erection, a distraction, and then when he sucked in a breath and loosened his grip on her wrists, Jamie shoved him away and broke free. Chase laughed and caught her around the waist with one arm, jerking her back to his chest.

"I don't think so, sweetness. You could've done a little striptease for me, and I'd already be inside you, making you come for me." Jamie couldn't quite stifle a whimper. "But no, you had to play tough girl, hard to get. So...we do this the fun way."

"Fun for who?"

Chase dragged a finger down her chest, between her cleavage, and then traced the rim of the bra cup. "Fun for me. It'll be fun for you...eventually. But you might get a bit...desperate before I'm done with you."

He tugged the cup down and a breast popped free; he did the same to the other side, and then began toying with the nipples, one and then the other, pinching and rolling, flicking and cupping each breast with the taut bud caught between his middle and index fingers. Jamie's breath caught, and she couldn't stop herself from arching her back into his touch. He slid his hand down her belly, dipped his fingers beneath the denim to cup her mound over the silk of her panties. Jamie froze as he stroked the damp line of her entrance with one

finger, making the silk even wetter. She found herself panting and on the verge of begging him to put
his finger inside her. She didn't beg, and he didn't
touch her skin to skin. He seemed content to stroke
her through the silk, digging in slightly to put pressure on her clit. Her hips writhed on their own,
despite her attempts to stop them.

"Chase…" she heard herself whisper, and then
clicked her teeth together on the rest of the plea.

"Yes, love?"

She only panted in reply, resting her head back
on his shoulder.

Chase released her hands, withdrew his fingers
from her jeans, and placed her palms flat on the
wall, pulling her hips back until she was forced to
take several steps backward. She was now standing
as if she'd been arrested, feet shoulder-width apart,
palms flat on wall.

"Stay like this," Chase ordered, his voice gentle
in her ear.

"Or?"

Chase's finger trailed up from her hip to her
side, and then up to her armpit. Jamie tensed, realizing what the punishment would be if she moved.
He ever so gently traced her underarm, and she
choked back a giggle, flinching away.

"No, no! Please don't tickle me," she said,
putting her hands back on the wall. "I hate being
tickled."

Chase rumbled in amusement. "Good to know."

Jamie cursed herself for having given him leverage. She lost her train of thought when his fingers came back around her belly, both hands dipping beneath both denim and silk to cup her flesh, one hand remaining on the dip of her hip. His middle finger dove down to press against her clit, and Jamie hung her head, gritting her teeth against a whimper. He circled her once, twice, and she couldn't stop a single gasp from escaping.

"I want to hear you," Chase said.

So, of course, Jamie decided to make a game of her own out of how silent she could stay. He made wide, slow circles around her throbbing nub, and she had to clench her jaw to keep from panting. He increased his assault, circling faster and faster, and, just as she was about to lose her own game, he stopped. That was almost her undoing. She wanted to beg him to keep going but bit her lip to keep quiet.

He unbuttoned her pants, then slowly unzipped her fly. She tensed, waiting for the pants to be pushed down, but he didn't do that. Instead, he skated his palms up her sides, cupped her breasts in both hands, tenderly kneading the soft flesh. He abruptly unsnapped her bra but left the straps on her arms. Jamie wriggled her shoulders, hating the feel of the loose straps, but Chase stilled her with a single press of his palms to her shoulders.

Her breasts were hanging free, unsupported now, but the bra was still partly on. It was driving her nuts, but she forgot that soon enough as his hands came back up to cup her breasts, now stimulating her nipples until she was shifting in place, holding back moans. And then his touch was gone again, sliding down to her hips, pushing the pants down to her knees and leaving them. She lifted her leg to pull the pants off, but Chase made a negative sound in his chest.

"Leave it," he said.

Jamie blew out a sigh of exasperation that nearly turned into a moan of appreciation as he began to massage her buttocks through her panties. It wasn't an erotic touch, oddly, the way he kneaded the muscles there, but it still turned her on even as it relaxed her. Of course, she couldn't get much more turned on, she didn't think. Then he slid his palms under the silk to caress her bare skin, and she realized how wrong she was; she could get a *lot* more turned on. He traced the crease between her ass cheeks with one finger, and she found herself wanting to spread herself wide to allow him entrance. She didn't, though, and he didn't press in. She was almost disappointed.

He pressed his erection against her backside, leaning in with his mouth to her ear. "Soon, sweetness." He writhed his shaft into the crack, the zipper and button scraping against the silk. "Soon I'm going to be deep inside you...here."

"Soon, like now?"

Chase made a noncommittal sound. "Maybe, maybe not. You want me to?"

"Maybe." Jamie tried to sound blasé, but couldn't quite manage it.

If she was being honest with herself, she *did* want it. A lot, actually. His two fingers had been intense enough, but if he managed to fit his entire huge cock into her? It would be...mind-blowing, she was sure. As long as it didn't hurt, and she knew for a fact he wouldn't do it if was going to hurt.

"You lie," Chase murmured in her ear. "You want it. You're a dirty girl. You want my cock in your ass."

Jamie hung her head and bit her lip to keep from responding. Chase abruptly shoved her panties down to her knees with her pants, and then carved a line up the outside of her thigh to rest at the apex of her hip.

Chase murmured in her ear, "Which way should I go? This way?" He slid his finger toward her core. "Or this way?" He ran his fingernail back toward her ass.

Jamie wanted him in both places, so she didn't answer. Not that she would've answered anyway. He took her lack of answer as freedom to do both.

One hand curled forward to cup her mound, now pulsating with heat and dripping wet. His other hand clutched one ass cheek and then the other before digging his fingers in between her thighs and ass. Jamie wanted to widen her thighs so he could touch her more freely, but her pants around her knees wouldn't let her, and neither would her own determination.

He moved both hands simultaneously, slipping one long finger into her pussy and the fingers of the other hand deeper between her thighs from behind. Jamie allowed herself a long breath in and then out as he circled her clit. Then, abruptly, both hands were gone, and so was his presence behind her. She started to twist to try to locate him, but his voice at her left ear stopped her.

"Mmm-mmm. No moving," he admonished her.

Jamie clenched her jaw around her sarcastic comeback and waited. He took one of her hands in his, slid her bra strap off, then repeated it with the other side. He stepped away to hang the bra off the bathroom doorknob. Jamie watched him, then snapped her attention back to the wall when he returned to his place behind her. He knelt down behind her, kissing her spine on the way, then each buttock, then underneath each one. He wrapped his hands around the front of her thighs, stroked upward until his fingers brushed the line of her entrance. Jamie's breathing became more labored as he slid his hands down and then back up her legs, stopping again just at the apex of her thighs.

"Step out of the pants," Chase instructed.

Jamie obeyed, stepping on the cuff of one pant leg and tugging her foot out, then did the same on the other side. She was naked now, trembling with anticipation. She waited, and waited, but Chase did nothing, just knelt behind her with his hands on her thighs and his mouth pressed in a stilled kiss to the rounded outside of her ass.

Then he was gone. "Don't move," he ordered. "And don't look. Close your eyes."

Jamie closed her eyes, listening to a zipper of a bag *zzzzhrip*-ing open, then the sounds of clothing being rummaged through. She smelled him, felt his presence. Cloth touched her eyes, tied behind her head. She opened her eyes, but all was dark. He tugged her hands away from the wall and guided her to a different position, standing her in place and leaving her, then spinning her a few times so she was disoriented but not dizzy.

"What are you doing, Chase? What's going on?"

He didn't answer. She heard a soft footfall to one side and then the other; she smelled him as he passed by her, and then the scent was gone with the breeze of his passage. A finger trailed across her belly in one direction, a palm slid over her ass in the other. Lips pressed to hers briefly, gone as soon as she began to respond to the kiss. Fingers carved over her hips and into the wet folds of her core, stroking slowly and languorously, then were gone before she could begin to respond. His lips touched hers, tilted slightly sideways, and this time stayed until she opened her mouth, his tongue sliding in and tangling with hers, tracing her lips.

He was gone again, and then Jamie heard a zipper, cloth rustling and falling to the floor, and then she caught his scent and felt his presence in front of her.

"I'm right in front of you," he said. "Touch me."

She reached out, found hot flesh. She explored the area and found it to be his elbow. She followed his arm to his shoulder, his neck, devoured his bare torso with both hands then, over the toned bulk of his muscles, the cut and rippling perfection of his abs, down to his hips. He was naked, thank god. She felt the cool, hard, tautness of his ass, cupped it, clutched it, then reached around to grip his erection. She stroked him a few times, and then he pulled away.

"Come back," Jamie said, "I want to touch you more."

He ghosted back into her outstretched hands, and she caressed his body all over, pressed her face to his chest, kissing across it, touching his shoulder with her lips and running her tongue over the small bead of his nipple, tracing the grooves of his abdomen with her mouth, falling to her knees and laving the hollow of hip, finding the V-cut and worshipping it with her fingers and her tongue. She paused, turning her face up to him, as if to look at him through the blindfold. She could almost see him in her mind: absurdly, gloriously gorgeous face turned down to look at her, his brown eyes wide and dark and glinting with unrestrained desire, his broad, hard muscles rippling as he held himself still for her touch, tribal tattoos across his biceps and forearms. She kissed his thigh, then skated her palms over his taut ass, pulling him closer, closer, until she felt the heat and iron and silk of his cock against her lips. She kissed him, smiling at the gasping intake of his breath, then took him into her mouth and slowly lowered her head, taking him deeper and deeper, relaxing her throat and going deeper yet.

"Fuck, Jay, what are you doing?" His voice was thick and quavering. "Don't gag yourself! Jesus..."

He lost capacity for speech then as she backed away, sucking on his tip, and then downed his cock once more, deeper than before, until she felt his close-trimmed curls against her face. She backed away slightly, then bobbed her head until he hissed and pulled himself away.

She smiled up at him, licking her lips. Judging by the fraught silence stretching between them,

Jamie knew she'd made her point. She stayed on her knees, waiting, hands on her thighs, face turned up to where she knew he was. She could feel his intense gaze on her.

Then she felt his hands on her arms gently lifting her up to her feet. His mouth touched hers, his tongue spearing through her lips in a demanding kiss. She melted instantly, moving to let him curl her into his embrace, but instead of his arms around her, she was swept up off her feet.

"Omigod, Chase! Put me down, you lunatic! You'll break your back!"

Chase just laughed and walked with her in his rock-solid arms—no hint of trembling or straining—and set her slowly onto the bed. He kissed her breastbone, then suckled her nipple until she gasped and moaned, switching to the other breast and doing the same, scraping the sensitive peak with his teeth until she whimpered. He moved down her body, kissing as he went, and when his mouth reached her mound, Jamie eagerly slid her legs apart, cupping his bald scalp and shamelessly pulling his mouth to her hot, wet sex. Chase chuckled at her eagerness, and the vibrations of his laughter had her lifting her hips to press herself into him. He teased her with his tongue, light butterfly-gentle flicks against her clit, followed by slow, fat licks of her entire opening, then a darting tongue tip into her channel. Then his fingers curled into her to stroke her G-spot, and his mouth worked her throbbing nub until she was bucking underneath him, moaning a nonstop sound of need as she drew closer to climax. She held onto his head for dear life, holding him tight against her.

"Oh, god, Chase! I'm gonna come right now!"

And then he was gone.

"Where are you going? Come back here!" She writhed on her back, reaching for him, growling in frustration. "You can't do that!"

She heard him moving around, and then her hand was enclosed by his hand, something cool and soft wrapped around her wrist. Her arm was drawn back and over her head, a pause and the sound of rustling, and then she felt his presence move around the bed to the other side. She reached for him, only to find her right hand stop abruptly, as if...

"Did you just tie me to the bed?"

"Maybe."

Her left hand was held in his unbreakably gentle grip, tied to the bed, and then he was gone once more.

"Chase Delany. You *cannot* tie me up and blindfold me and then just leave me here on the edge of orgasm. You'd damn well better come back here and finish what you started." She heard the tinge of desperation in her voice but couldn't quite manage to erase it.

Chase's voice came from across the room. "Oh, don't you worry, my love. I'll finish you off. When I'm ready."

"What are you doing way over there?"

"I'm looking at you. You're tied up and naked and at my mercy. I'm deciding what to do to you. You're so fucking sexy like that, all spread out for me...I could come right now, just looking at you."

Jamie spread her legs apart and writhed on the bed, an invitation. "You better not come. I want it. I want you. Give it to me."

Chase's voice was closer, now. "You want it? You want my come?"

"God, yes. All of it."

Closer yet. "Where?"

"Anywhere. Everywhere." His fingers grasped her ankle, and she sucked in a sharp breath; his palm ran up her thigh, and Jamie wantonly spread her legs apart for his touch. "There. Inside me."

His weight settled on the bed, and then she felt him climbing up her body to kneel over her. "What if I want it somewhere else?"

Jamie lifted her body, wanting his skin against hers, wanting pressure on her aching clit. "Anywhere. Just...finish it. I want you."

She felt something hot and soft and broad nudging her sex. Jamie moaned, arching her back to get him deeper. He matched her thrust to move away, and then replaced his tip at her entrance. "Be still. Don't move. Don't make a sound."

Jamie froze, clamping her lips together. He moved his cock in circles, rubbing her clit with his crown. Jamie's body wanted to writhe in circles with him, but she forced herself into stillness. He moved himself faster and faster, and then pulled away, leaving Jamie gasping, head craned back in desperation. She wanted to plead with him.

"Stop moving."

"I can't help it."

"Try. The more you move, the more you make those sexy little sounds, the longer it will take. I can't take those moans. I'm so close to coming, Jamie. If you keep making those noises, I'm done."

Jamie felt him nudge her throbbing clit, and she had to flex every muscle in her body to keep still, biting her tongue to keep quiet. He circled her hot, hard nub again, and she felt the pressure of impending climax building up. Without warning Chase drove himself into her, a fast, hard thrust, fully impaling his thick shaft inside her. Jamie shrieked in surprise and pleasure, and he pulled himself out.

"I'm sorry, I'm sorry," Jamie gasped. "I'll be quiet. Give it back, please."

He slowly entered her again, and Jamie wrapped her fists around the cords binding her—neckties, it felt like—and held them for leverage to keep still as he slid his pulsing shaft into her drenched slit. She bit her lip until she tasted blood, but she kept quiet, and he buried himself to the hilt, his hips bumping hers. He held there, and she heard his breathing, fast, ragged, as if he was barely staving off his own orgasm. Jamie flexed her vaginal muscles as hard as she could around him, clenching and releasing in a pulsating rhythm.

"Fuck, Jay. Fuck, that's incredible." His breath huffed hot on her throat. "Do it again."

Jamie clenched him tight again, flexing hard as long as she could, and then releasing with a gasp of exertion. Chase kissed her throat, then moved down to her breast and kissed the mounded flesh with soft, wet lips. Jamie struggled to contain her groan as he sucked her nipple into his mouth and flicked it with his tongue.

She nearly screamed when he drew back and slammed in, then twice, a third time, and with each hard thrust Jamie fell closer to orgasm. He plunged deep a fourth time and then withdrew completely, and this time Jamie did mewl in irate frustration.

Chase's body slid down hers, and his mouth pressed to her sex. Jamie stifled a whimper as he licked and lapped and laved her aching clit in arrhythmic flicks, driving her mad with the need for pressure, need for rhythm.

She was desperate now, so close to climax, but held away from the edge by his endless teasing. She was drawing close now, and she struggled to hold absolutely still and remain completely silent, hoping if she could keep him from knowing how close she was he might send her over the edge. He settled into a rhythm finally, licking directly against her throbbing nub. She called on every shred of will she possessed, but as she neared climax, her traitorous body bucked beneath his skilled mouth, and the delicious wet pressure of his mouth was gone.

"*Dammit!*" She couldn't stop the cry of crazed need from escaping, either.

He laughed, a predatory rasp in his throat, sinuously gliding up the length of her body, the slick tip of his cock dragging up her leg to nudge against her entrance.

"Are you ready for me?" Chase asked, his voice an almost inaudible whisper in her ear.

"Yes!" She let all of her desperation into her voice, let herself abjectly plead with him. "Chase, *please*, please...no more. No more. Just...be with me. Come with me. Come inside me. Shit, come *on* me, if you want. Come on my tits, or my face or anywhere. Just let me go, let me touch you."

Chase's tongue flicked her earlobe, and then his mouth kissed her ear, her jaw just behind it. Jamie panted, thrusting her pussy against the tip nudging her slit. He kept away until she went still and then nibbled her neck, sucked her shoulder near her armpit hard enough that she'd have a mark later. She tugged on the ties binding her, wanting to feel his back move, feel his ass rippling, wanting to draw him in. She thrashed her head, trying to dislodge the blindfold. She curled her legs around his hips and jerked, but it was like trying to move a statue.

His breath returned to her ear. "I'd never degrade you that way, my love." His whispering voice was sweet and tender. "Never. Now, tell me where you want me to come."

She twisted her face to bite his earlobe. "Inside me. In my pussy. Now. *Please.* No more teasing. No more games."

He nudged in, a tiny movement that had only the very tip inside her, but it was enough to make her whimper.

"Like that?" he said, his voice a low rasp.

She could feel him trembling, holding back, straining for control.

"Yes...god, yes. Just like that. More. More." She fought for stillness. "I'm begging you, please, more."

Chase fluttered his hips, a series of slow, shallow movements that had Jamie flailing in paroxysms of delight, moaning. He kept up the tiny thrusts, barely moving in before he was pulling back. Jamie wasn't about to complain since it was better than nothing, but she wanted, *needed* more. He'd brought her so close so many times now, had her rising up and up and closer and closer until she was nearly mad with raging pressure, pent-up climax. And these butterfly thrusts weren't going to get the job done.

"Chase...stop teasing me." Her voice was a broken whisper.

He laughed again, the same low gravelly rumble of leonine amusement. "Teasing? This isn't going to do it for you?" He thrusted even more shallowly, if possible, the tip barely moving between her labia.

"You bastard. You know it's not." Jamie jerked on the ties, but only succeeded in tightening them around her wrists.

Chase froze. "A bastard, am I?" He pulled out, barely stifling a hiss that told Jamie he was teasing himself as much as her.

He lowered his mouth to her breast, cupping it with his hand and flicking the nipple with his teeth. His other hand snaked between their bodies, a single finger racing around her clit. Jamie groaned and writhed in frustration, in pleasure, in confusion. What he was doing felt amazing, felt incredible, but she needed *him*. He didn't stop when she bucked beneath him to the tempo of his licking tongue and flicking fingers. He didn't stop when she began to arch off the bed, and he didn't stop when she began to let full-voiced cries escape.

"Oh, god, oh, god, oh, *god*," Jamie cried, finally cresting over the verge of climax.

At the very moment the wave broke over her, Chase plunged into her, hammering deep in a single thrust. She screamed in delirious ecstasy, curling her legs around his ass and clutching him with all the considerable strength in her legs. Wave after wave crashed through her, the pressure releasing in an inundating barrage powerful enough to leave her heaving sobbed breaths.

Chase didn't relent as she came, however. He drew back and pounded in, unleashing another scream from her, and then he did it again, and she couldn't scream, could only gasp for breath. He began a driving rhythm, and Jamie tried to keep up, tried to thrust back into him, but the blasting waves of climax weren't letting up, were only intensifying with every thrust of his cock. She had her fists wrapped around the ties tightly enough that she was sure her circulation was suffering.

"Untie me," Jamie pleaded between ragged sobs.

Chase never slowed his plunging thrusts, reaching up with one hand and deftly untying her right wrist, then shifting his weight to the other hand and releasing her left. As soon as each hand was free, Jamie clawed at his back, pawing at his sweat-slick skin, gripping his bulging biceps and pistoning hips and tensing buttocks. She smeared the sweat on his scalp, dragging his face down to hers in sloppy, desperate kisses, missing his mouth a few times and not caring. She wanted his skin, his sweat, his body. She clung to him, driving her hips into his madly now as she began to match his furious rhythm. She was panting wildly, each breath a loud moan.

Her climax had never retreated completely, and she was shuddering with aftershocks every few moments. Then, as he began to pump faster, Jamie felt the aftershocks morph and burgeon, turning into yet another orgasm. She clung to Chase's neck, her legs locked around his back, holding on to him as she rode out the orgasm, struggling for breath as the waves grew stronger, ripping through her like a tsunami.

The climax receded slightly but didn't dissipate completely. Chase shifted positions slightly, slowing his pace but still driving deep. He brought his knees beneath him, slid his palms beneath Jamie's ass, gripping her hips and lifting. She moved down the bed toward him and arched her back, lifting her hips to meet him, reaching back to grip the headboard with both hands. Chase held her hips up, plunging hard and deep. Jamie's voice rose in a sound that wasn't quite a scream, a high-pitched keen of rapture as his cock filled her deeper than she'd thought anyone could be. He drove in deep this way a few times, and then, against all sense, thrust shallowly, pivoting his body so the broad head of his cock struck her G-spot dead-on.

Less than thirty seconds later, Jamie came again, and this time she couldn't bear it, couldn't stand it, couldn't even ride it out. All she could do was release a guttural scream and rake her fingers over his shoulders.

Tears of raw overwhelmed emotion tracked down her cheeks, and she didn't bother to wipe them away.

Chase's movements grew rough and clumsy, and Jamie recognized the signs of his impending release. She planted her heels on the bed and met him thrust for frantic thrust. She moaned his name in his ear when he finally released her hips and collapsed forward onto her, grinding raggedly and arrhythmically, growling and groaning with every thrust.

"Chase, baby...oh, god...come for me." Jamie held the nape of his neck and the back of his head, her body wrapped around his. He came with a counterintuitively soft sigh, slamming his pulsating cock into her with almost brutal force. "Yes, yes! Hard, I love it like that, so hard."

Chase couldn't speak as he came. Jamie felt his hot seed hit her inner walls, and his thrusting became deep-driving insanity, frenzied and wild. His pelvis crushed her clit, and she felt another impossible orgasm wash over her, impossible, absurd, and spastically potent. She bit his shoulder, dug her fingers into his back, and pounded her core against him, their hipbones crashing like colliding tectonic plates, slow and unstoppably forceful thrusts.

All the while, liquid heat filled Jamie, wash after wash spurting from Chase into her cleft, and she took it all, clamping down on his throbbing cock with every ounce of power she had within her.

"Jamie...oh, god, *fuck*, I love you so goddamn much." Chase's voice was gravelly and ragged in her ear, his thrusts finally slowing, abating. "I love you...so much. You—god...you shatter me so wonderfully, Jamie."

He rolled with her so she was cradled against his chest. She was a dribbling mess, but she didn't care. Nothing mattered but closeness, the warmth of his huge hard body radiating like a furnace against her sensitive skin, his manhood softening and throbbing against her thigh, his palms skating softly over her shoulder, his fingers tangling in her sweaty curls...

Jamie fell asleep more contented than she knew how to understand. She felt full in her heart, in her soul, in her mind, beyond exhausted, wrung limp and sated to surfeit.

"Promise me this will never end," she whispered, her voice muzzy and heavy.

Chase threaded his fingers through hers. "I promise you this will never end. You and me...this is just the beginning."

"Please?" It was a mumbled reply, meant to be a thankful sigh of relief, coming out as something else.

Chase just tightened his grip on her and kissed her eyebrow, and she heard his breathing even out as sleep stole over her.

TWELVE

JAMIE FUMBLED FOR HER ringing cell phone. By the time she found it on her bedside table, it had stopped ringing. Figured. She struggled to a sitting position in her bed, wishing she could've stayed asleep for a bit longer. She'd driven from Chase's show in Milwaukee straight to Detroit, where she worked a nine-hour shift before finally going home. All this had been on barely four hours of sleep. She'd woken up at oh-dark-thirty to pee and had ended up pinned beneath Chase's hard body, his sleepy eyes tender and lustful. She couldn't—and didn't—say no to him, so she'd never gone back to sleep.

Now it was Tuesday morning—Jamie glanced at her phone and swore—okay, fine, Tuesday afternoon...and she was still feeling groggy and in need of sleep. She'd crashed hard when she got home, but it had been a broken and not entirely restful sleep. She'd kept partially waking and finding herself alone in bed.

Two nights with Chase, and I already miss him in my bed, Jamie thought. *I've got it bad.*

The voicemail notification beeped, and Jamie played the message. "Hey, hooker, it's me," Anna's voice said. "Haven't seen you in forever, and I miss your face. Call me. Or better yet, lunch at BD's at one? 'Kay, good. See you there."

Jamie leapt out of bed, swearing. It was twelve-twenty. Knowing Anna, she'd show up at Mongolian Bar-B-Q at one and expect Jamie to be there. Showering and dressing in record time, Jamie skipped makeup except for the basic blush, mascara, and lip gloss, and bolted out the door. As she expected, Anna was waiting with a diet Coke when Jamie showed up ten minutes late.

"There you are," Anna said, getting up to hug Jamie. "Wondered if you'd gotten my message."

"Yeah, sorry I'm late," Jamie said. "I had a bit of lie-in."

Anna laughed even as her face wrinkled in confused frown. "'A bit of a lie-in'? Starting to talk like Ian, are we?" Anna shook her head, chuckling. "Shall we carry on to the table and have a spot of lunch?" She said this with a terrible *faux*-British accent.

Jamie frowned. "Did I say that?"

"Yeah, you kind of did."

Jamie tilted her head back and groaned volubly. "I can't believe I actually said that. That was one of Ian's favorite phrases."

Anna cast a quizzical look at Jamie as they scooped uncooked chicken and vegetables into their bowls. "Was?"

Jamie bit her lip. She wasn't quite ready for that part of the conversation, but Anna knew her too well for Jamie to be able to dissemble for long. "Yeah, well…you know what I mean."

Anna scooped teriyaki sauce into a ramekin and set the dishes on the counter for the grill guy. "Maybe I don't." She dug her cell phone out of her pocket and tapped a message, then sent it and turned back to Jamie. "You're being purposefully vague, and I don't like it. Spill, sister."

Jamie watched the grillers show off with their grill-sword things, trying to come up with a suitable response that would still buy her time. In the end she just sighed. "How about I ignore all interrogative queries until after I've eaten?"

Anna frowned, shrugging. "Okay, guess I can handle that. But I get the feeling I'm not gonna like this very much, am I?"

Jamie couldn't answer that. She accepted her food with a smile for the sweaty but good-looking young guy behind the grill, tossing a couple dollar bills in the tip jar and banging the gong. Anna was true to her word, letting her eat in peace. When they'd both finished, Anna toyed with her chopsticks and leveled a serious look at Jamie.

"Okay. We've eaten. Now...*spill*." Anna stabbed Jamie's hand with the chopstick playfully. "Ian didn't knock you up, did he?"

Jamie sighed, half-laughing. "No." She took a deep breath. "Ian and I broke up about an hour after I got to Chicago, actually."

Anna's brow wrinkled. "Really? I thought things were going well. I was half-expecting you to tell me you were moving to Chicago."

Jamie shook her head. "It was never going well, Anna."

"What do you mean?"

"Ian...the whole thing with him. It was never going to work, and I knew it from the get-go."

"I don't understand. You seemed to like him. You were always talking about him whenever we hung out."

Jamie rolled her eyes. "Yeah, well...I was trying to convince myself everything was fine."

"So you broke up with Ian on Friday...it's Tuesday, and I know you work every Monday...so what happened Saturday and Sunday?"

"Actually, technically, he broke up with me, but I was gonna do it soon anyway."

Anna waved her hand dismissively. "Irrelevant. Where were you the rest of the weekend? What are you not telling me?"

"Um." Jamie tied a knot in the empty paper wrapper from her drinking straw, not looking at Anna. "Nothing?"

"Fuck you, hooker. Give me the truth."

"You can't handle the truth."

"Okay, *fine*, Tom Cruise." Anna scooted her chair back and prepared to stand up. "I'm going to the bathroom. If you can't talk to me, I get it. Or really, I don't, but I'm not gonna try to drag the truth out of you. You've either avoided the truth or outright lied to me every time we've talked for, like, months now. I'm getting sick of it." Anna left, her messy blonde braid hanging down her back, swaying as she walked.

Jamie put her face in her hands, groaning in despair. "This is gonna suck," she muttered to herself.

Anna came back and sat down, crossing her arms over her chest. "Last chance, Jay. Or we're fighting for real."

Jamie took a deep breath, shredding the straw wrapper between shaking fingers. "I ran into Chase after I left the restaurant where Ian broke up with me."

"Shit." Anna's eyes slid closed slowly. "I knew it. I *knew* it. You fucked him, didn't you?"

Jamie looked up sharply. "It wasn't just *fucking*, Anna."

"Whatever, Jamie. You slept with him. You had sex with him."

"It's not...it was more than that." She could barely manage a whisper. "I can't even explain to you how much has changed for me. It feels like...I don't know how to put it into words. It's hard to believe it was just a single weekend. Two days. Two days, but everything is different. *I'm* different. He changed me, Anna."

Anna drew a long breath and let it out slowly. "Yeah. He has a way of doing that, doesn't he?" She reached out and took Jamie's trembling hands in hers. "I'll bite my tongue as long as I can, but you have to talk to me."

Jamie nodded, pushing back the huge weight of emotion bearing down on her chest. "I'm in love with him, Anna. I have been since Vegas. I tried so hard, *so goddamn hard* to deny it. To pretend it wasn't true. I did. I swear to you, I didn't want this to happen, but it did. We both tore ourselves apart for months trying to act like this wasn't inevitable. Ian...he was just an attempt to be okay without Chase, and it never had a fucking chance in hell of working."

"And Chase? How does he feel?"

"He did basically the same thing. Hooked up with some girl from around here named Tess. He was in Chicago for a show, and she dumped him, pretty much at the same time as Ian dumped me. We were both hurting innocent people with this, Anna. Tess, Ian? Neither of them had any part of Chase or me. But now that Chase and I...happened...you're hurt. I don't know what to do."

"He loves you, huh?" Anna's voice was small and tight.

"Yeah."

Anna didn't answer for a long, long time. "Shit. I—shit. I don't know how to deal with this. It's not like he's my boyfriend and you went behind my back with him. I'm married to Jeff, and I wouldn't change that for the world, but...it's *Chase*. You know how hard that whole thing was for me."

Jamie half-shrugged, sniffling back a tear. "Yeah...I know. But...you don't know what I went through trying to act like I don't need Chase."

"No, I don't, because you weren't talking—"

"How could I talk to you about it? About him? You still care about him. I know you love Jeff with all your heart, but you can't sit there and tell me there's no part of you that doesn't wonder what could have been if you hadn't run away from him in New York. What was the right choice in this, Anna? I tried the right thing. I tried to walk away from him. I *did* walk away from him. So many times, I did, and it nearly broke me every time. That kiss in Vegas. It was one of those moments that define you, that change who you are, what you want in life..."

Anna sighed. "I know the feeling all too well."

"Every time I saw him just made it worse. It's not just an attraction. I don't know what to say. It's...*need*. I was completely exhausted last night, but I still couldn't sleep right because he wasn't there, and I'd only spent two days with him. It's like...I don't know...like he's inside me."

Anna stood up abruptly and walked out of the restaurant, wiping at her face. Jamie slumped forward, resting her head on her arms on the tabletop for a minute, then followed Anna out to her car. She slid into the passenger seat and rested her head on the seat back. Next to her, Anna had her forehead pressed to the steering wheel. Her shoulders shook.

After a while, Anna sat up and scrubbed her face. "I...I love Jeff. I don't want anyone else. He's...he's perfect for me. But goddammit, Jay. You're right. I do sometimes, in very pit of my heart, wonder sometimes. I ran before he had a chance to explain, and later I realized he probably hadn't done anything wrong. But by then it didn't matter, because I was in love with Jeff already."

"I know."

"But...how can I ever look at Chase without that little niggling worm of doubt popping up? How can I look at him and not see us—him and me? You're my best friend, Jay. I want to be able to ask you about things with your boyfriend. We're supposed to have dirty little secrets about our men together. I want to ask you...I mean, I know what Chase likes, and I'm guessing I can imagine how the weekend went, and—" Anna shuddered and ducked her head, "—But then I think of him and *you* in bed together, and I get sick. It's not jealousy, exactly. I don't know *what* it is, but it hurts, Jay. It hurts."

Jamie leaned across the console between them and hugged Anna. "I don't know, either. That's how I feel when I think about you and Chase together. I mean, like...he's *mine*. I don't know what I'm gonna do while he's on tour. I'm already going insane, and it's been less than twenty-four hours since I saw him. And sometimes you come up, and it's awkward. And I...I don't know, Anna. This is what's been tearing me apart about the whole situation. I love him so much. I've never been happier in my entire life than when I'm with him. Nothing else matters except being in his arms. But I have to live life and so does he, and then everything comes crashing back down around me and..." Jamie rested her forehead against Anna's shoulder. "Reality sucks."

Anna laughed through a sob. "Yeah, it does." She leaned her ear against Jamie's head. "Don't take this the wrong way, Jay, but—fuck you for falling in love with my ex." After a silent moment, Anna shoved Jamie away playfully. "It was pretty amazing, though, right?"

Jamie dragged in a deep breath and let it out with a shriek and whole-body freak out. "Anna, it was so far beyond incredible! I didn't know it could be like that. I didn't know..." She took a deep breath and tried again. "He took me places I didn't know the human body could go." She said this last part quietly, lending intensity to the statement.

Anna sighed, almost wistfully. "You two are perfect for each other." She picked at her thumbnail, keeping her gaze cast down. "I never said this to anyone, or even admitted it to myself out loud before now, but I kind of felt like he wanted things I didn't know how to give him. He was just so crazy and intense and...it was exciting and fun, but it was overwhelming sometimes. I think that's the largest reason I ran. Emotionally, yeah, there were things there I couldn't figure out how to face, but I think unconsciously I was a little overwhelmed by the things he wanted to do with me, *to* me."

Jamie rubbed her palms on her thighs. "Yeah, see, for me, that's exactly what I need. I've been so...closed off, numb...and just bored with sex, with men in general. Chase makes me feel alive. Like I've just been dreaming until now, and Chase is reality."

Anna giggled, a little hysterically. "This is a strange-ass conversation." She twisted the engagement ring and wedding band around her finger. "Jeff is exactly what I need. Being with him, making love to him is...it makes me feel cherished. He takes his time, he's so slow and sweet and thorough, and he can get a little freaky sometimes, but mainly, it's just...so completely what my soul and my heart and my body need." Jamie wasn't sure what to say to that, so she kept silent until Anna blew out a harsh breath and turned to Jamie. "I'm trying really hard to be cool about this. But...I'm upset. I'm confused. I'm hurt. I'm kinda angry, actually. I mean, I know this wasn't something you intentionally chose, so it may not be *fair* for me to be pissed off, but it's hard to ignore how I feel just because it's not 'fair.'" Anna used air quotes when she said the last word.

"I'm sorry, Anna. You have every right to be pissed at me. I get it. And yeah, I didn't ask for this, but...I can't—I don't know what to do. Just don't make me choose between you and him, please? I couldn't—couldn't do that. I love you, you're my best and oldest friend. But Chase? He's...I feel like he's my future."

"I'm not gonna make you choose, Jay. I wouldn't do that. But I need time. I need to talk to Jeff about this. Just...give me time." Anna stuck her key in the ignition but didn't turn it. "I'm not gonna lie,

Jay. The more I think about this, the harder it feels like it's gonna be, the first time we all get together."

"It's gonna be—"

"Impossible." Both women said the word simultaneously, and then laughed together.

The gaiety quickly faded, and Jay pushed the passenger door open. She got out and paused, bending down to look at Anna, her hands on the roof of the car. "I don't know what else to say besides I'm sorry, and thank you." Jamie felt like she'd said some version of that last phrase a thousand times in the last few days.

"Thank you?" Anna asked, her face screwing up with the tension of someone trying not to cry.

"For trying to understand. For being my friend anyway, despite this. I can't shake the feeling that I've betrayed you somehow. Unintentionally maybe, but still." Jamie felt her voice break.

Anna squeezed her gray eyes closed around stubborn tears. "BFFs, no matter what." She reached out her fist, and Jamie bumped it with hers. "Now go the hell away before you make me ugly-cry."

Jamie sniffed and laughed, then turned away without another word and drove home. On the way, she realized that, despite the number of times she'd apologized to Anna, her friend had never said it was okay.

Probably because it wasn't.

Anna might not have been actively in love with Chase, but old, dormant, and mostly forgotten feelings still had the potential to cause heartache.

Sitting at home, catching up on her DVR'd episodes of *Teen Mom 2*, Jamie found herself wishing she could quit her job and just follow Chase on his tour. Or fly out to wherever he was for each show and be with him that way. Or...anything other than sit at home missing him, jealous of the fans who got so much of his time and attention.

She Googled his tour dates, switched shifts around with the other assistant manager at work, and bought a plane ticket to St. Louis, where Six Foot Tall was performing next. The ticket nearly cleaned out her savings, but she'd just paid rent, and all of her other bills were up to date. Everything else could wait.

THIRTEEN

CHASE FINISHED HIS LAST ENCORE NUMBER and stepped off the stage, the screaming of thousands of fans bolstering him despite his exhaustion. The band's tour schedule was brutal. The last several weeks had been a whirlwind of nonstop shows back to back, sometimes with a few days in between. Demand for Six Foot Tall was growing exponentially, and there was talk of the band headlining a show in Detroit sometime soon. Jamie had met him for almost every show, Chase paying for her airfare and hotel stays. Their relationship had deepened over the last two months, but it was still very much like a long-distance relationship. They spent more time talking on the phone or texting than they did in person, and they rarely had more than one night together in a row. Chase needed a break. He needed a few consecutive days spent not on stage, not warming up or writing new material or traveling. He needed private downtime with Jamie, without the specter of the next show looming, cutting short their time together. Jamie understood, of course, and never complained. She came to every show she could, and was traveling almost as much as he was, flying all over the country to meet him. Chase's credit card was racking up serious frequent flier miles.

That night's show was one of the rare and blessed dates that was followed by three days in a row off. He'd already booked a suite for the two nights he had with Jamie. They were in Phoenix, Arizona, and the next show was some tiny club somewhere in New Mexico, an unplugged acoustic set. He accepted a towel from the stagehand and wiped his face and head with it, searching the backstage area for Jamie's wild red curls. There she was, facing into a darkened corner, her phone pressed to her ear, finger plugging the other. He sidled up behind her, wrapped his arms around her waist, and kissed her neck while she finished her phone call.

She hung up and stuck the phone in her purse, then turned in his arms and met his lips with hers. "Hey, baby. Great show!"

Chase smiled into her lips. "Thanks. Who was that you were talking to?"

She shrugged. "Work call. The M.O.D. messed up the inventory order, and I had help her unfuck it."

"Gotcha. So, ready for three days and two nights alone with me?"

"God, am I ever," Jamie said. "Are we staying here in Phoenix?"

"Yep. I have a suite booked. I'll meet the guys at the next show in New Mexico."

"And you're in L.A. after that?"

Chase nodded and pulled her into a walk out of the building where the limo rented by the label was waiting. "That's gonna be a huge show. Biggest yet, I think. If that one goes well, our agent says we might get a headliner billing at the Palace."

Jamie lit up, gripping his arm in excitement. "Really? That would be so huge! Headlining in your hometown? I bet it would sell out."

Chase laughed. "Yeah, probably not, but nice try. We're a long way from selling out the Palace, baby."

Jamie shoved him playfully. "You so would. I've heard people talking about you guys. You're getting a lot of radio play on the WRIF and 89X."

Chase glanced at her. "Really? Jim told us we've been getting more air time, but I guess it didn't quite register what that meant." He handed her into the limo and slid in next to her. "It's kind of weird. For as much as I'm all over the country, I still feel isolated from reality in a way. We're playing in front of sold-out crowds, but they're there to see the other bands as much as us, if not more so. We play, and we keep going. We're getting paid a shitload of money, but it's not really *real* most of the time, you know? Someone tells you, 'You're getting a lot of radio play,' and you're all like, 'Oh, that's great,' or whatever, but it doesn't *mean* anything most of the time. It's not like I'm in those cities hearing our songs on the radio, you know? Right now, it feels like the whole word is broken up into the bus, the stage, and you, and nothing else even exists except in theory."

Jamie turned on the limo seat and draped her legs over his, curling her arms around his neck. "You're building a brand, baby. A name. Recognition. It'll all pay off. It already is paying off. People are starting to know who you are, on a household level." She nuzzled her face into his throat. "And now none of that matters."

"No?" Chase asked, tangling his fingers in her hair.

"Nope. For the next few days, you're mine. You're not a rock star as of this moment. You're just my Chase."

He sighed into her hair. "Your Chase. Perfect."

The limo dropped them off at the hotel, where they ordered room service and drank two bottles of expensive white wine. They sat side by side on the bed, finishing the last of the second bottle.

"How long can you keep this up, Jay?" Chase asked, apropos of nothing.

Jamie tilted her head to rest it against his shoulder, swirling the wine at the bottom of her glass. "I don't know. Like you said, my life feels compartmentalized into work, airports, your shows, and hotels. I love traveling, honestly, but...it *is* getting exhausting. I'd give anything to spend a week on a beach with you." She tossed back the last of her wine and set the glass aside before turning to straddle Chase. "I'll do this as long as necessary. As long as this is your life, your career, this is how I'll see you."

"Do you even see your friends anymore?"

Jamie shrugged. "I have lunch with Anna when I'm back in Detroit. I went out with Lane and his partner Matty the other day. The rest of the people I called my friends? They weren't really friends. They were drinking buddies. I only drink with you now. They don't call me or try to catch up. The only people who keep up with my coming and going anymore are Lane and Anna, so they're really all that matter."

"Funny how that happens, huh? When you're gone all the time, the fake friends have a way of getting culled out." Chase slipped his hands beneath her shirt to run his palms on the hot skin of her back. "It works for me, though. The guys are my friends. The roadies and the driver, the security guys, they're friends, too. Jim, our agent. You. That's about it."

"Who else do you need, really?"

Chase kissed the base of her throat. "Besides you and the band? No one. Who else is there?"

Jamie reached down and peeled her shirt off, her curls bouncing down to hang around her shoulders. She'd let it grow recently, and it was now almost to mid-back. Chase loved her hair, loved to hold on to it, run his fingers through it, grip it in his fist as he made love to her.

He'd been planning this night for a while. He'd hinted at what he wanted to do with her, and she'd not demurred. He skimmed his hands over her shoulders, across the lace of her bra, feeling the hard beads of her nipples, then reached behind her to unhook her bra. He felt his cock twitch and harden as her heavy breasts fell free. He took them in his hands, cupping them, kneading the silky flesh, grazing his thumb across her nipples. He flicked a nipple with his tongue, a featherlight touch, and Jamie gasped sharply, arching her back.

She shifted her weight backward and unsnapped his pants, unzipped them, and gripped the waistband of his pants and boxer-briefs, tugging them down. Chase lifted his hips, and she slid the garments down to his knees, where he toed them off and kicked them aside. She peeled his shirt over his head, and then shimmied down his body, her soft breasts brushing his skin. All thoughts left his mind as she took his erection in her mouth. She worked her jeans and panties off while she licked and kissed his cock, and then they were both naked together. He let her work his cock for a second, and then drew her up so her face was level with his.

"I have plans for you," he told her.

"Oh, yeah?" Her voice was low and sultry, and her eyes hooded.

She rolled over and lay on her back, posing for him. Her palms skittered over her breasts before moving down to cup her sex, teasing and inviting. "What kind of plans?"

Chase hopped off the bed and dug in a pocket of his suitcase, producing a bottle of lubricant and couple of condoms. "Plans that involve this."

Jamie's eyes widened and her nostrils flared, her tongue running over her bottom lip. "Oh. Oh, god. Okay." She sat up, then moved to her hands and knees.

Chase laughed, crawling across the bed toward her. "Eager, are we?" He curled his hand around her hips and drew her to him, so his cock slipped, upright, between the firm, soft cheeks of her ass.

She writhed into him.

"Yes…" she breathed. "So eager. You've been teasing me about this for so long."

Chase sucked in a hard breath, pulling his hips away to caress her ass with his palms, sinking back on his haunches behind her. "It's not teasing. It's… getting you ready for it."

"I'm ready." Jamie watched him over her shoulder, biting her lip.

"Not just yet," Chase said. He skated his hand over her spine, then around her ribs to cup a breast, working his other hand between her legs to trace her damp heat with one finger. "First, I need this. I need to taste you. Feel you come. I'm so hard for you, I couldn't last long enough to get deep enough, slow enough in your tight little asshole."

He fingered her clit, feeling her juices begin to flow. He circled the sensitive nub, tweaking a nipple as he did so, and within minutes Jamie was quivering and rocking back into his hand, near to orgasm. Before she came, she reached behind herself and found his cock, guided him into her silky wet folds. He was throbbing already and had to hold back after only a few slow strokes. She began to thrust back into him, and the feel of her ass pushing against him brought him to a boiling point all too quickly. He slowed then, clenching his teeth and forcing himself down. He reached for the lubricant, squirted some onto his fingers and slathered it against Jamie's tight anus, massaging at first with one finger. She moaned in ecstatic relief as he nudged his finger in to the first knuckle, then began to whimper when he worked a second finger in, liberally working her entrance with lube.

"Fuck me, Chase. I want it. Fuck me in the ass."

"Not yet, baby," Chase gasped. "Come for me first."

He began to stroke into her pussy, sliding his fingers in and out of her ass gently, in sync with his thrusts. She began to buck hard against him, and Chase had to focus all his strength in holding back his own orgasm as she let go, whimpering softly into the blanket as she climaxed.

He pulled out of her folds then, and reached for the condom. Jamie took it from him, ripped it open, and handed the roll to him. He slid the latex over his cock, gritting his teeth, and then smeared himself with lube.

Jamie craned her neck to watch him. "Now, Chase? Please?"

Chase pulled his fingers out of her slowly, and then settled the tip of his cock against her asshole. "God, yes. Now, my love." He hesitated, though.

Jamie rolled her hips, inviting him. "What is it?"

Chase held her hip in one hand, meeting her gaze. "This is both of our first time for this."

Jamie quirked an eyebrow. "Really? I didn't realize it was yours, too."

"It is. This is something we're doing together."

Jamie swiveled her hips into groin. "I'm ready, love." She bit her lip, her hair hanging down to one side, bouncing lightly as she moved. "I need you inside me, baby. I want you in my ass."

Chase searched her eyes for hesitation, trepidation. All he saw was love and desire.

Jamie watched Chase grip his shaft by the base and gently probe her anus. She forced herself to relax, even though her belly was fluttering with nerves. She wanted this with him. Especially now that she knew it was his first time doing this, too. Lust burned through her, dark and dirty. His fingers inside her back there were always intense, every time. She never came as hard as when he was knuckle-deep in her ass, and she loved the feeling. Now he was finally about to put his cock inside her, after weeks of promising.

She admitted, deep down, to being a little afraid. He was huge, and that entrance was small.

She felt a hint of pressure, and tried not to tense. His breathing was ragged, as was hers. A bit more pressure, and then the now-familiar feeling of tightness and penetration and stabbing thrill, shooting pleasure. This was more, though, so much more. She twisted her head back to look at Chase. He had his head thrown back, his spine straight, his thick, beautiful cock held in one hand,

his other on her hip, steadying her. His eyes were
closed tight, sweat streaking his scalp and forehead. His muscles were straining, and she knew he
was holding back. He nudged in a little farther, and
Jamie felt a gasp escape at the pulsing invasion. She
was stretched wide, so wide. It hurt, just a little,
but the pain was laced with a lovely thrill, delicious
desire, and hot need.

Jamie reached forward and jerked the pillows
toward her, stuffed them beneath her belly, propping herself on one elbow. With her other hand,
she touched herself, a gentle circling of her clit
at first. She moaned, and Chase slid in another
inch, prompting the moan into a loud groan. He
growled, tensing, freezing. She felt herself adjusting, loosening. Her fingers pulled pleasure from
her core and sent it out in hot waves, turning the
stretching into filthy need.

"More, Chase." She barely recognized the ani-
mal growl of her own voice.

He gave her more, slowly. She moved her fingers faster, now, in the confident speed of a woman
touching herself, the way only a woman can pleasure herself. Chase let go of his shaft and gripped
both hips, then bent slightly over her and tweaked
a nipple, once, and it was enough to bring Jamie
nearly to the edge. Chase thrust again, and she felt
him to be all the way in then. He held still for a

moment, gathering himself and giving her time to finish adjusting.

Then he drew back with aching slowness, and Jamie felt a lightning bolt shoot through her, like an orgasm multiplied by a thousand. She shrieked, then bit the comforter, stifling her building scream. Her mouth went wide, but no sound came out.

Chase reached the apex of his pullout, hesitated, then began the slow plunge in. A squeak scraped out of her throat, and Chase took that as encouragement to let the thrust in morph into an immediate withdrawal.

Jamie needed him to move faster. Each slide was an agony of ecstasy, and if only he would give her more, faster, she knew it would get better. Her mind was so scrambled by need, she couldn't get words out of her mouth. She tried to speak, she really did, but all that emerged was a whimper. He plunged in, faster now. He pulled out, paused, and Jamie felt the cold touch of lubricant, and then he stroked in again, incrementally harder. Jamie keened, a high-pitched sound from the back of her throat, and pushed back into him as he thrust in.

"Oh, god, Jamie. Oh, god, you're so tight. So... so fucking tight," Chase growled.

His fingers dug into her hips and began to tug her back into his thrusts. Jamie let herself moan, then felt a scream building again. The pressure inside her was a mountain, heavy and overwhelming, huge and sun-hot, fire in her belly, lava in her core. She shook all over, and now she was moving with him.

Jamie shoved the pillows away, stretched her arms in front of her and let go, gave in to need. She rocked into his plunging shaft, a scream bubbling up. His hand slid up her spine, his touch achingly gentle in counterpoint to his rampaging thrusts. Brushing over her shoulders, he tangled his fingers in her thick copper curls, caressing and massaging at first, and then he gripped a fistful and tugged her backward, holding close to her scalp and jerking in time with his thrusts, his other hand still clenching the flesh of her hip. Chase was growling now, wordless and primal, and Jamie matched his feral sounds, gasping and grunting as he slammed into her ass.

"Chase…" His name grated past her lips, dragging more words with it. "Fuck me hard, Chase. Fuck my ass so hard…"

"Jamie, *fuck*, Jay. I love you." He pulled her back by the hips, hard, giving her a slamming thrust, flesh slapping against flesh, and a scream ripped from Jamie's trembling lips.

The sound of her scream set Chase free, unleashed him. He drove in without restraint now, and Jamie rocked forward as he pulled back, slammed her ass into his body on the in-thrust, crying out as the tensing, shaking, quivering muscles of her buttocks crashed into him.

The pressure was an inferno now, volcanic heat, titanic and unstoppable. She felt the crest rising within her and let her front half go limp on the bed, half-supported one arm, reaching down with the other to touch herself once more.

Now the touch of her fingers on her throbbing clit was nearly too much, an overwhelming erotic shock to her shattering system. She was splitting apart, bursting at the seams. Screams were ripping from her throat in staccato ululations, peaking as he plunged deep, hard, and fast, quieting as he drew back. He was roaring nonstop now, a leonine rumble as he began to pump with manic speed and crushing force, and as hard as he was fucking her, Jamie needed more, craved more, lifting up with her core and thighs and slamming down to meet his thrusts.

Lust bled into love, need and desire bled into starvation-like hunger for the way he filled her and stretched her with every thrust. She felt tears squeezing from her eyes, salt drops of overwhelmed ecstasy, pressure of her impending climax leaking from her tear ducts.

"Jay...I'm gonna come..." Chase's voice was rough and thick.

She couldn't summon coherency. "Yes...yes!" That was all the sense she could make as she rocked into his thrusts, her fingers a blur on her clit, teeth clamped on her lip so hard she tasted blood.

Chase lost his rhythm, thrusts stuttering and frantic. He drew back, paused, and then slammed home hard enough that Jamie was bumped forward off-balance, then jerked back by his hands at her hips. She let him control her body, acquiescing willingly to his primality, his dominating power exactly what she wanted. He made a sound in his throat, and she felt his cock pulse. She came in that instant, screaming louder than she ever had, not caring who heard. The pressure was a tsunami roaring through her, magma rushing through her core, wave after wave clenching her muscles around his cock.

He pulled back and then rammed into her again, throwing her forward, a sustained growl coming from his chest. She was pulled back again and felt another wave of orgasm rolling over her as he blasted into her ass a third time, and this one had them both screaming, his voice even louder than hers.

She felt him thrust once more, softer now, and then a last, soft fluttering push, and then he was still. Jamie couldn't support her weight, not with arms or legs. She was still impaled by him, held up by his hands. She sobbed ragged breaths, whimpering.

"Holy…fuck," Chase gasped.

"Love you…so much," Jamie managed.

She cried out when he began to draw out. He was achingly tender as he withdrew, and she wanted to cry out again when he left the bed and stumbled to the bathroom to toss out the condom and wash his hands. She murmured in pleasure when his heat and weight settled behind her, spooning her. She turned in his arms, and he cradled her close, holding tight for long minutes. Her lips turned up, touched his, and then she let tears of…everything… fall as she lost herself in his kiss.

His hands roamed her back, her hip, her ass, her thigh. She bit his lip when he pulled back, sighing as his fingers tangled in her sweaty curls.

"Did I hurt you?" Chase mumbled.

Jamie took his face in her hands, fixed her eyes on his hesitant brown gaze. "*No*, love. No." She kissed him with all the affection and tenderness she had. "You were perfect. So incredible. I can't even describe what I just experienced. It wasn't just an orgasm, it was…a super-gasm."

"Good. I kinda lost control." He sighed in relief. "I was worried I'd hurt you."

Jamie reached down and curled her fingers around his softened cock, knowing his refractory period was almost over already. "I love that you lost control. *Love* it." She bit his chin, then kissed his shoulder, squeezing his cock in soft pulses, feeling him harden. "This time, though, I want it slow and gentle and soft. I want to ride you slowly. I'm gonna ride you until you come apart beneath me."

Chase rumbled in laughter, leaving his fingers threaded in her hair, letting her touch him. "Damn, girl. You're insatiable."

"Complaining?" Jamie asked, caressing him into full erection.

"God..hell, no. I love that about you. I love that you initiate as much as I do." Chase tilted so he was on his back, drawing Jamie on top of him. She straddled him low on his thighs, leaning down over him so her breasts hung down to brush his chest. She kissed him, slowly at first, then losing herself in his mouth, the wonder of his hands on her skin. She sighed into the kiss as he thumbed her nipples into taut beads. She gasped when he shifted his hips so his pelvis applied pressure to her clit, which drove her nearly over the edge from the very start.

Jamie arched her body away from his, fisting his rigid cock slowly and gently, then lifted up on her knees and pulled his shaft back toward her. He stilled, her breasts cupped in his palms, waiting. Jamie knelt above him with his crown poised at her nether lips. Her mouth was slightly open, her breath coming in shallow puffs, her gaze locked on Chase's. One hand propped her weight up on his chest, the other gripped his shaft at the base. His hands tensed, then relaxed, began roaming her body, sliding over her spine, clutching her hips briefly, grazing her face and tracing the line of her throat. She waited, waited, the very tip of him nestled between her labia. When his fingers darted down between their bodies to circle and carve and caress her clit, Jamie sank down on his thick length, abrupt and swift, without warning or preparation, moaning on an exhale as he filled her channel. She settled both hands on his shoulders, holding herself still at full impalement, drawing deep breaths, meeting his gaze with unrelenting vulnerability.

She was lost to this man. She'd been telling the truth when she promised him she'd meet him at every show she could for as long as it took. Nothing mattered but him. She shifted her hips back and forth, settling him deeper, feeling so full of him, physically and emotionally, and wishing she could be even more filled by him, wishing she could drown in him, hold all of him within her body, let his essence merge with hers.

Chase groaned, fluttering his hips in restrained thrusts, wanting to plunge up into her but holding back, relinquishing control to her. Jamie sat back, balancing on her shins, stretching his cock away from his body. He moaned, wincing as she pulled him as far away as he could go. He spread his palms on her thighs, fingers digging into the firm muscle and soft flesh. Jamie rose up with her thigh muscles, pulling him nearly out but not relaxing the stretching of his cock. She sank down and rose up once more, then began a slow rolling rhythm with her hips, rocking her core back and forth over his slick, solid shaft. He moaned continuously as she rode him, clutching her thighs and rocking into her.

Jamie kept the pace slow and soft, balancing above him, her eyes locked on his, her hands resting on his on her thighs. Chase traced up her torso with one hand, cupped her full breast, and tweaked the nipple, causing her to gasp in pleasure. His other hand delved down between her thighs to where their bodies joined, one long finger lazily caressing her clit. Jamie began to pulse above him faster as he fingered her closer to climax, and she felt his stretched, strained cock begin to throb, saw the tension in the lines of his face and the veins in his neck. A crushing pressure ballooned into life within her, centered on her core, and it only built with every stroke of his fingers, every throbbing plunge of his thick shaft inside her soft, sex-slick slit. She was breathless already, and when she came, it was with a gasping, keening cry, arching backward. She clutched her breasts, one hand resting over Chase's, encouraging his caressing grasp. She rolled and rocked on his body, but still she didn't relax forward.

"Jamie...I can't—can't come like this. I'm—pulled back too far," Chase said, panting.

She smiled wickedly, pinching her own nipple and sliding up and down his cock slowly, torturing him, feeling his need for release. "I know, baby," she whispered, bending forward while keeping her hips tilted back. "You're not going to come until I'm ready to let you."

Chase arched and humped up, seeking relief, but Jamie followed his movements, keeping him stretched far enough to prevent him from coming. He groaned and grunted, arching into Jamie's still-slow rhythm. His eyes squeezed shut and sweat streamed down his forehead, his breath coming in harsh pants, his fingers fisting in the sheets at his sides. All was forgotten but for his need for release. Jamie watched him carefully, measuring his desperation.

As she sinuously impaled herself on his shaft, she felt yet another climax burgeoning inside her, and she pressed two fingers to her aching, hyper-sensitive nub, skyrocketing the pressure into sudden supernova heat. Her other hand went to her breast, rolling her nipple between her fingers, hard, just this side of painful, and she began to slide on his cock with increasing speed. Urgency filled her, frenzy overtook her. This climax would be intense, she knew. The pressure was unbearable, fire in her belly, lava in her veins. She held it back, slowing her pace on Chase's body, letting the heat and pressure build yet more.

"Jay...please...*fuck*, I'm dying. I'm gonna explode." Chase's eyes were feral slits in his face, his voice a rasping growl like a rockslide.

"You wanna come, baby?" Jamie whispered the words, pleased with how sultry she sounded, even to herself. "You wanna come inside my pussy?"

"Fuck, yes. I need it. Let me go, please. *Please.*"

Jamie tilted her hips even farther back until Chase cursed out loud, and then she relaxed the tension slightly, ever so gently. "Beg me," she whispered, each word a breathy moan.

Chase laughed. "I *am* begging you. Please let me come. I need it. I need you."

"You have me," she said.

"Promise?" His eyes were wide now, brown pools of fire locked on her.

"Yes, Chase. I promise." Jamie tilted and slid up his cock so the thick shaft pulling wet against her clit shot lightning through her core; then, feeling the climax crest inside her, she paused at the apex, his crown between her lips. "I love you. Forever."

"Forever." He tensed, still, frozen, waiting. "I love you."

"Come with me." Jamie fell forward on the last word, slicing her core down around his cock in frantic rhythm.

"Oh, fuck, oh, fuck, oh...*fuck*!" Chase thrashed into her wildly, and she felt his seed spread through her in a flood of wet heat.

She bit his shoulder, meeting him thrust for frenzied thrust, her body flush against his, only their hips moving as they climaxed together.

Chase's arms were steel bands around her back, one hand fisted in her hair at her neck, the other curled around her waist, holding her tight against him as he crashed into her core, spurting deep with every thrust, filling her, filling her. She wept against him, overcome by physical sensation and emotional flood tide, love for Chase pounding through her in place of blood, need for all of him firing in place of synapses. She sobbed, heaving in the rhythm of their frantic, pounding pace. She felt her body clench around him, felt her womb contract and her muscles clamp and her core clench.

She felt her her heart expand, and she knew if she hadn't been already, she was irrevocably *his*.

After a timeless eternity of mutual climax, they went still, Jamie collapsed on top of him, still impaled by him, filled by him. His breath huffed in her hair, his fingers toying with tangled curls, tracing her skin, the lines of her hips.

Neither spoke as sleep stole over them. Jamie eventually shifted so he slipped out of her folds, and she slid off him and curled into his arms, more contented than she'd ever been. It seemed every night she spent with him saw her more full of his presence, more contented with life, with love.

She wondered muzzily how she could find any further happiness, how she could be any more wonderfully full of Chase.

FOURTEEN

CHASE TRIED TO CALM HIS NERVES, tried to force himself into relaxing. It didn't work. He was uneasy, unexplainably anxious. Well, his anxiety was partially explainable: Six Foot Tall was headlining at the Palace of Auburn Hills that night. It was their first headliner venue, and it was their hometown. It was also nearly sold out. The guys were amped, and so was Chase, but the other source of his nerves was less pleasant.

Jamie had been off lately. Just...distracted, almost distant. Snappish, at times. He'd asked her if anything was bothering her on a number of occasions, but she always denied it.

Matters weren't helped by the fact that she'd had the other assistant manager at her work quit, leaving her to cover most of the shifts on her own. She'd only been able to get away to see him twice in the last two months, and most of the time he tried calling her she could only talk for a second, or was so tired she fell asleep while talking. He'd been busy, too, of course. They'd done an interview in *Revolver*, played on Conan O'Brien's show, as well as their usual aggressive tour schedule.

But none of that mattered to Chase if something was wrong with Jamie.

He sat backstage at the Palace, watching the seats fill up, plucking strings on his guitar. He'd played the guitar most of his life, in a hobby sort of way. He was a singer more than anything, but if he got a few minutes of downtime before shows or on the bus between venues he would pull out his old acoustic six-string and play. He wrote most of Six Foot Tall's songs that way, although he'd never played the guitar on stage for the fans. Kyle, the guitarist, was talented enough for six people, so there was never any reason for Chase to play on stage.

This time around, he was working on a song, but not one for the band. He'd written the lyrics over the last couple of weeks, tweaking them here and there until they were perfect. Now he was putting them to music, and he was almost done putting the finishing touches to the melody. He wasn't sure when he would sing the song, since it was a special piece he'd written for Jamie, and their relationship seemed strained as of late.

He glanced back down at the black-and-white composition book he wrote his lyrics in, made a note, changing a chord. He soon lost himself in the song, and didn't emerge again until he heard someone approaching from behind him. He closed the notebook just as he felt Jamie's arms slip around his neck, and her lips touched his jaw. He reached up over his head and pulled her down for an upside-down kiss. Jamie moved around his body without breaking the kiss, sitting on his legs facing him, and the kiss deepened.

His body responded immediately, thickening against the button fly of his leather pants. Jamie clearly felt his response, shifting on his lap to rub her core against him. He moaned into the kiss, and wished they were alone.

"God, I missed you," Jamie whispered against his lips.

He sighed in relief. "I've missed you, too," he said. "So much. I really love this kind of hello."

Jamie smiled, her lips tightening and curving against his. "Want to go somewhere more private for an even better hello?"

"The bus is empty," he said. "The guys are out to dinner."

"Let's go." Jamie stood up and pulled him up by his hands.

He shrugged his coat on and led her to the tour bus, into his room, locking the door behind them. When he turned around from locking the door, Jamie already had her coat, shirt, and pants off and was clawing at his zipper. He let her strip him naked, and then he unhooked her bra and slid down her panties while she stroked his cock with her fist. Before he could stop her, Jamie had dropped to her knees and had taken his cock between her soft, perfect lips, running her skilled tongue around his tip, caressing his base with her hand and his balls with the other. He let her take him deep a few times, and then when he felt himself rising too fast, he reached down and lifted her up by the arms.

"Enough," he growled. "I need to be inside you. Now."

"Then take me," she breathed.

He kissed her, reaching down between their bodies to stroke her silky, wet folds with his fingers. She was juicy and dripping and incredible, ready for him. He pushed her backward onto the bed, positioned her at the edge of the bed with her legs over his shoulders as he knelt between her thick, powerful, perfect thighs. He felt his cock twitch as she gasped when he lapped at her sex, then nearly came when she whimpered again. He licked and flicked her into a frenzy, curling his fingers inside her channel in a "come here" gesture, and she obeyed, coming immediately, arching up off the bed and keening as she fell apart under his mouth. At the crest of her climax, Chase rolled Jamie onto her stomach and plunged into her, fisting his hand in her wild, lovely red curls, loose like he loved her hair. She moaned and rocked back into him, humping her back and pushing hard against him.

"Fuck, Jamie. You feel so good."

"Oh, god, Chase. Fuck me hard. I need it. I need you." She settled onto the bed, rising up on her tiptoes and falling down as he thrust up. "Come inside me. Right now. Don't wait."

Chase couldn't help but obey her command, pumping hard, once, twice, a third time, then found his release buried deep inside her, watching sweat bead on her spine. She crawled away from him, up onto the bed, and rolled to her back. He stood panting, slumped forward, breathless and still shuddering with the aftershocks. Jamie spread her thighs apart and held her hands out for him. He slid up her body, his still-hard cock pushing easily back into her wet folds. He kissed her lips, one hand planted on the bed next to her face, the other cupping her cheek.

He slipped his tongue between her teeth, sighed in his throat when her feet hooked around his waist. He needed her again, and soon. His hand found her breast, cupped and hefted its weight. He thumbed her nipple, then pinched it.

"Ow, not so hard," Jamie said. "My nipples are sensitive."

He gentled his touch but found himself wondering at her complaint. She'd never said anything like that before. Usually she liked it when he pinched her nipples, and he was always careful not to cross the line into real pain. He knew he hadn't pinched her too hard. He went back to kneading and caressing her breast as he kissed her, beginning a subtle shifting of his hips, testing his hardness. She tensed her vaginal muscles around him, and he felt himself hardening. Her breasts seemed slightly heavier, he thought. He looked at her, took in her beautiful face and lush body.

They definitely seemed bigger. Not that he minded. He caressed her body, stroking her face and sides and belly, and then, his palm pressing over her stomach, he found himself wondering if her belly seemed firmer, harder beneath the padding of silky flesh. He returned his attention to her breasts, and this time Jamie pulled away from his kiss.

"What?" she asked. "Is something wrong with my boobs?"

He shook his head. "No. They just seem a little bigger than normal. I like it."

Jamie froze, her vivid green eyes searching him. "Are they? I've been really busy lately, so I haven't been working out as much. I might have gained a little weight."

"That wasn't what I—you're beautiful, baby. Perfect. I love your body, love your big breasts and perfect hips and amazing ass."

She smiled, but it seemed forced. "Thanks, babe." She shifted her hips and curled her arms around his neck. "Make love to me."

He pushed aside his thoughts and stroked into her. "I love you, Jamie."

She pressed her lips against his shoulder and her body shook, almost as if she was crying. She spoke with her face in his neck, meeting his soft and steady thrusts. "I love you, Chase. So much." She pulled away, and her eyes were wet. "You love me forever? No matter what?"

He frowned, slowing, but she ran her hands down to his ass and pulled him against her, encouraging his faster pace. "Of course. No matter what. Always." He felt himself rising to climax, and Jamie's harsh breath and frantic hips told him she was close, too. "What's wrong?"

She shook her head. "Nothing. Nothing." She clawed her hands into his ass and jerked at him, as if she needed him closer. "Just make love to me. Don't stop...please...never stop."

He pressed himself hard against her, his base crushing her clit, rolling deep into her. "Never... I'll never stop. I promise. God, Jamie...come with me."

"Yes! God, Chase." She whimpered, buried her face against his neck once more, and held him more tightly than she'd ever done before.

He burst into her, filling her with his seed, thrusting hard several times, feeling her walls clench around him, her legs tense against his thighs, her fingers digging into his ass. She was sobbing, and he knew something was wrong.

He took several deep breaths, then pulled out. "Jamie, baby, what is it? And don't say 'nothing.'"

She shook her head.

"Honey, talk to me."

"I'm fine, Chase."

He pulled her over, cradled her against him. "Bullshit, Jay. Something's up."

She sighed deeply. "I don't want to talk about it right now."

"Are you okay?" He put his fingers to her chin and tilted her face up so he could search her jade eyes. "Are *we* okay?"

Her eyes wavered wetly, jumping from side to side as she gazed at him. "Yes, oh, god, yes. It's nothing like that. I'm not about to break up with you or anything like that."

He sighed in relief. "Thank god." He glanced back down at her. "Don't put it off till after the show, if that's your plan."

She took his face in her hands and kissed him deeply. "That's not it. I promise you, I vow on my soul that's not it."

"But there's something you're not telling me."
It wasn't a question.

She ducked her face then. "Yes, baby. But just
trust me, okay? We'll talk after you perform. Please
don't worry, okay? It's fine. We're fine. I'm fine.
We're all all right."

"You know that's just gonna drive me crazy
now, right?" He pulled her against his chest to hide
his frustration. "I'm gonna be wondering what's
going on."

"Just try to forget it for now, okay? If it was
something urgent, you know I'd tell you."

He sighed. "Okay. Fine. But we're going out
alone after, and we're talking."

"Absolutely."

They were silent then, Jamie ruminating on
whatever was on her mind, and Chase going in circles in his head trying to figure out what it could be.

He dozed with her in his arms, and a thought
floated through the back of his head, an idea.

No, he thought. *That's not it. It can't be.* He
held her close, breathing in the familiar scent of her
shampoo and her body lotion and the musk of sex.
But if it was?

He tried to honestly consider the possibility
running through him.

If it was that, I'd be happy. Among other things.

An unknowable amount of time later, he heard
a knock on the door. "Chase, dude," came Gage's

voice from the other side. "We gotta be onstage to warm up."

"Coming," he rumbled.

Jamie stirred in his arms. "Gotta go already?" she asked sleepily.

"Yeah. You stay here for a while."

She pursed her lips for a kiss, and he gave her one, slow and deep and passionate. "Okay, baby. I'll see you up there. Love you." Jamie pushed his shoulder to get him moving.

Chase forced himself out of bed and got dressed, knowing if he didn't, he'd get lost in her, lost in the kiss, lost in a third round of lovemaking. He slipped out the door with his boots, which he didn't remember taking off in the first place, and glanced back at her. She was dozing with one hand draped over her stomach.

He paused, watching her sleep, wondering.

Jamie woke up alone in the bed on the tour bus. She stretched lazily, listening to the thump of the distant bass and drums of the opening acts. She crawled out of bed and stepped into her panties, then hooked her bra under her breasts, spun it around and slipped the straps on, tucking her breasts into the cups. She put her pants on, but left them unzipped and unbuttoned. There was a mirror on the back of the door, and she examined herself in it, turning sideways to look at herself in profile.

She wondered if he'd noticed the changes in her. Probably. He was observant like that. She ran her hands over her belly—still flat, thank god—then hefted her breasts. He'd obviously noticed her breasts, but he might've bought her story about gaining weight. Which she had, just not for the reasons she'd given him. She'd been working out more assiduously than ever, taking up yoga with a vengeance.

She wasn't ready to tell him yet. She knew how important this performance was to him, and she wanted him to put his whole attention on the show. If she told him, he'd be too upset to focus. It was why she hadn't said anything yet. He was consumed with interviews and TV appearances, show after show. Obviously she couldn't tell him via text, and she hadn't been a hundred-percent sure when she'd seen him the last couple of times.

She was sure now, of course. Doctor-verified sure. Nerves and fear fluttered in her belly at the thought.

She wished she knew for sure how he'd react when she told him. God. Would he be happy? Afraid? Mad? The last possibility was the one she feared most. That wasn't like him, but...she couldn't be sure. The band was just starting to reach their true potential. This was the worst possible timing for this news.

For her, too. She'd been shouldering a huge burden at work, taking the place of two people. The GM had hinted that she was being considered for a regional position, which would make Jamie the only real choice for the next GM. Now was not the right time for this.

Except...you couldn't really pick the timing in these sorts of situations, could you?

Jamie finished getting dressed, fighting off panic.

She'd been pretending she was okay, trying to put on a brave face for Chase until the time was right to tell him, but she knew he'd noticed a change in her. Of course, he thought it meant something was wrong with her, or that she was going to dump him. She needed him more than ever, but—if she was going to admit the deep, dark truth—she was terrified he'd leave her to figure this out on her own.

If the pattern her life had taken thus far kept up, that's what would happen. The man she loved would abandon her at the time she needed him most. She didn't think he would. Her gut told her he'd be what she needed, he'd stick around for this. But...the fear remained.

This was the one eventuality she'd always been afraid of. It was why she was always so careful about protection and about taking her pill every day. She didn't need this, didn't want it. Not yet. Maybe not ever.

But now here it was, her worst fear realized.

She slipped her coat on and stepped out into the late December cold, shivering deeper into the wool jacket. A Palace security guard met her half-way across the parking lot.

"Mr. Delany sent me to escort you backstage, Miss Dunleavy." His voice was a throaty croak. The guard was short, stocky, with a bald white scalp and kind dark eyes that hinted at capable confidence.

"Thank you." She extended her hand and shook his. "Jamie."

He squeezed gently but firmly. "Gary."

His smile transformed his face. He wasn't an attractive man, but he had a spark of charisma that drew her, made her like him. She followed him through the Palace underground to the entrance to the backstage area. The last opening act was still performing, a lively local rock band. She found Chase sitting in a dark, lonely corner, plucking at a guitar.

She stood beside him and rested her hand on his shoulder. "I didn't know you played the guitar. How the hell did I not know this?"

He shrugged. "I don't play much. Usually only when I'm writing a song, which I only do on the bus, lately."

"What are you playing?" she asked.

He shrugged again, shook himself, and reached out to close a notebook on a stool in front of him. "Nothing. Just a song."

The notes he'd been playing had been haunting and somehow familiar, even though she knew she'd never heard the song before.

An awkward silence sat between them. He was obviously brooding on the news she hadn't told him.

"Chase, look, I'm not trying to keep anything from you—" she began.

He cut her off. "Then just tell me. Whatever it is, I'd be better of knowing. This not knowing is killing me."

"But this show, it's so important. I don't want anything to get in the way."

He set the guitar down and grabbed her ams. "Nothing about you, nothing about us could ever be in the way."

She nearly caved, nearly told him, nearly blurted out the two heavy words. But she didn't. Afterward. That was the best time. Once he got on stage, everything else would vanish for him. It always did.

When he realized she wasn't telling, he sighed. "Fine. Afterward, then."

He stood up, clearly irritated. The opening band had finished, and the crew was resetting the stage for the main act. Chase's gaze burned into her, digging at her secret. She wanted to tell him.

She rushed into his arms and felt a soft rush of comfort in his embrace. "I love you, Chase. Just hold on to that until we can talk after you're done, okay? I love you, and everything's okay."

Except it's not. She fought back the flood of words bubbling on her tongue.

"Let's go, Chase. We're on!" Gage appeared, smacking Chase on the back.

"Coming." Chase turned and pasted on a grin for Gage, mimicking his best friend's exuberance.

Jamie saw through it, though. He was worried.

She met his eyes when he turned back to her. His dark eyes locked on hers, and she saw a heady, dizzying depth in them. *He knows,* she realized. Her mouth opened, but nothing came out.

"Just tell me," Chase whispered. "Say it."

She couldn't. The kick drum pounded onstage, and the guitar twanged and whined as Kyle tuned it in.

"Chase! Fucking come on! Hometown head-liners, motherfucker!" Gage appeared once more, and this time physically grabbed Chase by the arms and pulled him away from Jamie. Gage met Jamie's eyes and smiled apologetically. "Sorry, Jamie. I'll give him back after the show!"

"I love you!" she called after Chase. "Kick ass!"

He smiled, and then he turned toward the stage and she saw the transformation happen. He shook his head, rolled his shoulders, hung his head back on his neck and drew a deep breath, shaking his hands. Then he stood straight, arms loose at his sides, leonine and powerful and graceful. He strode onto the stage, accepting a wireless mic from a techie on the way.

Jamie found her place just off stage, where she could see everything but remain invisible. The lights were down, thousands of people filling the seats and the boxes and the pit near the stage. The crowd was screaming, shrieking with anticipation. Jamie felt nerves flutter through her at the thought of being out in front of that many people. *No, thanks.*

A single spotlight clicked on, bathing Chase. He was wearing his signature tight, faded, black leather pants, heavy black combat boots, a white button-down dress shirt with the sleeves ripped off, thick black leather wristbands glinting with silver spikes. His head was freshly shaven, glistening in the spotlight. His gorgeous face was limned in the light, and she could see him composing himself, pushing everything away. He just stood for a moment, bathing in the applause. From her vantage point, she saw him flick a finger at the drummer, a subtle gesture, and the drums kicked into life, a pulsing heartbeat rhythm. The crowd went even crazier. He raised his head, looking out over the sea of people, and the volume of the audience raised even more. They were in a frenzy, and Chase was eating it up, pulling into himself like oxygen.

He spread his arms wide, and Jamie was deafened.

Then Kyle plucked a single string, sending a long, high, wavering note over the crowd, which Gage underscored with a throbbing bass note. Kyle watched Chase, drawing out the single note. Chase slowly brought the mic to his lips, and Kyle held his pick poised over the bridge of his black and red electric guitar. Chase drew a deep breath, held it, mic to his lips, and then on some signal Jamie missed, Kyle brought the pick down to produce a wild rush of noise, a huge, deafening power chord. At the same time, Chase belted a wordless note, half-sung, half-screamed.

And then it was on. The song took off, a popular radio single that everyone knew. Jamie sang along, trying to relax into the show.

Song after song, and Chase was on fire. He was turning his anxiety into heat, energy, and Jamie knew this was their best performance yet.

Finally, one of their artistic numbers came up, a long instrumental song written by Gage and Kyle. Chase stepped offstage and found Jamie.

"You're amazing," she told him, kissing him.

"It felt good. We were on." He was wired, almost vibrating with energy.

"*You* were on." She rested her hands on his back, meeting his gaze.

The song soared, providing a dramatic counterpoint to the tense silence between them.

"Tell me," Chase said.

"Not yet," she whispered.

The song ended, and the crowd filled the silence with roaring applause. The band left the stage and downed bottles of water, then met for shots. Gage beckoned to Chase, who backed away from Jamie. Gage handed him a shot glass, and the guys all clinked glasses and downed their shots. Chase turned back to Jamie.

"Please," he said. "Tell me. Say it."

The crowd was insane, wild.

Gage appeared. "We gotta go back on."

"One second," Chase said without looking at his friend.

"We don't have a second. They're gonna fuckin' riot, man." Gage looked frustrated, sounded irritated.

"Go," Jamie said.

"No. Tell me."

Jamie squeezed her eyes shut. "Go, Chase. A few more songs. Then we can talk."

Chase took her arms in his hands, ignoring the screaming fans. "I'm not going on until you tell me. Say it."

She was hyperventilating, fear boiling through her. She couldn't resist the pleading note in his voice. A tear slipped down her cheek.

She forced her eyes to his. "I'm pregnant."

He blinked, rocked back on his heels, his fingers loosening on her arms, blinked again, sucked in a deep, ragged breath. Then he blinked fast, as if holding back tears of his own. "I knew it," he said, more to himself. He pulled her against his chest. "You're positive?"

"I saw a doctor. No question. I'm eight weeks."

"Phoenix," Chase said.

"Yeah. Phoenix."

Gage grabbed Chase's shoulders. "I know something heavy just went down, and I'm sorry to interrupt it, but we have to go back on. They're seriously about to fucking riot. *Now*, Chase."

Chase struggled for composure, clearly fighting emotion. "Jamie, god…I—"

"This is why I wanted to wait. I'm sorry, Chase, I'm sorry—"

"Sorry? Fuck, no. Don't be sorry. I love you. I gotta go, but…shit. Fuck." He kissed her roughly, desperately. "I love you. I love you."

Then he was gone.

FIFTEEN

CHASE RAN THROUGH THE LAST PART of the show on autopilot. He felt a distant sense of amazement that he was able to function at all. He was numb. He was terrified. He was shocked. He was thrilled and excited.

He was happy.

He didn't know what he was, too overwhelmed by too many emotions to sort them all.

It all translated into a raging performance of their signature hit, ironically the number he'd written for Anna and performed in Vegas. He'd performed it so many times by this point that all emotional meaning had been leached out of the lyrics. Thank god for that.

The last notes hung in the air, settled over the wild audience like a blanket. The band bowed as Chase introduced them all, and then they began to file offstage. As he passed out of view of the crowd, Chase felt a bolt of inspiration hit him. He knew what he wanted to do. It was crazy, but it was inevitable once the idea hit him.

He grabbed his guitar and a little black box he'd been carrying around for almost two weeks. The house lights had started to come up, but then the tech saw Chase onstage with a guitar and lowered them, hit him with a spotlight. The crowd froze, returning their seats. Offstage, confused whispers echoed.

He turned, beckoned a stage tech over, and whispered a few requests. The tech scurried away and returned with a guitar amp cord, a mic stand, and two stools.

Chase adjusted the stand, plugged in the guitar, and then turned to the crowd. "This is unplanned, me being out here alone. I hope you'll bear with me for a few minutes." He lifted the guitar in a gesture. "A little-known fact about me is that I play the guitar. I don't play on stage because, shit, you've all heard Kyle. The guy can shred better than anyone I know, so why would I bother? But...this is a special occasion."

The crowd howled and clapped, then fell silent when Chase lifted his hand. "As you may be aware, this was our first show playing as the headlining band, which, of course, is fucking huge. Right? And we're all from the D, so it's extra special. You guys are awesome. I know I speak for the rest of the band when I say there's nothing like playing at home. And to be here? In the Palace? It's a dream come true. So yeah, special occasion." The crowd went nuts again, and Chase had to quiet them. "But that's not why I'm out here alone with my guitar. You guys are about to hear a song no one has ever heard before. Not even the other guys in the band. Will you let me play you my song?"

They screamed, and several yells of "yes!" rose above the din.

"Awesome," Chase said, readjusting the mic, fidgeting with the tightening knob, then strumming a chord. "This song is for Jamie. In fact, I think you guys need to meet Jamie. She's the love of my life, and she should be sitting here with me when I sing this. Jamie, come on out."

Gage appeared, pushing a stunned, terrified Jamie. She sat on the stool next to Chase, her green eyes wide.

Chase took her hand, whispered in her ear. "Just sit there and be beautiful, okay? You don't have to do anything but look at me and listen, okay? Just listen. This is what I was playing earlier."

Jamie nodded, sucking in deep, shuddering breaths.

Chase turned on the stool and moved the mic so he was half facing the crowd and half facing Jamie. Into the mic he said, "I've been working on this song for a while now, and waiting for the right opportunity to sing it to Jamie. Initially the plan was for it to be at a picnic or some shit, somewhere romantic where it was just us. But…" He glanced at Jamie and offered her a bright smile, "…but Jamie gave me some…news just a little bit ago, and that changes everything. Everything. So here it is.

"It's called 'A Six-word Spell.'"

Chase cleared his throat, then picked a simple but haunting melody on the guitar. He met Jamie's eyes and began singing in a high, clear voice, at the upper end of his register.

"A skein of kisses
Trails from my heart to yours,
Tangling our souls one with the other
In an endless web of heat and desire.
I hold you tight and whisper as we kiss,
You clutch me close with desperate fingers
As we drowse in the afterglow,
Drowning delightfully in satiety."

He paused in his singing and repeated the opening notes as an instrumental chorus, eyes locked on Jamie, his gaze unwavering and fierce. He saw the emotion in her eyes, the wonder and hope and stunned confusion. She glanced out at the crowd, then back at him. He smiled at her, then returned his lips to the mic and resumed singing.

"The days and moments and weeks that went before this night
Are but a dream, lost and burnt by the fire between us.
And now all that remains is love,
Our fingers twined as we sleep,
Our hearts beating as one.
Apart from you, I bleed.
Without you I mourn.
How can I bind you to me?
How can I seal closed the spaces between us?
With a six-word spell, a vow spoken:
'With this ring, I thee wed.'
Marry me, my love.
Be my forever."

Chase repeated the chorus notes again, playing through his own emotion, fighting a thickness in his throat, stinging in his eyes. Jamie's face was streaked by a flood of tears. Chase let the guitar go silent, set it down on the stage, and slipped off his stool, grabbing the mic from the stand. He had the little black box in his hand, and he sank to his knees in front of Jamie. She put her hands over her mouth, shoulders shaking.

"Jamie, I know this is totally crazy. This is probably not a really typical way to do this, but...it's the only way I know. And...I love you. Too much to let another day go by. That song was my proposal." He opened the box to reveal a one-carat, princess-cut diamond ring, simple but beautiful. "Will you marry me?"

The crowd lost it, and Jamie's whispered "yes" was lost in the screams and applause. Chase heard it, though, read it on her lips and on her face. He stood up and scooped her against his chest, holding the mic away so it didn't *thump* noisily. He kissed her, to the delight of the audience. He heard a question shouted by someone near the stage and lifted the mic to his lips.

"Oh, I didn't tell you what the news is, did I?" He glanced at Jamie, lifting his eyebrow in a silent question. She shrugged and nodded, laughing. "Well, the news is, Jamie is pregnant. We're going to be parents together. Now, just so there aren't any questions from you guys *or* from her, I was writing this song with the intention of proposing well before Jamie told me she was pregnant."

Jamie laughed, almost hysterically. She took Chase's hand, gazing at the ring on her finger, then glanced out at the crowd, which hadn't stopped screaming since the moment Chase asked the question. She leaned close to his ear and whispered, "Get me off this stage, Chase. I need you alone."

He grinned at her and looked back out at the crowd. He took her hand in his, turned them to face the crowd, and raised their joined hands. "I love you, Detroit. Thanks for putting up with my sappy proposal song. I hope you liked it." They screamed their approval. "Now, if you'll excuse us, we have some celebrating to do."

The screaming went on and on, well after Chase and Jamie had left the stage and the house lights had risen.

The moment they were offstage, Jamie shoved Chase with all her strength against the wall, slamming him into it so hard his breath left him in a huff. He was stunned by her sudden fierceness, looked into her eyes. The intensity he saw in her jade-green orbs left him breathless.

She kissed him hard, kissed the hell out him. Kissed him so fiercely he couldn't breathe, couldn't do anything but kiss her back.

"Did you mean it?" Her voice was a harsh, ragged whispered plea.

"Did I—? *Yes*, Jamie. I love you. I love *us*. I want to marry you."

"But not just because I'm pregnant with your child?"

"God, no. No. That just made me want to marry you even sooner. Now. Tomorrow. Next week. I don't know when. But...you're mine. And I want you to be mine forever."

"I am yours forever. I just...I was so scared." She ducked her head. "I'm *still* scared."

Chase laughed, a nervous chuckle. "Me, too. You're pregnant. We're having a baby. I don't know shit about fatherhood. This is…so unexpected."

"I know, I know it's bad timing, and I'm sorry but—"

"Don't apologize. Never apologize. This is perfect. Just like you." He pinned her with an intense stare. "You weren't afraid I would…that I'd run, or something, were you? That I'd leave you to raise our child alone?"

Jamie shook her head. "No, I know you better than that. But it was still scared of it. I couldn't help it." She laughed and cried at the same time. "This is just the worst possible timing. Your band is bigger than ever and still growing, especially with how this show went, and I'm about to be promoted to GM at work, and…I'm not ready. I don't…I don't know how to be a wife, or a mother. I never thought I'd get married. Really *really* never thought I'd be a mother. I don't know *how*. I'm not even sure I want to, but I'm going to be, like it or not."

"Unexpected, yes. Unwanted? No. I'm not ready, either. But we can do this together. Okay?" He took her cheeks in his palms, drew her close to him, and kissed her, gently and carefully. "I'm happy you're pregnant. Scared shitless, but ready to take this on with you."

Jamie thunked her head against his chest and went limp. "Thank god. I didn't know what you'd say. I didn't know—god. I've been so scared for so long."

Chase led her into a walk, took her to the bus and into his room. They needed privacy. Chase felt his own emotions spiraling out of control, needed time alone with her to process. To hold her.

To make love to her.

He pulled her down onto the bed with him and held her close. She nestled in his arms, then turned her bright gaze on him, her eyes burning.

"I need you," she whispered. "Take me."

Jamie's heart was pounding a million miles an hour. As if they hadn't made love a hundred, hundred times by now, as if she didn't know every inch of his body. As if she hadn't felt him settle above her just like this a thousand delicious times. She watched him peel off his clothes, lifted up to let him strip her, watched, rapt, as he stood, raking her body with his gaze. She couldn't take her eyes off his erection, pink skin ridged and purple-veined, broad head dark with rushing blood. He simply stood, breathing, each breath causing his cock to bob, beckoning her touch.

She resisted the call, waiting for him. She wanted his touch, wanted to follow his lead. Before Chase she'd always been the one setting the pace, initiating and leading, hoping the flavor of the night could keep up with her. They never could;

they could only try to last long enough to make it worth her time.

Chase? Oh, god. He led her—he set the pace and took away the need for her to make decisions in the bedroom. She could trust him, wait for him, follow him. She could lie on her back and just breathe, knowing without a doubt Chase would take her to heaven and back.

She held her breath as he knelt on the bed and crawled over her. She forced her anticipation-tense body to relax as he prowled on all fours between her thighs, his eyes dark and predatory, his thick, heavy muscles rippling. She lifted her chin, arched her back up into his touch, sucking in a breath as his palms skated across her belly.

The look on his face told her what he was thinking. She stilled his hand on her womb, her palm on his, breathing deep and watching his eyes shine. The gleam of love turned to the glint of lust, and Jamie led his hand down her belly, over her pubis, guided his fingers into an inward curl, her eyes going hooded as he took the cue, took her away from now and into ecstasy. He captured both of her hands in his and raised them over her head, lifting her breasts to his lowering mouth. His hand left her wrists, and she forced herself to remain as he'd placed her. His hand traced a line down her cheek; his mouth sucked her nipple into an elongated ribbon of shooting heat, and his fingers curled against her core and sent lightning thrilling through her womb. He pinched her nipple in his fingers, and now he set a complicated rhythm of suckling, curling, and pinching, a fiery trinity of sensation blazing like a comet through her body.

She fell willingly over the edge, bucking against his touch, biting her lip to remain silent. Chase didn't take mercy on her, kept her writhing with his mouth on her taut nipple, and as she crested the wave of her climax, he sliced into her, sent her juddering over the edge once again. He pulsed into her, deep and slow, lips worrying her nipple, fingers rolling the other, his hips pistoning with gentle force.

He knew what she needed, and he gave it to her. He raised his head and settled his torso against hers, cradled her head beneath his strong arms, held her in a hot embrace and moved with her, breathing her name in her ear, a prayer to their mutual pleasure. He met her eyes, locked gazes with her as they slid and slipped and tangled together, her arms scraping over his broad shoulders and lean waist, her feet catching at the tensing and releasing muscles of his ass, her lips stuttering on his neck and his stubble-rough jaw, her breath coming in hard gasps as he took her to new heights of need.

There were no words, no cries or screams or moans, only synchronous breaths in the silent room, only the sweat-slick sliding of trembling limbs and eyes locked in an unwavering meeting of souls.

They came in unison, each gasping the other's name, the only spoken words.

There was no talk after that, either. Only fingers tangled and resting on her belly, their eyes staring at her womb. Jamie's thoughts were running in circles, incredulity at the life growing inside her, fear of screwing up, fear of not being enough, joy at Chase's crazy, romantic proposal, at his unflinching devotion to her. His bone-deep knowledge of exactly what she needed and his ability to make her feel loved and cherished and protected in a way uniquely Chase's.

She heard his breathing change and turned her eyes to his face, relaxed and handsome in repose. Her thoughts wandered back to before the concert. He'd been the rock star, taking her with fierce, forceful, erotic power, and then he'd taken the stage with the same dominant charisma, working the already-pumped crowd into a frenzy. He'd bled out on the stage, left pieces of his soul in the audience's ears. Then, when she'd spilled the news to him, he'd turned an arena into a coffee shop, transforming instantly from rock star into singer-songwriter, using a simple, beautiful song to move every heart in attendance.

She held her hand up so the light caught the diamond and sparkled brilliantly. She felt an overwhelming rush of joy and fear bolt through her at the significance of the ring.

She let sleep steal over her, knowing Chase would wake up soon and want to go out with her.

Her last thought before succumbing to unconsciousness was, *What am I going to tell Anna?*

SIXTEEN

JAMIE CLENCHED HER HAND INTO A FIST in a vain attempt to still the trembling. *I can do this*, she told herself. No, she couldn't. But she had to. She was distantly aware of the bright beauty of downtown Rochester, every building bathed in multicolored strings of lights. The streets were busy, bustling with bundled shoppers, breaths puffing white in the cold December air. Christmas was a few days past, and Jamie had spent it with Chase. They'd both been introduced to each other's families, which was fine. Chase's mother was kind, small, dark-haired, with the same intense brown eyes as Chase. His father was absent from his life, a story Chase had shared late one night in a hotel in Indiana. His father had left with another woman when Chase was thirteen, and that had shaped his young mind and heart. It had also nearly destroyed, Kelly, his mother.

Chase had bought his mother a condo and a car, sent a huge check to her every month. He called her once a week.

Jamie's family was a bit more awkward an experience. Her father and mother were still together, somehow, but she didn't see them very often. She had a strained, almost nonexistent relationship with them, which was putting it nicely. Her parents had always made it clear they considered her a disappointment, when they bothered with her at all. Her mother had, during the last holiday get-together argument, called her a whore. Of course, her mother was the one strung out on prescription painkillers at the time, and her father stank of cheap perfume—the kind prostitutes wore.

Jamie had left and hadn't seen her parents since.

Chase knew all this, and had still been willing to go with her for a Christmas Eve dinner. The shock on their faces when she'd introduced Chase Delany—whom even they had heard of—as her fiancé and the father of her unborn baby had been worth the awkwardness.

Chase's mom, however, had taken the news with joy, hugging Jamie like a daughter and asking a thousand questions about pregnancy to which Jamie didn't know the answers.

Now Jamie was about to meet with Anna.

Jamie pulled into a parking spot and made her way into Gus O'Connor's. Anna was sitting at a high-top, sipping diet Coke from a straw. *That's odd*, Jamie thought. *Anna's not drinking wine.* They'd agreed to meet at Gus's, which had long been a favorite hangout of theirs. They always split a bottle Kendall Chardonnay.

Jamie hugged Anna and sat down across from her. Anna seemed even happier than usual, glowing, almost. The server appeared, and Jamie ordered a diet Coke and a burger. As the server left to put in their order, Jamie noticed a puzzled expression cross Anna's face. Much like the one that had probably crossed her own, Jamie reflected.

"So, I have some big news," Anna said, grinning from ear to ear.

Jamie knew instantly what Anna was about to say. "I have some news, too, but you go first."

Anna's features flickered in consternation, then shifted back to joy. "Okay, so you can't tell anyone yet, since only Jeff knows, but...I'm pregnant!"

Jamie smiled and squealed with Anna, asked the right questions about due dates and whether she thought it would be a boy or girl. She was happy for Anna, she really was, but in light of what Jamie had to say to Anna, her excitement was largely a show for Anna's benefit.

Finally, after they'd both eaten, Anna pushed her plate aside with a sigh. "Okay, hooker. Spill it. You said you have news, too."

Jamie twisted her paper napkin between her fingers, struggling for calm. "Well, um. It's kind of a twofold thing." Jamie had been trying to keep her left hand out of sight for most of the meal, and now she set her palm on the scuffed wooden table-top in front of Anna. "Chase proposed."

Anna blinked, and then her eyes widened. "Omigod!" She seemed more stunned than happy. "He did? Omigod. Jamie, that's...that's wonderful! That ring is gorgeous!"

Jamie grinned, a real smile this time. "Yeah, it is. Wonderful, I mean. And the ring *is* beautiful."

Anna's eyes narrowed, her gaze zeroing in on the diet Coke Jamie was sipping on at that moment. "Oh...shit. You didn't order Coke just because I did, did you?" She leaned forward, both hands on the table, her eyes blazing. "You're *pregnant*!"

Jamie ducked her head. "Yeah. Nine weeks."

Anna sank back in her chair, clearly trying to process the news. "So he proposed when he found out he'd knocked you up, huh?"

Jamie physically flinched. "No!" She scrubbed her face with her palms. "Well, yes, but it wasn't like that. He was going to propose anyway. He... it was—I'm happy, Anna. Be happy for me, can't you?"

"I'm just shocked, Jay. I don't know what to think. It was hard enough when I heard you'd slept with him. Now this? It's just a lot." She averted her gaze to the table. "If you're happy, then I'm happy for you."

"I am happy. I'm scared, I'll admit. I wasn't expecting this. Husbands and babies? Never thought they'd be in my future, but yet...now I can't imagine anything else. It just seems okay, with Chase. It's scary, but I know it'll be okay."

Anna nodded. "I know what you mean. I'm married to Jeff and everything, but I'm still scared. I don't know how to be a mom. I'm still learning how to be a wife."

Jamie tilted her head. "How is being a wife different from being a girlfriend?"

Anna laughed. "It's totally different. If you're dating someone, you know, in the back of your head, you can always just break up if things go wrong. You know, even if you're afraid of the process of breaking up, that you'll be able to move on. But once you're married, it's permanent. It's legal. Getting a divorce is messy and difficult and expensive, if nothing else. And...there's an element aside from all that. I'm his wife. I want to make him happy. I want to be everything he needs. It's not gender role thing, or a *Leave It to Beaver* thing. I'm not June Cleaver by any stretch of the imagination. But I still want to be the best wife I can be for Jeff. Maybe that makes me old school, or traditional, or oppressed by some women's standards. But it's what I want."

Jamie didn't answer for a long time. When she did, her voice was hesitant. "See, I don't even know where to start with all that. You know, for all the sleeping around I did before Chase, I've never lived with a boyfriend. I've never had a boyfriend long enough for that to be a consideration. Living with you was different. We were roommates, and we barely saw each other at home. I don't know the first thing about being married. Am I supposed to do his laundry and cook his meals? He's a rock star. I don't know how being married to him is supposed to work. I don't know how to be a mother. I'm terrified of how bad giving birth is going fucking hurt. I'm—I'm happy, but I'm scared."

"Don't take this the wrong way, but I'm just worried all this with Chase and you is happening too fast. He's a man on the move. He was just on Conan O'Brien, for fuck's sake. Headlining concerts, *sold-out concerts*, at that. How is he supposed to be a father? A husband? I'm not gonna lie—I'm worried, Jay."

"You think I'm not?" Jamie snapped.

"But this is what you want?"

Jamie sighed, holding back tears. "Yes. I love him. But regardless of what I want, I'm pregnant with his child, Anna. And he's not gonna just run off, you know that as well as I do. He wrote this song for me, and it was how he was going to propose. He had the ring and everything, for, like, two weeks. And then I found out I was pregnant but didn't tell him right away, because he was touring and it just never seemed like the right time, and I was scared of how he was going to react and— and then the show at Palace happened. He was so amazing, Anna. You should have seen him. But he knew something was up with me, and I didn't want to tell him until after the show, not wanting to dis- tract him or whatever."

"But that didn't work," Anna said.

"No, that didn't work. He looked so torn up by whatever it was he was thinking I was gonna tell him. I think he kinda suspected. So I told him, right near the end of the show. Right in the middle of the fucking concert."

"Like, he was onstage when you told him?"

"No, dumb-ass," Jamie laughed. "He was off- stage during an instrumental number the rest of the band was doing. He pulled me aside and begged me to tell him what was wrong. So I did. Then Gage dragged him back on to finish the concert, which he did. I don't know how, but he did."

"He's a consummate performer, if nothing else. The man knows what he's doing onstage, I'll give him that."

"So then the show ended and the lights were going up and everything. I mean, people were get- ting up to leave, and Chase just swaggers out on stage with a guitar."

"He plays the guitar? I didn't know that."

"Yeah, neither did I, oddly. I mean, he's a singer, and he writes all their songs, so I guess it shouldn't be too much of a surprise, but it was. So he gets a mic and a stool and plugs in the guitar and goes into this whole bit about how he doesn't usually do this kind of thing but it's a special occasion."

"Oh, shit. I think I know where this is going."

"Yeah, it's going there. So then he calls me out onstage with him. In front of a sold-out Palace crowd. *Me*. And then he sings this incredible song, which ended with him proposing, *in the song*. The song was the proposal. And then he showed me this ring and I said yes and we kissed on stage in front of thousands of people...god, Anna. It was the craziest thing that's ever happened to me. And he'd been planning on proposing that way all along, just not in front of a huge crowd, I guess. But then he found out I was pregnant and just couldn't wait."

Anna shook her head. "That would have mortified me, but...it works for you, I think."

"I was shitting myself, Anna. It was sweet and romantic and incredible, but...terrifying. I'm not even a performer like you."

They sat in silence for several long minutes, each thinking.

Then Anna spoke. "So we're going to have babies together, Jay. You realize that? I'm a little over nine weeks myself."

"That's crazy, Anna. You and me, both with men, both about to have babies. At the same time."

Anna threaded her fingers through Jamie's. "BFFs, Jay. This thing with you and Chase is tough, but... You're clearly happy with him, so all I can do is be happy for you. We'll be fine. It'll be fine, right? Our men will learn to be friends, and Chase and I will get over the awkwardness, right?"

"There's only one thing to do at this point, you know that, right?" Jamie took a deep breath. "We have to go on a double date."

Anna's eyes widened. "You do remember that Jeff punched Chase, right?"

Jamie winced. "It might be a little awkward, yes."

Both women giggled nervously at the prospect.

Chase tried to ignore the butterflies in his stomach as he and Jamie followed the hostess back to the booth in Andiamo's where Anna and Jeff were waiting. He held Jamie's hand loosely, forcing himself not to clench her hand as tightly as he could.

"Hey, it's gonna be fine," Jamie said.

"Yeah. I know."

"Just breathe and be yourself, okay?"

"It's been more than a year since I saw her last, and a lot has changed since then," Chase said. "In my head, I know it's fine. But I just can't help being nervous."

Jamie just squeezed his hand. Anna and Jeff both stood up as Chase and Jamie approached. Chase eyed Jeff warily, resisting the urge to rub his jaw where Jeff had decked him. Jeff seemed relaxed, but the tension in the corners of his eyes betrayed his nerves. Anna had always worn her heart on her sleeve, so Chase could easily see that she was every bit as nervous as he was.

Chase shook Jeff's hand, then turned to Anna. "Hi," he said.

His hands hung loosely at his sides. He wasn't sure if he should hug her or not, and Anna seemed just as confused. He settled for leaning in from far away and giving her the kind of hug he'd give to a great-aunt he didn't see but once every few years: careful, hesitant, and awkward.

"Hi," Anna said, stepping away.

Her jaw was tight, Chase saw. She was taking slow, careful breaths, hands at her sides, rubbing her dress as if to dry sweaty palms.

"You look great," Chase said. "Jamie told me you and Jeff are expecting, so...congratulations."

"Thanks. Yeah, we're pretty happy." She glanced at Jeff, seemed to draw strength from his presence. "I hear double congratulations are in order for you and Jamie. Engaged *and* pregnant."

"Yeah, thanks..."

Jeff pinched the bridge of his nose, groaning. "You two are so awkward right now, it's making *me* nervous." He put his hand on the small of Anna's back. "As much as I hate to suggest this, the only way for any of us to enjoy dinner is if you and pretty boy here go and talk this out. Get the awkward shit out of the way."

Chase rolled his eyes at the nickname, then nodded. "You're probably right, cowboy." He and Anna went to the bar, found seats side by side. "Mind if I have a drink?" he asked.

"No, go ahead. I could use one, but I'm saving my one half-glass of wine allowance for after dinner."

Chase ordered a whiskey on the rocks, and they sat in silence while the bartender poured it. Chase took a sip, then turned sideways on the barstool and faced Anna. "You really do look great, Anna. You're glowing."

She laughed. "Everyone says that about pregnant women, and I have to admit, I don't see what the hell people are talking about. Jamie looks happy, but glowing?"

Chase shrugged. "It's kind of a stupid phrase, isn't it? I mean, clearly you're not actually glowing, 'cause that'd be weird."

"Yeah, probably not too great for the baby, either."

They laughed together, and the tension seemed to ease. Then Anna drew a deep breath, and Chase knew the serious part of the talk was about to happen.

"I don't know if I believe that everything happens for a reason, but I want to preface this by saying that I'm glad things happened the way they did. I wouldn't change anything—"

"I wouldn't, either—"

"Let me finish," Anna cut in. "What I need to say is that I'm sorry for not giving you a chance to explain, back in New York. It seems like a million years ago, like it happened to someone else. But the fact remains, I wasn't fair to you."

Chase let out a breath he hadn't known he was holding, a breath he felt like he'd been holding since that day in New York. "Thank you, Anna. You can't know how much that means to me." He found her gray eyes with his, shocked by how familiar, yet how foreign, her eyes were to him, after all this time. "I didn't do anything with them, you know. Not that it changes anything, but...you should know. Those girls were coming on to me. I was pushing them away."

"I know that now. But then, all I saw was the thing I was most afraid of, happening. I heard you say something about not wanting me to find out, and—"

"What I was going to say was, 'I don't want Anna to see this and think I'm cheating on her.'" He sipped his whisky. "I was really mad for a long time, Anna. I felt so *wronged*, you know?"

"Like I said, I'm sorry. I didn't give you a chance to explain, then or later. But...I don't think it would have worked with us, even if there wasn't Jeff in the picture."

Chase nodded. "Yeah, you're probably right."

Anna paused for a long moment, then said, "Chase...do you still have feelings for me? Truly?"

He set the tumbler down and stared into the amber depths. "Now? No. Is there some tiny part of me that wonders what might have been? Sure. A tiny part. But the rest of me knows that if you left like you did, then we weren't meant to be. If you had wanted it to work, then you would have given me a chance to explain." He met Anna's eyes. "Do you, for me?"

"Like you said, there's a tiny part of me that wonders, but it's so insignificant in comparison to the way I love Jeff, and the way I already love this little life inside me, that it doesn't even matter."

Chase nodded his agreement, feeling the same way. He let himself really look at Anna. He could admit to himself that he was still attracted to Anna on some physical level, since she was a beautiful woman and was glowing with the shine of pregnancy, but it was the kind of attraction a guy would feel for a movie star, distant and idle. He'd been worried that if he saw Anna all he would be able to think of was the time they'd spent together. He was worried he'd have images of her in his head, the way they'd been together.

That wasn't there, though. All he saw was Anna, his fiancée's best friend. Those images had long ago been scoured away by the force of Jamie in his mind, in his soul, in his heart, in his body. If he closed his eyes and thought of sex, all he could see was Jamie, green eyes bright and copper curls wild as she came apart beneath him. There had never been anyone else but her.

"So we can be friends?" Anna asked.

"Friends," Chase answered, shaking her hand.

There was no spark when their hands touched, no electricity between them. He finished his whiskey, and they went back to the table, finding Jamie and Jeff deep in discussion about some movie or another.

The rest of the dinner was comfortable. There were still some awkward silences, but it was clear the bulk of the brooding tension everyone had been worried about had dissipated.

When they all parted, Chase gave Anna a hug, a real hug this time. "I'm happy for you," he said to her. "All I ever wanted was for you to be happy, and to see your own worth. Now you do, and I'm—I'm happy for you."

Anna stepped away from him, toward Jeff, but she kept her eyes on Chase, a tear shining in one eye. "You did, Chase. You helped me see my own worth, and that was a priceless gift. So...thank you."

She turned away before he could respond, and he was glad.

Jamie twined her fingers in his, gazing up at him as he watched Anna and Jeff drive away.

SEVENTEEN

JAMIE TRIED UNSUCCESSFULLY not to fidget while Kelly Delany adjusted the pins holding her veil in place. She couldn't help shifting in the chair, however. She was jittery with nerves and excitement. More excitement than anything else.

"Hold *still*, Jamie," Kelly hissed. "I've almost got it, if you would just sit still for five seconds."

"I'm sorry, Kelly. I'm just excited."

"Of course you are. But unless you want to marry my son with your veil half on, you'll sit still."

Jamie drew a deep breath and let it out slowly, closing her eyes and picturing Chase in his tuxedo. She tried *not* to picture herself helping him out of it; she wasn't quite successful in this, either, and she felt her belly flutter and her core grow warm at the images running through her head. She must have shifted unconsciously, because Kelly hissed as a pin came loose. Finally the veil was in place, and Kelly was standing back, admiring her handiwork. Jamie finally allowed herself to stand up, turn in place, and look at herself in the mirror.

She wore a strapless, high-waist dress, the material gathered beneath her breasts and draping over her curves. Her belly was obvious beneath the dress, but it still managed to conceal the slight bump while flattering her figure. Her hair was mostly down, the curls brushed to a shine and teased and sprayed into a luxurious fall of springy copper ringlets, just the curls around her face drawn back behind her head. She fought a rush of tears at her own reflection, at the realization that she was about to walk down the aisle and marry Chase.

She breathed deeply, pushed the welter of emotions down, and turned back to Kelly. "Thank you so much, Kelly. I don't know what I would have done without you."

Anna returned from the bathroom at that moment, and immediately held a crumpled Kleenex to her eyes. "Jay, you look—" she sniffed back tears. "You look incredible. So beautiful. You're gonna take his breath away."

"I hope so."

"I know so. Hooker, you sexy." Anna frowned. "I probably should stop calling you that, huh? Now that you're being made an honest woman."

Jamie glared at her best friend. "If you stop calling me 'hooker,' we'll be fighting. How am I supposed to know you're my best friend if we don't call each other names?"

Anna laughed and pulled Jamie into a hug. "Seriously. You look stunning. I can't believe you're about to get married."

"Me, neither. Now let go before you mess up my veil. Kelly might kill you if you mess it up," Jamie said, backing away.

"Fine, ho."

"Shut up, bitch."

Anna smoothed her dress over her belly. "Two pregnant women hugging. That's awkward."

"You're awkward."

Kelly stepped between them, fluttering her hands. "Enough, you two. We have a wedding to get on with."

Jamie took a deep breath, sobering. "Lead the way, Mom-to-be."

Kelly and Anna walked ahead of Jamie, leading her to the double doors leading into the chapel. Jeff was waiting by the doors, rugged and handsome in his tuxedo. Jamie took his proffered arm, let out another deep breath, then nodded. Kelly and Anna pushed open the doors, preceding Jamie down the aisle.

In the months between Christmas and the wedding date, things between Jamie and her parents had grown worse, a combination of jealousy over Jamie's happiness, hypocritical disapproval of her being pregnant and unmarried, and just plain cantankerousness. Eventually, Jamie had made the decision to have Jeff give her away at the wedding, and left her parents out of it. The moment she made the decision, she'd felt a weight fall away from her, and the well of happiness inside her had only grown deeper. Her parents had never been much to her besides a source of trouble and hurt, so the decision to stop trying completely had been a relief.

Now she walked down the aisle at a stately pace, the wedding march played by live string quartet. The chapel pews were about half-filled, mostly with Chase's friends and family. Jamie's aunt and uncle on her mom's side had shown up by invitation, and a few of her other friends, most notably Lane and his partner Matty. There was no bride and groom's side, although Chase's band and their girlfriends took up a large portion of the chapel on the right side.

Her eyes found Chase's. He looked stunned, his eyes wide, jaw slack, gaze wavering in shocked adoration. Jamie felt a hot bolt of desire for him.

That need—it was always there, simmering just beneath the surface. No matter how much time she spent with him, her hunger for his sculpted body and skilled hands and hot mouth never lessened.

If anything, she wanted him more than ever with every passing day.

His eyes raked over her a second time, and this time she saw the tender lover give way to the fierce fires of lust. She took his hands when she reached him, only halfway hearing the words passing around her. She barely heard as the minister spoke the words, and although she reacted in the correct places, her attention was focused on Chase, on his chiseled features, high cheekbones and strong jaw, blazing brown eyes and simple black plugs in his gauged ears, plain black leather bands circling his wrists beneath the sleeves of his tuxedo. His head was freshly shaved, gleaming in the light. His arms stretched the material of the suit, custom cut to fit his powerful physique like a glove.

The service passed quickly, to Jamie. They exchanged the standard vows, which Jamie made it through dry-eyed.

Then, after the minister pronounced them man and wife and they'd kissed, Chase turned to Jamie with a grin. "I proposed to you with a song, so it only makes sense that I marry you with one," he said.

A guitar was brought to him from somewhere, and he slipped the strap over his head, strummed the strings with the pick, adjusted the tuning a bit, and then took a deep breath, letting it out slowly. He strummed again, then set about picking the tune of song he'd proposed to her with. A YouTube video of his proposal song had surfaced and gone viral, so many people in the pews had probably heard it already, but Chase had a way of capturing attention and keeping it, no matter what he did.

He sang the song through, his eyes never leaving Jamie's. Then he got to the ending lines, which Jamie realized he'd altered slightly to suit the occasion. Now he sang,

"How did I bind you to me?
How did I seal closed the spaces between us?
With a six-word spell, a vow spoken:
'With this ring, I thee wed.'
You married me, my love.
You are my forever."

Now Jamie's emotions, contained up to this point, burst free. She flung herself at Chase as the last notes hung in the air, and he slung the guitar by its strap around his back to wrap her in his arms. He pressed his lips to hers and devoured her mouth, then pulled away, whispering, "I love you, Jamie Delany."

She grinned at the sound of her name joined with his, but she was still crying too hard to speak the words back. She just pressed her cheek to his and let him guide her out of the chapel. He stood with her on the steps in the bright spring sunshine, his arms strong around her. Now, alone with him, albeit briefly, she was able to speak.

"I love you so much, Chase. So much." She rested her chin on his chest and gazed at him, letting her eyes take on a lustful, playful burn. "You look so hot in that tux, by the way."

Chase rumbled in laughter. "You, in that dress... I'm not sure how I'm gonna make it through the reception without pinning you against a wall and fucking your brains out."

Jamie smiled lasciviously, reaching between their bodies to stroke his zipper, feeling him come to life under her touch. "So don't."

"Seriously?" He quirked an eyebrow at her.

"Would I joke about such a thing?"

He kissed her again, but their embrace was broken up by the doors opening. They pulled apart and greeted the people streaming out of the chapel, thanking them for coming and exchanging other pleasantries. Eventually the last of the attendees were gone, and she and Chase, along with Anna, Jeff, Kelly, and Gage, the rest of the bridal party, took the requisite pictures.

The reception was long, loud, and fun. She ate, danced, and mingled for hours, always mindful of her promise to Chase. Finally she found a moment to slip away to the bathroom. She paused in the doorway, catching Chase's eye. He grinned at her and nodded. She watched him casually break off a conversation with Gage's girlfriend's brother and make his way toward her. She scurried ahead of him, waiting until she reached the end of the hallway. He caught sight of her, and she ran ahead. She heard his rough chuckle of amusement as she bustled ahead of him in as fast a run as she could manage with her dress. She came to another corner, waited until he was in sight of her, then ran ahead. Finally she came to a darkened but unlocked office at the farthest end of the reception hall, far away from the crowd and the staff. She made sure he saw her enter, then leaned back against a wall, breast heaving, laughter on her lips.

Chase burst into the office and caught sight of her, his eyes glinting with predatory amusement. He was barely panting, despite having jogged after her across the building. He closed the door behind himself, the *snick* of the latch closing deafening in the silent room. He simply stood there for a moment, hands loose at his sides, head tilted slightly as he devoured her figure with his gaze. She felt his eyes like heat on her every curve, felt his lust for her, his raw, potent desire as a palpable force.

She didn't move a muscle, simply stood with her back pressed to the wall, chest heaving, breasts straining against the white chiffon of her dress, her breath coming in deep gasps—from anticipation and desire now rather than exertion.

Chase swallowed the short distance between them in two long strides, pressing his hips against hers, his forehead bumping hers, palms flattened against the wall to either side of her face. She brushed her hands up his torso, resting them on his shoulders.

"You're beautiful, Jamie. Breathtaking. A goddamn vision."

Jamie smiled. "Thanks." She slid her mouth across his, then bit his lower lip. "So. Gonna fuck my brains out now?"

"Yeah, sure am."

She breathed a sigh. "Oh, good."

He chuckled, then lowered one hand to her waist, across her belly, then up to her breast. Her breath caught as she forgot to resume breathing. His fingers tugged the cup of the dress down and her breast up, baring one dark pink nipple. He lowered his mouth to it and flicked it with his tongue. Jamie's breath returned with a gasp.

His hand curled into the fabric of her dress at her hip, bunching the material, gathering it, revealing her legs an inch at a time. He pulled the dress up past her hips, and then his breath stopped with a long groan.

"*Fuck*, Jamie. You haven't been wearing any panties this whole time? Jesus. *Jesus*, Jay. It's a good thing I didn't know until now, or we wouldn't have made it through the wedding."

She laughed, reaching between his arms to unbutton his tuxedo pants, then slid the zipper down. Jamie bit her lip as she dragged his boxers down to his knees, freeing the erect weight of his cock. She circled her fingers around him, sliding down his length and back up. Chase sucked in a breath, closing his eyes briefly. When he opened them, they were on fire with need. He slid his palm around the back of one of her thighs, lifting it up to his waist. Then he moved his hand to her other thigh, and Jamie's eyes widened, realizing what he intended.

"God, are you crazy? You can't lift me up—"

She was cut off by him doing exactly that. Jamie clenched her legs around his waist and braced her back against the door, wrapping her arms around his neck. She was split immediately in two by his impatiently thrusting cock. Jamie lifted her face to the ceiling and whimpered in her throat, filled and stretched and impaled and completed by his manhood in her sex.

Chase buried his face in her breasts and crashed up into her, heedless of her weight, his palms cupping her ass beneath the draped dress. She'd been filled by Chase before, had felt him drive deep in a thousand different positions, but never had he been this deep. The base of his cock pushed perfectly against her clit as he drove into her with short, hard, piston thrusts. Her fingers curled around his nape, her palm flattened over the bald dome of his scalp, and she found herself lifting up and sinking down to meet him, her mouth pressed to the front of his head, muffling her cries.

Chase grunted and growled into the soft flesh of her breasts. Jamie lifted up and sank down with an exponentially increasing urgency, and the chorus of sighs and gasps coming from them both filled the tiny office. Jamie felt the delicious heat and pressure coiling in her belly, the weight and lightning of impending climax, and she knew by the constant growling coming from Chase—from her husband—that he was close, too.

"Now, baby," Jamie whispered. "Come with me."

"God, yes," Chase answered, and she felt the liquid heat of his essence fill her at the same moment that her entire being exploded from within, wave after wave billowing through her. She cried out into Chase's shoulder, biting the rough fabric of his suit coat, and he in turn muffled his bellow of release in her cleavage.

Chase held her aloft for another moment, then extracted himself from her folds and let her slide down to her feet. He held her dress up around her hips with one hand and reached to snatch a handful of Kleenex from the nearby desk with the other.

He cleaned her carefully and thoroughly before letting her dress down.

She smoothed out the wrinkles, although by this point in the night it didn't really matter, watching as Chase made himself presentable once more.

He grinned at her. "How are your brains, Mrs. Delany?"

"Very thoroughly fucked out, Mr. Delany, thank you." She adjusted his tie for him, and he rubbed her upper lip with his thumb.

"You'll have to fix your makeup," he said. "You're a bit...smudged."

Jamie nodded, glancing down to make sure she was presentable. She looked up, feeling Chase's gaze on her. "What?"

His eyes were blazing, his fingers flexing into the fabric of her dress at her hips. "I just...I guess it just struck me that we're actually, factually married now. You're mine. Really mine, forever." His voice was thick with emotion, and Jamie felt herself melting at the unusual sight of tears in his eyes. "I don't know how I got so lucky, Jay. You're... so much more than I could ever have dreamed for myself. I don't know what I'd do without you. Thank you for marrying me, Jay. I just...I hope to be the husband you deserve."

Jamie threw herself against him. He was open with his emotions, with her at least, but she'd never seen him bare himself this way, raw and completely vulnerable. She wanted to say something back, something equally as dramatic and poetic, but words escaped her.

"You already are, Chase. You wrote it in your song. 'You are my forever.'"

He pulled her into a kiss more potent than anything they'd ever shared before, a scorching, melting, soul-merging kiss that left them both breathless and bated.

"We'd better stop now, or our guests will start wondering what happened to us," Jamie whispered.

Chase's hands skated around her waist to cup her ass. "They're all drunk already anyway, most likely," he said, his voice rough with renewed desire. "Let them wait."

"Fuck 'em?" Jamie asked, laughing into his mouth.

"No," Chase said, turning her to the desk and bending her over it, lifting her dress. "I'm gonna fuck you."

"Oh, good." Jamie lifted her hips, giving him access as he freed his erection and rubbed its length against the seam of her ass. "I was hoping you would say that."

Chase slid into her, and she moaned, writhing back against him.

"God, Jay. You feel so good," Chase growled. "So fucking tight."

"I love feeling you inside me," Jamie breathed. "Don't stop."

"Never."

"I want you like this forever. Deep inside me."

Chase's palms caressed her hips and then pulled her into him. "Forever."

They breathed together, moved together, and then their rhythm stuttered and they came together, gasping in unison, panting.

When he slipped out of her, Jamie straightened and turned in his arms. "Forever? You promise?"

"Yes, my love, I promise. Forever."

THE END

About the Author

JASINDA WILDER is a Michigan native with a penchant for titillating tales about sexy men and strong women. When she's not writing, she's probably shopping, baking, or reading. She loves to travel, and some of her favorite vacations spots are Las Vegas, New York City, and Toledo, Ohio. You can often find Jasinda drinking sweet red wine with frozen berries.

To find out more about Jasinda and her other titles, visit her website: www.JasindaWilder.com.

Made in the USA
Monee, IL
12 April 2021